FORCE

hurry up and save yourself.

Joargenson, Candice
(author/publisher)

NEW ADULT FICTION | SCI-FI/FANTASY

www.instagram.com/candicejoargenson

Cover: Coffee Rain
Typesetting: Cambria
Book Design: Myself

ISBN: 978-0-646-71821-7 (paperback)

Second Edition

FORCE

THE ULTIMATE WEAPON
BOOK ONE

CANDICE JOARGENSON

I'll be the villain that the hero in me needed to fight.

—Abstract 'Nashvillain'

Hayden,

No one can take away the story we have written,

and all I can say, is every day I can't wait to write more.

Table of Contents

PROLOGUE

ACE

The high-rise building loomed above as I strode into the lobby, my strident steps filled with rage. Long, large strides that propelled me forward with an unmatched temper ready to tick over. My knuckles tightened, my expression guarded, my stature unapproachable.

I was done with the Ultimate Weapon; I was done pretending this omnipotent entity existed.

Throughout the past seventeen years of my life, weight, after weight, after weight had been pushed down into my torn and tired shoulders. Every day forced to produce a lethal weapon that simply did not exist. I had wasted years of my life, had sacrificed everything for this responsibility I never wanted.

The hatred I felt towards Kobi was otherworldly, was next level. I despised him for what he had done, for the divide he so swiftly and unremorsefully cut straight through us.

Even before birth, Felix and I were together, our young lives intertwined before we even breathed the Earth's air. We had once loved one another with a brotherly urgency that Kobi had severed, severed by constantly forcing us to use our powers against one another, to destroy the connection we shared.

Still, he praised me. Praised me for this superhuman power I never wished to have. I held the powers of light, of goodness and kindness, but it was wearing thin, destroying my mind, plaguing my withered heart.

My brother held the powers of dark, of lifelessness and defiance. He could turn against them all and they wouldn't even bat an eye. But instead, he stayed glued to Kobi's side like the Ultimate Weapon would save him, too.

The elevator dinged, and I stormed out into the below bunker, my shoes thudding against the floor as fury blurred my vision. "It wasn't her!" I yelled the second I spotted Stanley at his desk.

The old man jumped in fright as I slammed the file down hard, gripping my hands against the table until my knuckles paled.

I shut my eyes tight, breathing heavily as my mind contorted my power. I was at the end of my tether. I was furious for having this responsibility I *never* asked for.

Felix thought I was perfect. He thought my life was perfect.

Kobi had told him numerous times that I would be the one to find this great omnipotence, that I wasn't the disappointment, that I would succeed where he had always failed.

It drove my brother against me; it submerged him into a pit of despair and began a targeted rage towards me. He must've known it was Kobi he should've been enraged with. He must've known it wasn't me who drove this divide between us.

I needed the Ultimate Weapon.

Needed their divinity to finally free me from Kobi's selfish and deceitful hold. I would rebuild our shattered brotherhood. Felix and I would finally escape.

We would leave this wretched city and start our lives anew. We would no longer be exploited, no longer be pitted against one another for the inhuman powers we possessed. We would have a real chance of starting over, of existing within the world as normal human beings.

Perfect. It would be nothing but perfect.

I stepped back from the bench and yelled, flinging my arms out against its cluttered surface. A split-second moment before everything atop it collided, and clattered, and crashed against the ground.

The sound echoed throughout the enclosed bunker, ringing loudly in my eardrums for mere seconds before everything faded back into silence. The glass glistened upon the off-white flooring, my mind travelling back to the time I'd broken a window at home.

Home... I hadn't thought about that manor in months. That estate I could no longer stand, that toxic environment I refused to at times even acknowledge.

I'd wanted out since I was seven, since my mother offered our home to that sick, intimidating, vicious man. She'd allowed Kobi's tests to be conducted on us, inadvertently allowing him to destroy our tight-knit family.

Every day, he pushed for a new breakthrough. Every day, he mistreated us into giving our unyielding compliance.

We were tired, worn-down, worn-out. All we had ever wanted was to live the lives of two ordinary teenage boys.

Instead, I had lived almost every day in this bunker since I was ten. I refused to go home, refused to be condemned. My mind had fractured in on itself, my body a soldier to the years of refinement.

I wanted my brother. I didn't care about this lethal weapon, I didn't even care about Mum, and I couldn't have cared less about Kobi.

If I hadn't been so scared, so useless, I would've used my powers against him long ago, but what would I have achieved? Would I have borne the blood against my hands? Would I have failed and been locked within a cage to starve, and beg, and die?

I knew violence wasn't the answer, I knew I was better than that, but just how much longer was I going to allow myself to passively comply with these cruel mistreatments?

My sneakers lifted from the floor as I collapsed atop a leather chair, unable to stand any longer. I was exhausted, I was tired, and I was done. I didn't want to keep trying every single day for the same taunting conclusion—the Ultimate Weapon did *not* exist.

Felix and I existed as the imbalance, we were the unwilling ones who doomed the universe of creating its almighty entity, its all-powerful weapon. I screamed at just the thought that I had inadvertently caused all this.

"Ace, my boy, what on Earth is wrong?"

I fell eerily still and peeked up at Stanley. The old man puffed and wheezed, his cheeks flushed, his lips dry. I searched his emerald eyes for comfort, for something that would drive me from this forever-long course. He knew I was drained, depleted. That's why he'd allowed me to burst in here full throttle and perform my little tantrum.

My head hung low as I collapsed further against the chair like a rag doll void of limbs. "Ace, come on, pull yourself together!" His vibrant shirt and polka-dot tie refused to match such a coarse bellow. "You need to compose yourself."

I let out an exasperated huff, calming my body until I resembled nothing more than an empty shell. I looked up at the old man, my facial expression blank as I heard the wheels of the chair grind against the broken glass beneath me.

A mess that without a doubt would take me longer to clean up than it had to make, but I had felt a twinge of satisfaction watching the pieces hit the floor and simultaneously shatter.

Stanley was right, though. He usually was. He knew me better than anyone, more than Felix, more than my own mother.

So many months on end we had spent down here together, trying to piece together the mysteries of the Ultimate Weapon. It was all part of the Legend of Millennia; a legend started at the birth of creation. A weapon designed to restore the balance within the universe.

When my mum gave birth to twins, Felix and I, we became the imbalance. We were gifted—*though I say cursed*—with these inconceivable powers. The powers of our ancestors.

The planet hadn't destroyed itself, so we knew the Ultimate Weapon *had* to exist. Somewhere... otherwise, the world would've collapsed.

It would've returned us to the start of creation, to dirt, to dust, to debris. It would've punished mere mortals, would've set upon Earth a doomsday humankind was incapable of surviving.

And yet, their power should've been known to us. I should've felt the electric pulsations driving me towards them, but there was nothing. Not a flicker, a twitch, a phantasm.

I felt Felix's power; I felt it like an icy chill that slithered across my bare bones. I had grown so used to that feeling, I usually forgot it even existed.

The Legend of Millennia only restored itself every millennium.

Meaning, that since the beginning of time itself, only two others of this unimaginable power have ever existed. Hardly anything else was factually known.

However, Stanley sought to find the promised answers. He had devoted countless years to conducting his own research, gathering what he deemed as evidence from a few arcane journals. They belonged to a man known only as Alistair; the very man believed to have held the power during the 11th century.

It all sounded like false fables to me, and day by day, I was becoming more convinced of that, but Stanley undoubtedly believed in this research. He believed we would find the long-awaited entity.

I'd exhausted so many human beings born when the new millennium began, and so far, had found no such entity. I was sick of the outcomes constantly filled with disappointment; I was tired of the gruelling explorations that seemed to never end, nor suffice to this responsibility I had been so unwillingly bestowed.

I respected Stanley's determination, his certainty, but a part of me thought after so many years, it was bordering on nothing but hopeless stupidity now.

Although, simply put, Stanley would never stop searching, and Kobi would never stop forcing me to comply with that. I was incapable of forging my own path. I envied the way Felix believed, the way he paid no mind to what others thought. And yet, he hated *me* for being granted the powers of light. Jealous, one could only assume, of the attention focused solely on me.

He had no idea how much I truly didn't want it. He had no idea how much I longed to break the chain and be free of those responsibilities, how badly I wanted to rebel against this state-of-the-art facility and watch it crumble.

I needed to stay in control, to be calm and collected. I couldn't let my anger flood my vision; I couldn't let it win. I had to remain composed, to play my cards right, to make smart moves.

"Yeah," I said unsteadily. "I'm okay." I forced my voice to calm, focused my mind to settle. Stanley looked my way proudly, but his green eyes remained pained with worry. He knew I could fake it till I make it, and he knew that I did.

"It's just—I can't help but question if this Ultimate Weapon simply doesn't exist." I heedlessly shrugged as I eyed the old man with a doubtful expression. "I know everything we've researched goes against that very idea, but why can't I sense their power, why can't I feel them?" I sighed defeatedly, getting lost in the hazes of uncertainty that crashed against my tarnished mind like waves on the shore. "Why can't I *find* them?" I shuddered.

"I discovered something today," Stanley piqued my interest. I glanced across at him curiously, my blue eyes unsure. "Something good." He nodded in eager anticipation. "We've exhausted almost all options," he stated matter-of-factly, like I didn't already know it myself. "I found a buried file, and it's getting increasingly more interesting the further I dig." The gleam within his eyes glistened with hope. "A file, a girl, a very interesting case."

My anger subsided, my doomsday mindset fading slightly.

He shuffled over to his desk and sat down, the chair lightly squeaking. He clicked against the keyboard, bringing up a photo of a young redheaded girl.

Her hair was frizzy and tangled, her brown eyes shielded and panicked, her clothes dirty and worn. "*This* is Johanna Tolmer." I rolled the chair closer.

"She looks homeless," I concluded, glancing intriguingly at her wide brown eyes. They seemed to have held so many secrets, seen so many things, lived through so many lifetimes.

"She's in the system," Stanley continued. "Five foster homes since 2011. The peculiar thing, she doesn't have a birth certificate. The woman who adopted her filed the papers on the date in question. She was a nurse who worked at the largest hospital in the city."

Stanley turned and faced me straight on, like he couldn't bear to miss my firsthand reaction. I watched him steadily and waited readily. "A young girl comes into the hospital, severe labour pains, 39-weeks pregnant, but the baby isn't delivered. In fact, there's no record of her baby ever being born." I creased my eyebrows in doubt, the cogs in my head turning.

"You think the girl had the baby and gave her to the nurse?" It seemed unreal, unnatural. "Why would she do that?"

"The staff claimed she wanted nothing to do with the infant. The nurse, the lady who adopted Johanna, was married and barren. They could have potentially struck up a deal," Stanley paused, pondering his own words quizzically.

"Johanna lived with Luciana Tolmer, and her husband, Daniel, until their sudden deaths in 2011," he summarised. "Since then, she's bounced from foster home to foster home. She doesn't seem to be doing well. There have been a few allegations of abuse, but no investigations undertaken. She has a growth abnormality and has been categorised as 4'11", a below-average height."

I slouched my backbone, placing my hand to my temple to contemplate this new information. "You think she was born January 1st, 2001, but her mother didn't want a record, so they just swept it under the rug?" I spoke slowly, trying to piece together the unfolding jigsaw like a wrong assumption would wreck it.

Stanley sighed and slumped his shoulders. "We have very few avenues left, Ace. Johanna is in the city… somewhere. She was last seen at Coombe Park," he paused and considered his next words carefully. "What if the Ultimate Weapon has been here all along?" That same hopeful gleam returned to his worn and wrinkled face. Even after all the verbal abuse from Kobi, even after all the falsehoods, Stanley still believed without a doubt that the weapon was out there.

I looked back up at the screen and eyed the bedraggled girl. She had full lips, perfectly arched eyebrows, and the pinkish tinge to her chubby cheeks.

"Get me every file you can on her."

If she truly was the foretold, I would finally have a chance at the freedom I'd longed for with Felix. I would finally be rid of the one person in my life who made it miserable.

Was this girl the ticket to my freedom or the permit to my purgatory?

Starting today, I would learn all there was to know about one Johanna Tolmer and I would brave heaven and hell to finally reach my saving grace.

For the two days that followed, I read all there was to this girl. I learnt about her past, about her parents, about her fosters.

Any abuse was noticeably absent, but I could tell from the faces in her photos, and from the expressions of the other children, it hadn't been a pleasant experience.

Having a power like mine, it didn't make me immune to pain. I still felt it; my body still reacted. Only, I healed at an extraordinary speed.

Bruises clotted to the surface of my skin and then faded, cuts scarred for mere moments before invisible fingers stitched them up, burns heated my skin with a fiery temper seconds before turning to ash. I wasn't untouchable and I knew that. Felix knew that, even if he tempted fate and walked a line so thin.

This girl—*this miraculous, sad, disobedient girl*—was now my aim. I hoped she could save me, I hoped she could restore the closeness to my brother I once had.

Time had ticked away so mercilessly as our brotherhood sustained knockout punch after knockout punch. Our brotherly feud beyond even my understanding at times, forged long ago by lines drawn and lines crossed.

Kobi the skilled puppeteer of all that transpired.

"You have a name?" Kobi entered the bunker as if on cue. His black hair flawlessly gelled, his tailor-made suit impeccably crafted, his facial expression undeniably fierce.

Stanley nodded, his salt and pepper hair shifting. "Yes, but we have had hopefuls before," he reminded him. There was no venom to his tone, no spitefulness, just a matter of fact that every scientist knew.

Kobi ignored his words and scanned the files. There was a lot for a girl of only seventeen years. "Right." He looked on with disgust. "What is she? A harlot?" He cackled, but neither I nor Stanley found any humour in his judgemental words.

A large file had always meant something sour to Kobi, like you couldn't have lived a life so documented unless you were committing wrongdoings. He was so closed-minded, it literally hurt.

"You might not want this one to be the Ultimate Weapon," I chimed in with a cool and collected tone. Kobi turned and looked down at me, his tanned face twisting with annoyance, but at least he finally acknowledged my presence.

"And why not?" he hissed, his tone laced with tamed furies as I stretched my legs out to appear unbothered.

"Because she was abused. She won't be easy to mislead with stories of superheroes and fairy tales." I flicked the remaining file onto the table.

The pages slightly spilled, causing Kobi to reach for Johanna's unbecoming photo. He sneered at the image, outwardly repulsed by her improper appearance.

"The abused can be misled. You find out if *she* is the Ultimate Weapon. We are running out of time," his voice darkened.

"Running out of time for what?" I sat up further in the chair, my eyes daring his. He crumpled the photograph within his fist and threw it against the table.

Kobi was more immature than me, more immature than Felix, even at the best of times. Thirty-something and he acted like he was fifteen. He was childish, manipulative, explosive.

He'd only abused me to the point of hospitalisation once, but that was enough for me to fear him. That day, Stanley was the one who had to convince my mother to let me go to emergency care. I was nine years old.

I had now grown. I saw the world differently, saw the coldness it bore, the unhappiness so many felt. Love was a luxury that so few were ever granted, and I had doubted from day dot my mother had ever truly loved the evil and vile man that stood before me.

Kobi side-eyed Stanley, then glared at me once more like I was nothing but the dirt beneath his designer loafers. He turned and made his departure.

The sliding doors closed shut and I scoffed, slamming against the frayed chair. "I hate him!" I bellowed like it would grant me a fraction of liberation. "I should've taken him out years ago," I begrudged.

The way I felt was valid, however, I also knew I was as incapable of using my power for malicious intent now, as I was when I was seven.

"I know..." Stanley quipped. "But you're better than that." He shook a stern finger my way as I rolled my eyes. I knew his words true, but it still made me angry. Made me feel like I was powerless when I was one of only a selected few ever granted such an impressive inhuman ability.

Compared to the Ultimate Weapon, I was weak, but compared to humankind, I was far stronger.

In the past two millenniums that had birthed this formidable weapon, they'd been unable to harness any real power. This imbalance had changed so much. This birth of twins had set a ticking time-bomb out into the public.

We knew whoever held the almighty power was one not to be trifled with, one not to be challenged. I wished so much for there to be a step-by-step guide.

There was so much I now knew about this troubled girl, so much useless information to process if she turned out completely human, completely useless.

I knew I was being unkind. It wasn't her fault; it wasn't mine. Kobi was the one to blame, the one consumed and fascinated with this unmatched power created so long ago.

I only prayed Felix and I would make it out alive.

"Tell me the plan," Stanley's voice rang loud. I looked over at him glumly.

"She's currently a runaway, but was last seen at Coombe Park, like you said. I guess I'll rent a shitty motel and pay my dues. I can tell this girl won't be an easy one to convince if she's truly our all-powerful entity."

I sighed deep, knowing a challenge awaited me. "I'll just have to ask all the dumb and idiotic questions I always do. Please, wish me luck," I fussed, slipping off the chair noticeably.

Stanley chuckled. "You're very dramatic, but you'll be fine." He smiled my way with that ever-present hopefulness and gave an encouraging thumbs up. "See you in about a week's time."

His old-fashioned tunes faded into the background as I slipped past the sliding doors and headed up.

Next stop—*ultimate defeat.*

CHAPTER 1

RED

The wire fence shook as I flipped my body over and slammed my feet harshly against the ground, landing catlike. I shot up, my breaths rising and falling at an unsteady pace as I forced my feet forward beneath me.

Every bone in my body shook as each nerve trembled and every muscle quavered.

I didn't think I could keep going like this. Everything in my life had already fallen to pieces. Every exhausting day *trying* to be better, *trying* to force myself to believe in more.

I didn't. I don't think I ever truly did.

All the wasted lies, all the nonsensical excuses, all the swayed contradictions. They should've saved their breath instead of filling my overloaded and wound-up mind with their empty words. Never again would I put my trust in another. Never again would I bear another scar from those same sick and delusional individuals who wanted nothing more than to hurt me.

I was done letting the world mutilate my wounded skin and done fooling myself that it was only going to get better. But if only it could be that easy, that straightforward, to simply build a stone wall inside my mind. To let everyone that hurt me stay in the past, to let them drown with my demons, to *understand* how I felt.

The world was nothing but a cruel, and violent, and pointless place. I wanted to change who I was. My past *and* my future. I just wasn't sure if I could. If I could detach myself and turn away from all I'd ever known. It seemed perfect, but not easy.

Three months gone and I still couldn't move on. I was terrified they would find me, scared to death they would hunt me down and force me back.

I had to be brave, and determined, and fearless, but all my life I'd been told I couldn't be any of those things. All they did was let me down and abuse me every time I dared to be something more and someone better.

I had to let go, completely and utterly. Fly off the cliff, dive into the abyss, and grow wings on the way down. I had to believe within myself that I could be better, that I could challenge the demons tormenting my mind and win.

Believe that this fractured form could become whole again.

The only problem—I was running from something within me and fighting something I couldn't see.

My feet stilled beneath me, and I exhaled hard against the atmosphere, lifting my chin. The wind was cold, the sky overcast as raindrops threatened the clouds with their weighting presence. It was only a matter of time before the skies broke and a downpour ensued.

I had so much rage within me, so much pent-up, explosive vehemence. I'd once bared my bruises like they were trophies, like I had won. Only because I never had the courage to admit the truth.

They weren't victories... not even close. They were malicious, painful, deceitful acts set upon me by those who had no such right in doing so. A line that was crossed more times than I could count.

All I had to do was close my eyes and I was there, teleported into the middle of a warzone. The crashing of furniture, the searing of cigarettes, the booms that ricocheted as I felt impact.

Why did the world try so hard to suffocate us with fairy tales of callow heroes, when life and living were nothing but hell? Existence shouldn't have hurt this damn much—survival shouldn't have been this damn painful.

The world was backwards; it just didn't make any sense to me. Life was supposed to be beautiful. So, why the hell wasn't it?

I lowered my head and darted my bloodshot eyes around the park, analysing my surroundings before I moved into the haphazard light formed by a damaged lamppost.

I wasn't too sure of the time, but I knew it was late.

My exhausted mind blurred as I slammed back on that all too familiar park bench, huffing out a ragged breath. I lifted my knees to my chest for warmth, pulling the hem of my hood further down my forehead as I snuggled back into the slender wooden beams.

There had to be more to my life than *this*, more than struggling each day to just get through it. There had to be more than ending up on this same park bench almost every night, but I didn't know how…

I rested my cheek upon my cold hand and glanced at the deserted thoroughfare. No one was here, like always. Sometimes, I'd stay here until the sun came up, burning its almost hopeful glow against me. It made me sick, holding hope to another hopeless day. It should've shielded itself behind the clouds, hidden and unharmed.

Wasn't that the way?

A deafening thunderbolt awoke the skies, and I gasped, looking up. Droplets lashed against the soil with a powerful vendetta as bulletlike droplets drenched everything around me. They ricocheted off every object, bathing the stone paths and garden beds with malleable rivers.

I slammed against the damaged bench and screamed, throwing my head back in anguish. Raindrops slithered down my face as my voice unwillingly faltered.

A rowdy crow squawked within the distance as it perched its large body atop the twisted branch of a half-dead tree, one it had so stubbornly claimed. Usually, his solitude brought me comfort, but not today.

The chipped wood snatched to my torn trackies as I slipped against the beams in defeat. I dug my head into my hands, letting the freezing cold and soaking wet take me completely over.

"Are you okay?" My mind collided as I looked up, startled and alarmed. Ready to fight or ready to flee as my knuckles clenched and my mind reeled, but he just stood there. A boy about my age, holding high a bicoloured umbrella, with a concerned expression painted almost perfectly across his flawless features.

Calm. He was calm.

The umbrella hovered between us, keeping the rain at bay. I tilted my head and looked up at him with sudden scepticism as a wave of tranquillity seized me, my clenched fists slipping open.

This couldn't be real... could it?

I swiftly stood, hoping my height wouldn't appear docile. "Are you okay?" he repeated, glancing down at me with uncertainty.

My bottom lip slipped moments before I cleared my throat and shrugged defeatedly.

"No." It was as simple and as complicated as that.

My life had never been easy, had never been what I believed I deserved. There had to be something more, something within my conceivable comprehension.

I needed to be able to take off and never come back, to hold the power of forgiveness inside my heart and leave my past exactly where it was... but all the memories, all the abuse, every bruise and each cut would never fade completely, as if my own body was forcing me to remain exactly where I was.

Overwhelmed and overcome with the anger, the rage, the hate that pounded within me like a beating drum. Everything they had done, everything they had let pass them by.

Why didn't they help me? An abused and mistreated little girl left for dead. No wonder my life had turned out like this.

I gritted my teeth and clenched my knuckles once more. I tried to let go, tried to mend every vault, but each was shielded within my mind with a minefield of memories surrounding.

I just couldn't do it.

All the anger made me who I was; I was terrified of who I was without it. A face of the faceless, nothing but broken asunder that couldn't amount to anything more than shattered and meaningless pieces.

My backbone urgently straightened, my stomach pounding in and out at an alarming rate as my heartbeat rigorously hammered through my ears. I swallowed hard, my knees threatening to buckle beneath my malnourished weight.

I stumbled forward, unable to see straight, unable to function, unable to comprehend a single thing as uneven blurs of wretched fragments invaded my mind and left me screaming from within.

The wind violently howled as I frantically grabbed at the hood of my jumper. I dug my jagged nails into my scalp, trying in vain to halt the incoming tornado of destruction. The one that forced its way inside my congested mind, no matter the precautions I took to eschew it.

Why did I always do this to myself? I had to be stronger than this, powerful enough to overcome all of it.

"Hey?" The stranger grabbed my bare wrist and our eyes interlocked, bringing a wave of eerie calmness sweeping across me, bathing me in an unknown feeling I just couldn't place.

I should've been terrified, but he had the softest blue eyes that seemed to sparkle with specks taken from the universe's skies—*calming, vibrant, so sincere.*

They didn't bore into me like they were slicing my skin to find bone, no, they just simply looked. Filled with a hope for tomorrow I hadn't seen in years.

My breath hitched as I broke away, yanking my wrist in haste.

I shifted my gaze downward, eyeing the weathered bench instead, examining where erosion had withered away at its wooden planks, where cracks ran through its concrete base, where weeds now forced themselves to grow between.

"I'm Ace," he introduced, his blond locks shifting with effortless ease. His pastel-hued eyes now seemed unsure, like secrets grew beneath that I would never know of.

Ace, he'd said.

He sounded so genuine, asking me for my own name in return as if it was a simple question with a simple answer. Maybe once it could've been.

"Red," I responded as I ran my hand up my soaked sleeve. My gaze transfixed against the motion, not daring to falter as he tilted his head and leaned in closer.

"Did you say Red?" he double-checked.

My hand stilled as I took an unsteady breath. I glanced up at him, peeking at him past my hood, trying to remain pokerfaced. I nodded, curt and stiff as my whole body nervously trembled. I just hoped he couldn't tell.

A broad smile beamed across his cheeks, his expression seemingly amused. "And I thought Ace was a weird name," he replied, a joyful chuckle blending with his tone.

He was so carefree, enjoying the storm that tugged roughly at his umbrella. It didn't make sense to me, this boy or this meaningless natter. He was odd, strange, peculiar.

The raging storm around us felt a thousand miles away, like we were built behind a solid glass barrier. Protected from all the world knew as harm and together in unison.

"We should get out of the storm, or I'll freeze to death!" I suddenly announced, breaking away from my overloaded head as the weight of my drenched jumper seeped against me. The feeling uncomfortable and cold.

Ace nodded after a heartbeat, his eye-catching smile diminishing as he looked around.

It was difficult to see beyond the outskirts of the parklands. It was a dingy neighbourhood with an infamous reputation of being the city's worst. I'd say that's the real reason they never bothered putting up enough streetlamps.

Ace moved away abruptly. Off he went, immersing me in fierce raindrops once more. It made me feel lost, abandoned, but it was stupid. He didn't know me, nobody did…

Although, it had been nice, talking to someone who smiled in my direction, who didn't criticise me for my name, or for the way I dressed, for the way I spoke.

For the way I simply was.

I stepped away, feeling almost defeated. "Are you coming?" My limbs stilled midmotion as I looked back, eyes narrowed in doubt and lips fallen open in an almost pleading hopefulness.

He was turned back to me, holding the umbrella's handle with both hands to steady it.

"Come on," he uttered, cocking his head sideways. His words a kind gesture to a tormented mind like mine.

It was risky to follow him into the unknown. I had always gone with my gut, although it had never gotten me through unscathed.

Ace sighed, looking down momentarily. "I've seen you here before, sitting on that bench. Most nights you look like you've had all the life beaten out of you."

He knew.

My eyes widened, my body trembled, my voice shrieked. "How the hell do you know that?" Apprehension and uncertainty clouded my mind like a sudden infestation as my knuckles clenched and my eyes furiously narrowed.

Soundlessly, I dared him to say more, dared him to elucidate, but the way he stood, stared, and silenced… *foolishly perplexed.*

I tried to stop the anger that crept and gnawed away at me, but I couldn't. It was like a powerful tsunami that swept across my jaded and misconstrued mind. I winced, as though I'd been hit. I couldn't stop the anger that consumed me, that swallowed me up and left me gasping for air.

I wasn't strong enough for that, and I feared I never would be.

Rain slammed against me, causing my clothes to stick to my skin. I felt overwhelmed, hot, then cold. I wanted to scream, cry, shout, and sob. Every emotion jumbled within my head, leaping, bounding to be brought to the forefront. To the battlefront of all I'd ever deemed as war.

My hands gripped the coarse material of my hood, my nails clawing at my head. I tried to take a breath, but everything consumed me. I couldn't breathe, I couldn't think. Why was I like this? Why was I breaking apart in front of the one stranger who'd been nicer to me than anyone had in years?

The only thing I knew to do was run. I didn't look back, I didn't curse, I just ran. Ran with what felt like a mountain on my back, pressing me into the cracked concrete below.

I slipped, crashing into the dirt and stone, and for the briefest moment, everything went black.

My vision blurred momentarily as I winced, pushing myself up and onto my worn sneakers. I was calm again, my emotions subdued. I felt numb, stupid, like nothing in the world mattered. Why did I run? Why did I *always* have to run?

"I'm so sorry." My breath slammed against the atmosphere in disbelief as I sharply turned.

There he stood, puffing hard with cheeks slightly red and eyes glassy. "It was an expression; I didn't mean to offend you. I'm really sorry." He exhaled a shaky breath, a cloud of white momentarily visible before his lips.

He had the pinkest lips, curved with a cupid's bow. His face slim, pale but warm. High cheekbones and a well-kept posture.

"How old are you?" Of all the things I could've asked, I somehow decided on that.

"Seventeen," he answered, subtly swaying the umbrella so it shielded us both from the rain that had now died down to a gentle drum.

Seventeen... how was that even possible?

"Can I walk you home?" he offered. "I feel terrible for what I said."

"I don't live close."

He smiled, a selfless and assuring beam that lit up his face, causing his pastel-hued eyes to sparkle with even more intensity. "I don't mind," he stated as he promisingly reached for my hand.

I stilled, looking up at him with fractured belief. It hurt. Inside, it hurt like hell. They taught me not to trust, to forever be afraid, but was that really the way of the world? Nowhere outside those four walls had I seen such distrust, such cocooned defiance and abuse.

Our eyes locked, my whole universe teetering on the edge.

Was I brave enough—*even for a moment*—to let down those defences and take his hand within mine? Was I daring enough to wrap my insecurities and doubts around a stranger and not dangle in the in between, neither here nor there?

I was a masterpiece forever hidden, a secret never heard, a girl forever trapped in limbo. Always on the move, frequently on the run, constantly afraid of my own shadow that danced in the night.

Who was I, where did I belong, what was my purpose? The same unanswered questions that plagued my mistreated mind like an incurable disease.

I gritted my teeth and lowered my head as anger, and hate, and confusion surged through the anxious spaces within me.

Tears built behind my brown eyes, but I *refused* to let them go. Everything tangled, everything entwined, everything mismatched. *Confusion.* Confusion that drove me to the edge, each and every time.

Ace knelt before me, placing his hand over mine. Warmth slid through me, comforting but unnerving. I wished I knew, knew the answers within my mind that left me silently crying out for help.

"It's okay," he reassured, a soft smile meeting his lips. I timorously wrapped my rough fingers around his smooth palm, rising to my feet. My hand wet and sweaty against his as my heartbeat rapidly pulsed.

"That way," my voice cracked as I glanced across the abandoned park. "I live that way."

CHAPTER 2

RED

We walked side by side, Ace's red and white umbrella shielding us from the rain that rhythmically bucketed down from above.

He didn't say much, but then again, neither did I. I just focused on the ground beneath me where my sneakers needed to tread. I didn't quite know what else to do. I was nervous, unsure. He made me feel funny, a funny I'd never felt before. It was unexplainable, baffling.

I could tell he wanted to ask me about before, about having the life beaten out of me. It wasn't something I could simply answer.

It was five foster homes worth of abuse, neglect, and disappointment. It was behind the barrier I shielded from the world to get away from all the sympathetic glances and broken promises of salvation.

It was to hide the scars, the cuts, the bruises that scarred my skin like permanent tattoos. It was to escape those never-ending nights of waking up in cold sweats, overtaken with fear and overwhelmed by situations I had no power to change.

When I was brave enough to ask for help, they had laughed. Others had faked promises with grins smeared across their faces, whilst others had simply believed I was lying.

They would look at me with disgust and annoyance; would tell me I was ungrateful. Ten years old and forced to fend for myself.

Why hadn't anyone listened, why hadn't they cared? Was I not good enough, was I too loud, too dejected?

"Hey," Ace spoke, cutting through the silence that had somehow become comfortable.

My expression softened as I looked at him, really looked at him, forcing all the insecurities and torments far back within my overexerted mind.

For now, I was okay.

I nodded determinedly, then realised it hadn't been a question. I looked towards the ground, my cheeks reddening with embarrassment, but he just softly laughed. The sound was odd but comforting. It reminded me of those I'd once laughed with.

My eyes trailed along his jawline as he observed onward.

There was something mysterious about him, something mystifying, something I couldn't quite place. People avoided me, they went out of their way to avoid me. They saw me walking down the road and they intentionally turned away. They were disgusted by me, even though they didn't even know me. They judged my appearance, my clothes, my weight, before they'd even said a single syllable to me.

I knew I'd been through too much to care how strangers felt, but beyond that iron exterior and fortified heart, there was a soundless part of me that did. I didn't want their sympathies, their sorries, I wanted their respect.

I wanted to be passed down the street like I was just anybody else, but I knew it could never be that simple. I wasn't just simply 'anybody else.' *I was me.*

A messed up, confused, meaningless individual that the world couldn't stand. That some days, I couldn't even stand. I had fought my battles and survived through so much to just be here, to just be breathing. I had dealt with demons far more malevolent than I ever could've imagined, and in the blink of an eye, been left with nothing but hardship, hostility, and heartache.

"Are you okay?" Ace wondered as water overflowed the pathway ahead of us.

I stared directly into those starry blue eyes of his, unaware of my brazen act as I lost myself within a perplexing puzzle. Inwardly, I gasped, looking away in haste.

"Felt like you were looking straight through me," he muttered, an awkward chuckle blending with his masculine tone.

I allowed my cheeks to pale before turning to meet his soft expression. "And what do you think I would find?" I asked, inwardly grimacing as we stepped across the puddle caused by the blocked drainage.

He hesitated for a long moment, words pounding at his head. Unexpectedly, he half-smiled, taking me aback in confusion.

"You'd find me." He tilted his head to the side, watching me in the faint glow of the nearest lamppost. "At least, that's what I hope." He looked conflicted suddenly, thoughts hammering at his skull. "Do you—do you believe in superpowers?"

An odd thing to ask a stranger.

"Why would I waste my time believing in made-up stories and fairy tales?" Especially, when all I'd ever known was hell, and all I'd ever seen of people was evil.

"Maybe you should," he stated with an encouraging tone, like a simple sentence would change my mind on the subject.

"Ill-fated hope, misguided belief, corrupted faith," I groused as I trekked forward. "That's all believing in fairy tales gets you."

Ace's brows creased inward with uncertainty. "What was your favourite one growing up as a kid?"

I exhaled an uneven breath, remembering one moment. "Tiffany," I muttered, looking down with sudden sadness. "She told me I would be Ariel, a mermaid princess. She explained the whole story to me, the characters, the plot. It was her favourite. Although, she couldn't be Ariel because she didn't have red hair," I reminisced, my heart growing cold. "I've still never seen it, but I know it would be my favourite." I trailed my gaze along the kerb, tears behind my brown eyes.

"Tiffany," he echoed, as if he himself was trying to recall.

I stopped, feeling small raindrops collide atop my hood once more. Ace stilled, turning back with confusion as I stared underfoot, seeing nothing but fractured stone and years of neglect.

"She was someone I once knew..." I forced the solemn words free from my throat, feeling a cold sensation slither over my skin. I shivered, wrapping my arms tightly around my belly.

The world hadn't been kind to Tiffany. She was my best friend, my blood sister, my partner in crime. We were going to take on the world together and finally free ourselves of the evil that had leeched itself against us.

I was the only one who made it out of that house alive.

Ace placed his hand upon my drenched shoulder, lowering his head to investigate my glassy eyes. I caught my breath, eyeing his hand against me. "It won't always be this hard," he said as I took a sudden breath.

I wanted to believe him, every single part of me did, but this was reality and he, just a solemn stranger. This was the cold, hard, unremorseful reality of this doomed world, and nothing he said could truly ever change that.

My shoulder slipped from his grasp as I started up the footpath once more. He jogged up behind me, angling the umbrella between us as he steadied his pace.

"I never met my dad; he died before I was born."

"What?" I exclaimed, his words catching me off guard.

"It was a workplace accident. Unfortunately, that was all Mum ever told us." *Us?* I briefly wondered. "I went searching through her things when I was younger, hoping to find a connection to my father, but it was strange, almost like he didn't exist at all. I didn't find a single photo, no clothes, not even any hand-me-downs." He shrugged defeatedly. "I don't know if she hid them or just threw them away."

"That sucks," I muttered, unsure what else to say as I lowered my head, zeroing in on the raindrops that ricocheted from the umbrella's exterior. Why would he tell me that? Trust me enough to know something so personal?

"My parents died in a road accident," I announced. If Ace could be this honest, I could try to be, too. "Worst day of my life, and I was only ten years old." I laughed, but it wasn't funny. It was a memory pressed so far into the background of my mind it burned just being said aloud.

Ace sighed and glanced my way, his eyes filled with a genuine sincerity. "Things like that, I think they make us who we are," he said slowly, carefully, like I would protest and need to speak my piece.

I just nodded.

We walked a bit further in silence, hearing only the rain fall and the odd car that passed by. They would drive up the water-covered road, their headlights painting a golden glow of rippling colours in front of us before vanishing back into darkness.

Usually, I walked these streets alone, nothing but the complexity of my mind to keep me company. It was nice, though, having someone to walk with, even if for the most part we didn't speak.

I had a good feeling about Ace, he made me feel calm.

All the years I had fought against the demons to keep my anger at bay, but tonight, it had almost been easy. It alarmed me and soothed me. I knew it wouldn't last, but I prayed that it might.

I stopped outside a rundown and dilapidated motel.

"This is me," I announced.

Its rock walled exterior sat deteriorated and decayed, towering over the overpopulated garden beds. The garden, perhaps a word too kind, was filled with dead plants, bug carcasses, and overgrown weeds that meshed together and slid up the side of the rotting rock. Almost as if they had an urgency to reach the top and win the race.

Alongside that fine architecture, the entryway tunnel lay in disarray, with rocks chipped away from the numerous years of weathered deterioration.

Past that, the bitumen courtyard reared outward in a challenging response. Its ramshackled appearance overtaken with potholes, tossed pebbles, and discarded trash.

Cobwebs and dust invaded each crevice, and at night, stray cats patrolled with an iron fist, but it was as close to a home as I would ever get...

I half expected an impolite or belittling comment, but he simply smiled my way. "Be safe, Red." He gave a slight nod and was off, a moment of concord unexpectedly passing between us.

"Ace!" I called. He turned, his eyes searching mine with hopeful anticipation, like there had to be more. "Same to you." I allowed myself to bear just the ghost of a smile.

He responded with a wide and charming grin. One I knew had the power to stop traffic.

Maybe—*just maybe*—there were genuine people in this world. Kind, sincere, accepting people just like Ace. He had talked to me, had had an actual conversation with me, had even walked me home. Why, it made me laugh, not in a sarcastic way, but in a sincere one. Maybe it was a shame I would never see him again.

Ace... my mind pressed. *I hope one day we'll meet again soon.*

I slammed back on the uncomfortable mattress, staring up at the leaking, broken ceiling as my mind drifted. I felt nothing, just an eeriness of calm I couldn't place, and springs that dug into my backside.

It was getting better, my mind. The bad thoughts were slowly withering away into the furthest reaches of my overloaded brain, never to be thought of again. I could do this. I could be hopeful and optimistic.

Like Ace. Like Red.

A bang reverberated through the room, causing my chin to lift and my tired eyes to peer grouchily at the wooden door about to burst with one, hard knock. I exhaled an annoyed huff and walked towards the entryway.

For a split second, I hoped it was Ace, but I quickly pushed the thought aside. Irritated at myself for even thinking it.

"Lira?" I questioned.

"Who was that guy with you?"

"None of your business." I huffed, darting my gaze away.

Lira smiled her toothy grin and pushed past, letting herself in. I closed the door and twisted around as she sat against the rickety bed, suddenly looking apprehensive.

"I'm worried about you, Red." She twirled her manicured fingers around her blonde hair. "You've been acting differently." She chose her words carefully. "I know you're improving, but I'm worried," her voice strained.

She took a deep breath in, centring her thoughts. "I'm worried that it's only a matter of time before you do something impulsive, regretful. I—" she broke off abruptly.

"You're a good person, Lira. I know that, but I've got this figured," I told her sternly.

"No," she shuddered. "You don't! I have seen your anger. You don't know a life without it. All this—*you're pretending*. I know how they treated you, I do, but I fear you can't leave it all behind and move on."

"Why the hell not?" Sudden anger erupted from the pit of my stomach as vile and fictitious insects invaded my windpipe.

"Red—" she interrupted.

"Don't *Red* me! Who the hell are you to judge me?" I roared, seeing red as I choked on my own hateful words. "I'm trying here, you know that!" I couldn't stop the onslaught, the word vomit that spewed from my mouth and imploded from within. "I never asked for any of this!" Lira clambered to her feet.

"Red, I know," she raised her voice, her arms outstretched.

She was the picture of perfection. You wouldn't have any idea she came from a neglectful home. Her hair was glossy and vibrant, her skin smooth and sun-kissed, her attire new and designer.

All the money from this motel went to making her happy, and I was envious of that. She had a home with adoptive parents who loved and adored her, who treated her as their own and tried so hard to give her everything.

"Get the hell out!" It wasn't a question, I wasn't asking.

"You're always disappearing on me, always at that damn park! I am worried about you. Look, I know you don't want to hear this, but you need to work this out before you start seeing someone. You're toxic." She gasped for breath as if an invisible hand was suffocating her, and for a moment, I wished it was mine.

"*I'm* toxic?" I laughed in her face, amused by it all. "You are always on my fucking case, always flaunting your *perfect* little life in front of me!" I spat like a child.

It was a dumb thing to say to her, to someone who'd helped me when I ran, but in that moment, I was furious.

"I am your friend! You need to hear this from me."

"No, I don't!" I bellowed. "Get the hell out!"

"You keep blaming the world for all your problems. Look at you, Red, you finally have the chance to be rid of your past and you're letting it suppress you. You can't escape it."

I shook my head manically. "How the hell have I done all that just by talking to a stranger?" The anger reared from within me, contorting and manipulating, ready to burst like a volcano that had been idle for too long.

How dare she invade my space and accuse me, blame me, fault

me, for *trying?* Of all the things in my life I'd done wrong, trying was the only thing I'd ever done right.

Only I didn't know who I was without the anger, without the provoking voices inside my head, without the weight of a devastating past I needed to overcome.

One day, I knew, I would wholly overcome it. I would leap into a world full of freedom, justice, and joy. A place where it would be possible to meet people, *kind* people, like Ace, who didn't come crashing into my room when they saw me trying.

No, I was too toxic, faking my improvement instead of prevailing. It was people like this, like *her*, who didn't believe in me, who shoved me to the ground the first chance they got.

No, I was better than that, better than all of this. I was trying, but I was terrified. I clung to those harmful emotions, because I feared I wouldn't be strong enough to fight without them.

I was always fighting, every moment of each day. The determination like an unmoving rock lodged within my core. There had to be a way.

I had been wronged by so many people, blindsided and scared. Left with no one to stand by my side, to take my hand and tell me everything was going to be okay, even if they didn't believe that it was.

My life had been a constant struggle, back and forth, day in, day out. I had needed an out, an exit all my life, and no one had ever had the decency to ask me why.

Why I was covered in bruises, *why* I cowered away at every motion, *why* I cried each time I was forced to go.

"Doesn't this just prove what I'm trying to say?" Lira pleaded, breaking through my mind like a freight train set to derail. "Look at the anger consuming you. You'd be lost without it! You'd be lost without them."

Them?

I glared at her now, my heart aggressively beating as my veins clotted and hate swelled within me.

She knew *nothing.* One neglectful home and she acted like she knew them all, like she knew *everything.*

In that moment, I detested her, I hated her.

Hated the way she'd burst in here full throttle, accusing me of pretending when I was *trying*, trying the only way I knew how, flawed as that may be.

My life had nowhere else to go but up. It was the only direction I had left. I dared myself to be better, dared myself to overcome all the pain they pressed against me.

I knew I deserved to be treated better. To be treated like I was good enough, smart enough, worthy enough to venture through this life unharmed, untouched, unbroken.

"Get out!" I furiously screamed as starvation burned against my overworked lungs. I wanted no part of her hero charade. I wanted her out; I wanted her gone.

"I am trying to help you—"

"No!" I screamed. "You're only *pre-ten-ding.*" Venom laced my words as my eyes seared into hers, almost blackening.

Lira had saved me from my own filth, had saved me from dying, homeless and alone, and now she was nothing more than a passing phase within my meaningless story. It should've broken my heart, should've pierced me like a knife, should've completely unravelled me... but it didn't.

If I meant nothing to her, she meant nothing to me.

I held the door open, no sign of forgiveness against my odious stare as she shuffled out sadly, tears dotting her rose-pink cheeks.

I slammed the door hard before I screamed at the top of my lungs, luring the hate out of me, pressing my stomach in so tightly, trying to force myself to puke.

She was *wrong*. Wrong about everything.

She knew nothing about what raced through my broken mind. She'd given up on me, *so what?* Been there, already gone through that. It wasn't a game, yet everyone seemed to play it like it was.

But I was *done*. Done letting others rule over my mind and misguide my thoughts. I was my own person, and I'd be damned if I let anyone control that.

They did nothing to help, they did nothing to make me who I was today, they did nothing but break my bones, bruise my body, scar my skin. I scoffed, my mind fuming with something beyond rage.

Red was the colour of blood, of fire. It was the colour of my own redemption that I would pave the way to. I wasn't just going to survive; I was going to conquer. And no one was going to stand in my way.

I glared at the girl in the mirror before me. Nothing more than a frizzy haired, rage overtaken, bloodshot eyed catastrophe. Just like how the world saw me, but I would make them see me for who I really was.

For a determined, fearless, and powerful prodigy.

My hands violently struck the table, the flimsy wood splitting as tears slipped from my eye sockets. I hated the way I looked, hated the way I was, hated the way my life had unfolded before me. I hated *everything* about myself, I had not one redeeming quality, not one likeable trait.

My head shot up, the girl in the mirror daring me to attack. She was pathetic, she was unlovable, she was nothing but rage.

I could not stand her anymore!

My fist slammed against the mirrored glass, shattering the solid compound with a deafening echo. Glass fragments rained down, covering the damaged table and stained carpet below as I glared at my knuckle, open mouthed.

The pain pumped through my bloodstream as scarred flesh and red specks spiralled against it like a ripple. A piece of jagged glass protruded out, and I gritted my teeth, pulling it free.

A crestfallen sigh escaped my lips as I looked back to the mirror, the broken pieces reflecting a mosaic-like shape. My pale face was now shown by several shattered counterparts with haunted disfigurations.

I looked away, hanging my knuckle beside me in defeat.

"Why did it have to be me?" I uttered, looking out the cracked window to a darkened sky. I breathed in, then out slowly. "Believe in superpowers?" I snorted, glancing again at my bloodied hand. "Don't be so stupid."

A cruel mindset overtook my vapid thoughts as I curled up onto the bed, allowing my drained and exhausted mind to rest.

I awoke the next morning and sat up, wiping at my tired eyes as sunshine collided against the thin curtains, streaming into the room like a river of gold. A defeated sigh fled my lips as I heaved myself out of bed and onto my feet.

My knuckle was even more bruised, tender, and scarlet than the night before, the contusion an unsightly representation of my inept temper. I clenched slowly, pain spiralling through me.

A cold feeling enveloped around my bones as I leant over to the nightstand and plucked an old tee shirt from the top drawer. I twisted it around my knuckle and hand, tearing off the excess with my teeth, before I looped it through one last time and tied the fabric into a tight knot.

I took one last look at the destroyed mirror, then headed out the door, the morning mist awakening me with its shivering presence. I gritted my teeth, not allowing them to chatter as I started up the concrete path. I was determined to make today better than yesterday and determined to keep the anger at bay.

My feet shuffled up the footpath, but suddenly, they stilled. A gust of wind forced my hood back, my body trembling. I peeked up almost weakly at the skies above, at the sunlight that streamed in through the buildings and pierced through the early morning fog.

Nothing was amiss, but something didn't feel quite right. My heartbeat quickened and I felt weary, placing my hand to my head to remain upright. The world tumbled and turned, spinning on its axis like it always had, but I could *feel* it.

I could feel the core of the universe as it entwined with everything around it. I could feel the slight shift of momentum as it continued along its forever-long course.

Everything connected, everything intertwined, everything belonged... *everything except me.*

A car horn blared, and I jumped, gasping in fright as I anxiously turned. A silver car was idle down the road, a man impatiently flapping his hands about whilst jabbering to a young girl.

I turned forward and took a deep breath in, calming my jittering nerves. Something was about to happen, something big, something that would forever change me. I could feel it, feel it like a pebble in my shoe, a thorn in my side, a burr in my saddle.

It was unmistakable, and *it* was truly terrifying.

CHAPTER 3

RED

Midnight. Park bench. Did I ever have anywhere else to go? I'd avoided Lira all day. I had nothing to say to her. *Nothing.*

Anger momentarily flooded my mind as I thought back to last night, back to the vile words she had spoken. It made me furious to hear her tell me I'd be lost without them. I knew precisely who she was talking about.

My last foster parents, Norman and Cocoa. My mind shook as I lifted my sleeve slowly, timidly. Black and blue laced my arms like defaced latticework against my skin. It hurt so badly. Bruised layer upon bruised layer, wounds I feared would never abate.

I grabbed the end of my sleeve and pulled it down harshly. No matter how hard I tried to forget, my body always forced me to remember.

They were sick and twisted people who longed for power and authority. I hated them. My whole body ached and ached because of them, because of what they'd done. Of all the things they cared for, they had never once cared for me.

Just like the shop that put me there.

Why had no one ever taken the time to listen to me? Instead, they blamed me for nothing but false accusations and lies. I was forced to shield myself away, forced to beg, forced to rely on only myself. They never bothered to listen, never bothered to care.

I sighed heavily, feeling the cold air press tight against me, invading my burnt-out lungs.

One look at my naked body, and they would've seen… they would've been *forced* to see. To see all the ugly, hurt, and evil the world had driven down upon me with its never-ending torment. They took away my childhood, took away those years of felicity and freedom.

From the moment I turned ten, all that followed was pain, and suffering, and agony. Every day, I envied the life I was supposed to have with my parents. The life I was supposed to have before it was all taken away in one swift and unforgiving moment.

Metal had collided with a deafening and disbelieving pierce as headlights flared like rippling fire. It had weakly illuminated the heavy rainfall that pelted down maliciously as men in blue uniforms guided me towards pulsating lights of red and blue salvation.

After that, everything changed. My world submerged in chaos, turned a complete one eighty. I had lost the only two people who had ever learnt to love me.

Devastation, nothing but devastation.

"You're back again," Ace's soothing voice broke through my tarnished mind. I snapped back to reality, glaring at him with a blank expression. It was strange to find myself out of my own head. I lived within there for days on end.

He awkwardly smiled as he stepped up on his tiptoes, then back down in a rhythmic pattern.

"What are you doing?" I snapped, the motion triggering sudden irritation.

He stilled. "Can I sit?"

He wore such smart attire. A collared sweatshirt that was neat and uncreased, alongside light wash jeans and stark white sneakers. Ones that looked new off the shelf. *Was he rich or just pretending to be?*

"Knock yourself out." I turned away like I didn't care.

His ear-length hair was neatly combed, his preppy attire well-pressed, his physique strong and salubrious. He was the picture of perfection, torn straight from a magazine.

Whilst I... I wore damaged trackies and an oversized jumper with holes and stains, as well as sneakers that seemed as if they'd fall apart if you looked at them too long.

But what did it really matter? Ace was going to walk out of my life as swiftly as he had walked in. Unaffected, unbothered, completely unfazed. That was just how it worked. That's how it had my whole life.

I stood up and walked off. He called after me, but I ignored his request. He was only going to reject me, or hurt me, or leave me like everyone else had done previously. There was no use in denying that, not even to myself.

Ace appeared before me. I halted, surprised, as I stepped back a few paces. "*What?*" I snapped with arms outstretched. "What do you want from me?" I bellowed from the pit of my burning core.

My frightened mind was nothing but a hazy and harmful labyrinth of mismatched memories that blended reality and delusion. I had no idea what truly transpired. No idea what my true intensions were.

I was terrified, blinded by rage and scared out of my mind. I had no idea how to break the mould and be free of my own binding chains. Especially, when all I had to do was close my eyes to be catapulted right back into combat. I had bruises that would never heal, next to haphazardly healed bones that would disfigure me forever, nearby cuts that surely laced my organs. But I was here, they weren't. I had to be the one holding me back. *Right?*

Hyperventilated breaths pounded from my lips as my body violently trembled. Nothing ever made sense! Why did everything only blend into one hazy blur after another? There had to be clarity. An unmatched moment of recollection. A beating drum to halt the past and dim its overpowering clasp.

"Red?" Ace grabbed my shoulder, and I gasped, bloodshot eyes widening with fright. "Everything's going to be okay," he instructed. My fearful look flared as my entire body stood eerily still, my vision fixated. His eyes were otherworldly. *Calm, beautiful.*

My mind went numb, my devotion tearing me apart from the inside. Who was I without the anger? Without the hate of everything they'd done to me... my blood boiled, searing its way up my windpipe, ready to erupt. But I bit down on my lip, forcing the burning word vomit back down. This was not the place, and Ace was not the person.

Suddenly, he reached for my cheek.

I inhaled a razor-sharp breath, his touch soothing to a girl covered in bruises and only ever touched with malicious intent.

I knew I should've been terrified. Should've taken off at a million miles per hour and not dared to look back, but something inside me, something I hadn't felt in what seemed like a lifetime, urged me to stay.

Everything within me—*the good, the bad, the ugly*—it just fell away like crumbling rocks from a mountain moved by something inhuman.

My bottom lip slacked as our eyes met, really met. Could he tell how terrified I was? Could he tell how this girl before him, with red hair, broken faith, and battered clothing was ready to collapse from the demons weighing upon her shoulders?

I stumbled forward and crashed into his broad chest, closing my eyes. I let out an unsteady breath, feeling waned. What was the meaning of life? Moments like this? I frowned, perplexed, as I peered upward, tears behind my haunted eyes.

Ace placed his hand behind my head, pushing me further into his chest as my eyelids drooped, my mind focusing on the comfort of his touch.

I felt his heartbeat; felt the way his chest rose and fell with each battered breath as his hand caressed the back of my head gently.

Was this what healing felt like?

Could I hold onto it? Could I grasp onto it for the rest of my miserable life as tightly as I feasibly could? *No.* I wouldn't let myself be so selfish.

I pushed myself off him and stood, resolute, as thoughts tumbled and scattered within my dense skull. But I just looked blankly forward, begging myself to numb the emotions.

Vulnerability only got you injured; it only got you hurt! I knew this. I knew it backwards and forwards, upside down and inside out.

Our gazes locked, and I smiled softly as hurt shone through my tearful eyes. I blinked and sniffled, looking anywhere but at him.

"You're going to be okay," Ace muttered.

Alarm bells pounded within my brain as I looked to him abruptly. "Do you really believe that?" I asked of him, desperation clawing at my insides. I *needed* to know, was there really any hope for someone as hopeless as me?

"Yes," he proclaimed, a sure smile meeting his lips.

A held breath escaped me, my body lurching forward as tainted memories swirled like untamed cyclones within my brain.

I didn't have to be broken like this. I didn't have to be battered, or bruised, or beaten down. It would get better; I would get better. Everything was going to be okay, even if I had to force myself to believe it. *I could, I would.*

I swallowed hard, pushing every emotion down within the pit of my stomach as I straightened my backbone and looked to the dark skies above, the moonlight illuminating my pale face.

A happy, positive chuckle left my lips as rainfall swiftly broke from above, drenching me in its cold and familiar embrace, as Ace's umbrella popped open. I lowered my head, our eyes meeting once more. His full of apprehension, and mine of purpose.

A wide smile beamed across my face as my mind ignited with a bold new determination. I was going to change my past; I was going to rewrite my future. Everything was going to be mine for the taking. Everything was finally going to be okay.

"Walk with me?" I asked as I reached for his hand eagerly.

He hesitated, eyeing my bandaged knuckle. "What happened?" I followed his gaze and shrugged indifferently.

"Slammed the bathroom door shut on it." I didn't even mean to lie, but it had fallen so easily off my tongue. I awkwardly coughed. "No, I'm sorry." I glanced up, meeting his concerned blue eyes.

"That was a lie. I punched a mirror. I was angry." I stilled for a moment, remembering all those times I had lied about my scars.

"Hey," Ace soothingly voiced. "I'd love to walk with you." He lifted his hand to meet mine. I softly smiled as that same head-strong determination returned to my wide brown eyes.

Ace's firm grasp slipped from my sweaty palm as we reached the motel. I stumbled past the entranceway, my backbone abrupt-ly straightening.

Instantly, I froze. Ice filled my veins as terror engulfed me like flames. I was unable to move, unable to flee, as the blood ran from my face, my already pale complexion becoming ghostly white.

Fear coiled its way around my inactive body like vines, pain-fully binding my motionless stance to this one, neglected spot. The breath fled from my overworked lungs as my heartbeat faltered. I fiercely shook, powerless to stop myself as my mind went numb with terror. I was disorientated, traumatised.

It couldn't be them, anyone but them.

"Jo-*hanna*," he taunted as the foul stench of my foster father's boozy breath awakened a frightful terror within me.

I tried in vain to fight against the fearsome monster, to tear myself away from the immense fear that collided against all I had ever known. Tomorrow wasn't going to be any different, it was never going to get better, I was never going to be okay.

This was my life, my living hell, my endless abyss. Trapped within the confines of my own chancy demons, with a future I could never quite grasp, a past I could never be free of, and lesions from which I could never heal.

"*This* is where you've been? *This* is what you've been doing?" Norman roared, the sound bombarding me from every possible angle.

A single breath pounded into the atmosphere as I fearfully shuddered. Panic welled within the pit of my stomach, unmoving and unchanging, as my mind unwillingly floundered.

I could sense Ace's confusion, his misperception, his fear, but as much as I inwardly fought against my own tormenters to save him, I just couldn't win.

"Do you have any idea what we've been through since you ran off?" Norman furiously screeched as he took a step closer, secretly threatening to beat me one more time.

"You are nothing but a stupid, worthless, pathetic excuse for a human being!" My bottom lip trembled, but I refused to cry.

"Who the hell do you think you are?" Ace suddenly roared, but I couldn't break my sight away from the burning eyes of someone who had abused me.

It was like watching a car mangle, a plane crash, a ship sink. If I so much as blinked, I would be left with nothing but the aftermath of chaos and destruction.

Norman was right in front of me now. His face etched with rage, his pupils abnormally wide, his mouth turned to a near-permanent snarl. He spat and wiped his mouth, his bloodshot eyes never leaving mine.

I shook uncontrollably as fear, trepidation, and terror tore at my insides, screaming at me to run, but I couldn't move. Dread entrapped me, forcing me to this one very spot. I begged for Ace to run, to escape, to leave me and all my pain, wounds, and abuse in the past.

Norman seized my skinny arm, unremorsefully twisting his long and filthy fingers around my bruises. Then, he squeezed. I winced in pain, an avalanche of tears behind my glassy eyes as I failed to flee.

He threw me down and kicked my stomach in hard as I sucked in a lungful of breath. I clutched my belly in vain as he pounded his boot repeatedly against it. Blood splattered from my mouth as thoughts of better places clouded my mind with tearful memories. Was this it? Was I going to die?

I welcomed it. I wished for it. I couldn't live like this anymore.

Each pathetic day *trying* to be better, *trying* to change. It was exhausting, fatiguing. Like a riddle I was unable to solve, a boss I was unable to defeat, a weight I was unable to lift.

"Get off of her!" Ace bellowed irately.

He shoved Norman away from my crippled figure, punching him square in the nose. They scuffled as Cocoa stepped back, useless as always, with a foul and crooked expression.

"Get up!" Ace ordered, exuding authority.

I slammed my open palms against the concrete, heaving myself up with all the strength I could muster. I grabbed Ace's hand and forced us into a haphazard run as his discarded umbrella caught within the sudden surge of wind.

Every inch of my body threatened to buckle beneath my undernourished weight as I forced my limbs harder. We had to get away. *We had to escape.*

"I'm not done with you yet!" Norman's voice boomed violently against the night as he waved his fist within the air.

Ace glanced across at me with a fearful and unknowing expression as our hands abruptly parted, and we sprinted down the pathway like that of athletic joggers.

No matter my attempts, I couldn't bring myself to meet his wide blue eyes, couldn't tell him of all the horrors I had faced within a failed system.

Breaths pounded from my windpipe at an alarming rate as I turned a sharp corner and dropped, my face colliding against the concrete below.

My eyes opened drearily as raindrops fell against the puddles merged with my own blood. I slowly stood with Ace's help, forcing my feet onward with a scuffle.

Suddenly, a car engine roared. I gasped fearfully, my hair hurling in all directions as agony and anxiety, pain and panic, discomfort and dread, poured into every frightened inch of me. Without delay, I took off in a futile flurry.

Within that fleeting moment, I wished it was true…

I wished that superheroes really did exist and that fairy tales really did come true. That everyone met their Prince Charming and had their happily ever after in a world of make-believe.

A world of make-believe…

I wanted a world like that to press down against me so tightly it suffocated me. I didn't want to forever feel pain, to be nothing but a victim within this meaningless and painfilled life.

Ace followed directly behind me as I led us down a murky alleyway, hiding behind a filthy dumpster. He collapsed beside me with a heavy thud and a lungful of breath he unevenly exhaled.

I slammed my head against the brick wall, begging for it to be over. To be done. To be finished. I couldn't live like this anymore. They found me, they knew where I was. They would never allow me to escape them again. They were going to find me; they were going to force me back inside that malodorous house.

Every day, they treated me like an abomination, like their own personal boxing bag. They starved me, then beat me half to death when I asked for a crumb.

They would show me off to their friends, daring them to add more bruises and scars to my ever-growing collection.

My body was left permanently disfigured from the beatings; broken bones healed with dirty rags and wooden rulers. Alongside those improvised casts, sat the bruises, the cuts, the burns that would take years to heal.

If it was possible for them to heal at all...

"Who are those people?" Ace pleaded for an answer I wasn't ready to give.

I could never speak out of the horrors within that house, of the beatings daily that left me yearning for death. No one ever listened, they never *cared!* How was I truly meant to speak out and be heard, when each time I tried, they accused me of lies and deceit?

I couldn't do it again, I wouldn't! If I returned to that house, I would die there. I knew it, they knew it. It was their ultimate power move, my own zugzwang.

They would claim their victory. They would bury me beneath those floorboards and continue to walk all over me. And to make matters worse, to add insult to injury, the system would do nothing to stop them.

'They come with great recommendations,' they'd said. Why did they never *believe* me? Even in death, I would never be avenged.

I lifted my hands to my face and inspected them; they were well-worn and covered in bloodied scuff marks. My fingernails remained uneven, with dirt and blood stuck beneath them.

I couldn't remember how many times I'd broken my fingers over the years. If I looked closely enough, I could see how disproportionate they were to one another. One stretched out a little far, one wouldn't completely straighten, whilst one was a good centimetre shorter than its counterpart on my other hand.

Dark clouds weaved and tangled as I sighed, peering upward. My hands dropped against my knees as cold air filled my lungs and prickled my throat.

I reached my hand up and stroked my red hair, my fingers twisting around its frizzy mess. My mother had adored my hair, had constantly mentioned how it was red like fire, how it stood for determination, fearlessness, and a fiery temper.

Ace shifted towards me, his need for answers as desperate as mine once was.

But unfortunately, there wasn't an easy way to tell him I'd spent my whole life on my own, trusting only myself to make it through the scalding hellfire. I never forced another within that tangled web of lies, of abuse, of pain.

I huffed out a breath and slipped back with defeat. Nothing I did was ever going to erase the past. Nothing was ever going to shatter those memories filled with fearfulness and fright. Nothing was ever going to bring back those two human beings who loved me more than I ever thought possible.

My body swayed wearily, but up I stood.

I kept my hand fixed on the brick wall, maintaining my lopsided balance as my posture unwillingly slacked. I breathed out slowly, trying to ease the ache beating at my entire body like a pounding thump.

I spat out a pile of blood. It latched onto my teeth, painting them red. My chin dropped as I wiped my mouth with my sleeve, smearing the blood along my lip as I glanced up the abandoned path.

All I had ever wanted was a home, a safe place to call my own. A place where I could be myself, where I could slip away from reality and live forever in my delusions—*happy and free.*

There would be warm and yummy meals waiting for me at supper time and a hot shower for whenever I was cold. I would stay in bed all day with a cosy blanket over my head, a warmth that would cradle me like a baby wrapped in satin.

Silent tears rolled from my eyes, splashing against the concrete below. My mind was a jail that trapped me into obscurity. I tried to shut it off, those memories of the past, but it never remained that way.

My history was as connected to me as my own limbs. It was an inescapable cell. Bathed in shadows, concealed in darkness, hidden in madness.

"Ace," I instructed as our gazes interlocked. "Stay here, they only want me. I can't risk your life, I won't." I shook my head at a dizzying speed.

"Use your power," he pleaded, his eyes piercing against my fractured soul. I glowered at him, dumbfounded.

"I don't have any power," I hissed. "I have no authority, no say. I'm not eighteen. The police will order me back into that house and leave me for dead. I have finally found my freedom, and I won't give it up without a fight. I just need to outsmart them. I've done it before; I can do it again." A determined breath escaped me as I lifted my chin.

Ace looked up, tears behind his pastel-blue eyes. His busted lip that was only moments ago red and swollen, now appeared to be completely healed.

I didn't understand, and I never would. He was from a completely different world with a completely different life. He would find better; he would achieve greatness. My pain was a barrier for all I ever wished to accomplish. A never-ending sentence to a penalty I did not deserve.

I saw the spark within Ace, I saw his strength, his misunderstanding, his potential. *I refused to lead him down the rabbit hole with me.*

"Don't follow me," I ordered callously as I forced my backbone up harshly, my skeleton threatening failure.

My body stumbled up the putrid alleyway, my mind forcing my reluctant limbs onward. The frigid air knocked against me with its freezing touch, but I gritted my teeth and stumbled out into the open.

There I stood, disfigured and alone, but I would rather face them and bear the brutal consequences of my own undoing than hide away within uncertain shadows.

I scanned my surroundings best I could as terrified breaths travelled up my throat, colliding against the bitter cold air. Within that moment, I felt paralysed with fear. They were coming for me, and I couldn't see through the darkness.

Horns blared and headlights flared as their familiar automobile drove onto the footpath, flattening signs. Through the windscreen, I eyed two darkened silhouettes with grinning teeth.

I gasped and hurtled for safety, agony tearing through me as I forced my limbs harder. Ace would be okay. He would not be punished with fists that longed to imprint my scarred and bloodied flesh.

My wet clothing thudded against me, pushing me into the concrete below. With battered breath, I ran. Ran with everything I had. Every jaundiced memory, every hit, every broken promise of better days ahead.

I wasn't sure why I kept trying to save this futile and pointless life. There wasn't any reason! No one would miss me. No one would care. No one would *even* notice.

Silent tears rolled down my cheeks as my legs gave way beneath me. My empty stomach roared with excruciating pain as I forced myself back onto my feet. Ace was still too close.

I looked back as the car neared. They wanted to chase me; they wanted me to suffer within their game of cat and mouse. And when they were done, when *they* were satisfied, they would force me into that car and take me back, beat me until my body threatened them with my last breath.

How much longer was I going to force myself through this same unending hell? There was an answer to solve all this, and yet, I was too scared to take it.

I was too scared to die.

Every day the thought passed through my mind like clockwork, but I always told myself I was better. I would defy them, I would succeed. I would find peace, I would be free. It was a useless invocation, and I knew it, I'd always known it. I was only stupid, foolish, delusional to believe such impossibilities could truly come to pass.

My past held me captive long before my foster families even entered the equation. I was doomed from the moment I took my first breath within this misgiving world.

I stumbled onto the main road, my sneakers pounding the terrain below as I took off towards the park, eyeing the illuminated shrubbery and overgrown pathways.

The roads sat empty, and the walkways bare, as my hysterical gasps broke against the universe. I felt overtaken with an immobilising fear that plagued my mind and made me dizzy.

Rain slammed against the asphalt, sending booming noise all around as car wheels screeched behind me. The bridge reared into view, the determination unmoving inside my fractured core as I leapt over the barrier rail and peered into the dark watery depths below, adrenaline pumping through my bloodstream.

I swallowed hard, looking back as the vehicle skidded and drifted my way. I hesitantly leaped, my frightful scream piercing the air as Norman's out-of-control car hit the bridge with a deafening crunch.

Frigid winds whipped past my tattered form, scattering my hair, flinging up my jumper, seconds before I hit the freezing waters below. It slammed against my frame like solid ice.

My body jolted, my mind convulsing, as gravity forced me further and further below.

I was desperate to reach the surface, afraid of the creatures that lurked only inches beneath. I tried to breathe, tried to fight, tried to escape the downward current, but no matter my attempts, I just couldn't win.

Invisible hands clasped around my manic form as my arms wildly flailed. I could feel myself *failing, falling, fading.* I could feel

the cold infiltrating every personal part of me.
    I closed my eyes and let it.

CHAPTER 4

ACE

The most deafening boom violated my eardrums and I winced. It was like a crunch, like metal hitting metal with a strength and force not meant for this world. The sound rang loud throughout the night, causing dogs to bark, lights to switch, people to stir.

Before long, ambulance sirens beckoned within the shadow of the night, contorting the dark and star-speckled sky with pulsing colours of red and blue.

I hurried from the alleyway, jogging to where Red had diverted their vehicle. Obviously, Red was a nickname, a way to elude anyone in discovering her true identity. I couldn't even begin to imagine what her life had been like, the things she'd gone through at the hands and mercies of others.

The man that attacked her tonight was Norman Bryce, and his wife, Cocoa Evans. Unfortunately, I recognised them from my research, but I couldn't tell her that.

Red was a runaway, and she was right about what they would do if they found her. She was underage and under their control.

Part of me was thankful she wasn't the Ultimate Weapon, but another part of me longed to see her again.

There was something so magnetic about her, something stand-offish and unafraid. She was one not to be toyed with, but I knew that's how the system had treated her all along.

My blue eyes popped as I spotted their black car lying lifeless against the bridge, crumpled and wrecked.

As I advanced, I caught a glimpse of a paramedic in the midst of resting a white sheet over Cocoa's motionless body, whilst the rest of their team guided Norman onto a stretcher.

"It's a miracle you've lived," one of them commented.

Norman moaned, his enraged face now scarred, and cut, and bloodied. *Unrecognisable; a shell of who he was only seconds ago.*

His wife was gone, and he'd only barely survived the accident himself. If he ever caught Red, he would make her pay. He would blame her, beat her. *He would bury her.*

"Excuse me? I need you to take a step back," a police officer addressed me. "We need forensics to sweep the area before any evidence is destroyed," he explained. He was tall and slender, with a well-groomed moustache and goatee.

"It wasn't a high-speed accident... you think someone caused them to lose control?" I pressed, indirectly searching for Red within the chaos.

Was she crushed beneath the car, was she even still alive? She knew they would hunt her down; knew they would hurt her. She'd ordered me to stay put, to keep safe. Now I longed to see her battered smile and blood-stained teeth.

"The man said someone caused him to lose control, a young girl, but I'm not entirely sure of his babblings." The officer doubtfully shrugged. "We didn't find any girl."

Relief filled my veins as I quickly thanked the gods above, but if the car was aimed at the bridge, where the hell was she?

He motioned to the cameras observing the area. "Those don't work, either." Suddenly, his expression shifted. "Might there be a reason why *you're* out so late?"

"Just taking a break from my studies." I shrugged indifferently, acting unfazed. "Exams are coming up, so I thought some fresh air might do me good," I lied, eyeing his name tag that read GARY.

Gary nodded, pleased with my justification. "Did you see anything?" he queried. I shook my head.

"No, I didn't, but I heard a car rev and tyres screech. The sound from the impact was deafening," I expressed. It was part truth, at least.

Gary completed his rounds with the caution tape, swiftly making his way back towards the remnants of the car.

The more I took in the unsettling scene, the more my mind attempted to deny it. It was chaotic, perturbing. I couldn't believe it myself that Norman had survived such a fatal collision *or* that he'd immediately blamed Red for it.

Inwardly, I scoffed. It was unbelievable, idiotic. Norman was a vile and uneducated man with a short and violent temper. How he came to be Red's foster carer, that I'll never know.

Speaking of, where the hell *was* Red? Was she safely back at the motel, was she under a hot and heavy shower, was she curled up within a warm and cosy bed? I prayed for her safety; however, all my hopes fell against unknowns.

She didn't even know me, and yet, she had unhesitantly put me above herself. She was strong-willed, cunning, brave, but she was lost. So, so lost.

When she'd touched my hand, there was warmth, there was an

electric feeling that surged through my fingertips.

I wanted to see her again, wanted to pick her up and protect her from all the world knew as harm. She was a beautiful soul lost to the torments of the world.

It was unfair. It was all so damn unfair.

My feet led me absentmindedly into the building and towards the elevator that shone alongside the manufactured glow of down-lights.

I idly poked at the button and waited for its arrival, taking in the lobby that sat empty, the usual bustle of beings now cocooned within an uncomfortable silence.

There were so many times I had walked these halls within the early hours of the morning, but tonight, they felt exceptionally lonely. I glanced down at my mobile, disputing the clock that read 5am.

My hand dropped, my mind longing to know if Red was okay, if she had survived the brutal actions of those who promised to pro-tect her. I could tell her life was hard, could tell there was so much hate she felt.

She'd been so fuelled with determination, powered by an ur-gent essence of change. She had even spoken about her parents, though brief, but I appreciated every raw emotion she expressed.

Her parents had lost their lives in a tragic car accident around Christmas time. The 23rd of December, to be exact. Red was left orphaned and alone after witnessing the horrendous happenings from the backseat of their family car.

Her statement to the police had been truly horrific. She'd reported seeing the vehicle flip, shielding her ears as the windows shattered, screaming as the freezing cold crept in. She was only ten years old at the time.

The elevator dinged and the doors opened. I stared into the boxed confinement like it was a metal prison waiting to lead me to Kobi, to once again bear the bad news of no Ultimate Weapon.

Stanley had been so sure this time, so positive and upbeat. He was growing old, was slowly becoming less and less mobile. Although, I'd never dare speak it. I had spent so many years by Stanley's side, so many late nights, so many caffeinated days, so many deep conversations between us.

I turned and glanced at the outside world, so free, so vast and wide.

No matter where I ran, *if* I ran, I would never be able to leave this planet, would never be able to travel to the stars and beyond, would never be free from Kobi completely.

An unnerving chill ran up my spine.

"You're finally back." Felix peeled himself off the far wall as I inwardly gasped, watching his half-hidden figure separate from the shadows. He stretched his neck out and watched me with interest.

Abruptly, he clicked his tongue and turned away, his eyes that were usually so full of contempt, lain simply dull and pale. He seemed tired, not even making the effort to hide his exhaustion. "No weapon?" he questioned coolly as he flipped his elongated fringe away from his face.

I shook my head defeatedly, causing his mood to dramatically shift. "And they always said *I* was the disappointment." Contempt now burned within his hollow words.

He scoffed and strode past me in an aggravated manner as fury radiated from his shadow-like silhouette, similar to how smoke ballooned upward and bunched indefinitely.

He had since dyed his hair. It was now coal-black and trickled across his cheek like thinned and blackened icicles. One half had been substantially shortened, the other half a cascade of darkened strands almost to his shoulder. Alongside that, sat the unnecessary piercings. One that spiked his lip, one that stabbed his eyebrow.

I hated how he always went over and above to modify his natural appearance from mine. He must've truly loathed being identical.

I sighed defeatedly. Felix had no idea how I envied him, how I craved his unfettered lifestyle.

It was baffling how he always blindingly followed. He must've known how capable he was of revolt. He was strong-minded and powerful, a force not to be reckoned with.

He could defeat Kobi, he could win. Sure, his ability mightn't have been as strong as the Ultimate Weapon's, but he was always morphing and contorting his power to bend, and weave, and move with the shadowed defiance he bore.

He was proud of the strength he had achieved through his persistent training, and rightfully so, although Kobi had never been that impressed by it.

Kobi had the nerve to label him as weak, inept, dishonest. He really had been beaten down into submission. That disdain he felt, he should have focused that on Kobi, but instead, he thoughtlessly directed it towards me.

A fool's errand, no doubt.

He moved behind me like a shadow in the night, striding into the outside world with an effortless ease.

A dejected sigh escaped my lips as I pressed the button once more, awaiting the ding. This time, I stepped in without delay.

I entered the bunker, immediately hearing Stanley's light taps upon the keyboard. I smiled to myself, his presence calming my soul.

"Hey, Stan." I eyed the two lamps aglow, surprised the old man was awake at this hour. The automatic downlights Kobi had insisted on installing weren't even scheduled to activate this early.

Stanley swivelled his chair, grinning brightly when he spotted my blond hair and warm smile. "*Ah,* I thought Felix was back." He huffed, playfully scowling.

"What did he want?" I asked with a sharp snap as I rested upon the seat, placing my backpack beside me.

"He wanted to know if we'd found the Ultimate Weapon..." The sentence hung between us, a hopeful plead against his ageing tone of voice. I shrugged and eyed him with a defeated look, a look he knew all too well. He breathed coarsely, his posture sinking.

"She wasn't the one, but she could've been..." I murmured as I looked down with a mix of sadness and guilt. I wasn't sure where she was, wasn't sure if she was even still alive.

Stanley watched me with a curious look, then hummed joyfully when he realised my words intent

He turned back in his chair and once again typed away feverishly, the light clicks upon the keyboard relaxing my wound-up and overexerted mind.

I needed a rest; I needed a break. I'd been across the globe, yet I had never gone on a single holiday.

I'd seen snow at Christmas time, heard fireworks explode off the Sydney Harbour Bridge, witnessed the Aurora Borealis, smelt the saltiness of the Red Sea. Whilst, simultaneously, on high alert. My mind remained sharp, permanently focused on the next target, constantly overtaken with the debilitating thought of obtaining the Ultimate Weapon's location.

I lived, but I wasn't alive.

I'd visited beautiful and exotic places. Although, I was never given the chance to truly enjoy them, to celebrate with the locals, to learn their cultures and languages. I had experienced so many things but been deprived of so much of it.

"Ace, you need rest," Stanley offered thoughtfully.

I glanced up at him and rubbed at my tired eyes. Five days, I had stayed at that cheap and nasty motel. Four nights, I had rolled around on that thin and uncomfortable mattress. Half a day's time, most likely less, had I the pleasure of spending with that fearlessly outspoken redhead.

My body trembled as I slowly stood.

I placed my hand against the desk's metallic surface to steady my wobbling legs. "Are you alright?" Stanley waddled over to me, placing a secure hand on my back.

"I can't stop thinking about her," my voice shuddered as images flashed within my mind.

Her cinnamon-hued eyes that were filled with poignancy, her ghost of a smile that was only ever visible for seconds, her chubby cheeks that were an oddity to her otherwise slim figure, her rough hands that grasped mine with nothing but the gentlest hold.

I regretfully scanned the creases within my palm. There wasn't any excuse for leaving her, for turning away and returning to this mundane life of mine.

I had to know if she was okay; I had to go back.

I stepped aside and suddenly everything went black.

A groan escaped my lips as I sat upright in bed. The same cold, off-white, and lifeless walls surrounding me. I had tried over the years to cover them in posters, to stick colourful pops of artwork against an otherwise dull and blank interior.

I'd gotten tired of the rickety bed that I was forced to use, so I'd purchased my own and created a home within this tiny room. However, my double bed left only enough space to shuffle out down the side.

The room that remained was occupied with cube shelves, folded clothes, and random knickknacks. I spent most of my time out there with Stanley, anyway.

My tired eyes shifted towards the door as I smiled softly, then unsurely. I wanted to go to her, to that broken and bloodied girl. The one who wore her courage like a mighty lion and who stood bravely for her own freedom.

I flipped the large quilt back and crawled to the end of the bed. It was always so damn cold in these bleak rooms.

The hefty door squealed as I pushed it forward and entered into the main room. Stanley and Kobi stood in a heated debate that vanished when they saw me.

Stanley eyed me first, as hopeful and optimistic as ever. Kobi's hardened stare, however, was the complete opposite. His selfish words now silenced and his expression visibly irritated.

"Keep the boy here," he ordered angrily. "Felix will be here by nightfall. We reconvene then." The hint of disdain clear against his tongue.

"How are you?" Stanley shuffled over to my side as Kobi departed. I waited until he was gone to speak.

"What happened?" My eyebrows creased with uncertainty.

"You fainted," Stanley conveyed. My face responded with a surprised look before my mouth even had the chance to form a reply. "You were talking about Johanna—"

"Red," I interrupted before I knew the word had left my lips. Stanley eyed me with an unsure glance, proceeding anyway.

"Yes, Red," he corrected himself.

I smiled warmly, observing him with an earnest feeling that shifted deep within my heart.

That was the kindness within him I envied. A kindness he offered to all living, breathing things. Alongside that, a goodness he saw in everyone he came across, even words he didn't challenge when he didn't quite understand their meaning.

I hoped one day to be even half the man he is.

"You told me you couldn't stop thinking about her," he added, grinning his gap-toothed smile as he clasped a steady hand atop my forearm. He was like the father I never had. A light in my life so blindingly bright and so charismatically cheerful.

"Come with me," he ushered, leading me towards the old and ripped couch that Felix and I had hauled down here years ago. "Tell me about her."

And so, I did. I doubtlessly spoke of the girl I'd met in shadows, within stormy raindrops, under thunderous claps. How different she was to the girl I read about on paper.

"But I don't know what happened to her." I finished with painful words and a grim expression. "I need to know where she is, I need to know that's she's okay," I whispered almost soundlessly.

Stanley slid his large spectacles back upon his face and took a steady breath. "Yes, most definitely," he muttered, looking around the room quickly. "But Kobi has ordered you here for the rest of the day."

His words quieted as he stirred inside his subconscious, thinking up a plausible plan. "However, I'm sure I can smuggle you out tomorrow, perhaps I am in need of another library book." Stanley winked, pleased with his plan and proud of his tomfoolery.

Tomorrow... my heart raced. *I will go to her tomorrow.*

CHAPTER 5

RED

Nightfall fell upon the world as I awoke under a veil of stars, coughing and spluttering against the mud beneath me.

Every inch of my body ached as indescribable pain threatened to send my entire system into convulsion. I glimpsed at the water, watching as it lapped alongside the small dirt rise, deadly and untamed. Somehow within those icy depths, I had found myself here.

I sat up slowly as hyperthermia sliced through me, causing my entire frame to uncontrollably shake.

I rested my forehead upon the mud and shut my eyes tightly. Everything ached, everything hurt. It was worse than the pain I'd endured when I was beaten half to death. I didn't know if I could stand.

Suddenly, I puked, over and over. My brain fuzzy and flawed, my organs painful and pinched, my body cold and condemned.

Why did I do it? Why did I leap so surely off that bridge without any safety net to catch me?

I was as useless as a pebble, as dumb as a rock. I had nothing to fight for, nothing to live for, but everything to die for.

They couldn't hurt me if I was dead. No one and nothing could.

I would finally be free. No longer a slave to this unfair and unkind universe. It was what I wanted—*it had to be.*

So then, why did I bother searching my screaming head for answers, for even questions, for *anything,* if all I ever did was convince myself to keep fighting? To keep living, to keep trying? I was drained, depleted. I was done.

I fell against the mud and my puke, lying there for what felt like a lifetime. Rain continued to speckle down soothingly beside my bruised skin, pooling in a puddle around me.

All the injustice I faced, all the sleepless nights I suffered, all the misery I caused... I missed my parents, those two loving souls who took me in and gave me everything.

I thought about them daily; about the life we could have lived and the love we could have known. I missed the way I baked with my mum, missed the way I played soccer with my dad. I missed their smiles, their laughter, their warm forehead kisses goodnight.

My stomach rumbled and I winced.

I was starved, parched, immobilised. Why did I even bother? Why did I even try? Read the writing on the wall? Fuck the wall and fuck the writing. All it held was an impending doom I could never outrun.

It would be so easy to stand in front of an oncoming car and be crushed by its weight. To stand atop a high-rise building and drop. To jump in front of a train and—

But I was afraid to die.

I was used to pain, to torment, and abuse, but death? Death scared me. I feared the unknown, feared the consequences of failing, the penalties that would forever become permanent.

I feared what I did not understand.

And peace... I didn't think it would ever be possible for me to feel, or fully understand, what peace truly meant.

Was it the feeling when all the anger vanished? Was it the feeling when all the overpowering thoughts inside my skull ceased? Was it the feeling of incomprehensible calm when all I wanted was to scream my lungs out?

I knew how to be a failure, a hindrance, a mistake. I knew how to explode in rage when the furnace within my body blew. I knew how to ignore those few people that wanted to help me. I knew how to turn my back and walk away when all I wanted was to turn and run towards them. I knew how to be broken, how to be insecure, annoying, temperamental, and destructive. *I knew how to be all the things that slowly destroyed me...*

I didn't know how to be better. Didn't know how to change.

And so, I gave up. On myself, on living, on everything. My body was just the last to go. I didn't need to be scared anymore; I didn't need to be frightened. I was going to free myself. I was going to ascend into the heavens above and be reunited with my parents.

Panicked breaths tore from my dried lips as I hoisted myself up the uneven surface, my fingernails clawing at the lush vegetation and muddy soil beneath. It squished between my fingers and gathered under my nail beds.

My body threatened failure, but on I pushed, higher and higher, until I reached the top.

I stood, my soaked jumper cold and heavy against my hot and sweaty skin as my glassy eyes examined the illuminated road before me. The rain had subdued, but the roads still glistened with watery droplets and a slime-like texture.

I made my way towards the middle of the bridge, slipping on

the wet concrete as my eyes darted to the damaged barrier rail. I placed my hand against the scuff mark newly embedded within the concrete slab. There was an accident here for sure.

My hand contracted as I noticed a puddle of dried blood.

Dread coiled within my stomach, but I was unable to tear my disbelieving eyes away. I felt sick, queasy. I stepped back, my gaze never leaving that bloodstained puddle before I turned on my heels and ran like hell.

Images rocketed through my overloaded brain as I tried in vain to fight the amnesia. Just what the hell had I done? Terror escalated through me, shaking me to its very core as I slipped and stumbled against the footpath worn from years of decay.

I ran. *On, and on, and on.*

Everything went blurry, and for a brief moment, I was soaring, reaching for the heavens, yearning to reach my parents above. My body eager to connect, my arm outreached, my fingers strained to their max.

A train horn sounded loud within the distance. and I gasped, my shallow breaths pounding against the atmosphere. I searched within the darkness, desperate to find my incoming salvation.

Piercing headlights invaded my view, momentarily blinding as I darted towards the tracks without indecision, only determination. My head pounded, knees weakened, breaths fuddled.

I pushed myself further as everything inside my failing body cracked, caved, and convulsed with agonising pain. *This* was my solution, my salvation, my freedom. This was my answer—

My only answer.

The freight train closed in with exceeding speed, but I refused to turn my head away, afraid it would vanish into thin air. The click and clank of its weighted frame along the tracks roared as the horn sounded loud, piercing the atmosphere with its deafening wails. A noise that spiralled through me, causing my petite frame to flinch, as I descended the ballast covered slope. I forced my mind to quiet, my thoughts to empty, my brain to nullify.

I would no longer live within a painful world, I would no longer condemn myself to abusers or users, I would no longer hunger for food or wither away from dehydration.

I would free myself from the chains that forced me into their homes, into their lives, into their mistreatments. I would remove myself from all equations. I would show them I was unafraid of death and as manic as humankind could be.

To them, I would finally prove the unyielding courage that ricocheted through every broken part of me.

The front of the train slammed against me, causing my lungs to cry out in one enormous, excruciating screech. Pain encapsulated me in a crippling, disorienting, mangling form.

And then, I was glowing.

Agony tore through me as my body pulsed with an inhuman energy that buzzed, zapped, and jittered. I screamed out a brutal screech as orange waves violently propelled from my disfigured fingertips. It encircled a makeshift ball of alien entity around me as the entire world stilled and silenced.

The unbearable pain within my body buckled, my limbs breaking, my bones shattering, my flesh tearing.

I screamed out an ear-piercing roar as an enormous force field shot outward from my maimed figure, exploding from my inner self. It surged through all that stood as the crackling vibration ran outward like a haphazard ripple.

It was agony. *Intense, intoxicating, inescapable agony.*

The train warped and tipped across the tracks as streetlamps buckled from far away, sending broken pieces scattering below.

Each window shattered, every glass compound cracked, causing waves of crystal-like fragments to surge towards the ground like majestic waterfalls that glistened against the radiance of the moon.

I gritted my teeth and closed my eyes as the world quaked and shattered around me, like nothing I'd ever witnessed before. The universe was within me; I could *feel* it.

I could feel the power, the pull, of an unknown origin spiral through me and morph within my tattered and tarnished body. I was linked to the Earth, embedded within its core, fixed to its wobbling axis. I was ablaze with a power I did not know, a power I did not understand. A power that was seemingly impossible.

Superheroes, why did I think of superheroes?

Was I wrong for laughing at Ace's pitiful words of fairy tales? Was I mistaken for mistrusting my own biased thoughts of happily ever afters and worlds of make-believe?

I wanted death to reach up and snatch me, to tear me from this forsaken world indefinitely. I wanted freedom in its most vulnerable and deadly form, and no ill-fated, misguided, corrupted tale could ever truly save me from that.

Heaven or hell—it didn't matter to me. I did not seek power, revenge, or reincarnation. All I wanted was to be rid of this planet, rid of the sins and sufferings I had so unfairly faced. I wanted to be stripped of my miseries, doffed of my scars, remembered only in memory.

I did not wish to live beyond that.

CHAPTER 6

ACE

I could sense Felix's familiar snarl from across the room. I tried to act unfazed, tried to act as if it didn't immensely bother me.

We'd been summoned here by Kobi. Who now stood in the centre of the room, alongside Mum and Stanley. Mum was perched beside him with an unimpressed frown, her long hair dishevelled, her nails bitten down, her figure fatigued.

The air felt tight and tense, uneasy and unnerving. Had something happened I was unaware of? Had the Ultimate Weapon been unearthed? Had Kobi decided to set us all free?

I scoffed, rolling my eyes dismissively. Stanley had been pretty tight-lipped about this whole meetup, so I knew something big was about to go down, but what?

If it was anything to do with locating the Ultimate Weapon, I knew the old man wouldn't have been able to contain his excitement. He would have bear-hugged each and every one of us, even Mr Antisocial over there.

I glanced at Felix again, his arms crossed over his chest defiantly, his dark hair fallen in front of his eyes.

I mightn't have been able to see his lifeless stare, but I could feel it. Undoubtedly so. Part of me wished I could act as disinterested as he did, but mine came off as nothing but disingenuous.

Stanley had told me numerous times to stop comparing myself to him. He told me I was my own person who would, *and could,* achieve my own things. But I compared myself to Felix like it was a drug I was addicted to.

He was all I'd ever known, my competition from the day I was born. It was depressing and sad, but it was the truth. I felt meaningless without it.

Kobi began, but his words fell upon deaf ears as excruciating pain tore through my entire system. I screamed out an agonising screech as I collapsed against the floor on my hands and knees, unsuccessfully grasping at the hard and cold surface below.

I wrapped one hand around my belly and shrieked, echoed by someone else. I glanced up quickly as teardrops stung behind my wide blue eyes. Felix slammed against the ground, thrashing his limbs around in anguish and distress.

My vomit spewed across the polished floor as Stanley and Kobi rushed to my side. Their words inaudible as I cried, and puked, and shook with something beyond agony.

My power sparked against me like an unbalanced flicker, trying in vain to get a hold of my tortured body. I could hear Kobi shouting, could feel Stanley's hand against my back, could sense within me Felix's power trying and failing to secure him.

This power felt unstable, overwhelming. It did not feel like my own; it did not feel like Felix's. It knocked down every single one of my defences, driving me further and further into an endless pit of pain and suffering.

I couldn't disconnect, and my weakened ability could not combat it. It was omnipotent, wilful, strong. Had I not felt like death was knocking down my door, I would have been impressed.

Then suddenly, it stopped.

My power cooled and calmed the electric and catastrophic forces within me as I struggled for air. I breathed in deep, stabilising my emotions as I regained control over my limbs. I slipped back and sat defeatedly down against the ground, eyeing my vomit spewed across the floor.

My eyes lifted to meet Felix's.

They were scared, intense, knowing. *Knowing?* I concentrated, an omnipotent feeling infiltrating my senses, but it did not wish to harm me or hurt me. It did not wish to kill me. I gasped, my shaky eyes darting to his.

Our bodies simultaneously shuddered as our thoughts concurrently connected. "The Ultimate Weapon," we bellowed in unison as our minds pieced the puzzle.

In seconds we were on our feet, racing for the exit, ignoring their shocked soundlessness as we scrambled into the elevator, desperate to reach ground floor.

Felix pushed at the button like a crazed madman, over and over, until the doors dinged and opened. We surged into the lobby and dashed through the pools of people. We were manic, anxious, overwhelmed with the urgency to reach our destination.

I could feel the power, the pull, the proximity—*I could feel the Ultimate Weapon.*

We darted outside and jumped into one of Kobi's cars, Felix at the wheel. He revved the engine and skidded out the parking bay, driving recklessly towards our powerful entity that signalled in the night.

The headlights reflected across the wet roads as overhead lights briefly invaded the car with an artificial brightness.

Felix's side profile was partially visible as the above lights illuminated his face for brief moments between. I watched his throat shift as his breaths pounded into the atmosphere in an aimless manner. I could sense his concern, his trepidation, his eagerness.

A sudden gasp escaped my lips as he turned a sharp corner on two wheels. I banged against the side of the door, immediately straightening my posture. I reached behind and grabbed the seatbelt, buckling myself securely in place.

Felix glanced my way and laughed. *Laughed.* I hadn't heard that sound in what felt like forever, that sound that lit up his face with a glowing and happy gleam. I had forgotten what that looked like.

"Bet you've missed my driving," he said playfully. I made a face and lifted my hand, grabbing the assistance grip firmly. "You feel it?" he asked in a serious tone, his face now void of any enjoyment.

"I feel it." I nodded curtly as my blue eyes scanned the road ahead, unsure of what inhuman entity awaited our arrival.

Felix skidded the car to a harsh and abrupt halt moments before we barrelled into the dark and silent night.

No aeroplanes loomed above us, no sounds echoed from beyond the shadowy veil, no single creature stirred. "You take that side of the park; I'll take this side," I directed, arm outstretched in explanation.

Felix nodded, flipping over the stone wall fearlessly and into the darkness that loomed ahead. I darted to the other side of the park.

The electric pulse was strong here; I was almost on top of it. I could feel it jolt through my veins, run through my blood, spark through my system. It was divine and daunting, powerful and perplexing, calming and concerning.

An excited anticipation drove me onward as I jogged to each section of the park, searching, praying, hoping.

Was I really going to find the Ultimate Weapon?

After all my failures, after all those sleepless nights, after all the devastating losses. Was I truly only moments away from coming face-to-face with this weapon of supreme power?

I never should've doubted Stanley, I never should've disbelieved his research. He knew all along, he believed, he kept his hope alive. He knew this powerful entity existed, and he *knew* I would find them. So did Kobi. Mum probably did, too.

Would this discovery cause everything to shift, everything to change, everything to combust? Would Felix and I save our friendship, our brotherly bond lost so long ago? Would Kobi no longer have any need for us?

Would I escape his harsh mistreatments, my mother's disapproving eyes, the bunker I had forever longed to elude?

Hyperventilated breaths pounded against me in cold puffs that clouded before my lips momentarily. My fists clenched and unclenched nervously as I clambered up an old telephone booth, observing the still and silent night.

A drop of blood oozed from my finger, and I gasped, pulling my hand back in worry. I jumped down, my sneakers landing in a loud crunch of broken fragments. They sparkled against the faded lamppost light as I looked down at them eerily.

Vast arrays of shimmers glistened from far away as I lifted my chin and glanced across the parklands. It was as if every glass compound had shattered, raining against the ground like fallen stars snatched from the night sky.

I noticed then, the patrol cars and officers chatting amongst themselves, eagerly addressing the situation at hand. I crept low and moved closer, eavesdropping on their conversation.

"—Said it was like a bomb. She reported seeing all the windows shatter simultaneously as a large orange orb emitted a ripple into the parklands. I'm not entirely sure what to make of it," he uttered, his features perplexed.

"The report I took from the gentleman over there was eerily similar," the female officer spoke instructively. "He told me he saw this blinding light, like an orange wave, which ran outward and shattered the windows. He said it was quite supernatural-like."

A heartbeat passed between them. "Do we think this is Mr Holloway related?"

I gasped, then quickly covered my mouth. They thought it was to do with Kobi. It made sense, obviously, but I had no idea he had ties to the police force.

All along, had he been manipulating Felix and I into compliance all whilst entangling his dishonest misdoings within every law enforcement organisation?

Did the Army know, the Marines, the Air Force? Just how far did this devious scheme go? And how come I had never noticed it before, had I really been that blind to what was going on this entire time?

I knew we had connections to the government. I knew that's how our supernatural abilities were well-protected from outsider groups, and how Kobi had managed to secure the funding for the makeshift empire he created off of them.

But this? This felt next level, this felt deceitfully and strategically planned out.

What malicious intentions awaited the Ultimate Weapon? I felt sick just thinking about it; I felt ill just trying to fit all the seemingly meaningless pieces together.

The Ultimate Weapon was omnipotent, an entity designed to never unleash their power within the known universe. But what would happen if they did?

What if the imbalance Felix and I had inadvertently caused had destroyed the limitations of their unmatched ability? What if that doomsday was still entirely possible?

An orange orb that emitted a power strong enough to shatter every window... an orange wave with blinding light that rippled against the darkened night... the Ultimate Weapon had awakened, and I was positive the world was not ready for their insurmountable supremacy.

"*Ace!*" Felix bellowed from the darkness.

I shot up onto my feet and ran, my elbows pumping. I could hear the glass lodged within the tread of my sneakers, shifting and breaking, as each shoe slapped against the ground.

I sprinted towards Felix with urgency. We were in over our heads. The Ultimate Weapon was not made for this world, was not made for humankind.

"Ace, over here!" Felix called, waving his arm within the air as his voice grew louder. I slowed, breathing hard as I glanced at the mangled and inhumanly moved train.

"It's weird," Felix stated. "It looks like it ran the tracks, but the tracks aren't damaged. It's like someone just picked it up and placed it gently on the slope, but that dent—that dent is fascinating." He clicked his tongue in wonder as a moan echoed from beyond the fallen train. We shared an apprehensive look before we hurried to find the owner of the muffled echo.

An elderly man sat up drearily, holding his head. His shirt was untucked and messy against him, his tie dirty, his overalls scuffed. He was clearly the locomotive driver.

Someone had placed him here against the track ballast with a tattered and stained jumper beneath him. One that certainly didn't match his well-pressed uniform.

"Sir, are you alright? What happened?" I queried, reaching tentatively for his back to support his hunched position. He was old and wrinkled, his hair grey and thinned.

"I, *um*," he stuttered with a coarse and worried tone. "I don't understand what happened," he croaked, shaking his head.

Felix stepped closer, arms crossed, listening intently. I knew the police would be scoping the area, but I couldn't rush the old man for information.

"There was this shadow, a girl, *she*—she jumped in front of the train. I didn't have time to stop or even react." He sobbed, tears escaping his copper-coloured eyes. He sniffed and stifled his cries.

"When the train and her collided, there was this moment, like a slow motioned act, everything moved in milliseconds. I heard her scream as this bright glow flew out from around her, encircling her like a bubble. She was in so much pain. Then, I felt the train sway, and something lifting me, placing me down gently in the cold. But I was weak, exhausted." He leaned into me, his voice hot. "And a little scared." He swayed back. "I didn't want to open my eyes; I didn't want to witness what I thought was death." His expression flared with a fearful flicker.

"Can you stand?" I smiled his way, trying to ease his distressed thoughts.

"I can try."

I guided him onto his feet and down against the large sleepers. He weakly stood, grasping my sweater as firmly as he could.

"What's this?" an officer exclaimed as they peered down at us with a too-bright flashlight.

We shielded our eyes as Felix stepped aside, signalling the old man and obsolete train. The officers gasped in unison moments before one swayed back and radioed the situation in.

"Are you okay, sir?" the female officer asked, descending the slope with unsteady footing.

"I am unsure," he muttered gravely.

"Ambulance is on the way, sir, they'll get you checked over soon." She looked to us sharply. "Do either of you two know what happened here?"

I opened my mouth to speak, but Felix beat me to it. "No," he muttered dryly. "We found the train and the old man this way. My brother and I are looking for our dog." I couldn't believe how easily the lies rolled off his tongue.

The officer turned to me and narrowed her eyes with suspicion. I nodded, perhaps a little too eagerly, but it was enough for her to be convinced. "Speak to Officer Neil. He'll take your reports, then you can go find your dog," she instructed as she aided the old man.

I glanced at Felix quickly before we ascended, his expression unreadable, but at least he didn't look displeased with me. We reached the top of the slope as sirens wailed against the darkened skies.

We recounted our stories to Neil. I went first; Felix went second. We weren't unfamiliar with officers, or reports, or punishments. In the beginning, Felix and I had really given our all to making everything difficult for Kobi.

Unfortunately, it hadn't lasted long.

We learnt from an early age our abilities and how we differed from those around us. We were known to few as 'Supers.' Not quite superheroes, not quite human beings.

We were somewhere in between, a place not yet designed, a term not yet invented. With expectations, and consequences, and responsibilities far too big for our adolescent expertise.

"She must be the Ultimate Weapon," Felix mumbled as we slid into the warm embrace of the car. I nodded, continuing to survey the area for any signs of movement or activity. We couldn't return with nothing.

We still sensed the Ultimate Weapon's presence, but not as strongly as before. The inhuman connection remained, the invisible string that tied us together, the intangible chain that kept us linked.

"We can't go back empty-handed," Felix added, as if reading my own depressing thoughts. I nodded, reluctantly agreeing.

CHAPTER 7

RED

As I wandered, my body didn't ache, my bruised limbs didn't pulse in agony, my scarred knuckle didn't bleed. My body simply reacted to every step I took with a newfound confidence, acting seemingly on its own impulse with nothing holding it back.

I hadn't felt this kind of unrestrained energy in years. I felt like I could take off in a sprint and not face fatigue. Like I could hike the highest mountain, swim the largest canal, combat the deadliest creature.

But there was no way to explain it, no way to put into words what I had felt, what alien glow had radiated from my bare fingertips with an agony that felt like death within my bones.

I stepped out into the roadway and stilled, glancing at my arms unsurely. They seemed odd, less painful, less colourful, almost as if the scars were fading. I touched against my softened skin, doubt creeping across my spine with a prickly sensation.

A car horn blared, and I gasped, thrown against a silver bonnet. I slammed across the glass and flipped over its roof, falling hard on the ground like a rag doll pulled by an invisible string.

I gulped, on my feet in seconds as break lights shone within my fearful eyes and tyres screeched against my eardrums.

A middle-aged man jumped out, his face flushed and tone furious with indignation. "What the hell is wrong with you?"

He stilled, stunned, staring at me with deep apprehension. "You're—*okay?*" he stammered, confusion gnawing at his expression as he eyed me up and down with uncertainty and bewilderment.

Suddenly, a large figure collided against me, almost striking me down as irregular breaths tore from their lungs.

"Are you okay?" *Ace.* His tone piqued with panicked concern as his eyes grew wide with worry and his breaths tumbled unevenly from his perfect lips. "Where does it hurt?" He examined my shaky form, searching for any signs of pain or injury as his fingertips trembled against me.

I didn't know what to say, I didn't know how to explain the inexplicable. My body had seared with energy, had surged with a power unknown to me.

I stood, mute, for once completely speechless as his doubtful eyes met mine.

"Is the car alright?" someone asked the man from afar.

I glanced over to see a boy that looked strikingly like Ace. Only the hair colour, unconventional hairstyle, and noticeable piercings were a stark difference to the stately boy who stood before me. And their eyes... they seemed greyer, duller, *darker.*

The man stepped back and glanced at the damaged hood before shaking his head stiffly. "Bit of a dent in the bonnet," he expressed, agitation lacing his tone.

"How much?" Ace's look-alike questioned. "Six hundred?"

The man hesitated. "I, *uh,* I'd say that's a little too much," he commented, his honesty refreshing.

The enigmatic boy slipped his wallet from his rear pocket, flicking through the multitude of notes. "Some extra for your discretion, then." He eyed the man with a fierce and dark expression. One even I wouldn't dare cross.

The man stood agape for a moment too long, then nodded nervously. The boy smiled, the slightest mouth upturn, before handing him the notes. He retreated to his car, accelerating into the night without so much as a second glance.

Ace looked to me abruptly, his blue eyes filled with concern, but I lowered my head and looked away from them both. I hugged at my fragile body tightly; afraid I would shatter at any given moment. I held my breath, pinning my lips down in place. This wasn't real, it couldn't be.

Nothing hurt. Nothing ached.

"Ace?" I asked timidly as I looked up. He nodded softly as he placed his hand carefully against my shoulder, lowering his head to my height. "Am I dead?" The two boys shared a fearful and knowing glance between them.

I hesitated as I lifted my hands to my face and flipped them back and forth, examining their grainy and unusual texture. "My scars—they're healing." My tone trembled as horror embedded itself within my unstable system.

I gasped loudly, stepping back as I glared at my wounded arms in astonishment, watching as the bruises and scars, as the burns and cuts, all completely healed. Unsteady breaths tore from my lungs as I retreated further and further from Ace's propinquity.

Fear shook me to its very core as bare, unharmed, and pale skin shone beneath the glow of the overhead lights. I screamed and grabbed at my stomach, circling around as everything scattered within my head like a jar of toppled marbles. My eyes shut tight as I bent down, gritting my teeth hard.

"Red, *Red!*" Ace yelled, grabbing my shoulders firmly.

I shot upward, my eyes wide and fearful as I stood eerily still, my mind screaming at me from within, but his gaze remained against me, coating me in a secure, safe, and unfamiliar feeling.

"What is happening to me? I can't *feel* anything," I cried. Ace gasped, his eyes widening with fright as his mouth fell agape.

Terror spread through my bones.

"Come with me," he ordered, reaching for my hand in haste. We both gasped as a spark of electricity jolted from against our fingertips. I pulled my hand to my chest, the feeling within my numb fingers charged by an unseen force. Ace reached for my hand once more, this time not emitting any haphazard effects.

"That's Felix, my twin brother," he added quickly. I glanced over at the stranger sheepishly, our eyes meeting for mere uncomfortable seconds. He nodded stiffly, pursing his lips.

I looked back to Ace and followed his lead, my gaze now fixated on my bare, freckle-covered arms. It had been years since I'd seen those imperfect freckles.

Rain drummed against us as we ventured through the park.

The whole time Ace and Felix spoke, but I didn't catch a thing. I was baffled, terrified, numb, and so, so scared. I had lived almost half my life with those bruises. With those burns, cuts, and scars they had enforced upon me.

Mutilations I believed I would possess for the rest of my miserable life, no matter how hard I fought to heal them.

Ace steered us towards a vacant parking lot, ushering me into a sleek and shiny car. I fell into the leather seat, quiet and still. I pulled up my tee shirt as Ace slipped into the seat next to me and Felix into the back.

Nothing. I pulled down the fabric, reaching for my trackies as the car engine roared. I lifted the ragged material hurriedly and inwardly gasped, my mind flattened like a tsunami hell-bent on human obliteration.

Nothing. Not one single scar. Not one faded bruise. Not one ugly scuff mark. Startling realisation slammed through me as I reclined into the seat, sinking like quicksand.

My frame subtly shook, but I forced myself to look straight ahead. I couldn't bear to look down, not again, not after all those years of bearing those brutal marks.

It had been so long, a constant reminder of a never-ending hell that looped indefinitely. They told me I would never see my pale-coloured skin again. They told me they would kill me long before I ever had that chance.

"I'm going to puke," I blurted. Ace gasped, immediately pulling the car against the kerb. I opened the passenger side door and vomited, over and over, for what felt like an eternity.

I wiped my mouth with my tee shirt, slowly resting against the seat with a throat that burned.

"Red?" Ace asked tentatively.

I bit down on my lip hard, tears threatening to loosely slip as Ace watched me carefully, placing his hand lightly against my arm. The interaction heartfelt, the motion gentle, the gesture kind.

A drop of orange blood dripped from my lip, and I gasped. One single droplet, and then, nothing. I felt no pain, no discomfort. Only undeniable unease.

Ace swallowed hard. "You were abused," he whispered, tears within his own pastel-hued eyes. I kept my face firm, not daring to react. "Every day... it would seem."

I felt the heat within the car, felt Ace's soft expression, then Felix's pressing stare fuse against me. Everything was happening too quick, too soon. *It was all too much.*

Tears filled my glassy eyes as a single sob escaped my dried lips, my pained mind seeping through the cracks of my iron-built exterior.

Ace's face fell, his fingers tapping against the steering wheel rhythmically. He looked away momentarily as cold air swept in through the open door.

"I would close my eyes and pray, every night, to be granted one wish. Just one, only one." I lifted my head and stared at the night sky, watching the stars twinkle, the clouds roll by, the planet shift.

A coarse breath left my lips as I looked back, our troubled eyes meeting. "To feel no pain." I smiled a broken smile. "Now, I can't feel pain, I can't feel anything. They broke me, all of them. I ran off energy I didn't have, fought every day for something I didn't want. I was exhausted," I wept. "I *welcomed* it. I *wished* for it. I was gone. I was dead, but then... I woke up." My brown eyes shook as my voice trembled. "I woke up," I echoed hopelessly.

Living was misery. It was pain, suffering, and I was being forced to keep enduring it. Existing in a world I faltered to. Life was only supposed to be temporary, but there I was.

I did not understand why. Why I was being penalised, why I was being punished. Why those bruises I wore like battle scars had all but faded. A constant reminder of cruelty and brutality.

Gone—just like that.

"You killed yourself," his mortified expression a perfect match to his shaken tone. It was half question, half statement, although deep down, he must have known the answer that lay in wait.

I touched upon my arm softly, cautiously, pressing my fingertip against the naked skin. I traced my freckles, the way I used to, creating constellations against my dotted skin.

"You can't help me," I abruptly stated, no hint of doubt within my unwavering tone. I lifted myself from the seat, aiming for the outside world.

Ace grabbed my arm urgently, causing my eyes to snap back to his. "No," he declared, looking across at me longingly. "Did I cause this?" His tone shuddered against my unsure expression. "I left *you*. I deserted *you*."

I snorted, slipping once more within the warmth of the car. "I told you to, Ace. It wasn't your battle, wasn't your problem. This isn't on you," I conveyed as his tense demeanour slightly relaxed. He exhaled deeply, releasing his hold. I shifted against the seat, unsure what to do.

"Please, don't leave, Red. You're the one I've been waiting for." I narrowed my eyes, feeling distrustful. "I need to take you to see someone. I know what's happening to you... Felix and I, we *know*."

"How could you?" I snapped as my heavy heart went toe-to-toe with my mistreated mind. My emotions held captive before my own gormless divergence.

There was a long pause before he spoke again. "You're the Ultimate Weapon."

"I'm *what?*" It sounded comical, stupid, amusing.

I shook my head savagely and pulled away, slipping within the darkness. Ace jumped out and darted in front of me. "Red, please, nothing is going to make sense from here on out unless you listen," he implored, his eyes pleading. "You're immune to pain, you're not hungry, or thirsty, or covered in bruises. You feel *nothing.* Your body healed before your very own eyes. Red, I asked you for a reason, asked if you believed. It isn't make-believe, isn't ill-fated hope—superheroes exist, but not like you think, not how you know."

"*Shut up!*" I cried, fear latching itself against my malnourished core. "You don't know *anything!*" I blurted, panic burning within my overworked lungs as my body convulsed.

I was so confused, terrified, lost within a maze I didn't even understand. How the hell could this be real? What supernatural fuckery had truly caused my bruised limbs and burnt flesh to heal before my own two eyes?

It wasn't real, it couldn't b*e. I refused to believe that.*

Confusion bubbled within me as I lifted my hand, gnawing on the fingernail of my thumb, grinding my teeth against the solid compound like it would break me not to.

Who was I without the abuse—without the handprints and scorch marks of evil present against my skin?

I had long given up on tee shirts, on shorts, on dresses, on anything that didn't shield my body away with oversized cotton and polyester. No matter the season, the weather, the time of year. I did what I had to do to survive, did what I had to do to protect my abusers. I could see now how stupid I had been, but back then, I had thought an abusive home was better than no home at all.

So, I protected myself from the concerned stares and whispered murmurs of others. Of those who asked if I was okay, then backed away with contrite expressions when I had told them no. But it wasn't just them who did me wrong, it was the whole screwed up system I was forced to be part of, when all I ever did was begged to be loved.

A sharp tickle suddenly stabbed against my throat. "Stop that." Ace whacked my hand away from my face. I gasped, anger sweeping across me like a sudden shift in tectonic plates.

I clenched my fist, ready to let my wound-up mind shriek. "You ripped off your nail," he uttered, staring at my hand with disturbed disbelief.

My limbs stilled midmotion as I narrowed my eyes in confusion and glanced down at my thumb. My bottom lip slacked as I stared at my hand with deep apprehension.

I held my breath, daring it to suffocate me, daring it to end my torment within this endless afterthought of existence.

"Red, listen to me," Ace sharply stated as Felix exited the car and stood watch.

"*No!*" I bellowed from the pit of my burning core, my eyes like daggers as I backed away from them both. "I don't need to do a damn thing, Ace. You explain what the hell is happening to me!" I roared as uncertainty crept along my trembling form, my stomach pounding in and out with each frightened breath.

"Listen, Red, this isn't going to make any sense to you," he proclaimed, stepping closer as panic spread across his flawless features.

"I don't care—just *explain* it!"

A piercing sound suddenly ricocheted through every terrified inch of me. It vibrated within my entire body, crushing my organs, squishing my cells, sending agonising pain spiralling through me.

I fell to my knees as my hands began to abnormally glow. I screamed, but my vocal cords were silenced, my body aching for any form of release as I glared at my glowing hands with trepidation. Trepidation that threatened to blow me into a whole other dimension.

Energy lashed like wild waves against my inhuman form as I forced myself up and onto my trembling legs. Ace and Felix stood, frozen in place. Terror sprawled across their faces as the entire world shook around me, sending me further and further into a dark and inescapable abyss.

"Make it stop!" I bellowed as I watched my fingertips emit a terrifying glow. It pulsed against me, forceful and bold.

I was breaking apart, splitting down the uneven cracks of my own excessive state. I'd seen hell on Earth, seen violence, assault, been threatened with blades against my throat and knuckles that gripped my skin until it turned blue. But never before had I seen power expel from my fingertips and entwine into the atmosphere around me, beckoning like a beacon in the dark, forcing itself to be known and forcing me to believe in the unbelievable.

I had never wasted my time believing in the unknown, believing in the revolutionary and extraordinary. I'd spent my whole life just trying to believe in making it through to tomorrow. And most days, I didn't think I could.

Life was hard, unforgiving, and unkind. It tormented me at each step, my body a prisoner to the aches and pains it bore from years and years of shattered refinement. But I used that rage, that wroth within my bones to drive me on, day in and day out. The anger the only thing that had ever made sense to my tarnished and fragmented mind. And I held onto that with everything I had.

Heavy breaths pounded from my lips as I collapsed against the footpath. I held my stomach tightly and placed my forehead upon the concrete below.

I focused on calm, on stillness and peace. I whimpered, forcing my body to obey as the abnormal glow oozed back within my shaky hands. Teardrops slipped uncontrollably onto my cheeks, desperate to reach the ground below. One after the other, over, and over. Droplets eager to be freed, to be torn from the numbness of my mind.

I gulped and sat up, falling back on my butt. I wiped at my eyes with the back of my hand, gasping at the strange orange droplets that spotted against my bare arm.

Ace sank beside me and reached for my shaky limb, slowly lowering it. I glared at him steadily, waiting for him to speak, waiting for him to explain.

There were no words, no explanations within my disrupted mind. Not after my whole world had just crumbled, broken down into nothing but dust, and debris, and fragmented hope.

"You died, Red," he softly began. "You're the Ultimate Weapon now," he muttered dryly, sounding as if he himself didn't believe those words. "What more proof do you need?" He looked directly at me then. His face pale and his pastel-hued eyes fearful, like he was hiding behind a tsunami of emotions he couldn't rectify.

What more proof *did* I need?

I needed it to be false, fictitious. I didn't want to believe in it, didn't want to even acknowledge it. People were born, they grew old, and then they died. It wasn't possible to live beyond that, it wasn't possible to live without pain, without malice, without consequence.

I couldn't accept this, I couldn't allow myself to believe in this idiocy, because there was no way to run from that. From a truth that had so indelicately latched itself against me with a strong-handed fist.

Every bone in my body had broken, every limb torn from its socket, my own flesh had tightened so hard it split from my skin.

There was no way in hell I could convince myself otherwise, but I did not believe in fantasies, I did not believe in prophecies, I did not believe in superhuman abilities.

I did not even believe in myself.

"Dr Stanley Pattison. He's taught me all I know."

"About me?"

"Indirectly, yes. They call us Supers. We're part of the imbalance; that's why we're like this. Although, our powers are a lot different to yours, a lot weaker," he conveyed as I eyed Felix, who rested against the car, poised and alert.

"I still experience pain, and I didn't have to die to be this way. I was born with these abilities, I was born a twin, the cause of the imbalance." He sighed heavily, continuing reluctantly. "It's to do with the Legend of Millennia, an old tale that began at the start of creation."

"Start of creation?" I echoed, disbelieving. "Am I being punished... by some old legend... for something totally coincidental?" Sudden aggravation laced my tongue as Ace curtly nodded.

I scoffed, but at least he wasn't lying about it.

"Legend foretold that long ago two brothers went to war, one of good and one of bad. Their powers of light and of dark scorched together, devastating the Earth, destroying all that stood, so too, themselves. This battle led the universe to create the balance: the

Ultimate Weapon."

I blocked the anger out of my system, listening intently, trying desperately to retain the information before it slipped away like a balloon string from a child's slimy palm.

"Each millennium, an entity with the powers of the Ultimate Weapon births, unknowingly to what lies within them. They grow up, live a normal life, and then they die. A balance that is renewed every one thousand years," he paused.

"When my mum birthed twins, it created the imbalance. We weren't one entity, so the power split in two, returning Felix and I to our ancestral powers of light and of dark. The Ultimate Weapon, therefore, came to be nonentity. However, the universe had to restore itself, meaning you became the byproduct of that imbalance, and somehow, unlocked the formidable powers of the Ultimate Weapon within. A power that is strong enough to send us back to the Stone Age or millenniums into the future."

"Why me?" I argued thoughtlessly.

"You were born when the third millennium began, January 1st, 2001. You share the same birthdate as us. I don't know why this title befell you, I just know that it did." He glanced across at me longingly.

I shook my head in irritation. "I don't know what you think I'm capable of, but I'm not," I declared bluntly.

"Come with me," Ace urged, his pastel-blue eyes yearning for my acceptance. "Please, Red." I swallowed hard, shifting my hand roughly upon the loose gravel, desperate to feel the pain. "Stop," he ordered, grabbing my wrist, but his harsh tone held hidden empathies.

I felt like a statue. Frozen in time, blockaded in place. There for all to admire, but none to really understand. A fractured form of something once whole but now confined to a barrier built behind solid glass and iron balustrades.

Vulnerable. Vulnerable to the very core.

I placed my hand within Ace's, feeling his body warmth run through me like a deadly toxin. My eyes lifted to meet his as his breath hitched, his frame trembling ever so slightly.

"I want to see it," I requested. Ace narrowed his eyes in confusion. "I want to see your power."

"Not here," he uttered, sounding defeated. "It's not made for this world, Red. Our ties to the government secure our safety, but we have rules we must follow." He deeply sighed, a heavy burden resting upon his shoulders.

Felix caught my eye as he shook his head pompously. Although, I had no idea what it meant. "They'll already need to cover up what has happened tonight," Ace continued.

As if on cue, sirens echoed against the darkened skies, filling the atmosphere with their suffocated wails that ricocheted inside my eardrums.

We both looked up the road, seeing red and blue lights illuminate alongside the dim nighttime surroundings. They shone within my scarlet eyes, beckoning to be seen.

I winced, looking away as they darted past.

"We're not untouchable, Red." Ace turned back towards me as the world grew silent once more.

"Then what are we?" I shot up onto my worn sneakers, anger spiralling through me as I glared at him with a pleading look, begging for an answer.

"If I'm dead, I can't die again!" I bellowed belligerently. "Why the hell am I still here? Just what the hell is the point of pointless?" I screamed at him, and for a moment, desperate for him to hold the answer, but deep down, I knew it was never going to be that simple, that meek.

Life was cruel—I knew that. I'd lived each useless day within the midst of that. I was more fractured than full, more broken than built, more scattered than sculptured.

Each day I dared myself to keep going, to keep fighting the demons not only in my head, but the ones that welcomed me into their homes with lies, deceptions, and angelic halos that covered their devil horns.

Every moment filled with malice, each hour strewn with nothing but instability, and each moment that passed, one I could never recover.

"You're not pointless, Red. You never were." My eyes shot to his, burning like ripples of fire against a straw field.

"How the hell would you know that? You don't know me!" I yelled, seeing red as my knuckles furiously clenched. "This isn't some fantasy world, Ace," I proclaimed, filling the open space with the echoes of my enraged temper. "I've been alive for a lot longer than the few days you've known me, and I assure you, it wasn't all sunshine and lollipops—it was fucking hell!" My vision blurred with fury as my chest heaved in and out with agitated breaths.

He knew nothing about me, nothing about my life, nothing about my future. "Don't you dare," I sneered. "You know *nothing,* so I suggest you shut your damn mouth before you really regret it."

Ace swallowed hard, feeling uncomfortable as he shifted his weight from one foot to the other. "I'm sorry," he conveyed. I narrowed my eyes with suspicion, watching him carefully. "No, you're right," he announced to my surprise. "I don't know anything about you. Anything about your life, about your past." He glanced up at me then, his body falling eerily still, his eyes fixated on mine. "But there is one thing I do know, Red—you are the Ultimate Weapon, whether you choose to accept it or not."

I was scared. I was terrified. This wasn't real, it couldn't be. Superpowers didn't exist. Death was inevitable. It was the unfiltered truth of a broken world twisted within the illusions of heaven and hell.

Death was all we could ever be sure of. It was the end of the line, the last call, the final countdown. It was unavoidable certainty, the rarest form of reality, and it was inescapable.

And yet, there I stood with an alien glow within me, a temper ready to blow, and a mind fractured from years of neglect. I could not escape it even if I tried. It was woven into the very fabric of who I was.

"Take me to see that doctor," I bade. Ace nodded, reaching for my hand within the darkened night. I realised then, the silence, the shadows, the feeling of solitude that befell the fallen sun. I glanced up at the moon, large and bright, taking up more space in the night sky than seemingly possible.

Did I reflect that in my own life? I dared to be outspoken, to be noticed, to be challenged. Most of the wounds that had befallen my skin had been from the result of my own temper, of my own words and actions, or was that only what I had been told to spare their own notions of right from wrong?

I looked back to Ace, trailing my eyes from his head to his chest, to his outstretched arm and slightly curled fingers. He held himself with such promise, such kindness.

If I took his hand within mine, who's to say I wouldn't become attached? Who's to say I wouldn't hold his well-being above my own?

He was gentle, surprisingly so. And kind in a way I'd only ever seen my mother. Ace felt new, but in a familiar way. He felt safe, in an intriguing one.

If I was truly this all-powerful entity, like Ace had forewarned, what would become of me? Would my own recklessness destroy me, would the system continue to do nothing but fail me, would I unravel this world with the injustice and hatred I felt towards it?

If I was truly this formidable being that had been foretold, then just who in the hell would be able to stop me?

CHAPTER 8

ACE

There was no excuse for what I had done. I had lied to her. Lied straight to her face, lied right in front of Felix. I knew who Red was. Knew about her past, about the abuse. I also knew that her parents weren't really her parents, a fact I wasn't sure she was even aware of.

Above all, I needed to gain her trust, I needed her to know I was by her side.

And so, I'd lied. I was nothing but a perfect stranger to her. I couldn't come at her with seventeen years of knowledge about her life. She would have freaked, and rightfully so. I just hoped this poorly laid plan didn't backfire.

It seemed the anger within her was explosive, destructive, unpredictable. It warped her thoughts and contorted her decisions. I had to tread cautiously; I had to be careful.

Red wasn't just a girl with a red-hot temper anymore; she was a girl with a power strong enough to blow this entire Earth to unrecognisable pieces. I couldn't allow myself to push her that far, I couldn't allow myself to trigger those unstable emotions.

She sat beside me, poking, picking, pushing at her bare skin.

She traced along her freckles, felt the bones within her skinny wrists, judged the way her fingers perfectly aligned. Her life was never going to be the same, but then again, neither were the lives of Felix and me.

I eyed him within the rearview mirror, watching as he stared at Red with a steady curiosity. He'd pushed the dishevelled hair away from his eyes, examining her with a clear view, studying the way she touched her skin with deep apprehension.

His company tonight had been most enjoyable. I had missed that, had missed the way we worked together. It had been a long time since he could stand being in the same room as me, let alone the same car.

I let loose a steady breath and looked forward, watching the road as we headed back to headquarters.

An uneasy feeling surged within my stomach, and I pulled the car over, bringing it to a slow and easy standstill. Felix and Red both looked my way questioningly.

"What are you doing?" Felix barked, glancing out the window unsurely.

I twisted back around to face him. "Are we sure about this?"

He shot me a puzzled and impatient look. "What the hell are you talking about?"

"Delivering the Ultimate Weapon to Kobi," I answered as Felix glanced at Red doubtfully. I did the same, her tiny stature holding tight to so many dangerous and destructive capabilities.

I knew everything ever documented about her past... but I didn't know anything about *her*. I felt obligated to protect her, to safeguard her. I didn't want to lead her into the arms of Kobi so doubtlessly. I wanted my brother—*of course I did*—I wanted my freedom, but was I willing to hand over an innocent girl just for the slim possibility of that?

I knew Kobi. I knew his twisted ways, his deceptive words, his hazardous views. Add that with the information I'd pieced together from those officers, and the plan that awaited her became crystal clear.

He was going to use Red as a weapon. He was going to pass her around until she had destroyed everything except for herself. He was going to ruin her mind, manipulate her thoughts, and coerce her into using this unmatched power for violence, bloodshed, and war.

It was unbelievable just how long it had taken me to realise the full extent of Kobi's deceit. I was nothing but a pawn within a losing game, and now, I had sentenced Red to that same cruel fate. For too long, I had only thought about myself, about my own selfish feelings. I never considered the Ultimate Weapon as their own person, and never as an impetuous and temperamental girl.

"We need to think about this." I eyed Felix bleakly as my eyes communicated the unspoken words.

"Think about *what?*" he argued. "I didn't just hand over six hundred bucks for you to finally grow a conscience. We have been searching for the Ultimate Weapon most of our lives, how can you just throw that all away now we've finally found her?" His voice sparked with venom, and honestly, I couldn't blame him for it.

"I heard those police officers talking tonight. They know Kobi," I stated firmly.

Felix shook his head, a manic expression against his cold eyes. "And that's news to you?" he barked.

"Kobi has the whole damn world wrapped around his finger.

She is the Ultimate Weapon, she's indestructible. Do you have any idea how many wars she could win, how much peace she could inspire?" He eyed me furiously. "This isn't just about *us;* it never has been. We are not powerful enough." He was shouting now, filling the car with a loud and obnoxious screech.

"Why are you talking about me like I'm not right here?" Red bellowed angrily. We both fell silent and glanced across at her timidly. Her face was etched with anger, her bottom lip stiff, her fists clenched. "What the fuck did I just become?"

Suddenly, an ear-piercing wail filled the confines of the car as an electric and haywire force field expelled out around us. Felix and I gasped, breaking away from our overloaded and overexerted minds as orange waves buzzed and jittered within the vehicle.

Red's eyes glowed inhumanly bright as her hair weaved with that same unstable energy. Her bones cracked, protruding from the naked skin as her flesh burned and blistered.

I rammed against the door as scintillated waves darted uncontrollably around us. Her power was compelling, powerful. I could feel the strong connection between us; I could feel the way my body pushed and shoved me in her direction.

She shrieked as a searing sensation inched up her pale arm, scorching the hair clean off. She convulsed, her body trembling violently against the leather seat.

I reached out and touched her, the electricity lapping at my hand. It was hot and painful, burning the sensitive skin against my fingertips.

Red collapsed, her force field blinking out of existence like it never even was. She leant against the car door, breathing heavily and haphazardly. "Pain," she squeaked through her uncontrolled breaths. "Do you feel *any* pain?"

How she looked my way was heartbreaking, teardrops that stung at the corners of her eyes, her bottom lip that violently trembled, her pale cheeks that glowed with red splotches.

I inhaled hard before answering. I wouldn't lie, not again. "Red," I began. "I don't feel pain when I use my power, neither does Felix. Like I said earlier, we were born this way. Our bodies have always just—*known.*" I shrugged a shoulder.

"We experience pain when we get injured, but it's rare, and we heal quickly." I peeked back at Felix then, his eyes unsure. "Most of the time..." I added as an afterthought.

He seemed awestruck and alarmed. He didn't know all the things I did about Red. He didn't know about the abuse; about the years and years of ill-treatment she encountered. He didn't know of her brutal past.

"Then why do I?" She fearfully shook; seemingly afraid the pain would return just by being spoken of. She lifted her knees to her chest and rocked, backwards and forwards, backwards and forwards. I didn't know what to say, didn't know how to help her.

"Because you committed suicide, probably," Felix uttered from the backseat. Red gasped and spun around, her eyes wide and intense against Felix's. "It's literally self-destruction, why would the power within you allow such brutality?"

He was so sure of his harmful words. "Watch," he instructed. He lifted his hand, filling the car with a shadowy and lifeless mist that bunched like billowed smoke alongside us, morphing and distorting into shapes and figures.

His eyes darkened exponentially until they were completely black, the veins within his body following that same discoloured pattern. He looked like a tiger, white sickly skin against lines of black scars that twitched and pulsated grotesquely.

"Our powers are within us, but they are also independent within their own right. We cannot use our power against itself, we cannot try to force it out of us, we cannot destroy it."

Red eyed the shadowy creations with admiration as they hovered around us. "There are consequences if we try. We are blessed with these abilities. We can learn from them if we allow them to grow, and change, and alter." Felix lowered his hand, the lifeless fog ceasing, along with the unnatural discolouration against his flesh.

Red watched, open-mouthed and in awe. I was surprised she wasn't disgusted. Before today, I had witnessed only a few others observe Felix's powers, and they had all been sickened by his ghastly appearance. One had even vomited.

He was an entity of darkness, possibly even of death. When he used his abilities, his hair turned as black as his eyes, but you could hardly tell now he'd dyed and defaced those natural locks.

"You will never be able to use your power without pain, because that's how the power began, how it birthed. That's how the imbalance within you renewed itself. I'm sorry," he muttered, looking against Red's upset face. "I really am."

I stared at Felix in disbelief. He had never been this open or honest about his powers with me. He seemed like a completely different person. Was he faking it, twisting the truth, luring her in so he could ultimately destroy her?

Red hung her head low, her gaze trailing the floor. "I don't want to live like this... I'm supposed to be with my parents." She suddenly gasped, feeling around her neck. "My necklace—" she yelped. Her eyes blazed into mine, frantic and anxious. "I need you to take me back to the motel," she desperately begged.

I nodded, sensing her distress. I put the car into gear and signalled my U-turn, uncertainty playing within my mind.

The overhead lights briefly illuminated the windscreen as I thought back to all those times I'd discussed my abilities with Felix, and he in return.

It felt unnerving, unnatural for him to be so truthful, and to know so much about trying to destroy the powers within us. Had he once tried? Was he talking from firsthand experience?

It was an impossible task to read his facial expression within the reflection. His eyes were so shielded; his face so void of emotion.

There was so much that now intrigued me, so much I desperately yearned to know, but Felix had shut me out long ago. Had drawn the battle lines within the sand. How could I change what had happened between us? How could I rewrite all those past wrongs?

I had mistakenly believed if I listened to Kobi, if I obeyed his orders, Felix and I would finally earn the freedom that we'd both longed for. And yet, maybe that mentality had always been flawed.

Instead, I should've prioritised my brother's well-being over obtaining the Ultimate Weapon.

My tired eyes glanced at Felix's reflection within the rearview mirror, a sympathetic expression against my features and regretful mindset against my thoughts.

One I didn't know if I would ever get to voice.

CHAPTER 9

RED

Was Felix correct? Had I doomed myself the moment I jumped in front of that train? I felt conflicted, doleful, overwhelmed.

I wanted to scream my lungs out until they smoked, wanted to fall to my knees and plead forgiveness, wanted to watch this self-incrimination burn and warp like wildfire on a blustery day.

Every emotion I'd ever experienced, I foolishly wore on full display, daring the world to provoke me, urging it to challenge me, taunting it to attack me and my blazoned battle scars.

Only now, my body pulsed with electric waves, my fingertips burned hot without heat, my bare flesh blinded me with its un-bruised surface. It was only a matter of time before I cracked under the pressure like an inundated hull.

Ace turned at the stoplights, the wheels spinning within my brain as I held my breath tightly within my lungs. I never again wanted to step foot inside that motel, but there was no way I could leave it behind. It was the only valuable thing I'd held onto this entire time.

He pulled the car up to the kerb, but I hesitated, my fingertips hovering alongside the door handle.

I felt afraid, uncertain. What if Norman returned? What if he was already there, lying in wait? A shadow within the darkness, armed and ready to encapsulate me with mangled visions and disfigured values?

But I had bigger problems now…

Suddenly, a bang reverberated from the bonnet. Ace, Felix, and I gasped, looking straight ahead. "What the hell are you doing?" Lira bellowed with hate against her pretty features.

I swore under my breath and opened the door, stepping into the cold air without indecision.

"This is where you've been?" she yelled, her hair messy, her eyes glassy. She intruded my personal space, but I shoved past her, beelining for my rundown room.

She trailed behind me, hot on my heels with strides filled with fury. "You are not welcome here anymore!" she shouted as a few porch lights flickered on.

I huffed and ignored her, fastening my pace. There was only one mission on my mind as I reached for the door handle, but it was locked. I stood back, kicking the door in with one mighty boot.

The wood split, slithering down the flimsy piece like patterns woven into the sand. I barged into the room, eyeing the broken fragments of glass that remained against the stained carpet.

I reached the bedside table, pulling the drawer free. There it was. The silver necklace and '3' pendant. My heart skipped a beat as I slowly held it up, watching the pendant dangle.

I closed my fist around it, shoving it into my pocket as I spun around in haste. Lira stood in the doorway; her temper ready to blow. "Why?"

"Why *what?*" I retorted. "Why do you keep feeling the need to constantly interfere with my life?" I shrieked, anger gnawing away at me, seeping into the cracks within my fractured mind. "I never asked you to!"

"The police came here tonight, looking for you. Just what the hell did you do?" She scoffed, flipping her hair behind her shoulder. "You need to figure out what the hell you're doing with your life before you go and fuck up the lives of others."

The anger within me flipped, buckled, pulsed with a feeling beyond rage. "Fuck up the lives of others?" I repeated, scorching the words into her furiously.

"What about everyone who fucked up *my* life? Who abused me, tormented me, who took me for granted each and every day?" I roared from the depths of my fiery core. "You weren't *there!* One neglectful household and you act as if you've seen all the brutality the world has ever held." I gritted my teeth and clenched my knuckles as red invaded my vision.

My skin seared like molten lava had been poured into each pore. I couldn't control it, the sweeping feeling of salvation, the red-hot pulse of electricity, the eternal touch of brutality.

My body felt fuelled with power and control. A feeling of pure, hypnotising, thrilling freedom that I longed to forever hold. A feeling of euphoric proportion that left me dizzy, and drunk, and high on a power I yearned to capture.

My scream pierced the air as I crumpled to the floor in agonising pain. It was as if all the pain that had healed against my skin now slammed through me. Over, and over, leaving no inch of me untouched by the deadly force that burned deep into the most protected parts of me.

I stumbled to my feet as pain and an orange glow engulfed my entire self. My hands flew open, a supernatural power surging from my fingertips as the unnatural radiance imprisoned itself within the room, weaving like fierce waves about to slam against a ship's mighty hull.

An extreme shriek tore from my throat as forbidden tears invaded my scarlet eyes. I twisted and turned, thrashing my limbs in vain as a phantom force snatched me five feet into the air.

Lira screamed out a fearful pierce, rushing from the room like a ravenous wildcat. Ace caught her bedraggled form, calming her down with hushed words of comfort and a kind smile of reassurance.

My body mimicked an elastic band, stretching and contorting in impossible ways as the room erupted into a misty haze. My entire body fearsomely shook as I hurled my head back, opening my burning eyes.

I caught a glimpse of myself within the mangled mirror, a reflection of pure terror, of something nightmare fuelled and monstrous. I shook frightfully before I forced my eyelids shut, breaking them away from the unrecognisable and inhuman form that stared back with eyes ablaze.

Punished, I could only assume, for being born into a world that I never truly belonged. All I wanted—*all I wished for*—was to be reunited with my parents. To be safe, unharmed, and once again feel loved. I wanted this nightmare, this hell, to be over, to be done. I wanted to be free of these chains, of these consequences to actions that hadn't even been mine.

For once, I wanted the world to be kind, to deliver me to a haven I had forever been kept from...

The ground kissed my face as I landed with a violent snap of fractured bones, but up I stood, unscathed, unbruised, unharmed. Perfectly okay *on the outside.*

My head thudded violently within my eardrums as I gulped down a large breath and ran from the room, fear welling up inside my throat like an unmoving stone.

I sprinted across the open courtyard, desperate to reach the car and change my fate.

Ace stood, stepping away from Lira as I darted past. "*Red!*" he bellowed, stepping in rhythm behind me, but I paid him no mind as I forced my limbs harder, my feet quicker. This was all a dream, a hellish nightmare that I would soon awaken from.

Ace was wrong. Felix was wrong.

The car reared into view moments before I knocked against its sleek exterior. I jumped into the driver's seat and put the car in gear. With the handbrake released, I flattened my torn sneaker down on the pedal, taking off in less than a heartbeat.

The wheels screeched as I gasped, fear breaking through in hyperventilated breaths. My throat burned as my scarlet eyes filled with tears that shone against the overhead lights.

Felix shot up from the backseat urgently. "What the fuck are you doing?" he screamed.

I shook my head as my mind spun. I had no idea what I was doing, no idea why it had to be me. *Why* it always had to be me! My life wasn't a gift, I wasn't blessed. I was a tragic mess, a useless shell of a person with nowhere to go and no one to count on.

Year, after year, after year, I dwelled in my own guarded solitude, shielding myself from daybreak, away from the sun that burned hot and the people that denied me everything. No matter what I did, there was no escape from this life.

Not even death wanted me.

Felix barrelled into the passenger seat. "Red, listen to me. I know you're scared; I know you don't understand what is happening to you, but you *need* to calm down. This isn't something you can just run from!" he bellowed frantically as he grasped the dashboard for support.

"I don't want to run from it!" I threw my head towards the steering wheel and screamed as I tore two hundred up a seventy zone.

I was falling apart, collapsing into a mosaic mess of a thousand shattered pieces. Pieces that I no longer cared to salvage, to save. I turned the wheel, forcing the road black beneath my tyres as I headed up the main road.

My vision blurred as my mind thundered from within.

I couldn't live like this anymore. All I'd ever done and all I'd ever known had been wrong. And yet, the way they treated me; the abuse they constantly inflicted upon me... *how* had that never been wrong? It was always me. I was always blamed for daring to stand against them, for daring to believe I deserved better.

They won. In the end, they *always* fucking did.

"Red, you cannot die, you are already dead!" Felix's frightened voice rang loud within the compacted space.

Maybe he was right, maybe this was nothing but hopeless stupidity, but if there was so much as a sheer chance, I had to take it. I had to know I tried as hard as I could to join my parents above. To ascend into the heavens like I had planned.

My worn sneaker slammed harder against the pedal as orange tears slipped from my enflamed eye sockets. I sniffed, wiping the fallen droplets away.

Before me, a high-rise building appeared, its solid structure looming over me, threatening me, provoking me.

"Red, *stop!*" Felix cried in vain as I looked away, gritted my teeth, and closed my eyes.

Within seconds, we violently collided.

The building crushed us from above as the vehicle crumbled like clay around us. The sound as fierce as rapid thunder and as violent as gunfire.

I exhaled sharply and opened my eyes, my vision hazy as a distant alarm assaulted my eardrums. I fell from the seat and onto my knees, crawling out the broken and mangled window.

My legs wobbled as I weakly stood upon the rubble, looking out at the shattered glass that surrounded my disfigured form. The car lay unrecognisable, the lobby almost the same as the wreckage sat perched within its entryway.

It wasn't possible to survive an impact so deadly, and no matter my attempts, I couldn't lie myself around this one. Couldn't fake it, ignore it, or even pretend.

They were right; this was real. *I was unable to die.*

Breaths pounded from my lungs as anxiety struck my core. It left me flustered, agitated, overtaken with uncontrolled energy. I inched back from the crumpled mess, feeling overcome with guilt.

The deep cuts, broken limbs, and hideous wounds against my maimed body healed rapidly and painlessly, as if patched up by invisible fingers.

I grimaced at just the sight of it. At the broken bones that seeped back into my flesh with a sloshing sound that made me want to puke. None of my injuries were covered in blood, only dotted specks of orange that oozed like oil against water.

This power was embedded within me, it was inescapable, unchallenged by simple human limitations.

No one could save me. Not now, not ever.

I was doomed, doomed from the very moment I came into this world, bloodied, scared, alone, unloved. Abandoned at birth, left to fight my own way through this hopeless world.

My feet scrambled for the outside world desperately.

Felix moaned and pushed himself away from the car's interior, bloodied and bruised. I approached him quickly, pushing away my own selfish thoughts of abandonment.

I crouched beside him, touching the deep cuts that trailed his skinny arms. He huffed and I glanced up, looking into his blue-grey eyes as he leant against a broken support beam.

His pale face was now speckled with scratches, his forehead smeared with a large gash, his teeth stained with droplets of blood.

"It's going to take more than that to kill me, but I have to say, that was a pretty solid effort." He chuckled then grunted, shifting his weight painfully.

It was slightly alarming just how similar he and Ace looked. The same facial features, same cheek bones, same defined lips. Crafted from the same captivating beauty.

I felt sick suddenly. I was prepared to die, and I was prepared to take Felix with me. I was selfish, horrible. Maybe Lira was right, maybe all I was ever destined to do was hurt others and destroy their lives.

Someone like me... I was better off dead for so many reasons, but Felix? I had no right to choose whether he lived or died. Ultimate Weapon or not, I had no right to decide that.

I sat down next to him, looking into the ruined building. The fluorescent lights buzzed and malfunctioned, hanging down on broken wires. The large glass panels sat shattered and mangled, covering the ground like a shimmering sea. The jaunty signboard lay dented and damaged, pinned under the weight of the crushed car.

"You'll live?" Felix nodded curtly, wincing from the pain.

"I heal faster than a normal human being, but not as fast as you. You'll heal immediately and barely even notice it." I glanced across at him sadly, studying his cold eyes and his jet-black hair now riddled with speckled glass.

"How do you know so much about this power?" I pressed.

He was so different to Ace, so brutal and raw. They were like day and night, like hot and cold, like fire and ice. Complete opposites within, but identical on the outside.

Felix chuckled, the gash against his forehead slowly healing. "I did my own research, not your usual Stanley and Ace stuff, but I wanted to know all I could about the Ultimate Weapon. I could tell Ace was over it, that he wanted to find you just so he could repair our broken brotherly bond." He snorted imprudently.

"He doesn't know how wrong he truly is," he continued. "He doesn't know what your awakening really means. I've studied Kobi, I've watched him from the sidelines like a shadow. I know what awaits you, I know the plan." He exhaled hard and gave me a sympathetic look. "And it isn't good."

"What awaits me?" I echoed his words, searching his face.

"You can't die, you don't bleed, you no longer ache. You are incapable of feeling pain," he expressed. "You are the strongest and most powerful being that has ever walked the Earth. Don't you understand how deadly that makes you? Don't you understand how much potential that holds?" He turned and watched me with a steady look, his eyes empathetic.

"Ace doesn't know, does he?" Felix shook his head slowly.

"I shouldn't be telling you this, but there's another doctor working for Kobi. One with… unethical means. Ace and Stanley don't know about her, not yet, their job has always been solely to find you." A strained smile met his lips. "You're a player in a game, Red, only you can decide how far it takes you. You can choose to be good, like Ace, or follow blindly along for your own safety like I do. Either way, you can't escape this," he conveyed, slight trembles within his tone.

I appreciated his honesty, but I didn't know what I was meant to do with everything and nothing, all at once… I was a clean canvas, a pristine figure, a piece of masterful work gnawed down to nothing but bare and unbroken bones. Never again would I feel the rough skin of another violently impact with mine. Never again would I wait mere moments to see black and blue rise to the surface of my skin. Never again would I beg and bargain for food or water.

It was as if my own self had turned off the ability to feel physical pain. I should've been thrilled, should've been happy, but I wasn't. I was scared. I was scared out of my mind. I didn't know how to live without feeling the pain of exactly what it meant to be human.

"Why have you never told Ace?" I glanced back at Felix then, surprised by the now smoothness of his face. His cuts and scars all healed, nothing but the blood remained.

"He wouldn't believe me. He's so angry at me, although he'll never admit it. He thinks your power will free us, but it won't. If anything, it has made this whole situation far worse." Felix stood, crunching the glass beneath his combat boots.

"You're the only one with the power to set him free, to set us all free." He reached his hand down to me.

I hesitated for a moment, eyeing against his palm restlessly. I forced a smile and touched atop his skin, a brief immobilising sense infiltrating my system.

He pulled me to my feet, quickly slipping his hands into his pockets. "I had to act like I resented him to get the information I needed from Kobi," he added impetuously. "Although, now that I have it, there isn't really much I can do. Like Ace said, we're weak. Our powers don't hold much strength in this world, yet we're labelled dangerous enough for the need to be under frequent surveillance." He jiggled his jacket, causing the glass fragments to fall away from the leather material.

"You need to be careful, Red, and so does Ace."

"I'm not ready for this." I shook my head stubbornly.

"I know," Felix uttered, his voice low. "But you have to be."

CHAPTER 10

RED

Was it too late for someone like me to be saved? I'd been blindsided my whole life, compelled to view my existence as nothing but a cruel joke.

I was tormented by decisions made for me. Trapped within the choices of others. Conclusions concluded by everyone but me. How was I meant to break away from that? How was I meant to change? Was it even worth trying?

Confusion swirled within me like a hurricane. I wanted to run, I wanted to stay. I wanted to hide away, I wanted to fight to the death… but this power had already impacted me so much. I would be nothing short of a blatant fool to ignore their warnings.

If Felix was right, and I had no doubt that he was, we were all in for a hell that had never been seen. I wanted to protect him, Ace, too. I sought to restore their bond, heal their resentment, see them through to the completion of their desires.

Sure, I mightn't have fancied Felix's stark attitude, but Ace was nothing but warm-hearted. He held such promise within himself, such optimism and light. He was the good in the world. I could tell from the way he spoke; from the way he acted.

He helped others, he prioritised their needs over his own. He didn't want to fix me, he wanted to help me, guide me. Maybe he felt obligated to.

But I feared for people like him, those hopeful and kind. The world crushed people like that—*harshly, cruelly, unforgivingly.* I would know, I was once one of them.

A heavy sigh escaped my lips as I glanced at the skies above, glistening with stars of faraway places. Of universes, of worlds so different to my own. Heaven and hell. Recovery and relapse. Pleasure and pain. Where did I fit, where did I belong?

Why did the universe *choose me* to hold such power against my battered and bruised fingertips? Why was I the one gifted the title of the Ultimate Weapon, when there were so many out there who begged to be saved by something inhuman?

My mind was a complex place, and I doubted peace could ever be achieved. No matter what superhuman forces accompanied me.

A cab pulled against the kerb and Ace rushed out. The silent night filled with the worried echoes of our names. Felix was fine now, standing beside me as if untouched by my harmful act. He huffed and shook his long fringe free of shattered fragments.

I glanced at my open hand, boring my eyes into the wrinkles against my palm, daring them to glow. Daring them to react. Daring them to rewrite my future.

Ace's hand slipped within mine. I exhaled sharply and looked up, letting his blue eyes into the deepest depths of my shattered soul.

He made me feel, feel a way I'd never felt before.

Was Ace safe? Was he the person who would stand by me, protect me, keep me from the demons that brought me to the brink?

"It's going to be okay," he soothed as his gentle expression, warm smile, and peaceful tone perfectly blended the sentence together like a honey and cinnamon brew on a cold morning.

He lifted his free hand to my cheek, brushing lightly against it. I felt tingles, waves of electricity as my heartbeat quickened, like someone had pulled the rug out from under me.

I reached up and wrapped my fingers gently around his. They felt warm, silky, and for a moment, it was like the whole world had stopped. Slow motioned to a point of near standstill.

It was me, and it was him.

His eyes moved past mine and his breath caught, the dismantled lobby an unsettling sight to behold. He stepped back and swallowed hard, placing a worried hand to his forehead. "Kobi's going to be *so* mad about this."

"Isn't he mad about everything?" Felix remarked, mordantly amused.

"Your power—" I hesitated. Felix glanced my way with an eyebrow curiously raised.

"Go on," he inclined as I lifted my chin.

"Your power feels like death," I reluctantly proclaimed. "I felt it when I touched your palm." I positioned my hand against him, breathing in deep the aromas that surrounded us.

A shadowy mist crept along his skin, leaving goosebumps as it brushed against the surface of my fingertips. His veins protruded with an inky texture as his eyes darkened.

His power was inside me; I could feel it. Could feel the stark sensation of darkness, of destruction, of defiance as it consumed my tattered being from within.

My eyes opened, revealing inhumanly black irises. A perplexed expression overtook Felix's face as I dropped my hand, his power ceasing. I rubbed at my eyelids, feeling discomfort.

"How did you do that?" he muttered dubiously.

"Beats me." I shrugged, glancing his way coolly. His pale eyes sliced against mine, eager for explanation. "You're wrong about your abilities," I proclaimed. "Your power is as strong as mine."

They shared a nervous glance between them. "How could you possibly know that?" Ace interposed, knitting his brows close.

"I, well, I can harness it," I replied awkwardly as I witnessed their faces turn ghostly white. "I'll show you." I closed my eyes and held out my palm.

I focused on Felix, on his power, on the darkness within him. I focused on the way it festered; on the way it contorted. I opened my blackening eyes and stared straight ahead.

My fingers twitched as my veins blackened with something in-human, the darkness arising against my skin. The eerie mist over-took my body, encircling my hand. It pushed, and pulled, and pulsed with a faint electric glow.

I concentrated as I forced the darkness above, into the sky, higher, and higher, and higher. It fanned out like a veil of cloth, pooling upon the city skyline. A blanket of darkness that flickered with orange specks of electricity.

The power felt alight, but dimmed, disrupted. Was there some-thing inside of him that sentenced it into submission? Something that affected these abilities and weakened their strength? Was there an outside force that toyed with Felix's control over a power I thought was unable to be governed?

"What the hell are you doing?" an angry screech filled the air. I gasped and extinguished the power, slamming back into reality rigidly. Ace and Felix were turned away, watching the man fearfully as he strode towards us.

He wore a tailored suit with black locks overly gelled, the strands looking as if they would snap under the slightest of pressure. His stern eyes pierced through mine, causing a restless squirm as he lessened the space between us.

Ace and Felix backed away silently. They seemed anxious, vulnerable, their eyes pinned to the ground below.

The stranger stilled a metre before me, holding his hand out confidently. He towered over my tiny form like a wave about to swallow me whole. "Kobi Holloway," he introduced.

Kobi.

I crossed my arms in front of my chest defiantly, my knifelike stare an undaunted display. I refused to be threatened.

This was the man who wanted me, who wanted to exploit the powers within me, who wanted to control the fearsome abilities of the Ultimate Weapon.

Little did he know what I was capable of, little did he know of the warfare I had been subjected to almost my whole life. I'd battled man many a time before, I'd dealt with more monsters than I could count. *He* would be no different.

Kobi licked his lips, eyeing me up and down like predator to prey. He tried to intimidate me, but I wouldn't allow it. He had no idea how many times the shop had displayed me, displaced me, discarded me. I had been training for a war my whole life, only now, could I see why.

"Johanna Tolmer."

My eyes widened as the breath seized within my lungs. "What the fuck did you just call me?" Ace winced as my knuckles instinctively clenched. "You *knew?*"

Ace peeked up at me timidly, his eyes glassy and regretful as my furious expression flared, waiting impatiently for justification that never came.

"It wasn't by chance you met me on that park bench," I spat through gritted teeth, the realisation hitting hard. "You knew who I was! You knew I'd been abused, knew I'd suffered at the hands of others. You were just waiting for me to *die!*" He flinched as the last word escaped my lips.

I snarled and shoved past them, stepping into the darkness without hesitation. "Who said you could leave?" Kobi turned, placing his hands neatly before him as Felix's eyes flickered between us.

I stilled and spun back slowly, my demeanour fierce and enraged. All that held me together was the sliver of possibility that Ace didn't know I was going to kill myself, that this wasn't some planned out scheme on his behalf.

Kobi cleared his throat. "Don't you want to know how powerful you are? Don't you want to witness all you can achieve? Don't you want to make them pay?"

I lifted my chin as an uneasy feeling swept across my battered mind. "The simulation will help you," Kobi proclaimed with a twisted and untrustful smirk. "The simulation will tell you how powerful you are."

So many conflictions battled within my brain, so many unanswered questions, so many hopes destroyed and foolishly rebuilt. I missed the days I mimicked happy people; the days I pretended I was joyful, healthy, fortunate and free. I missed the days I wished on falling stars, on white horses, on 11:11's.

And all for *what?* All for nothing but hope. A foolish hope that persisted through every downfall. The hope of a better life, a better situation, a better world.

Newsflash—it never got better. It got easier, I got tougher. I spoke my mind when I should've stayed quiet. I questioned my own sanity when I should've questioned theirs. I hid away from the world when I should've waged the war inside me.

I gave up on myself. I gave up on a better life. I gave up on living. What else was I supposed to do? Take their abuse and thank them for it? Pave my own way to being a more productive boxing bag? It wasn't fair, it wasn't right. I didn't ask to be born into this world, I only asked to be loved in it.

All I had ever wanted was security, stability, but all I received was the opposite. Had it really been my own fault? Had I really caused all of this to spiral out of control?

I talked back, I acted tough, I refused to play their little games. I was everything I needed to be, all at once, and it destroyed me. Turned me black and blue. My body covered, my mind numb, my feelings ignored.

When I finally had the courage to kill myself, I woke up. Was that destiny, fate, or a cruel joke to a girl bathed in bruises with broken faith?

I didn't want to keep fighting this battle in vain. I wanted to let go; I wanted to destroy myself. And I had... I allowed the demons to win, the voices inside my head to succeed, the monsters within to run rampant.

I was a puzzle piece forever torn from its own completion, left to wither away under discarded trash. I was nothing.

Why did I always let my demons win? Maybe because this was

a battle I was never meant to. I was always on the losing end, always left behind, always the butt of the joke.

Maybe it had been a sign? Maybe I was supposed to just accept it? Never question it. Let it be the unavoidable truth; let it destroy me. Destroy me like I always did, destroy me like I always had. *That* was the unavoidable truth, as poetic as it was devastating.

What I felt towards the world was anger, annoyance, aggravation. I wanted this insufferable globe to pay for its sins. I wanted redemption, vindication.

I wanted war.

But what would it get me? I had no home, I was still broke, still depressed. All the power did was reinforce those facts. Ace would come for me, as would Felix, so would Kobi. I couldn't run forever. Not from this. Yes, what Ace did was wrong, and I was mad at him for that, but could I really blame him for it? What would I have done in the same situation. Would I have lied? I now perfectly understood why he'd told me to use my power.

His eyes met mine, watching me with a hopeful and pleading expression. Felix told me to be careful; told me I was the one that could save us all.

I smiled softly, causing Ace's blue eyes to widen in surprise. I shifted my body to face Kobi straight on. "If you hurt Ace, or Felix, I will destroy this entire fucking planet," I warned.

Kobi nodded his agreement, his smile ever so slightly shifting. "As you wish." He bowed his head acceptingly, but I knew better than to truly trust an enemy.

CHAPTER 11

RED

"If you're under my roof, you're under my rules," Kobi ordered as he punched at the elevator key, looking back at me with an unimpressed snarl.

He'd ordered me into his own car for supervision, demanding Ace and Felix travel together in a cab. To no one's surprise, we arrived before them.

"I'm the one with the power. I get to decide my own rules," I snapped as I silently observed the dark and empty building.

"You don't have any idea how powerful you are," he hissed.

"And if I walk back out those doors, neither will you." I kept my voice low, my tone serious. I crossed my arms in front of my chest, for a split second their naked newness unrecognisable.

I glanced at the front desk, peering at myself in the mirror's reflection. I stepped towards it, ignoring the complaints that rang loud from Kobi. I flipped over the counter and landed with a tiny thud that echoed throughout the vast space.

My eyes transfixed against the reflection, hypnotised by the transformation.

I was still covered in dirt, vomit still stained my tee shirt, holes still poked their way through, but my face didn't harbour any imperfections. My acne was no longer noticeable, the dark circles under my eyes no longer visible, the shade of my skin no longer sickly.

This body didn't feel like my own, my appearance permanently changed. I no longer knew the girl within the mirror; no longer recognised the hands I glanced down at.

For years, I'd yearned for that. Desired nothing more than a clean slate to redo my whole life. Now, there I stood, the reflection reflecting a figure seemingly unaffected by evil intent. A body that looked pure, untouched, pristine. A body that didn't feel quite like mine.

Within those scars, I'd found comfort, found release. I got addicted to the way it felt, obsessed with the way their cruel intentions painted me like a work of art. I found solace in that pain, relief in the way I rewired my brain to obey their inflictions.

"What are you doing?" Kobi grumbled as the elevator door opened. I straightened my backbone and looked across at him.

"I was healed," I informed him sourly. He shot me a puzzled look in return. "I was covered in bruises. They healed. I'm a clean slate now." I laughed flippantly, purposefully acting insufferable to this stranger Ace and Felix had been so afraid of. I'd seen those looks before. I knew what they meant.

Kobi studied me with a sinister expression as I returned to the lift. "I will honour our deal," he began as the doors clunkily reopened. "I will not harm Ace or Felix, but in return, I need compliance."

My options were limited. Regrettably, I didn't have much of a choice. I needed to follow his rules, but at least I had his word he wouldn't harm them. *Not directly, anyway.*

"Why can't Ace and Felix use all of their power?" I asked, inspecting him watchfully.

His eyes changed briefly, momentarily, like a sudden gust of wind had derailed him, but as swiftly as it had happened, he was back to officious. "How could you possibly know that?" His voice cracked as he awkwardly coughed.

"Because I can harness their powers," I stated, catching him off guard. "I haven't Ace's, not yet, but I was bound to Felix's abilities. I know what he's capable of, and I know it's being restrained." He looked uncomfortable suddenly, fiddling with the collar of his shirt. "Why don't they know how powerful they truly are?"

The elevator dinged and Kobi hurried out, colliding against the cold air of an underground bunker. He fixed his tie, running a hand along his hair to flatten a fallen curl. "Stanley!" he bellowed as I slipped from the elevator, feeling unsettled.

I couldn't understand why he had wasted years of his life searching for me, searching for *my* whereabouts, when he was well aware of the limitations placed upon Ace and Felix's abilities.

Especially, when he knew their powers had the exact same potential to be as insurmountable and as indestructible as the Ultimate Weapon's. There had to be a reason for his methodical manhunt, but what? What could I do that Ace and Felix couldn't? What made me so damn special compared to them?

"Dr Stanley Pattison," an old man introduced himself, reaching out his hand eagerly. "I've done a lot of research on you, my dear." He chuckled as I shook his hand timidly. He had a firm grip for a senior citizen. "It's an honour to finally meet you." I half-smiled, feeling suddenly anxious.

Was it within this very room Ace first learnt of my existence? The thought alone sent an unwelcomed chill down my spine. It felt wrong, icky. He would have uncovered everything there was to know about my miserable life...

He would have discovered the information about my parents, about the accident, about the foster homes, maybe even about the abuse.

My insecurities poked at my tattered form, gnawing away at me feverishly. I squirmed, feeling uncomfortable and filled to the brink with tension. There was so much pressure from the outside world to be perfect, and I fell short. *Every. Single. Time.*

I hated how I was perceived by the world, how I was ridiculed, judged. And all for circumstances completely out of my own two hands. I'd grown up in foster homes, been abnegated, abandoned, abused. I'd battled every day of my life, and all for what?

All to defy death the one moment I was brave enough to defy myself...

Kobi hovered around us, but Stanley hardly seemed to notice. He had a soft-hearted gleam within his emotionful eyes, an enthusiastic and sunny feel. He felt comforting, kooky but kind. What I imagined a grandparent to feel like.

He wore a coloured duck tie, a buttoned-up shirt covered in bright mismatched patches, and circular-framed spectacles. "I really am glad to meet you," he repeated wholeheartedly.

I quickly nodded, unsure what else to do. This man probably knew everything there was to know about my life, and all I knew about him was he was old, a doctor, and apparently liked ducks.

"Please, sit." He wheeled over an old and frayed desk chair. I sat down cautiously as he took the seat across from me. "Can I get you anything?"

I shook my head silently as I glanced around the bunker. It was lifeless, empty, and massive. The cluttered desks were positioned closest to the entryway, and across the room sat an old-looking couch. Past that, was a hallway with a few spotted doors, and behind me, were two caged cells with large cream-coloured bars and built-in deadbolts.

I turned back sharply and exhaled raggedly.

"We rarely use those cells. I assure you, it's nothing to concern yourself about," Stanley explained, seemingly sensing my doubt. "Tell me about yourself," he ushered with an enthusiastic nod. I dithered. "You go by Red?" I nodded my agreement. "Why is that?"

A nervous breath escaped my lips as I tightened my knuckles anxiously within my lap. "There was a girl who bullied me in primary school. She would always call me Red, would laugh and point. After my parents died, a couple named Daxton and Kalila fostered me, then adopted me. When I was sent to my second foster home, it felt like I had lost my whole identity. I felt void, meaningless, invisible. I wanted to change who I was, and so, I did." I shrugged. "Now I go by Red."

Stanley smiled warmly, but it didn't quite reach his eyes.

In the beginning, Daxton and Kalila had been nothing but kind. They were rich and well-to-do. Those two years within their care, I'd become an equestrian, learnt to play the piano, and been gifted an education in one of the city's most exemplary private schools. I was spoiled rotten, and I loved it.

The money made things so much easier. My parents hadn't been poor by any means, but money had been tight, planned out, well-budgeted.

I was devastated, broken, and shocked when Daxton and Kalila sat me down at the kitchen table, with a packed bag full of my belongings, and told me I was leaving. I cried for four days straight. I later found out it was because Kalila was pregnant. It should've hurt a lot more than it did, but those four nights I'd cried until there simply wasn't a single tear left, had truly broken me.

"I'm sorry," Stanley muttered.

I peeked at him past my lashes. "It was a long time ago." I shrugged curtly as I sank back within the frayed chair.

There was a moment of silence before Stanley spoke again. "There are a few tests I'm needing to conduct today. The first will be drawing blood, the second will be entering you into the simulation." He reached back and grabbed a clear folder and pen, scribbling some information down.

"I have all your basic information on file, but I do need your consent. I know as a minor you cannot legally enter into a contract. However, we can make an agreement, and I can sign as a doctor on your behalf." My body squirmed restlessly.

I didn't like any of this, but what could I do, what could I say? Within myself, I knew blood no longer dripped from my veins, knew oxygen no longer filled my burning lungs. I just didn't know whether I was being freed or punished.

I needed Stanley's help. So, I nodded, forcing my body to obey. I'd lied my whole life. Protected those that deserved misery and penalty, faked scenarios, pardoned punishments, played dumb when I was well aware.

My mouth was a loaded gun, a brutal weapon, a ruthless saboteur. And I'd let them play me for a fool... *but not this time.* This time, I would be one step ahead. I was going to master my power;

I was going to free us all. Even if I had to fake it to make it there.

Ace and Felix entered the bunker, puzzled expressions against their wound-up faces. I eyed Ace doubtfully as he gave a reassuring nod.

"Please, allow me," Stanley offered.

I followed his motions as he organised the needle, his movements careful, concise. He placed a nylon strap around my arm and tightened it, then slid a needle into my skin.

No sting, no discomfort.

He pulled the syringe back, but it wasn't blood that oozed from my veins, it was the same glowing liquid that had leaked from my eyes as I'd cried, from my lip when it bled.

The syringe exploded, causing Stanley and Kobi to flinch as tiny specks of glass fell atop the floor. I watched in awe, unable to tear my disbelieving brown eyes away.

It wasn't natural, it wasn't normal. It wasn't blood. It wasn't rich, red, revolting blood. Something I'd seen drip from my own flesh too many times. The glow, the orange, the abnormality. It soothed me, it calmed me. It *protected* me. If I couldn't bleed, they couldn't hurt me, but if I couldn't die, was there an eternity waiting to make me suffer for it?

I slipped off the chair, my sneakers crunching the microscopic fragments of glass beneath them.

"That's not possible," Stanley voiced. His green eyes glassy, his tone uneven, his features perplexed. "I never predicted—" he cut off as his fingers grasped his chin in disbelief.

He shook his head and slipped his spectacles from his face, shuffling over to my clustered file. "What does it mean?" Kobi barged between us.

Stanley shook his head once more, slipping upon the chair. "I don't know yet," he wheezed. "Connect her to the simulation. I need to view her brainwaves," he instructed, worry lacing his cheerful tone. "Ace, my boy, will you set up the simulation?"

"I can do that," Ace confirmed, jogging towards an adjacent room. Stanley promptly stood as he fiddled with my overflowing file and booted up the desktop.

"What's a simulation?" I asked nervously.

Stanley stilled, glancing my way with an inquisitive gaze. "A simulation monitors the electrical activity within your brain, reporting the response back to us; the chart notifies us of the brain's frequency, amplitude, and shape," he paused, analysing my unsure expression. "There's nothing to fear, my dear, it's only science." He chuckled playfully as Felix stepped beside me.

"I've done it before," he interjected with an awkward side-eye. "It can be intimidating, but it isn't real. Simply put, it's a safe way to determine how powerful we are. That's it."

His cold eyes met mine as he shrugged indifferently. "You have nothing to worry about." He smiled a small but reassuring smile.

"Ready for you," Ace called across the wide-open space. I swallowed hard, eyeing him with a feeling that twisted and tightened deep within my gut.

He led me up a narrow passageway, a bleak and dull hallway that appeared to only grow. "It's not as scary as it looks, I promise," he reassured as we stepped within a cramped room. It felt cold, alarming. It played against my better judgement.

"Come sit." Ace led me over to the two leather chairs that filled the entirety of the room. "Lay down here and try to relax. I can sense your panic from here." He smiled my way encouragingly. I exhaled an exaggerated scoff.

"I don't trust it," I snapped, slamming against the cold and lifeless chair. I glanced around, eyeing the computer screens and multiple wire cables that hung limp.

"What am I going to see?" I looked directly at him, my muscles tensing, my stomach sick, my mind troubled. I swallowed hard and straightened my posture, trying to play it cool.

"It's a training course, of sorts. Built by Stanley himself. It's one of the only safe places for us to use our powers. You really have nothing to be concerned about. Felix and I have done this a handful of times, and nothing's ever gone wrong." He patted my shoulder gently.

"How much pain am I going to feel?" I whispered meekly. Ace observed me with an empathetic expression before a gentle smile met his lips.

"None. You're not able to feel pain in the simulation," he reassured as he brushed a loose strand of my hair behind my ear. It caused my entire body to nervously tremble.

Stanley walked in with a plastic cup full of liquid. "For you, my dear." He handed me the cup with a playful wink. I glanced at the blue solution hesitantly. "Drink it when you're ready," he added.

"How's it going?" He looked to Ace, and then the screens, reading the cryptic text with a focused demeanour. "Everything looks ready to go," he said with great excitement as he reached forward and grabbed a strange looking helmet covered in loose wires and cables.

I sat up, feeling frightened. "It's alright," Stanley echoed Ace's words as he slipped the device against my scalp.

On cue, the flavourless solution gushed down my dry throat. I scrunched up my nose, expecting the worse, but no rancid after-taste arose.

I passed the cup to Ace, feeling unsettled. He nodded my way with a kind and pleasant smile. "If anything goes wrong, we'll pull you right back out," he promised.

I blinked a few times, my eyelids growing heavy as I peeked up at Ace and smiled softly, an intoxicating feeling flooding through my system.

And then, darkness.

CHAPTER 12

RED

A blinking light shone within my eyes, and I stirred, peeling my sweaty body from the unpleasant material. The feeling vexatious against my skin as I wiped at my eyes, suddenly drowsy.

My trembling figure stood as I restlessly observed the four lifeless walls that surrounded me.

I glanced back at the bed, remembering all those times I had been in hospital rooms just like this one. I wondered then if anything would've been different had they just listened.

Blooming flowers sat alongside the windowsill, their colours vibrant and enchanting. I eyed them with contempt, watching as they rapidly wilted and died. Disdain slithered through me as I barged out the room, stepping into a cold and empty corridor.

"Simulation, huh," I muttered as I trekked up the uninhabited hallway, bypassing the walls that began to crumble and stain, falling away like leaves from a tree, almost poetically.

I placed my finger against the structure, imprinting a distinct line in the dust as I journeyed on. I didn't feel scared or on edge. I felt calm, eerily so...

The colossal structure groaned as ripples of fractured plasterboard snaked across each side of the weakened passageway, causing the adjacent rooms to groan and huff in response. Cobwebs, dust, and mould bunched against the supporting beams above, the hospital withering away to decay before my own two eyes.

The broken pivot door swung only halfway out as I shoved my way through and into a deserted waiting room, the faulty hinges groaning like nails against a chalkboard.

A surplus of old chairs lay positioned in a sporadic and messy way, the marmoleum flooring under my feet was both cracked and filthy, and the windows all-around were split and damaged.

I slipped up on the front desk, sighing loudly. What the hell was I meant to do now? Was something supposed to happen? Was there meant to be a sign, an ode, a play-by-play?

An annoyed breath escaped my lips. Even inside a simulation things irritated me. Nothing was ever simple.

Suddenly, the desk collapsed, sending me into the floor below. Down, and down, and down. I fell, lightly, softly, as Alice had fallen down the rabbit hole. I felt no impending doom, only stillness.

A prickly and unpleasant sensation ran up my exposed flesh as I was laid gently against asphalt. The sun now overhead, its golden glow seeping into my cold bones.

Now I felt uneasy, uncomfortable, unprepared.

I quickly stood, my sneakers heavy against my feet, my clothes cold against my skin, my hair sticky against my cheeks.

Fog loomed above, shielding the sun away as overhead lights hung low, weakly illuminating the road that seemed to stretch on for miles. There was almost a feeling of familiarity, but then again, didn't all roads look the same after a while?

A piercing scream filled the atmosphere, encircling the fog

around me like I was stuck in a blender.

I forced my legs into a sprint, running blind as I pushed my body onward. I felt lethargic as the sound of my sneakers hitting the concrete started to lessen. I stopped, heaving, my body frantic for oxygen as sweat broke across my brow. In and out, *in and out.* I had to stay calm.

I straightened my backbone and stepped within an open clearing, a fearful gasp fleeing my lips as my face paled and my mind reeled. I'd stepped straight out into suburbia, to the residence of my younger self. The house I grew up in, the house where I learnt what love truly was.

"Mum?" I meekly asked, hearing her sweet hums echo through the crisp air. I started up the driveway, then stilled.

I stumbled back, feeling distressed. "This isn't real," I mumbled, her hums intensifying. "*This isn't real!*" I shrieked, knuckles clenching as my temper blew red-hot within me. It escalated, extended, expanded within my overfilled head.

My own saliva choked me as a young girl appeared beside me. I glared at her with eyes wide and bloodshot as she stared back with brown eyes all too recognisable. I cleared my throat, trying in vain to ease my scattered and startled mind.

"Johanna," she cheerfully introduced.

"What is happening?" I muttered fearfully as I staggered back, collapsing against the ground.

I'd stepped back into my past... to *what*—stand face-to-face with the girl I will never be again? To give wisdom to my younger self? To lie, to deceive, to give false assurance? I couldn't be honest, not after everything that had happened to us.

If I could go back, if I could rewrite the whole story, would I even want to? Would I choose to forgive those that had abused us, neglected us, destroyed us? Would I pardon their improper behaviour with a newfound acceptance, or would I suffer all over again for sins that weren't even mine to begin with?

And what of my parents?

Would I want to see them one last time to only suffer their inevitable death a second time around? I knew if I went back, I wouldn't be able to survive it. Those same people wouldn't listen, those same families wouldn't care, those same protocols wouldn't protect me.

It wasn't the future this little girl was meant to have. It was defective, faulty. It hung against me like a mighty stone, unmoving, unchanging. Could I have done anything to stop it? To modify it, to alter it? To make life for this little girl bearable...

Five metres from my ten-year-old self and all I had were doubts, confusions, questions, troubles.

All I had was guilt.

I should've tried harder, should've done better. I was so angry at the world, at those who'd wronged me, but most of all, I was angry at myself. I should've run earlier. Should've packed my bags and never looked back. I should've started again, in a city I was nameless, in a place I could once again be loved.

God—I wanted to scream, pierce the exosphere with all the rage, and anger, and hate I'd had bottled up within me for years.

Just what the hell had I done that justified a punishment past death? That little girl, innocent and unaware, the world was going to break her like a glow stick.

Warmth built beneath my palms, and I gasped, watching as bright liquid oozed all around. It encircled me, surrounded me. It burned into the concrete, turning the solid compound into a malleable muck.

Panic soared through my windpipe, escaping in short and untamed breaths. The ground rumbled, the skies darkened, my younger self faded into obscurity.

I screamed and reached for her, my fingertips straining, my heartbeat quickening, as my former residence crumbled into the soil, almost gracefully. Along with everything that stood around it.

I found my footing and jumped, slamming into solid glass. I exhaled hard and looked up, glass above and sand beneath. An hourglass, I concluded fearfully.

My fist pounded against it, daring the compound to crack as speckled grains of sand slipped against me from above. It seeped within my sneakers and under my skin as my trepidation grew. I twisted and turned, ignoring the itch that danced above the surface of my skin, begging to be scratched.

A scream bellowed out from within me as I crouched low, hands above my trembling form. My head shot skyward as my whole body fearsomely ached and painfully ignited.

Waves of orange light propelled from my fingertips, shattering the hourglass with one mighty blow, as a force field reared from within me. Larger and larger it grew, until nothing else remained.

Electricity seared inside the bubble, whipping, lashing, zipping past me with intense speed. I stood, alarmed, awed, amazed by the immense power.

I lifted my arm, a bolt of electricity wrapping itself against me like a string abused by the wind. It slithered across my arm and coiled around my torso, descending at my leg.

I watched on in sheer amazement, my body buzzing with an

unknown feeling as I glared at my wide-open palms, studying the creases. I still didn't fully understand this alien glow, but I knew it was part of me, a part that was inescapable.

It allowed me to live beyond death, to defy Mother Nature. I was the result of an imbalance. Defective as it were. As powerful as they come.

The revelation should've thrilled me, should've felt good. But doubt festered within me. It polluted me, poisoned me, plagued me. And like every foster home before me, I feared I could never escape.

I shot up onto my sneakers and ran. Ran as fast as I could as their malevolent laughter closed in around me. It bombarded my eardrums like gunfire, it seeped into my bones with a rotten vendetta, it seared itself against my pale skin like flamed iron. It beckoned to be heard, forced itself to be challenged.

Suddenly, someone grabbed the back of my head. Fist full of hair as they slammed me into a brick wall. I gasped and cried, blood cascading from my bruised and wounded cheek.

I sank to the ground, fearful and small as mangled shadows loomed above me, laughing, whispering, distorting, grimacing.

Their yellowed teeth like spiked daggers, their shadows bony, their stature manic.

The shadows grew. Larger, and larger, and larger. I held my breath, scared to even breathe, as I recoiled before them. I closed my eyes tight, my knuckles clenched, my lips jammed shut.

I wanted to squeak out a cry, but my body refused. I shook my head, the blood splattering out around me. I felt the pain—the gentle drum, the slipping liquid, the burning pleasure.

A large hand slammed against my shoulder, and I screamed

out manically. Blinded by fear as I sprang onto my trembling legs and cried, piercing the exosphere with my almighty bellow.

I opened my eyes, and they burned, burned like fire, as my trembling palms flew open, expelling an upsurge of unforgiving waves into the simulated universe.

I felt insurmountable.

The shadowy demons shrieked as the alien glow captured them, forcing them into a newfound hell of inescapable terrors. They erupted into flames, weaving and dodging in vain.

I stood, feeling strong and capable. Feeling like for once, I wasn't the target, I wasn't the tragedy, I wasn't the terrified.

The electric waves of scintillated light pulsated around and against me, soothing my cheek, calming my fears.

I reached my hand out longingly, lacing my fingers within the supernatural buzz. Unexpectedly, the orange glow wrapped itself against my wrists. Tighter, and tighter, and tighter, it squeezed. I squirmed and shrieked, trying to break free.

The glow ran up my arms, lacing my pale flesh with all the bruises, and scars, and burns that had vanished before my own two eyes. I screamed out fearfully, watching the ugly distortion of colours seep back within my skin.

My head wilfully shook, desperate for the cruelty to cease. I fell to my knees, my body alight with intense agony as I sobbed and wept.

My frizzy hair cascaded down my face, cupping me in a faux bubble of security as my head slammed against the pavement and my chipped nails dug into the rough terrain.

Blood ran from my weakened body, sliding, snaking, shimmering against my pale complexion. Every exhale like knives against my throat as blood slithered down my arms like veins, squishing between my fingers.

I struggled for breath beside the increasing pool of blood as hyperventilated huffs escaped my lips, my stomach pulsing in and out with each passing second that ticked by with excruciating consequence.

Orange liquid spewed across the sidewalk as I vomited, my stomach heaving and emptying with a gross display of golden fluid that commenced an onslaught of overbearing emotions.

They jumbled within my overfilled head as hatred and pain overtook and overcame me. I wanted to give up, fall against the alien glow, and in an instant, be gone. Be lost to the world, taken by the wind.

"*Red!*" a voice screamed out urgently. I exhaled sharply and winced, glancing up with a painfilled expression as a blurred figure sprinted within my field of vision.

It was Ace. I knew it was Ace.

I kicked my legs, slipping against the blood. My head firmly shook, my dismal mind determined to break away. I caught my footing, propelling myself up and away from the oozing glow, from the drippling blood, from the impending doom.

My shaky arms wrapped around Ace's slender neck, hugging him tighter than I had anyone before.

I breathed him in deep, savouring his smell, latching vulnerability to it. I grasped onto him tighter, like claws against silk, and I *refused* to let go.

Tears slid from my enflamed eye sockets as my knees buckled, and I collapsed. Ace hoisted me up, holding me securely. He felt safe, he felt warm, he felt...

My tired eyes rolled into the back of my head. "Red, come on, stay with me!" His blue eyes blazed with worry as he cupped my face. A face now painted with an ugly blackeye, a puffy lip, a swollen cheek.

My mind was a battlefield and my body its battleground.

He hesitated, eyeing my abused figure with a sympathetic and unsettled expression as our troubled eyes met. He shook his head dizzyingly, fear overtaking his worried features once more. "Out of the simulation, we need to get you out!" His tone was off, shaky. His body language fearful, offset. But the way he touched me was nothing but kind. "Right now," he commanded.

The words didn't sound like his, they were too forceful, too bold, but I was in no position to argue.

I nodded weakly, then paused. "*How*—how do I do that?"

"Take off the helmet!" I reached up and slid the helmet from my head, crashing instantaneously against a cold, hard, and unforgiving darkness.

My body jolted upright to the sound of the helmet smashing against the floor. The screens buzzed and jittered, deep cracks embedded within their surface like a work of art.

I struggled for breath as I clambered to the side of the chair, knuckles white, mind unresponsive.

"*Red*—" Ace leaped out the adjacent chair and onto his knees before me. "Breathe, Red, I need you to breathe." I shook my head furiously, prickles invading my spine.

"You said none!" I screamed at him. "You told me I wouldn't feel pain," my voice shuddered. I shut my eyes tight, refusing to let the teardrops fall. "Why did I feel pain, Ace? *Why?*" I opened my bloodshot eyes, daring him to respond.

He was so meek, so defeated and sorry. "Answer me!" I yelled once more. "*Why* did I see my younger self? *Why* was I back at my childhood home? *Why* did the bruises—" I gasped, looking down at my arms fretfully. Only pale skin ascended my flesh.

My hands gripped the bottom of the chair hard, my body convulsing as I swayed, forwards and back, forwards and back. I felt so violated, so vulnerable, so vexed.

"You destroyed the machine." Stanley stood in the doorway, watching us with uncertainty. He looked so disappointed, so deflated, so defeated.

The anger, betrayal, and bitterness within me lingered, but I couldn't help but feel sorry for him. I relaxed my mind, cooling my temper best I could.

"The data is gone," Stanley began. Ace stood up beside me, his full attention now on the old man.

"We have nothing?" he muttered. Stanley slipped his glasses from his face, nodding slowly.

"My dear, under no circumstances are you meant to feel pain in the simulation, nor are you able to go into the past." He looked to me directly, his green eyes soulful.

"That's how I built it. None of that is meant to be possible, and yet," he stilled, his breath hitching. "I apologise, Red. I don't know how powerful you are, and I don't think it's possible to fully understand."

He took a shaky breath. "I was able to gauge a few pieces of data before the breach, and what I saw—" he paused a moment. "Was truly remarkable."

He smiled my way proudly, a short-lived gleam within his emerald eyes. "But unfortunately, I don't have the answers you need. It's impossible to collect such data on you. I couldn't test your blood, I couldn't check your amplitude, I couldn't get you out." He wheezed, looking away. "I think that's enough for today." He hobbled out the room sadly.

The silence that occurred between Ace and I was deafening. I didn't know what to say, didn't know what to do, didn't know how to break the tension. Part of me felt like I should've apologised. It wasn't his fault I saw my past, and it wasn't Stanley's.

Maybe I was the only one to blame...

Ace walked over to me and placed his arms against me, pulling me into his prickly pullover. I cuddled into his chest, my cheek irritated by the material, but I didn't pull away. Instead, I hugged him tighter, feeling secure within his warm embrace. I closed my eyes and tried to soothe my mind.

There were so many things I wished to change. Not only the situations, but my reactions. The way I spoke to other people, the way I treated myself. I leapt off that edge without daring to ask if I could survive it.

I had misplaced faith in myself. I was angry, filled with hatred, ready to duel with the devil if he so much as looked at me funny. *But where had it all gotten me?*

Not all the consequences I had faced were my own. Not all the scars on my body had been from others. Not every situation had required my input. I was so mad at the world. At its willingness to leave me bruised, broken, battered, and blamed.

I wanted vindication. Justification. I wanted to know *why.* I wanted to know why the world was so kind to some and so ruthless to others. Why I had drawn the short straw, the rough end of the stick, the worst end of the bargain. Why there was such a divide between humankind when everyone was meant to be born as an equal.

There were good people, who did bad things, and there were bad people, who did good things. Nothing scripted about how someone thought or about how someone acted.

Was it the indirection of the past or the ambiguity of the future that steered us towards our own conclusions of decisions we were forced to make?

"Relax, Red, you're okay," Ace uttered gently as he pushed me back and looked deeply into my wide brown eyes. I smiled up at him softly, grateful to have him.

I'd only ever daydreamed about people like Ace.

In that moment, I could've kissed him. The way he held me, the way he made me feel so safe. Nothing had prepared me for it. For the feelings I would feel, for the actions he would take, for the way my mind would rewire itself. I was no longer trapped within a painful world.

I wondered then what my parents would say, what they would think. A title such as the Ultimate Weapon wasn't an every day one. Would they be proud? Would they feel shame? I wasn't even biologically theirs, yet they loved, raised, and cherished me like I was. The whole thing was complicated. All I knew about my birth mother was that she was a runaway. She couldn't keep me; she didn't want me.

My mum was one of the nurses who worked that shift. The one who took me in, adopted me, gave me a home. She would always be my mum; my dad would always be my dad. I didn't care who that woman was. Luciana and Daniel Tolmer were my parents.

"Red?" Ace asked, his voice laced with tenderness. "You're crying." I gasped and wiped at my scarlet eyes, feeling the orange teardrops slither down my cheeks.

I coughed awkwardly. "I was thinking about my parents," I confessed, glancing up at him, but he was already looking at me. "Can you—" I hesitated, feeling foolish.

I'd known kids in foster homes longer than I had Ace, but none of them had ever had this type of influence over me. "Can you find out where my parents are buried?" I forced the sentence out. I wanted—*no, I needed* to finally know.

Ace exhaled softly, nodding gently. "It will take some time, but I can do that for you." He smiled at me doubtlessly, his blue eyes radiant.

Looking at him now, you'd never have guessed he suffered any mistreatment at the hands of others. He carried himself so surely. The preppy clothes, his clean-shaven face, that gleaming smile. He glowed in every room he walked into. He was radiating, courteous, understanding. And if I hadn't known better, I would've wondered if he walked straight out of my dreams.

It was clear that I'd been treated poorly, left to fend for myself. I'd formed alliances, broken promises, been left for dead more times than I had ever cared to count. And you could tell. One look in my direction, and it was crystal clear I had danced with my demons, chosen to hate when I should've chosen to love, and hidden away from the world in fear I couldn't withstand it.

I was a twisted tragedy. A manmade mistake. A pitiful project. Doomed from the very moment I took my first breath. And Ace knew it. I knew it. They knew it. I was fighting a war within myself that I knew I could never win.

Living was my purgatory, the inescapable consequence of my own action. That had to be the reason why I was here, sentenced to live beyond my suicide.

Like a ghost, I was unable to be seen, unable to be loved. I didn't understand what good this power was if I couldn't even use it. I felt so worthless, so pointless, so hopeless. I just wanted to scream.

The air pounded aimlessly out my throat as a dizzying spell overtook me. I stilled and placed my hand to my forehead, relaxing my breathing. I was distraught, upset, angry. My mind a roller coaster of emotions I couldn't counteract.

I wanted to believe that this power was granted to me by my parents. A way to hold me without existence, a way to save me without death, but I knew that it wasn't... and I knew I was smarter than that. But it still hurt, knowing they would never see me again, or whoever it was that I became.

Ace stood beside me with a warm smile, and I lifted my chin to meet his kind expression.

There was something about him—the way his hair perfectly fell, the way his features shifted as he spoke, the way he held himself with such confidence.

All my life, I had needed someone like him... someone to mend the bruises, patch up the scars, soothe the burns. Now there I stood, unable to feel pain, unable to bleed, unable to die, and only now did the world gift me a saviour that I damned well needed years ago.

I swallowed hard and whispered. "I'm going to send us to the brink of obliteration." *And I meant it.*

CHAPTER 13

ACE

I didn't doubt her words. I didn't doubt her ability to annihilate this world. I had seen the evil present against her skin. The bruises, the scars, the cuts that had laced themselves against her freckle-covered beauty.

When I first met her, I had no idea of those injuries, no idea of those heinous mutilations against her fragile form. She had covered them with clothing, like she probably had for years.

It was clear the system had failed her, but as much rage as she felt towards the organisations that had wronged her, she felt it more towards herself.

Red wasn't the only one abused, I would be a fool to think it, but she may have been the only one brave enough to tell of the atrocities. But that hadn't saved her, that hadn't relieved her.

She had been painted with brutality, marked with viciousness, touched with cruelty.

I wanted to ease her mind, I wanted to show her kindness and surround her with nothing but safety, but what could I do? Kobi would never let Red be, and she'd foolishly walked right into his cunning trap, right into his deliberate ambush.

Sure, he promised Felix and I would remain unharmed by his hand, but what about Red's? What was going to happen when Kobi forced her to use her abilities against us?

Within her, there was a power unmatched by this universe, unmatched by us. We weren't equals... at least, that's what we had always been led to believe. Except Red believed differently, she believed our abilities to be powerful, to be strong.

Did our powers really hold that much potential? Had Kobi been lying to us about it our entire lives? And what of Stanley, did he know? Was he the mastermind behind this guileful ploy?

I highly doubted it... but who would know these powers, and how to influence them, better than him?

My heart had momentarily broken when Red accused me of waiting around for her to die. Stanley and I had no idea the Ultimate Weapon would only awaken after death had taken them.

She was an unstable byproduct of an imbalance; there was really nothing to go off of when deciphering her powers or understanding her place within the universe.

But if she was now dead, did that mean she would never die again? Did that mean she was going to be forced to live forever in a never-ending immortality? Did that mean, unlike me, she would never age a day?

"Tell me what went wrong!" Kobi's voice echoed manically inside the enclosed space as Red and I ventured into the main room. Stanley stood nearest Felix, looking thwarted, as Kobi continued his unnecessary outburst. "What can the Ultimate Weapon *do?*" he demanded, his eyes darkening with fury.

"I don't know!" Stanley suddenly shrieked. "She destroyed the machine—the data is *gone!* The charts couldn't read her brainwaves. Essentially, her entire form is an immense compression of unstable energy." I stilled within the room, glancing across at Red. She looked anxious, chewing on her bottom lip, darting her fearful eyes between Stanley and Kobi.

She was nothing but power.

It made sense, in a completely nonsensical way. She wasn't human anymore; she didn't bleed, ache, or scar. She was a form of pure energy, of immense power and possibility.

Only, I knew she didn't want it. I knew she was frightened. I knew she had spent years working up the courage to flee, and when she finally had, she was trapped once more by circumstances completely out of her own control.

"*You.*" Kobi's malicious stare stilled against her. "Get here—now!" he roared, pointing a stern finger before him.

Red gasped, fear overwhelming her as she quickly glanced up and shook her head, her eyes communicating the words she was unable to form.

"Kobi, stop," I ordered, stepping in front of her. "The power is unstable." Kobi laughed, filling the tense room with a fake and manufactured sound.

"I know that much," he retorted. "Show us what you can do, show us the true power of the Ultimate Weapon, grace us with your fabricated design!" he screeched against the silent room.

His foolish words caused me to flinch. He must've known what a dangerous game he was playing, fighting fury with fury. Red was incapable of feeling pain; she was incapable of controlling the anger within her. She was a loose cannon, an idle volcano, a beehive just waiting to be poked.

I thought Kobi was smarter than that.

Before I even turned my head, I felt the electric buzz within the room. Felt the fearsome powers that thundered outward from her tiny form. Felt it like haywire zaps within my body, like manufactured sparks under my skin.

I held my breath and glanced Felix's way. His mouth was fallen agape, his stunned expression awed and afraid, his body inert. My wide eyes shifted to Stanley next.

The old man was fixated, entranced by the supreme abilities Red possessed.

His first time bearing witness to her immense and immeasurable power. It must've been surreal for him, life-changing and triumphant. After a lifetime of researching, documenting, estimating, and scouring the internet, he had finally found our greatly awaited Ultimate Weapon.

I breathed out a long breath and turned back, watching her magnificent and affrighted form in all its glory.

Red's eyes shone with orange pulsations as her hands propelled electric flickers within the room. She stood firmly with her face unchanged as the powers ignited from against her.

She gritted her teeth as her body violently quaked. Bones protruded from her pale flesh as her human skin cracked and seared, liquefying to reveal a glowing form of pure energy. One hidden behind stained and filthy clothing.

Suddenly, she shrieked, her enraged echo coursing through the bunker with a fierce rumble. The lights ominously flickered as she lurched forward in agony, her red locks weaving and waving within the glow that pulsed through her entire system.

She was a being of untouched energy, of pure electricity, of supreme endowment.

This was the Ultimate Weapon we had waited years for. *This* was the all-powerful, almighty entity that would either lead the planet to peace or drive the world to war.

She would never be challenged, never be controlled, never be concealed. She was the destined one. She was the hope of the Legend of Millennia.

Red collapsed to the ground with a hard and forceful thud, her glow blinking out of existence, replaced with her normal pale-skinned complexion.

I stood, disorientated for a few seconds as Felix rushed past me, skidding to his knees in front of Red. "You're okay," he muttered firmly as he picked up her head and held her for a few moments. She looked up at him weakly, their eyes meeting.

An unusual feeling slid through my bones, one unpleasant and agitated. I looked away, focusing on anything else as Felix seized Red's arm and hoisted her to her feet. She stumbled, shaky and fatigued.

"In the cell," Kobi instructed, his voice gravely unbothered. Felix and I shook with abrupt anger as Stanley looked across at Red, his eyes apologetic.

"She's not going in the cell!" Felix dared to challenge.

"*Oh,* yes, she is. She's a danger to everyone in this building. In the cell, now," Kobi ordered once more, his tone unchanging. "If you go against my rules, you'll be in there, too."

Felix glanced across at me with the same angered expression I wore. We both knew Kobi didn't give a damn about anyone above this bunker.

"It's fine," Red murmured as we lowered our eyes to meet her. "I don't care." *But she did.* You could tell that she did.

"Good," Kobi barked. "I will be back in the morning, be sure to document any findings," he stated like any of us cared.

Stanley gave him a small nod in agreement as he strode out the room and headed for the lift.

I was glad he was gone. I think we all were.

"I'll bring you some bedding," I offered with a smile. "It can get really cold here at night." Red nodded doubtfully, her smile thin and nervous.

"I'll fetch you some light reading," Stanley proposed, his dull tone slightly lifting. He shuffled over to his makeshift bedroom as Red shrunk into her oversized clothing.

I noticed then, the goosebumps against her skin, unwillingly remembering the discolouration that had festered along those skinny arms in the simulation.

They weren't real when I saw them, but they had been once. I shifted my gaze uncomfortably, examining the holes, stains, and scorch marks against her tattered clothing.

"Do you want some of my old clothes?" I asked before I'd even realised the words had left my lips. "Nothing too fancy," I added in haste as my cheeks started to blush. Red looked up in surprise. "Just might be a little nicer." I shrugged, trying to act unfazed and unembarrassed.

She snorted. "Wouldn't take much to be nicer than these." She smiled, her demeanour softening. "I'd really like that. These smell and feel horrible," she confessed. "That jumper I had, I scored that out a dumpster when I was fourteen," she stated almost proudly. "I was sad to see it go."

I watched her steadily, the way her face moved and stirred, the way her body shifted and changed. I may have known Red on paper, but in person she was completely different. She wore her heart on her sleeve and wore those abused mistreatments like armour. She was fascinating, defiant, resilient. She was like no one I had ever met before.

I needed to protect her, and I needed to apologise.

"Over this way." I cocked my head in the direction of my room, leading the way as she followed suit.

I guided her into my small bedroom, pushing the hefty door with a hard exhale. The door closed shut with a huffed squeak as Red awkwardly stood.

"Sorry, there's not a lot of space in here," I quipped as my shaky hands fiddled within my cube shelves. She mutely nodded, her eyes analysing the colourful posters as I flung a bunch of my old clothes onto the bed. She glanced at them quickly. "Pick what you want." I smiled her way.

Red inhaled sharply as she began sorting through the clothing. She placed aside a grey singlet, dark shirt, navy oversized jumper, and a pair of trackies. I passed her some new socks and a pair of pyjama shorts.

"These are new, I've never worn them." She took them from me slowly, our fingers brushing against each other's.

"Why are you doing this?" she asked as she bundled everything within her grasp. "You know you don't have to."

"I know, but I want to." I looked down, fidgeting with the cuffs of my sweater. Red waited, sensing my apprehension. "I, well—I want to apologise." She shifted uncomfortably.

"I shouldn't have lied about knowing you." I glanced up at her then, meeting her steady expression. "Before I met you," I coyly began. "I researched you, found out everything there was to know about your life, about you. I hoped you were the Ultimate Weapon, but after I found you, I hoped that you weren't."

I scooped up my remaining clothes, chucking them onto the floor in a messy pile. I took a seat on the sinking mattress, eyeing my fidgeting hands within my lap.

"I was wrong," I uttered sheepishly. "About everything... I hated my life. I hated having a power that felt so weak. I fixated on you, on this ideal weapon that would come along and fix everything I hated about myself. I thought, *'Good, now I won't be the centre of attention, the one who needs to have all their shit together.'* But now, I feel guilty for that."

My tone trembled, but I forced myself on. "You're your own person, you feel your own emotions, you act on your own impulses. You aren't afraid of what others think of you, you aren't bound by those that lay claim over your own power. You stand up for yourself. You defend yourself. You speak your mind even when it hurts. And... I envy that."

I paused and exhaled a heavy breath, willing myself to continue. "I didn't know who you would be, and I didn't know where to find you. I even doubted your existence towards the end. But if I'd known you, Red, I would've moved heaven and hell to save you."

I looked directly at her then, at the small and fragile girl who hovered within my doorway. "Move heaven and hell?" she echoed as orange teardrops slipped down her face. I nodded, sure of my words. She smiled gently. "Maybe one day you'll have to prove it."

I stood and stepped over to her, wiping away the droplets that fell against her pale cheeks. She was so beautiful, yet she didn't even know it.

We stared at one another for a moment too long. I hesitated

and stepped back, blushing hard as I ran my hand through my hair awkwardly. Red looked down, her frizzy locks tumbling in front of her reddening cheeks.

"Can I have a shower?" she asked nervously.

I keenly nodded, glad for something else to focus on. "Yeah, of course. Follow me." I squeezed past and led her once again into the hallway.

CHAPTER 14

RED

My body trembled as I turned the faucet off and slid out the shower, reaching for a microfibre bath towel. I screamed against it before flipping my crimson hair up into a spiral. Droplets slithered down my pristine spine as I placed my hands upon the basin.

There wasn't a single bone in my body they couldn't break. No surfaced skin they couldn't ink with colour. No part of my mind left unburdened, unscarred, unfractured, from the never-ending years of abuse. Of neglect, of stolen hope, of believing I deserved better and getting none.

Treated like garbage, discarded by the shop, turned away all those times I'd needed them most. I was starved, beaten, ignored. Abandoned by those who swore they would protect.

So then, why did I constantly question it? Question how I got into this position when I knew exactly how. They took away my innocence, my childhood, my life.

They took away my love of the world, of learning, of creation. And they did it without even a side glance, a double take, a second thought. I was nothing but damaged goods.

Alive in my own nightmare. And I had been for years.

I slipped into Ace's baggy clothing, appreciating their comfort and newness. I breathed them in deep, running my fingers up and down the smooth material.

They smelt like lavender and felt like Egyptian cotton upon my skin. I sank into their soothing feeling, wrapping myself up in the sleeves, thankful for Ace's kindness.

But fear still gripped me. It controlled me, it contorted me. Yet, over and over again, I told myself I wouldn't let it win. I had to stay calm, to be collected. Otherwise, I was going to send myself off that deep end quicker than you could say Ultimate Weapon.

I hurried out the bathroom, the steam suddenly suffocatingly thick as I stumbled into the hallway.

My wet hair was uncomfortably perched atop the back of my neck as my arms hugged at my waist tightly, bundling myself up within the warmth of my new jumper.

My feet stilled as I overheard Ace and Felix in mid conversation. "We can't put her in the cell," Felix argued.

"I know," Ace snapped. "But Kobi will be watching through the cameras. Don't you think it'll be Red who will have to pay for any disobedience?" He was right, but of course he was. He knew the game; he knew the players.

My body slunk against the wall, my breaths unbalanced. I couldn't help but think back to Ace's words, to his apology and his statement. Would he really have come for me if he knew? Would he have freed me, saved me? Would he have shown me love in a world full of hate?

My fingers touched tentatively atop the necklace as I pulled it free from behind my collar, fiddling with the silver pendant. There was so much I needed to learn about this power, so much I needed to know, master, and then prove. I just wasn't sure how far Kobi was willing to push me.

My breaking point had been reached a long time ago. I was lost, misguided, unassured, even though half the time I faked my own confidence and relished in my own defiance.

My past was behind me, I overcame the abuse, I made it out. I should have felt relieved, satisfied, fulfilled, but I didn't...

All the vile monsters they told me about during my childhood years were nothing compared to man, to woman, to humankind. They were the real behemoths, the ones who tormented minds and crushed dreams, who destroyed hopes and fractured hearts.

I wasted my life's younger years fearing the Bogeyman, Bloody Mary, Bigfoot. When all along, I should've feared those right before me. Those devils that used their malicious words as weapons against my young and grieving mind. Like Scooby-Doo had always tried to teach me, humans were the real monsters all along.

Was I destined to retrace those steps, to repeat that history? Was Kobi only the start of a deliberate and devastating downfall? But even so, what other monsters would I meet, what new evils would I witness, what further devils would I dance with?

The Ultimate Weapon was the most powerful entity within the known world, and yet, I still feared the corrupted mindsets and the brutal actions of humankind.

This infected globe, this contaminated planet, this polluted universe. Was it even worth saving? Was it worth World Peace, worth bending over backwards for? What if I brought battles, crusades, conflicts?

What if the Ultimate Weapon was designed solely for warfare, created to kill? I had the fury, the fight. I possessed the capability, the skill, the knowledge, and I *knew* it. But what would Ace think of me?

I wanted to be good, to do better. I wanted to control the anger inside of me. The anger that overtook me, overwhelmed me, overpowered me. The anger that brought me to the brink and sentenced me within an inescapable cell.

"Red?" Ace muttered.

I glanced up, swiftly tucking the necklace away. "I'm ready to do my time, Super," I joked, saluting.

Ace chuckled awkwardly. "We tried to make it comfortable, and also," he paused and reached for something. I hurried up the corridor and spied around the corner as something dense was heaved into my arms. "I present to you—Stanley's light reading." He smirked and patted the top page of the thirty-something science magazines. I grimaced.

"Does he want me to become a rocket scientist?"

"He can only hope," Ace responded with a sly wink.

The pages within my hands slipped and slid as I struggled towards the cell. They were all in pristine condition, all treated with the utmost care. Stanley must've been a genius after reading all these, and no doubt, doing so with extremely focused notetaking. I concealed a humorous smile. I'd never had any hobbies myself; I was moved around far too frequently to care that long for any one thing.

I stilled and looked around the bunker. Was this my home now? My newfound family? I wanted it so badly. I wanted to know that I was loved, know that I was safe, know that I was home. I'd missed out on so much, I'd rivalled so many... I didn't even know if I deserved a family anymore.

"Hey," Ace soothingly voiced as he lifted my chin with his finger and thumb. "Don't be too worried about the magazines, Stanley won't expect perfected notetaking by tomorrow."

His laughter filled the space around us, and I smiled despite my unease. He fell quiet as I met his pastel-blue eyes once more.

In that moment, I wanted to hold onto him forever. I wanted to wrap him up in silk and ribbon, and hold on forevermore. I wanted him eternally in this forsaken world I was destined to walk indefinitely.

Felix clicked his tongue, and we looked sideways, watching as he lifted his hand in a confused and irritated manner. Ace's hand slipped away, causing me to feel incomplete.

I waddled over to the cell and sat down, placing the magazines beside me in a slanted heap. The room was small, with a single bed, thin mattress, toilet, and basin. All very jail-like.

Ace closed the heavy door and passed me the key. I stood and grabbed it from his grasp. "Kobi can always see us, but the cameras don't pick up sound." He leant against the bars with a defeated exhale. "I don't want to keep you locked up like this, but—" he broke off.

A small smile met my lips as I nodded my head, silently reassuring him. He returned the gesture with a thankful smile of his own, his cheek pressed tight against one bar, his hair dishevelled against another.

"Use the key if you need to get out, just please don't leave." He eyed me apologetically. "I mean, you need a keycard to activate the elevator, but it'll just suck more for us if you try."

I eyed Felix watching us from afar, his black hair tousled, his demeanour unreadable. Sometimes, he was friendly, other times he was closed off and insolent. He was a difficult one to fully understand.

"You know where my room is," Ace stated. "Across from mine is Felix's, and Stanley's is at the end of the corridor. Just let one of us know if you need anything," he paused briefly, the cogs in his head turning as his fingertips clicked against the metal bars.

"*Oh,*" he remembered, handing me a flashlight off the desk as Felix stalked his movements like a wildcat. "Lights work on an automatic timer, off at ten, on at six. It's annoying, and Kobi refuses to let me change it. Some bullshit about being well-rested, I don't know." He shook his head and passed me the torch through the bars. "I think that's it."

"Okay." I fiddled with the flashlight. "Goodnight, I guess."

"Goodnight, Red." Ace smiled.

"Night," Felix echoed.

They made their way towards their rooms as I listened out for their receding footsteps and the closing of doors, but only one echoed throughout the bunker.

Ace hurried out as I sat against the thin mattress, the magazines shifting against my weight.

"Forgot something," he fussed as he reached into a drawer and fiddled with some pages, placing them out nearest Stanley's computer. He watched me from afar as he passed in front of me, a small smile playing on his perfect lips.

"Ace?" I asked timidly. He halted immediately and walked over to meet me. "How did you know?" He looked at me with a puzzled expression. "After I died... how did you know to come find me?"

He looked conflicted suddenly. "I, *um,* felt it," he whispered. I shook my head in confusion. "I felt your death." I gasped, my eyes widening as I jumped up and closed the space between us.

"You, *what?*" I shuddered as tears built behind my eyes.

Ace's composure slacked as he rested against the bars and glanced across at me longingly. "It was brutal, worst pain I think I've ever felt. Felix felt it, too. Took us both out, just like that—" He clicked his fingers, the sound echoing.

I stepped back from the bars and sank against the side wall, sliding down to my butt. I brought my knees to my chest, holding my delicate body tightly.

Ace crouched beside me and placed his hand through the bars, resting it against my knee. "We're connected, Red. You, me, Felix. We're an imbalance, we're all part of this," his voice stilled. "Although, I don't really know what *this* is."

He looked away, his blue eyes trailing the floor as I rested my head against the wall. "Why'd I have to die to be like this?" I questioned, even though I knew I would never hold the answer.

Ace exhaled softly, his expression unknowing, his smile unsure. "You didn't know I needed to die, did you?" I implored, eyeing him watchfully. He slowly shook his head.

Immune to pain, immune to the one thing that had kept me going for *so* long. I was jaded, broken, defeated. Beaten down to my brittle core, and then some.

My fingers fiddled with the pendant once more. We were the three musketeers, we were a family, I was complete. Why hadn't it lasted? Why hadn't it stuck? What had I done to cause such a catastrophic event?

If nothing in the world truly mattered, then why did that? It was love. It had to be. I loved my parents, I loved my life, I loved our pet rabbit.

Then in one split second, it was all taken away.

A car that rolled almost poetically against the night. A thunderstorm that felt almost erroneously designed. A moment that unmistakably changed the entire course of my life.

Some had asked if I'd seen the other side, if I'd met God, if heaven was a peaceful place. Some had filled my naïve mind with tales of heaven and hell, of the veil between the living and the dead. They would tell me how lucky I was, how my survival was such a blessing.

So, why had it never felt like one?

Within those first moments that followed the accident, all I could remember was the fearsome darkness, the icy cold, and my own screams that still sliced terror right through me.

Maybe I had always been held, stuck, suspended in animation. Unable to move, unable to feel. What did it mean to be human? Was it the pain, the peril? The certainty of death or the uncertainty of living? Was it the scars I had once kept, the pain I had endured through the hopeless and tragic years of my life, or was it simply just by breathing?

I grew up on my own, became an adult the day I stepped foot from the household I belonged. I was fractured, damaged, and all alone. I had no one to turn to, no one to love. Sure, I met people. I talked, I shouted, I ghosted. I ran my mouth like I had the right to, injured my body just because I could, scarred my flesh because I wanted to feel, because I wanted to take control of *something*.

If I'd died in that car accident alongside my parents, I would've unknowingly awakened. Ten years old with a power not made for this world. Would I have destroyed myself? Would I have finally lived?

It would have connected me to Ace, to Felix. They would have come for me, they would have had their Ultimate Weapon, and I would have had my freedom, my sanity, my purpose...

And my body. My own damn body.

I had threaded wounds into my skin, had hurt myself, cut myself, scarred myself. Had watched blood drip from my skin. I had taught my body to deal with the pain, to enjoy it. A feeling so intoxicatingly euphoric, it left me breathless. It hurt so bad and felt so good. But I didn't want to die. I wanted to show my strength; I wanted to cure the overbearing thoughts of suicide. And for mere moments, I had.

Some said I did it for attention, some said I did it for myself. Why had I done it? It was simple, really, it was because I wanted to feel something—*anything*—against the numbness that had penetrated my mind and left me dying from within.

It wasn't complicated mathematics, wasn't difficult to understand, it was as simple as one plus fucking one. It was the only thing I felt I had an ounce of power over.

I bled to show my strength. To distil my shattered heart. To feel human, to feel alive, to feel put together. I was so broken, adjusting to a world I had forever felt wronged by.

I had screamed at God; I had demanded my retribution. Demanded my freedom, my peace, my deliverance. But that was just the thing, wasn't it? *You could pray until your knees bled, and it didn't mean you'd be saved.*

"We were out looking at Christmas lights," I nervously began as Ace met my expression with a breathless concern. "My mum and dad, they meant the world to me. They rescued me. The day I was born, my birth mother abandoned me. My mum was a nurse who worked at the hospital. She took me in, her and dad, and they opened their home and their hearts to me." I felt the orange teardrops slip down my cheeks.

"It was really cold that December," I paused, willing myself to continue through the painful heartache. "The weather was stormy, but it was the only night Mum had off. We were looking at Christmas lights around the neighbourhood. We'd even stopped for snacks at this old roadhouse."

I breathed out a shuddered breath, remembering the bald man that served us, the woman with a smoke in her hand, the girl my age that recommended sour smog balls. All I had to do was call it to mind, and I was there—*the smells, the signs, the snacks.*

Etched inside my brain with so much pointless detail, the last place we had ever gone together...

"We were laughing about Dad's ridiculous jokes, we were singing along to Mum's favourite Christmas tunes, we were so happy in that moment, I remember thinking that I hoped it would last forever, that it would freeze in time."

I fixated on the science magazines sprawled atop the bed. "I don't know exactly what happened, but Dad lost control. The car flipped, the windows shattered, the icy cold seeped in. I screamed for Mum and Dad, but they were silent. I could feel blood on me, I could feel my whole world crumble into a thousand pieces, and I begged God to take me, too." I teared up, wiping at my eyes and nose with my jumper sleeve.

"It sounds a little different when it's not on paper." I tilted my head, glancing across at Ace. He patted at his glassy eyes as teardrops fell against his attractive features.

"Very different," he replied coarsely.

"I spent that Christmas in the custody of a case worker who had everything better to do." I huffed out a frustrated breath. "I had hopes, I had dreams, I had happiness. The shop took away everything I believed in."

Ace eyed me quizzically. "The shop?" A caustic laugh escaped my lips.

"The agency, for rehoming children. It never felt more than a shop sending out its orders. To me, anyway." I shrugged hard.

Ace stirred and reached for my hand, his fingertips entwining with mine. "You've been on your own for a very long time, Red," he spoke gently, his tone slightly muffled. "I feel your fire. I see your determination, your strength, your willpower. But I also see your hate for the world, your anger towards it, the fury you feel at its injustice." He leant back and exhaled hard, our solemn grip tightening.

"I won't tell you to stop feeling the emotions you feel, Red, but you need to bare your soul. You need to realise that those harmful things remain only in your past. You can start again. You can hope again, dream again, love again—you can feel *happy* again." Ace glanced up at me then, eyeing me with a hopeful gleam. My bottom lip trembled, my mind feeling vulnerable.

He understood.

Understood in a way I had always needed someone to understand. I could confide in him, trust in him, depend on him. He was there for me; he wanted to help me control the anger inside.

But what if I couldn't? What if I was a lost cause, a broken arrow, a defective machine? What happened if I couldn't be saved— did the story end, did the power within me implode? Did I become nothing more than fiction in a fairytale that had no happily ever after?

Teardrops slipped down my pained face as I forced a smile. Ace stood and walked over to the door, unlocking the deadbolt. He wandered in and fell to his knees before me. I watched him with unsteady breaths as he reached forward and took both of my shaky hands within his.

I swallowed hard as he leaned forward and kissed my forehead. "I won't let Kobi hurt you, I promise," he uttered against me. I held my breath tightly as my cheeks fiercely blushed, my mind overwrought. I kept my eyes low as Ace straightened his backbone, our hands disconnecting.

I glanced up shyly, feeling unsure of my own emotions. He looked to me with a small smile; his eyes filled with hope and sincerity. No matter what I did, no matter what I said, no matter how I acted, he was there for me. A constant within my collapsing life, a cutman within my corner, a player within my field.

"Goodnight, Super."

"Goodnight, Red."

It wasn't just me anymore, the decisions I made, the actions I took. It was all on them, too. They would suffer for my inability to heed.

They would take blow, after blow, after blow for my misdeeds against a system that had forever failed me. They would carry the burden of my revolt. They would endure torments made for me.

I could rebel; I could bring World War 3 if I deemed it to be. I knew I was powerful enough to do it, but what would happen to them? Would they be penalised, punished, possibly even imprisoned for acts that were mine and mine alone?

From now on, I had to think before I acted, be aware of the

consequences before I unleashed destruction.

I didn't want them to suffer for my behaviour. I *refused* to do that to them. I needed to learn control, to accept support. I needed to trust them. *Completely and wholeheartedly.* With the powers we possessed, we were forever connected. Eternity interwoven into this messed up, screwed up, fucked up situation.

I had spent most of my life searching for someone like Ace. Someone who would stand by me, who would put their faith in me, who wouldn't judge me for the tumultuous past I ran from.

I had begged myself for the courage to change when the system failed to protect me. Instead, I had solely stood, displaying my pain like battle scars as I rebelled against every authority I could.

For too long, I'd deserved more, deserved better, deserved an Ace. And now, there he stood. I could reach out and touch him, feel him, breathe him in deep. I could uncover all my ugly, present to him all the scars I bore, and bled, and burned for. I could stand with my mind naked, with my thoughts raw and my vulnerabilities uncaged.

But I was afraid for Ace. I was worried my tormented memories would not only destroy my mind, but his as well. If that ever happened, I'd never forgive myself. I had to believe that I could be changed, that I could rewrite myself into someone entirely new and someone unmistakably happy.

An untriumphant huff escaped my lips as I glanced over at the science magazines. I needed to do something whilst I waited for exhaustion to take me.

I crawled across the ground and reached for a magazine, settling back on the floor, cross-legged. I flipped the magazine open and began my epic journey of scientific pursuit.

CHAPTER 15

ACE

"There are rumours," Kobi snapped as he slammed his knuckle against the table. I stirred, watching the muscles within his tanned face contort. "The board members are getting sceptical. They want to know if we've found the Ultimate Weapon. I cannot keep them waiting!"

"Red isn't ready," I fired back unexpectedly.

I would've shut my mouth if this was anything to do with me, or my power, but this was Red.

"The simulation isn't even really a test, and she managed to destroy the whole damn machine. You can't just send her up there, she'll freak," I protested, my booming voice reverberating within my own tired mind. I'd tossed and turned all night long, unable to find sleep until the early hours of the morning.

"Ace is right," Felix chimed in. I glanced across at him, a surprised look against my features. "She's not ready and you know that. Her powers are unpredictable, unmatched. If something goes wrong, we might not be able to save you *or* your precious board members." Felix stretched against the chair, placing his legs atop the metal desk. The motion instantly angered me.

"She needs time," he concluded.

Kobi exhaled gruffly. "Time is a luxury that we don't have." He placed his hands upon the table and glanced between us, trying to act intimidating. "We have three days, tops."

We both let out a harsh exhale of astonishment. "You've been training us since we were seven," I cut in. "She won't be ready in three days, that isn't enough time," I quarrelled, my usual soft and timid voice ringing loudly within the bunker. Kobi shook his head dismissively.

"Three days," he demanded once more. I hiccupped a laugh of pure bewilderment.

"I went into the simulation, I got Red out! Remember that? You didn't see what I saw in there," I stated bluntly. "You're playing with fire if you think she'll be ready in three useless days."

I was glad Red wasn't awake to hear this. I'd checked in on her twice this morning, worried she would try to hurt herself when the realisation of what was now reality set in.

Kobi exhaled sharply. "You can have today with her, Felix can have tomorrow, and Stanley can have Wednesday," he concluded weakly as tension sliced between us, thick and heavy. "That is more than enough." His tone was like venom, spiteful and hateful, ready to strike. I gritted my teeth and clenched my knuckles, forcing the burning urge of rage back within me.

Felix stood. "That isn't enough time!" he bellowed at Kobi, his face red-hot, his temper the very same. "Do you want her to kill everyone within that meeting?"

He struck his palms against the table, and it shook. "*She* is the Ultimate Weapon, you cannot control her, you cannot force her to do anything she does not want to do! Her powers are unparalleled, erratic, deadly. Don't act as if you don't understand that!" Felix yelled, his eyes wide with anger, his demeanour standoffish and resolute.

Kobi leant off the table and stood inches from Felix's furious stance. I held my breath, looking between them. "Three days. Any blood will be on *your* hands," he sneered.

"I hope it's yours," an irritated voice echoed around us.

We glanced towards the cell in unison; shocked expressions shared by all three of us. Red stood, leaning against the bars with her cheek squished and her hair messy.

Suddenly, she straightened, her chin oddly angled. "I'll kill you in a heartbeat if you challenge me," she toyed with Kobi. I watched her with an unsure and alarmed look.

"Are you threatening me?" Kobi spat.

Red exhaled hard and shrugged as Kobi closed the space between them, peering down at her like a lion eyeing a gazelle. Red clicked her tongue and stilled, looking up at Kobi with an expression as hard as stone.

"Who do you even plan to show me off to?"

Kobi curtly swayed. "Board members, naturally." He swiftly stepped aside and returned to us.

Felix had slightly calmed, but he was still an active hive if poked. "The meeting is in three days; I have a lot counting on this. She needs to be ready," he stated cruelly.

"*Doubt,*" Red bellowed flippantly.

Kobi's eye twitched, but he didn't acknowledge her remark. He looked to Felix, then me, then made his departure. His sinister and silent stare confronting all on its own. I gulped down a held breath as the lift dinged within my eardrums.

"You seem different," Felix pressed as he strode over to the cell. I was glad I wasn't the only one who noticed it.

"Jail time will do that to you," she joked bitterly.

"Did you sleep well?" I asked, slinking past Felix's shadow as Red's wide brown eyes met mine.

She shook her head, her lips pressed tight. "I didn't sleep at all. My body didn't need it. Although, I do feel a little stir-crazy and over-energised right now."

She pulled a face. "I tried to sleep, but I just couldn't. My mind wouldn't turn off, wouldn't settle, wouldn't tire." She stilled and fiddled with her fingers. "Thank you for checking in on me, I presumed you were searching for any self-inflicted wounds." She dryly chuckled. I ran my fingers through my blond hair anxiously, ignoring Felix's persistent stare. "I was able to read about half of Stanley's magazines," she added.

I lowered my hand and glanced across at her with a dumbfounded expression. She smiled at me oddly. "He's been trying to get me to read those for years. I think I've read two," I admitted.

Red laughed, but the sound was off-key. "I had a bit of time." She stood and shoved the door open, stepping into the vast space. She huffed out a large breath and stretched her arms above her head. "I know myself," she began. I twisted around to face her as Felix leant against the bars, doing the same. "I won't be ready in three days." She stilled and our eyes met, her overworked mind wide awake and filled with worry.

I could sense her panic like I had before the simulation. Only this time, the consequences of failing were far worse.

"We know," I spoke gently as Felix stepped beside me.

"We can't teach you all that much in three days, but we can

hopefully train you enough to restrain that bloodlust for Kobi." He laughed. Red smiled unsurely, doubt festering within her.

I longed to know what she was thinking, longed to know all the compressed atrocities she hid within that tiny form of hers. Without the signs of insomnia against her face, without the dirt, vomit, or grime stuck to her clothes, without the blood-stained teeth and busted lip, she was gorgeous.

She didn't look sickly anymore. She didn't look exhausted, or worn-out, or hard done by. Her skin glowed, her hair shone, her pale complexion blinded.

She pulled her sleeves down quickly, as if sensing my inappropriate thoughts. I coughed awkwardly, looking away. "Felix and I will train you best we can," I tried to assure her.

"Our grandparents own a whole bunch of land in the countryside. We can head out there today and I can run over some basic ability training with you," I offered, watching her steadily. She nodded after a heartbeat, seemingly reluctant.

"I've got my own stuff to do," Felix interjected. "Just let me know tonight what you went over." I nodded at him surely. He shot me a conflicted smile and then looked to Red, nodding his head solemnly. She did the same in return as he headed for the elevator.

"You seem different today." I observed, careful not to poke the bear. She looked up at me with those wide brown eyes of hers and shrugged dismissively.

"I died, Ace. I don't know how I'm supposed to feel, or act, or anything, really." Her eyes flickered with emotional turmoil. "I'm the Ultimate Weapon. I can't be harmed, I can't feel pain, I'm indestructible..." her gloomy voice drifted like a discarded sailboat out at sea.

"I remember the moment I died, the moment the pain was so unbearable I couldn't wait for the end to come, for the Grim Reaper to reach out and snatch me. Every time I close my eyes, I feel that same disappointment, failure, contempt that I did the moment before I jumped." She breathed out slowly, scrutinising the wrinkles against her palms. "I wanted to die, Ace." My eyes met hers, they were honest and bloodshot, glassy and raw.

"I shouldn't have told you about my parents," she uttered. I sucked in a breath, feeling caught off guard. "It wasn't your trauma to bear." She half-smiled hopelessly.

"I want to know you, Red," I blurted rashly. "The *real* you. Not the one I read about on paper." I reached forward and touched her hands. They were cold, shaky. I tried to meet her gaze, but she looked away nervously, biting her thick bottom lip.

All I wanted was to wrap my slender arms against her and pull her in close. I wanted to reassure her, comfort her, soothe her. But unfortunately, I couldn't do anything if she wouldn't let me in, if she wouldn't open up, if she wouldn't demolish that stone wall within her bleeding heart.

She squeezed my hands gently, lifting her chin to meet my kind expression as tears built behind her eyes. "I can't get you out of my head," she uttered frightfully. "And that terrifies me."

"Come here." I pulled her into a tight embrace.

Red stood upon her tiptoes, wrapping her arms around my shoulders. She breathed out a shuddered breath as I closed my eyes and leaned into her tiny figure.

"Ace, I've lost everyone I've ever loved. Who's to say you won't be next?"

The smooth strands of her hair slipped effortlessly through my fingertips as I placed my hand upon her head. She smelt of my own shampoo and conditioner, a lime scented aroma with hints of coconut.

I didn't know what to say to her, didn't know how to mend her tainted heart. She deserved so much more, deserved love, deserved the world. I knew I couldn't fix her.

I knew that was a battle she needed to face all on her own, but I wouldn't leave her, wouldn't run, wouldn't abandon her. Maybe all she needed was to hear those comforting words.

"I'm not going anywhere, Red," I muttered against her. "You're stuck with me."

She was silent a moment longer. "I'm afraid to let you in. I'm afraid it will destroy you." I slipped from her touch.

"Destroy me?" I repeated her words, uncertain of them.

She nodded sadly. "I've gone through the worst heartaches, I've loved, I've lost, I've mourned for those I barely even knew. I'm grieving myself right now," she paused to catch her shaky breath as a loose teardrop escaped her eye socket. She flicked it away curtly as she lifted her chin and eyed me straight on.

"I care about you, Ace. In a way that's new, and weird, and alarming. But I won't allow myself to latch onto you. I'm lonely, I'm troubled, I'm depressed. I know myself, I either feel nothing at all or everything at once."

Her body trembled as she continued. "You know my whole life on paper, but you don't know what it took. I could've died when I was ten, I tried myself when I was thirteen. I swore for months I'd seen an angel, but I later concluded it was just a nurse in emergency care who looked like my mum."

She clicked her tongue, forcing her tearful eyes to remain open. "My foster dad almost beat me into a coma when he found out. I still have the—" Her slender fingers froze upon her wrist. "Scar," she muttered, her breath hitching. "No, I don't." Her head shook frantically as she sobbed, teardrops rolling down her pale cheeks.

"I don't have the scar." Hyperventilated breaths pounded from her lips as her entire body convulsed violently. "*No!*" she cried as she dug her head into her hands, her body shuddering.

My feet shuffled backwards, my glassy eyes watching her with growing trepidation. I couldn't understand why. Why she wanted the scars, why she wanted the ever-present reminder of brutality and violence against her pretty figure.

I fought to keep my own tears at bay as everything around her came undone. I reached forward with a slow glide, touching atop her shaky hands. "Red?" I murmured anxiously.

She resisted as I tried to pull them away from her face. "I had scars no one could heal, I had skeletons in my closet I was too scared to face. I had a life I wanted to live."

She stirred as her tearfulness eased. "I've lived every day with the lie that tomorrow will be better. And it never was." She lowered her hands and lifted her head, our eyes interlocking. "Until the day I met you." I took a trembling breath.

"But you need to know who I am," she continued. "The person my past forced me to become. My body may have healed, but my mind is as broken as when my parents died." I smiled weakly at her distraught face, trying to lessen her pain, even though I knew it was impossible.

"I told myself I needed to forgive, that I needed to move on, but I am still so enraged and damaged by what the shop did, and by what they didn't do. I rebuilt myself from the fractured, shattered, and broken pieces the system gave me. Why should I ever forgive them for that?"

"What about forgiving yourself?" I questioned, my blue eyes glassy and tearful.

"I don't deserve to be forgiven for the things I've done." She was so sure of it.

I fell quiet as I tried to understand the ways she thought, the ways she trusted. She was abused, repeatedly, neglected and forgotten.

Forced to bear those bruises and face those disfigurements for what she believed would be a lifetime. She was so small and innocent, her life so brutally redefined. But she no longer wore those bruises or felt the pain inflicted by them. Now, she had the ability to orbit within her own refuge, her own safe sanctuary.

She couldn't be blissfully unaware of that fact, but maybe she was too scared to acknowledge it, to admit the truth that was undoubtedly her new life.

I wanted to help her, to heal her. I just didn't know how. Her anger was interconnected with her past, with everything she had faced within the system, and within those homes of incomprehensible horrors.

She had a second chance at life, something so many people had prayed for, had begged for, and she was throwing it all away. And all for what? All because she couldn't handle not bearing witness to the contusions they'd inflicted upon her? All because she didn't know how to survive without the marks of refinement that had once been present against her butchered body?

Inwardly, I scoffed. Red was lost and confused. Reborn into a world where she was unable to feel the one thing she had felt for years.

Whether inflicted upon herself or by others, she coped, she dealt, she reinvented herself to survive within an abused and violent world. I couldn't be angry at her for that, for adapting, for enduring.

She deserved kindness, gentleness, and I vowed to show her those things. To show her there existed a world within this world that was free of brutality and cruelty. One filled with love, and happiness, and dreams that came true.

I would find her parents burial. I would offer her that closure and hope to end the hateful thoughts that bombarded her brain.

But first, I had to try my best to teach her in one day, what I had learnt across a lifetime.

CHAPTER 16

RED

My mind raced, compacting me tightly into those deadly spaces within me that I did not wish to journey.

I could feel myself self-sabotaging, but without it I feared I would suffocate. I would wheeze and battle for breath, I would abide by any debilitating woe.

I was no longer all alone; I no longer had to face those faceless foes solo. I had to move forward, I had to be brave, I had to start again.

My eyes peeked against my body anxiously. It didn't look like mine, didn't feel like mine. I felt like an outsider within my own skin, like the liquid that pumped through my veins wasn't part of me, like the heart that pulsed within my chest belonged to someone else, like the girl that inhabited my reflection was nothing but an imposter.

I didn't know who I was without those scars, without the constant reminder I could never escape my history. I was as toxic as the mould that grew against the beams of that basement. In fact, I might've been worse. I came in like a bulldozer, and I destroyed everything I touched and everything I loved.

Ace placed his hand over mine, a gentle reminder that I wasn't all alone in this.

"We're almost there." He smiled my way encouragingly.

A controlled breath left my lips as I relaxed against the passenger seat. I looked out into the vast fields covered in rocks and grass, in hills and wildflowers, at horses that galloped, cows that trot, sheep that grazed.

My time with Ace had only been short, but I already knew just how much he was worth fighting for.

I knew how much he deserved humanity, deserved gratitude. Of all the people in the world I could have been stuck with, I was glad it was him. And I was glad he opened his heart to me when there wasn't a single reason in my mind he should've.

I was so thankful for his benign treatment, but I feared the toll his tenderness would take against my mind. I knew within myself that I could be weak, that I could be complacent at the worst of times.

Ace's presence was exciting, alluring. I longed to be by his side, to be against his touch, but I didn't know whether these were authentic feelings. Secretly, I worried about dependence, obsession. I worried my mind was being spurious.

There were all kinds of loves within this world, like the love expected from your parents, the appreciation felt towards a partner, the passion sensed when doing something you enjoyed. Love was friendships formed, relationships gained, connections identified. But love was also indefinable, it was happy but sad, scary but safe, mysterious but knowing.

To me, Ace's love was the scariest, the most unknown.

I couldn't risk screwing it up. Ace, Felix, and I, we were bound by these powers of the Ultimate Weapon. We were tied by this formidable force, synced together, connected for all eternity. I couldn't risk the aftermath, or the harm, if these feelings turned out to be nothing but emotional dependency.

I needed to be in love, not in need.

My mind suddenly raced, and it caused me to wonder, was Ace only putting up with me because of who I was, because of who I'd become that day I took my life into my own shaky and incapable hands? Did he tolerate me because he had to? Did he treat me like a friend only because he felt obligated to?

I felt conflicted, unsure if any truth rang from my thoughts.

Was I here because Ace wanted me here or was I nothing more than an inconvenience with a power strong enough to slice the globe right through its equator?

I frowned. Why was everything constantly so confusing and why did I always seem to end up astray within these emotions that drowned me?

My unsure gaze trailed along the interior of the car, meeting Ace, watching as his hair ruffled against the wind, as his bright eyes scanned the road ahead, as he changed gears with such an effortless ease. He really did make me feel safe.

A small part of me still regretted being so open and honest about my parents, but another part of me knew I had needed to be. Besides those few conversations I'd shared with Ace, I hadn't mentioned them outside of my tiny mind in years.

It had been too hard, too forced, but now, it felt necessary.

It was thanks to the trust I felt towards Ace that I was able to ask him of their final resting place. I had dreaded the question since I was ten, a question I should've known the answer to years ago.

Now, just the thought of knowing their final burial brought tears to my eyes. I never had the chance to say my final goodbyes, to take flowers to their graves, to find closure after their parting. It felt surreal, bizarre in the most unexpected of ways.

Ace turned into a slanted driveway where a large stone wall and black iron gate guarded the entrance. He buzzed in a code before continuing up the drive.

The path twisted and turned, leading up to what looked like an old Victorian mansion.

Trimmed hedges, perfectly sectioned pine trees, and stone pathing lined the private road. The mansion perched overlooking the estate like an ominous tyrant.

It looked grand and artistically designed, but there was an eerie feel about it. A feeling I didn't like the sorts of.

I'd already noticed Ace came from money, but it didn't affect the way I saw him. He never held it above me, never made me feel lesser. He was always willing to help me out and ask for nothing in return. Even the clothes I currently wore were his. He was kind beyond measure.

Ace parked the car and the engine quieted. I tapped my fingers against the side of the door, my mind running at a million miles per hour. I feared what awaited me, feared the power I had three useless days to learn how to control.

"Don't get too worked up about it," Ace said comfortingly. "It'll all work out." I stilled my fingers and glanced back at him.

I feared new places. I feared new people. I feared new prospects. I was afraid of the things I didn't understand, the things I couldn't control.

My stomach suddenly swirled and somersaulted with a feeling of anxiety deep within my nervous system. I breathed out heavily, demanding the vile within my gut stay there. My head nodded quickly as I shoved the car door open, acting unfazed as I collided against the refreshing springtime air.

Ace and I stood outside the grand entryway. The mansion was immense with an asymmetrical design, large columns, overdone bay windows, and a slanted roof that trumped three storeys high. Alongside a fine stone exterior mixed with lighter tones of wood.

A man dressed in a well-kept suit exited the structure; his gloved hands folded neatly in front of him. "Good day, Ace," he conveyed.

"Hey Marty," Ace replied cheerfully. "This is Red."

"A pleasure." Marty bowed his head as an alarmed and anxious expression overtook me. "I'm a butler for the Hart family." My lips curled unsurely as my eyes shifted to Ace.

"Yeah… it's true. We have a butler," he clarified, running his hand awkwardly through his hair. He seemed embarrassed by it. "Come on, let's go inside. It's the quickest way to the back gardens," he spoke hurriedly, lowering his head timidly.

"I apologise, but Lady Stella is currently ill in bed. Does this matter require her input?" Marty interjected.

I couldn't imagine being a butler, having to be nice to everyone *all* the time. You wouldn't even be able to pay me to do it. I'd be drained after five seconds and given up by ten.

Ace shook his head. "Not today, Mart," he expressed. "I came around to show Red the gardens. We're going to be doing some dexterity training."

"Very well." Marty bowed his head understandingly. "If you

require my assistance, you know where I'll be."

He smiled and turned away, heading towards the side of the property where three groundskeepers were grouped in conversation.

It was a bizarre sensation seeing how dissimilar our lives truly were. Ace had been brought into a world of privilege and nobility, an existence remarkably similar to that of my short-lived stay with Daxton and Kalila.

I had tried over the years to ignore my daydreaming of that life, of the opportunities I could've been gifted, opportunities now bestowed upon their own daughter. But at the end of the day, it wasn't them I wanted. It was my parents. I questioned again what could've been if they hadn't died. We were financially apt, life was good. Pathways paved with prospects and promises.

I was set for life, or so I thought.

Ace and I stepped up the large concrete steps and onto the veranda. The wooden door was exceptionally large and meticulously hand carved. I analysed it for a few moments, admiring the handiwork of each detail.

Ace exhaled hard before he pushed the hefty door open and entered. I meekly followed, unsure of what awaited us.

We stepped into another century. The décor was Victorian inspired, with an abundance of patterns, ornamentations, and use of darkened hues.

It set off an unnerving and foreboding sense within me. I shivered, feeling a cold sensation glide across my now goosebumped skin. I glanced around nosily, scanning the room like an undercover agent.

Ace reached back and gently entwined his fingers within mine.

I looked down at my hand unsurely as Ace led us silently into the next room over. I could sense his unease, feel his tension, hear his rapid heartbeat.

I couldn't imagine it. He grew up in privilege and wore his kind-heartedness like a badge of honour.

He didn't wear his hate, or anger, or injustice against him like I did. He chose to be better; he chose to be kind. I saw that about him, I valued it, I envied it. I wanted to modify myself, but did a tiger ever really change its stripes?

Ace coughed nervously, and I gave his hand a soft squeeze, feeling his tension ease. I wanted him to know I was there for him; I wanted him to know I cared. That I would move heaven and hell for someone who treated me like he did, who showed me compassion, who challenged my toxic views, who stood beside me when everything faltered.

I'd watched a society collapse and a system do nothing but fail us. I knew I wasn't the only one mistreated, abused, lied to, but I was the only one who now had a means to destroy them all.

Only, what about Ace? He would take the brunt of their fury when I stood unaffected by their questionable morals and anathematised actions. His kindness didn't deserve such heartless consequence. He didn't deserve to feel the harshness of humankind for actions that weren't even his.

We exited the mansion, a fresh and comforting scent slipping against us. It was a warm November day, the sun hot, the birds active, the smell of spring fresh and flowery.

I glanced at the mansion with growing trepidation as we ventured into the picturesque gardens. A cold feeling stuck against my bones.

"Ace?" I asked as we trekked down a perfectly paved trail. Ace smiled and turned back to me, our entwined hands separating.

"Sorry," he uttered. "I get lost in my own thoughts when I visit here. Can you believe I once owned a horse?" He chuckled, the tiny lines in his face matching the movement effortlessly.

He glanced forward once more and breathed in deep, filling his lungs. "I miss the outdoor air. Especially in spring, the flowers grow like wildfire, the dull winter colours give way to vibrancy, the plant life rejuvenates."

His face fell. "After my mum met Kobi, everything changed. It seemed like even the seasons did," he reminisced as he turned to glimpse at the faraway city skyline. "There are so many memories out here, Red. I really can't wait to share them with you." I caught my breath, feeling flummoxed.

He turned to face me; an unsure expression painted across his face. "You ready for this?" I naïvely shrugged. "You have the ability to control your power." He spoke so surely of those words.

I skimmed his face as a strong zephyr blew against us almost ominously. "How long did it take you?"

Ace sighed, his heart weighing heavy in his chest. I waited for his response, but I didn't push for it. If he was ready to give an answer, then I was ready to listen. Words were hard sometimes. God only knew how much I related to that.

"Some days, I still don't know what the hell I'm doing," he answered honestly. "When you harnessed Felix's power, when you told him it was strong, I doubted everything I knew of my ability after that. Inside the simulation, I was labelled weak, so was Felix," he paused, catching his breath. "We've spent our whole lives with these powers, and within us they feel strong, capable, but we were told—*and convinced*—that they weren't." He sighed haphazardly and frowned.

"I need to ask Stanley about it, I just haven't had the chance," he continued. "He's way too concerned about you now." I glanced across at him defeatedly, feeling sorry for his inconvenience.

"I think it's amazing that you can control our abilities." He looked my way and smiled wide. "I studied you; I prepared for you. I thought I knew the powers of the Ultimate Weapon as well as I knew my own. But as it turns out, I didn't. Stanley's research, we thought we knew how powerful you would be. We thought the world would be ready for you... we thought *we* would be ready for you."

Maybe I was wrong. Wrong for the way I thought, wrong for claiming the abuse as the reason I was so unhinged, the reason my power was so unpredictable.

There were those, like Kobi, who tried to lay claim over this fearsome power, but I wouldn't allow it. I envied Ace, the way he didn't base his whole existence off something unseen within him. He chose to be his own person, to be bigger than the power he held.

Was this power a blessing or a curse?

I couldn't say for sure, but it was definitely something. And as much as I wanted to hate it, it brought me to Ace. It forced me to challenge everything I knew about myself, the things I hated, the things I liked, the things I felt. It forced me to face the abuse without ever having to feel it again.

I should've been grateful, but I wasn't. I knew that sooner or later I wouldn't be able to cope without imprinting my skin and causing my own self-imposed slaughter. I would miss the hurt, the ache, the blood. I would fall apart at the very seams where this power was trying so hard to lace me up tightly.

This fatal secret I kept, I needed to tell Ace, but I couldn't.

What if he didn't listen, what if he didn't understand the deadly truths behind these foul-tasting words? They were bitter and burnt, salty and saturated. And I couldn't bear to hear them said aloud.

"When you were inside the simulation, what did you feel?" I glanced up, stunned by his sudden bluntness. I stuttered aimlessly.

"Sorry," Ace mumbled, running his hand through his unkempt hair. "I didn't know how to ask it, and I thought it might help with understanding and controlling your power."

I humphed, still slightly astonished. "I felt pain. And fear, and this unmoving feeling of... death." I swayed alongside the bitter breeze. "I saw myself, and it made me question my past. Caused me to question everything I knew about myself, about the life of that little girl." My throat burned against the words, like the flavours of them harboured deadly toxins only I could taste.

"If I had to go back, had to do it all again, I wouldn't be able to," I voiced. "I wouldn't be able to survive it. I look back and all I see is a past I'd give anything to outrun." I closed my eyes and envisioned how my life was before, picturing all that I'd sacrificed, all that I'd done, all that I'd given up.

"Those people, that agency, they signed my death certificate long before I even knew what suicide was." I looked up and met Ace's hard and concerned stare. His blue eyes slightly faded.

Part of me wanted to sugarcoat it, make it less brutal, less impactful, but I couldn't. It was the harsh truth no matter what direction I looked at it, no matter what language I deciphered it. There was no point in lying about that.

Ace had saved me, had rushed into the simulation to get me out. He saw the mutilations against my skin, he saw the blood, the vomit, the alien ooze. He saw the terror carved upon my bloodied face.

Their malevolent laughter rang loud within my eardrums once more as a cold sensation ran across my skin like drippling blood. I breathed out slowly, forcing my mind to relax, forcing myself to move past the nightmarish occurrences within that fanciful hallucination.

If I'd met my future self, I would've remembered. Those shadowy figures—they mocked me, tormented me, haunted me, but they weren't real.

None of it was real.

"What did you see inside the simulation?" I asked quickly, trying to escape my tortuous mind. Ace swallowed hard, moving his attention to the flowers that grew beside the cobbles.

"I saw you." I laughed despite myself. "Well, not you—*you*—but I saw the Ultimate Weapon," he paused briefly. "I was able to use my powers without consequence, without limitations. It felt freeing, meaningful." He eyed the ants underfoot, watching as they unitedly scurried within a straight line.

"I always presumed my mind had gotten muddled up with the powers of the Ultimate Weapon, but maybe it had been my own strength and abilities all along." He touched against a daisy gently. "Maybe the powers within me can be beautiful."

"You don't think your powers are beautiful?" I questioned, the sentence strange on my tongue.

Ace snorted, retracting his fingers from against the foliage. "I used to think it was nothing but a curse. Nothing but a deadly and unpredictable disaster. I've always wanted to use it for good, to save people, to null wars, to bring peace. But I was manipulated into believing I wasn't powerful enough for that. I was told I was a freak to society. I was told to hide, and cower, and make myself invisible."

Ace eyed me doubtfully, confusion against his overworked mind. "I've always viewed Felix's ability as having the potential to be fatal, but mine, the powers of light, I've always felt like I was destined to help people."

He sighed defeatedly, and I knew a lot more hid behind that statement. "The powers of the Ultimate Weapon are mesmerising, but unnerving. You have the choice to bring world peace or world war. You can be good and hailed a hero, or bad and labelled a villain."

I fiddled with a sharp branch, avoiding eye contact. "Honestly, I've always felt like there was a villain inside of me that I needed to overcome. Never told anyone that, though. I don't even know if it makes sense to anyone but me."

I stepped away from the tree, watching him steadily. "How do you control your powers?"

He pondered the question. "There isn't really a specific answer I can give you."

"Ever kill anyone?"

"No," he answered. "But that's only thanks to Stanley and his lessons on how dangerous these abilities can be. Felix and I were eight when we met him, before then, we thought these powers were normal." He sat against a white concrete bench.

"Mum had home-schooled us and warned us of using our powers outside of the estate, but she'd never told us why. She never told us they weren't normal."

Ace looked up at the large oak tree, watching as the branches and leaves rustled against one another. The sound was loud, but peaceful. It reminded me of the beauty of Mother Nature, reminded me that everything within this world had the potential to be something beautiful... *everything except me.*

I lived past death, defied Mother Nature, rivalled humankind. It wasn't normal, it wasn't right, but there was nothing I could do about it now. I had to learn to live with it, to survive with this alien entity within me that was the consequence of my own suicidal act.

The concrete was cool against my open palms as I sat beside Ace and huffed out a noisy breath. The shadow of the tree rested beside us, shielding us from the sun that burned hot against the globe.

I squinted my eyes, glancing at the gardens beyond, at the endless rows of plants, and flowers, and bushes that seemed to perfectly align. Everything appeared to be lush and green, the flowers colourful and in bloom. I wrinkled my nose, inhaling the multitude of fresh aromas that danced upon the surface of my skin, sweet and enriching.

Next, I trailed my brown eyes along the cobblestone path, to the great white arches, large cement pots, and delicate trellis. It was really something out here. It was calm, peaceful, untroubled.

"From what I've witnessed," Ace began. "Your power is only out of control when you can't handle your emotions. So maybe, instead of focusing on controlling the power, you focus on controlling the anger." He glanced my way, a hopeful look within his pastel-blue eyes.

"I know you're right, but I don't want you to be." Ace tilted his head, a half-smile present against his lips as he looked me over carefully.

I eyed him back, my anxiety duplicating at a dangerous rate. "I have a lot to be angry for, a lot to be enraged about," I stated as my voice unwillingly trembled. "That's trauma that years of therapy couldn't even solve. I mean, sure, it's a solution, but the problem is bigger." I took a sudden breath. "I tried to get help, I really did, but I was turned away. I was labelled ungrateful and told to get in line. I don't want to be this unstable, this angry, but three useless days isn't going to change shit."

Ace nodded his agreement wordlessly, his expression disappointed but not surprised.

It was years of trauma, years of an ugly influx that built, and built, and built within my tattered heart. It wouldn't be easy to unravel, would be almost impossible.

"And maybe, I don't want to let it go." I eyed him straight on, my voice breaking. "Maybe, I don't want to give the anger up. Maybe part of me believes it's all I have left of my pointless and sad human existence." My pitiful words echoed around us.

Ace eyed me bleakly, placing his hand gently upon mine. His voice soundless, as the world around us soothingly spoke.

CHAPTER 17

RED

Time was the killer of all, but it wouldn't be mine. I defied the odds, I outran time, I challenged the very meaning of human existence. I was otherworldly, indestructible, the legend's omnipotence.

And yet, I was bloody miserable.

I folded my hand against my knuckle, leaning my cheek upon the bony surface. "You taught her *nothing!*" Felix bellowed.

He felt absent against my decayed mind, like a blurred mirage from miles away. He yelled at Ace, then Ace yelled back, their match muffled within my eardrums. Stanley tried to calm them, but his words were tuned out, ignored. Like I was doing right now.

I didn't want to listen to them fight, I didn't want to listen to them battle and brawl over my failure to control my own superhuman ability. I already felt useless; this didn't make me feel any better about it.

Felix said I should've used my powers, should've gained familiarity with them. He had a point, but then again, so did Ace. I was emotionally drained, psychologically exhausted, mentally done. I didn't want to think about this stupid power anymore. I wanted to forget, I wanted to close my eyes and float off into a never-ending slumber.

Their figures slow motioned against my mind, their voices inaudible, their scuffle jumbled. My thoughts drifted and wandered, surprisingly quiet and quelled. A long sigh escaped my lips as I trailed my eyes along the metal desk, observing the files and documents. They were sprawled across the table, my old foster photo present against a clear sleeve. I reached over absentmindedly and grabbed it, bringing the picture before me.

I really did look homeless.

My eyes were bloodshot, my mouth a snarl, my face dirty, my hair knotted. It was clear why no one had ever wanted to adopt this, it was disgusting. I tossed the photo into the trash and stood up.

I shuffled into the cell and shut the sturdy door closed behind me. The deadbolt clicked, causing Felix and Ace to pause and look my way with piqued uncertainty. They hurried between the space, thwacking against one another purposefully.

"Are you okay?" Felix asked coarsely.

I sat upon the bed, looking across at him gruffly. "I like Ace's idea." I exhaled an unimpressed huff as I lifted the topmost science magazine from the towering stack, resuming my readings from last night.

Felix snorted and shook his head. "It's stupid, you can't control your anger," he fired back without a single, fleeting care of my feelings towards the matter.

I slammed the flimsy magazine upon my lap and looked to him sharply. "And what would you suggest?" I hissed as fury flooded through my veins and tiredness wracked against my overexerted brain.

Ace glanced between us worriedly.

"Go somewhere abandoned, learn to manage your power, stop being so afraid of it." Felix clanged against the bars curtly.

"When I killed myself, *you* felt my death," I barked at him, eyeing him like a viper ready to attack, ready to kill. "What was that like?"

He clicked his tongue dismissively, exhaling hard. "It was painful, I puked a few times," he explained indifferently.

"It was agony for you," I snapped.

Felix reluctantly nodded. "Okay, yeah, sure. Maybe it was the worst pain I've ever felt, but what does that matter?" He eyed me with daggers, his blue-grey eyes filled with hostility.

"I feel that same agony, that same excruciating pain, every time I use my power. My consequence, *remember?* If you want me to use this ability—*you* make me angry." I exhaled a sharp snort, returning my attention towards the magazine.

I wished it could've been different; I genuinely did.

The anger brought out the worst in me, it brought forth the uncontrolled powers of agonising affliction that I just couldn't quell. "Now get lost, I'm busy."

Felix's eyes blazed with fury as he began shouting offensive remarks through the caged bars. I ignored his meaningless attack, focused on the theory of relativity. I couldn't be bothered faking my attentiveness. Not today, I was done with today.

Ace's silhouette caught my eye, and I glanced up, tilting my head in confusion. He looked across at me and smiled doubtfully. "I'm sorry about that," he muttered.

"You don't have anything to apologise for. Felix doesn't like your idea, so what?" I shrugged boorishly. "I doubt that's the first time." I sounded so rude, so conceited.

I stilled and lowered the magazine, taking a long and much-needed breath. "Ace, I am mentally *done* for today. I need a break from all the power this and the power that. I just need a moment alone, a moment to think."

He nodded sympathetically as Felix slammed a glass beaker against the floor. The ear-piercing impact ricocheted like gunfire within the quiet room, causing Ace and I to jump.

I huffed harshly as Ace stepped away. "What the hell are you doing?" he shouted over the newfound noise.

"What do we need science for if Little Miss Ultimate Weapon over there only wants to learn about her *feelings?* All she's going to need is some solid soul-searching!" he roared as he furiously threw a drinking glass against the floor. The shattered fragments rippled out, slithering like tiny crystal-like insects.

"Felix!" Stanley bellowed, fastening his pace to reach him.

"Stan, there's no point. He's in a mood," Ace expressed as he held an arm against Stanley's arched figure. Stanley paused reluctantly, eyeing the destructive brother with a disappointed and concerned expression.

Felix's cheeks brightly flushed as his breaths hitched in uneven patterns. He childishly flung a paperback book against the floor, smashed a few more glasses, and kicked over the bin.

The metal compound dinged against the sturdy table, sliding across the smoothed floor like a hockey puck desperate to reach the goal.

I grumbled aloud and placed my head within my hands. All I wanted was some *peace* and *fucking quiet.*

"Red?" I glanced up with an eager expression. "Come here," Ace ushered. I stood and unlocked the door, stepping over the broken glass, scattered documents, and tossed books.

Ace leant against my ear, his breath hot and tingly alongside my exposed neck. I trembled despite my resistance. "Go to my room and have a rest. Once Felix is done, I'll need to clean up." He pulled back, watching me with the softest blue eyes.

I nodded after a heartbeat, unsure if being in his bed was to help my understanding of these feelings towards him, but it certainly exceeded being out here with a seventeen-year-old having a temper tantrum. Especially one with such a dangerous superhuman ability.

Another glass shattered as I squeezed past Ace and Stanley. I gave Stanley a brief smile, but he hardly noticed. His scarlet eyes were fixated on Felix, his body motionless and stiff.

I entered Ace's room and deeply inhaled, allowing the aroma of him to seep within my system. I smiled intoxicatingly at the sensation before I fell atop the bed, the plush quilt catching my fall with cushioned resilience.

I shut my eyes, enjoying the silence the hefty door and fortified walls encapsulated me in. This was a feeling I wanted to stay forever.

"Red?" I stirred sleepily and sat up, wiping at my tired eyes as a blurry figure entered my vision, tall and handsome. I yawned and drifted back down to rest. "Hey, Red," Ace's tender tone filled my eardrums once more as a wide smile beamed across my face, euphorically possessed from the energy surging within my veins.

I swayed and leant against the wall as my eyelids drooped, my limbs flopping across the quilt. "It's nighttime," he whispered as he crawled onto the bed. I softly moaned, unsure why my slumber had been so rudely interrupted. "Do you want me to stay in the cell tonight?" he asked, examining my sleepy features.

I slipped back down on the bed, flipping the luxurious blanket above me like it was a tidal wave about to submerge me.

Ace stilled for a moment, watching me with a playful smirk before he shuffled back down the bed. I opened my eyes wide and grabbed his forearm urgently. He froze, unsure of my brazen act.

"Stay," I insisted as I weakly pulled his arm towards the pillows. "Stay with me, Super," my voice echoed within the room as sleep took hold once more.

I awoke within the early hours of the morning, a bleak and lifeless wall facing me. My eyes scanned the structure with confusion as I sat up onto my elbows.

The quilt against me felt thick and heavy as my stiff fingers bunched against it, feeling the various layers of comfort within.

I twisted around, gasping in shock at Ace's dormant body. My hand quickly covered my lips, muffling a shriek of pure embarrassment. I focused my mind, thinking back to yesterday's happenings.

I had been so exhausted, so drained and weary. I was annoyed at Felix, irritated by his uncontrolled outburst, when Ace had kindly offered me his room to rest. I vaguely recalled grabbing his arm, insisting he stay when he entered for the night.

I muffled another scream. *What had I been thinking?*

My cheeks blushed a cheery-red hue as my wide eyes shook, my body ablaze with humiliation. If I tried to leave, he might wake up, but if I stayed, he was eventually going to wake up, anyway. It was a lose-lose situation.

I lowered my hand from my mouth and scanned the room, analysing Ace's limited belongings. Colourful posters of bands I'd never even heard of lined the walls, and cube shelves with clothing and a few odd items sat nearest the bottom of the bed.

A photo of a young Ace and Felix was lopsidedly stuck behind the door, easily missable if you didn't know it was there.

They were both so young, so happy, their smiles wide, their locks dishevelled. They had their arms wrapped around one another, leaning in close to the camera lens. Within that moment, they were identical. They still looked strikingly similar, but it was clear they had grown into their unique personalities, into their own identities as time went by.

My gaze shifted to Ace, slowly, carefully, like his bright blue eyes would be piercing straight through me. They weren't—of course they weren't. He was deep within his peaceful slumber.

I smiled softly, watching his chest rise and fall, noticing the strands of blond hair that fell messily across his forehead, observing his perfect features from so close.

I leaned in, feeling his warm breath against me as I lifted my finger and traced along his cold cheek.

His sleepiness wrapped him up in a protected bubble, his mind free of mistreatments, free of worries and fears. He was so cute, so vulnerable, so touchable. He stirred and I panicked, scoffing at myself, annoyed at my own reckless stupidity.

I wanted to understand myself. I wanted to know if these feelings for Ace were real. I loved the way he loved, the way he cared and understood.

An uncertain huff left my lips as I slowly pushed the covers back, slipping my legs against the cold air. I cautiously crawled along the quilt, hearing the soft sounds of my weight squeak against it. I paused at the end of the bed and stood up gently.

My hand hovered near the door handle as I looked back at Ace. Even in sleep he was so perfect, so pristine.

I smiled and pushed the door open, trying to be as quiet as I could possibly be. "What are you doing?" I glanced up as the door fully closed.

Felix stood in the hallway, resting against the wall. His jacket was too large against him, his jeans too ripped, his combat boots too shiny.

"None of your business," I barked.

He smirked and gave me a knowing look, his pallid eyes playful against mine. I squirmed nervously, at least he seemed to be in a better mood.

"You ready for today?" he questioned, his manner shifting. I nodded. Although, after his outburst yesterday, I highly doubted it. "There's this abandoned building out of town, an old mill. We'll be training there." He leant off the wall and strolled past me, grazing by my bare and suddenly goosebumped arm. "Five minutes and we leave." I nodded instructively.

I met Felix by the elevator in the nick of time. I hurried into the metal box and adjusted my jumper as he punched in one of the highest buttons on the panel. I shot him a confounded look, but I didn't comment.

The clunky doors dinged open almost instantly, people filing into the compacted space with freshly brewed coffees and energised chatter.

They regarded Felix's presence, visibly ignoring mine like it was a noble quest as we were rammed into a corner beside one another. Our sleeves pressed uncomfortably tight.

The air felt suffocatingly thick, the smell of cologne and perfume overwhelming my senses. I winced at the sudden lightheadedness as meaningless babble filled the cramped space. I cursed at the creator of elevators.

The lift advanced and businesspeople entered and exited, wearing expensive looking suits, skintight dresses, and holding firmly to large briefcases and/or designer bags. It all seemed like an unnecessarily stressful rat race to me. Everyone was overdressed, hair overdone, makeup over-applied. This was the future so many dreamed about. For me, it was nothing but a nightmare.

Felix cleared his throat as the last person departed. "I guess morning rush was a bad time to leave." He hiccupped a chuckle and grinned amusingly. I grumbled under my breath, looking forward as the doors opened onto the 34th floor.

"What's the highest one?" I curiously voiced as I crossed my arms in front of my chest and departed the stuffy box.

"Kobi's penthouse." Felix rolled his eyes.

"Of course," I mumbled as I followed step behind him.

This storey was vast, with a long-carpeted hallway against oak panels that led to one colossal conference room.

We stepped inside the open space, and my jaw dropped as I eyed the sunlight that danced upon the city outside, bright and blinding.

I trailed my eyes along the large, wooden table within the centre of the room, at the almost one hundred office chairs that lined the edges, perfectly positioned.

My feet led me absentmindedly to the large windows that occupied the entirety of two of the four walls, my mind in awe of the heightened views. My eyes widened as I glanced at the bustling city beneath, watching a world that was filled with activity and liveliness.

I viewed the cars below, the bright yellow buses, the slow-going trams, the tiny specks of human beings as they travelled along the crowded footpaths, each with their own destination to arrive.

My chin lifted as clouds bunched along the faraway horizon, enveloping around the other sporadic buildings that stood equal to this one as aeroplanes silently ascended, their wings slicing through the skies with ease.

The outside world was so lively, so purposeful, filled with an ambition that had forever escaped me.

"This is where you'll come for the board meeting. It isn't too scary." Felix shrugged, stilling beside me. I shivered, slipping the aglet of the drawstring against my lips.

"Anyway," he exclaimed. "We'd better get on our way."

"Yeah," I uttered aimlessly, tearing my mind from the vastness of the outer world.

Felix parked the car, and we slipped out into the warm breeze, the midday sun looming above as we made our way across the abandoned car park.

We headed towards an old brick building that stood out like an eyesore against the reclaiming greenery. It was decayed and crumbled. Old and neglected.

I observed the tangled vines that crawled against the moss-covered stones, at the neglected rows of flowerbeds overgrown with weeds, at the discarded and uneven pebbles that lined the manmade paths.

A few fairywrens swooped in and out of the shaded areas as a gentle wind rustled by. I listened for the sounds of their tiny little beaks as they madly pecked at the vegetation below the soil. They were completely free. Unchained by laws, unaffected by politics. *They existed within their own, perfect world.*

I glanced up and squinted, eyeing Felix's half hidden figure against the intensity of the sun.

I placed my arm before me, eyeing him within the newfound shadows. "This place was abandoned almost sixty years ago." He twisted his body around to analyse the surrounding scenery. "Every time I come out here, it's somehow worse," he muttered as he made his way inside the dilapidated building.

I hurried behind him, moving into the awaiting unknown.

I stepped through, clutching the side of the old door frame, awe-struck by the beauty inside. The broken ceiling gave way to golden beams that spilled within the dusty area, covering the fractured flooring that lay cloaked in a sand-like texture.

Alongside that, shattered debris and tossed pebbles sat strewn atop the concrete floor, butting heads with the determined weeds that grew between the cracks and crevices of the once bustling building.

"It's beautiful in here," I commented, glancing up at the old and frail rooftop. It felt peaceful, calming, like a tranquil moment captured in a timeworn eternity.

I breathed the humid air in deep, certain I could smell the lingering aromas of crisp spices. "How did you find this place?"

Felix perched himself against a concrete slab and chuckled awkwardly. "Doesn't every tale of adventure start with a girl?" I looked across at him soundlessly, watching the way his body language softened as his mind reminisced. "Kobi was furious when he found out," he added, his smile diminishing. "Anyway, that's not why we're here." He focused on his hand, pushing the painful thoughts aside. His eyes grew exceptionally dark as an inky texture overtook his veins with a grotesque and murky shade.

Black smoke arose from his palm as he morphed the darkened puffs into animals. *A rabbit, a cat, a possum.*

The enchanted creatures weightlessly danced as I sat upon the floor, cross-legged, watching on in pure amazement. Their figures shadowy, and cloudy, and ghostlike.

Felix raised his hand, and the animals obeyed, pooling into one huge cloud that loomed above us. He opened his palm wider and grunted as the cloud surged outward at a lightning pace, submerging us in utter darkness.

My eyes widened in awe, in astonishment. I glanced across at Felix then, but I couldn't see him through the thick, black fog. A cold sensation slipped across my skin, but it was comforting. It connected me to Felix; it made me feel like I wasn't all alone.

I lifted my sleeves and raised my hands, urging the alien glow to appear. I concentrated, I focused, I cleared my mind of all nuisances, of all distractions. I shut my eyes and breathed in deep, allowing myself to slip against the powers inside me.

I thought of control, of restraint. I envisioned myself wielding the powers of the Ultimate Weapon without consequence. I imagined myself as a truly powerful entity, one not penanced by a painful power, one not punished by a choice made to end my lonely and miserable life.

An ear-piercing scream exploded from my lips as a mangled bone tore directly from my arm, jagged and aglow with spotted specks of orange droplets.

Felix's power blinked out of existence as he ran towards me, worry imprinted against his pale face. I puked, unable to keep it down, as I held my broken bone weakly. It seeped back within my flesh with an unpleasant and vomit-inducing squish.

There was so much pain, so much torture and agony. The otherworldly glow within my eyes faded as the buzz that electrified atop my skin vanished. I staggered towards the ground, breathing unevenly, ready to give up.

Felix crouched beside me, carefully touching his fingers along my arm. I groaned and pushed my body up against my palms. Debris stuck beneath them, but I was numb to the discomfort.

My bottom lip slipped as I eyed him with pusillanimity. "That really hurt," I whispered as Felix reached for my slender waist and hoisted me to my unsteady sneakers.

He stepped before me and placed both hands firmly against my shoulders, eyeing me straight on with a softened expression.

I told myself to remain pokerfaced, but I couldn't. I was strong, but weak. I was powerful, but powerless. I was indestructible, but ephemeral.

And I was fucking useless.

Orange teardrops slipped against my cheeks as I forced a forsaken smile. Felix leaned forward, resting his forehead on mine. "I'm sorry," he muttered almost silently.

"I appreciate that," I managed against my trembling lips.

CHAPTER 18

RED

"Can you drop me off at Coombe Park?" I asked of Felix, the sound of my voice alarming against the awkward silence we had been drowning in.

I had never been that close to Felix before, close enough to feel his breath on mine, close enough to notice the small details of his brooding face, close enough to witness the faint glimmer of his lip piercing. It felt as if he understood me a little better after today's events, even if it was just by a smidgen.

"I guess... just don't run off. And don't tell Ace," he voiced instructively. "I have a couple of things to get done," he added, his tone soothing. "Meet you back around five?"

"That's cool," I uttered as I eyed the digital panel near the centre console, the screen displaying three o'clock. The perfect timing for my adventure. I nodded eagerly, thankful for his trust.

Felix dropped me off by the parking lot, alongside the busy coffee shops and active hobby stores. I slipped free and rested my elbow atop the car door, the sunlight shimmering across its polished surface. "Remember, meet me here at five. You won't be the only one facing Kobi's wrath if you decide to run off."

I nodded dismissively. "Don't worry, I'll be here." I glanced up as a trio of giggling girls scanned the car and ogled at Felix. They shot me daggers, eyeing me with contempt. Inwardly, I grimaced, as I looked down at Felix once more. "Those girls are checking you out," I informed him. He placed his hand on the wheel and casually shook his head, a smirk playing against his lips.

"I'm aware." He playfully grinned as I humphed and slammed the door shut, slipping within the pathway of people.

I was glad he didn't pry about my whereabouts, because there was no single way in hell I was telling him I had my own dog walking service. It was embarrassing enough carrying around doggie waste bags.

My knuckle knocked against the wooden door, and I waited. Thankful to be doing something normal after the shitshow of days I'd had.

An old lady with greying hair and a wrinkled face answered politely. "*Oh,* hello, dear." She beamed. "I have Napoleon ready for you." She handed me the blue leash clipped to Napoleon's harness.

Napoleon was a short-haired Maltese. He was the easiest of all five dogs I walked. He was just shy of eleven years old, and wasn't very strong or agile, but he still had enough energy in him for our walks together. He was like a sixty-year-old man in human years, so I never pushed him more than he wanted to go. Sometimes, I even carried him home.

I walked each dog the same route to familiarise them with their surroundings, and so I could float up into my cloud of dissociation.

I wondered then if there was any point in continuing my dog walking. I no longer felt hunger or thirst, I no longer rented a rundown motel room, I no longer relied on basic human necessities to fuel my ageing body.

Napoleon strained against his harness, yapping at me madly as I suddenly stilled. I wasn't sure why, but something urged me towards the motel, towards Lira. I was still so angry at her, and I wasn't about to forgive her, but...

I pulled against Napoleon's leash, heading in the direction of the motel as apprehension coursed through my veins with a fearful and uneasy drift.

The clouds shielded out the sun overhead as I stilled before the rundown building, Napoleon eagerly sniffing the tree nearest us. I walked over to the pathway opposite the entranceway, peering through the damaged tunnel.

My mind drifted for a moment, remembering when I'd rounded that corner to see Norman's enraged and monstrous face.

I wasn't sure what happened after they hit that bridge. An ugly part of me wanted to believe they were both dead, another part of me just hoped for amnesia. Both of which I knew the abuse was talking.

My heartbeat quickened as I saw Lira exit the reception office, her adoptive parents close behind. They were an older couple, frail and slow, but unquestionably kind.

Her parents climbed into the car quickly, escaping the sudden chill within the air. Lira opened the car door, but stilled, a troubled expression against her pretty face.

She peered around anxiously, her unknowing eyes falling upon mine. She looked at me for a long while before she timidly waved and smiled.

I pursed my lips scornfully and walked off, dragging Napoleon away from the new and exciting smells.

We walked to the parklands, settling down on that familiar bench. The one riddled with graffiti, overtaken with weeds, the metal frame nearly rusted through.

Napoleon sat near my feet, occasionally lifting his snout to smell a new odour. I'd been dog walking now for three months, walking Napoleon for two. He was a good dog, a good listener, a good companion. Owned by a widowed lady in her eighties, her name was Paulette Hudson.

Paulette was kind, she had a passion for knitting and loved attending local farmers markets.

When I'd first met her at the Southside Dog Park, she'd invited me over for tea and biscuits, reminiscing of her time as a telephonist and her husband's adventures overseas.

She was a lovely old lady who volunteered her time at local thrift stores and charity centres, and even though she'd lost her husband, every memory she spoke of him included his cheeky smirk and dashing appearance.

It was plain to see how much they'd loved and adored one another, each aspect of their lives frozen in time with cheerful photographs, inspired love letters, and mismatched souvenirs.

For the longest time, I envied that, but now, I felt conflicted by it. I wanted Ace with me, I wanted him in my sight and by my side, but what if it was all to watch me undoubtedly fail?

Ace had so much faith in me. He challenged me, he offered me his help, his guidance. He wanted me to be better for not only myself, but for this power I was now and forever connected to.

He knew the importance of control, of managing your emotions. If I let him in—*truly, honestly, wholeheartedly*—he could really be the one to save me.

"Napoleon had a great time," I announced, handing Paulette the leash. Napoleon wagged his tail feverishly.

"*Oh,* thank you!" she exclaimed with gratitude. She reached over and handed me the twenty dollars, a whiff of her rosemary perfume colliding against my nostrils. I took the money from her ringed and wrinkled hand. "Next Tuesday, then?"

I nodded, faking my conviction.

She smiled my way as the door closed shut. I trekked down the pathway, placing my hood over my forehead and my hands into my pockets.

The wind whistled past me as I rested against the kerb, waiting for Felix.

Kobi's dark car pulled into the busy street, and I quickly stood, stepping within the roadway. I hoped he would notice my tiny figure alongside the cluster of activity.

Felix spotted my out-of-place stance and idled the car as I hurried over, slamming back with a thud against the warm and cosy interior. "Thanks," I breathlessly voiced, fiddling with the vents to blow the warm air against me.

A part of me expected a curious comment about my whereabouts, but he didn't mention anything. I preferred this, so I wasn't sure why I felt almost discouraged by it.

Felix pulled the car into a reserved park as I glanced up at the high-rise structure, squinting at the evening rays of sunlight that shone against the metal and glass compounds.

We entered the immaculate building, passing by the businesspeople who regarded Felix respectfully and overlooked my presence completely.

"You ever feel like you really don't belong somewhere?" I muttered under my breath, eyeing the lobby with irritation.

Felix glanced my way, a knowing look within his tired eyes. "Yeah, I know the feeling, but I wouldn't worry about any of these people. They don't matter in the long run," he paused. "I mean, they only care about me because of this power. Because Kobi has made it everybody's business to know how Ace and I are apparently so valuable and important." He exhaled an aggravated huff. "He acts like we need to be treated like royalty."

He leaned in closer as we passed the front desk, the receptionist addressing him by name. He opened and closed his hand curtly in response. "Once these people know you're our Ultimate Weapon, they'll be bowing at your feet." He straightened, giving me an assured nod. "Just you wait," he added at my disbelieving expression.

I crossed my arms in front of my chest and groused. "What good is a power when I'm powerless to use it?"

Felix shrugged a shoulder as he pressed the elevator button. "I think, and don't tell him this, but I think Ace is right. I think your emotions are too unbalanced, too unstable."

We strode into the lift in unison, Felix waiting for the doors to close before resuming our conversation.

"We've both had barriers to overcome, but nowhere near as brutal as yours. It seems cruel. You relive your death each time you use your power, yet you're unable to die from it."

He clicked his tongue. "Stanley's spent a lot of time teaching Ace and I the importance of bonding with our powers, of understanding their responses. I've spent most of my life trying to perfect my skill, whilst Ace has done nothing but hide from the powers within him, and I don't know why." Felix's eyes fixated atop the floor, thoughts pounding within his head. "Something must've happened; I just don't know what."

The elevator doors dinged open, and we ventured out, colliding against the cold bunker air. It felt as if I'd learnt so much today, details about Felix, stuff about Ace, even things about myself that I didn't know.

I wanted to understand their powers, I wanted to know how they controlled their emotions, how they balanced their inhuman abilities within themselves.

Felix's power was fascinating, defiant. It didn't play by any rules, it was in a league all its own. I envied that, envied the way he was able to use it so freely, the way he was able to explore, discover, learn what he was truly capable of.

I still hadn't seen Ace's powers in action, so I knew Felix's words to be true. For some reason, he feared the abilities within himself. He kept them grounded, compressed, hidden. *Why?* What was he so afraid of?

"How did you go today?" Ace stood before us; his slender fingers wrapped around a steaming mug. I stilled, trailing my eyes towards the striped cup. "Stanley made hot chocolates. Would you like one?" he asked with that joyous smile I had become a little too accustomed to.

I nodded once, and he hurried off to fetch me my own.

My gaze stalked Felix as he trekked towards the hallway in a noticeably unapproachable way. It seemed peculiar how his mood could be so easily wrought.

Ace returned with another mug and handed it to me gently. My fingers brushed against his as I took hold of it. He ushered me towards the old green couch, and I followed suit silently.

I sat against the distressed material, noting all the cuts and tears, the sewn-on patches and their uneven needle work.

In the last two days, I hadn't had anything to eat or drink, the hunger and thirst non-existent within my newfangled function. My body no longer craved those once needed necessities. It felt bizarre, unnatural. I had relied on food for so long, I had pleaded for it, I had begged. Now that feeling was all but dead and gone. And I didn't know whether to be grateful or terrified.

A keen smile met my lips as I glanced at the mug, letting the warm steam collide upon my chilled face.

"Thank you for this," I murmured as I took a sip of the sweet-smelling liquid. The hot chocolate flowed down my throat, but I couldn't taste it. I could feel the warmth against my tongue, but not the flavour.

I sat it down atop the coffee table and chewed on my hoodie's aglet once more. "Are you okay?" Ace eyed me unsurely.

"I can't taste it," I admitted with a sad shrug.

His eyes travelled to the mug, then back to me. He placed his drink down hesitantly, picking up mine. He took a sip, wincing at the heat before he quickly placed it down. A small burn mark now scorched against his perfect lips.

"You really can't taste that?" he uttered, worry now lacing his gentle tone. I shook my head solemnly. "The blue solution, the one you had before the simulation, how did that taste to you?"

I narrowed my eyes in doubt, forgetful of that bleak beverage. "Flavourless." Concern flashed fleetingly against his blue eyes before he looked away, his lips thin and doubtful.

"My tastebuds are fried, aren't they?" I wept as I buried my head into my loose-fitted hoodie. "How much more is the universe going to take from me?" I argued against my own fading hope.

CHAPTER 19

ACE

"Stan?" I asked, slipping within the spare seat beside him. He swivelled his chair and faced me, his smile warm, his eyes exhausted.

The digital clock nearby displayed eight o'clock. Felix had already barricaded himself within his room, arrogant as ever, and Red was taking a shower.

"Ace, what's going on?" he questioned. "Were the hot chocolates that bad?" He laughed wholesomely, and I smiled despite my troubles.

"I want to ask you about something," I began. I'd been honest to Stanley about so much, but this felt different. This felt scary, unnerving, and I didn't like it one bit.

"Our powers..." I slipped my fingers through my hair, an agitated twitch in my bones. "Are Felix and I capable of stronger powers?" My hands dropped into my lap as Stanley narrowed his eyes in confusion. "It's just—" I added quickly, urgently. "You examined us within the simulation; you know what our abilities are capable of." I watched him steadily, awaiting his reply.

"I don't fully understand what you're saying," he muttered.

I straightened my posture and took a deep breath in. "Red can harness our powers."

Stanley gasped, a hand to his mouth in bewilderment. "Are you sure?" he questioned, his scientific mind ticking overtime as he waited restlessly for my response. I nodded. "My goodness, that is, that is—" he stuttered, his mind unable to form his thoughts into words.

But that wasn't an answer.

"Did you know about the limitations?" I asked him directly. This time he had nowhere to run, nowhere to hide.

He slipped his spectacles from against his nose and fiddled with them worriedly. My mouth fell agape.

"Unfortunately, yes," he confessed with a devastated tone. "I'm truly sorry, Ace. I know you wanted to achieve so much with your power, but Kobi simply wouldn't allow it."

The old man's eyes peeked against mine, filled with a sadness I'd seen only once before. "He told me if I didn't abide by his rules, I would be gone. I didn't want to risk leaving you and Felix to his awful teachings. In a way, I thought I was protecting you."

He paused, working up the courage to continue as he slid his glasses back against his face. "When I created the simulation, and you and Felix first went under, I realised it right then and there. I was thrilled by the revelation, until I told Kobi of my findings. He was afraid you would revolt; he was afraid you would destroy any chance of locating the Ultimate Weapon. I restricted your powers, and I was forced to lie to you both. I am not proud of that."

Tears slipped down my cheeks as I swiftly stood. "Ace!" Stanley called after me, but I ignored his plead.

There were so many things within this lifetime I had longed to achieve. So much love, humanity, and peace within the world I had intended to convey. I had a plan, a purpose, a pursuit.

I had always sought to make a *real* difference—to feel accomplished, to feel proud of what I'd done.

I sniffled as teardrops ran from my saddened eyes.

"Ace?" Red tilted her head, her brown eyes suspicious, her perfect lips pursed. "You good?"

Her crimson hair sat wet and loose around her shoulders, her cheeks flushed from the heat of the shower, her bare skin blindingly beautiful.

I rushed towards her, wrapping her up in my firm embrace as I wept against her shoulder. She gasped and grabbed at my arms in haste, soon realising my actions intent. She pulled me in closer towards her tiny figure, snuggling into my sweater.

She held me for what felt like hours as my broken heart caved within my chest. I was so upset and hurt by Stanley's truth, by the limitations I bore for no reason other than Kobi's own selfishness.

I was so angry, so overwhelmed. All my life, I'd had access to this unmatched power within me, one that was beaten down into something meek, malleable, and meaningless.

I had mistaken faith in the Ultimate Weapon, had thought their omnipotence would come along and save me, would free me from this hell. Believed Felix and I would mend our broken brotherhood and finally flee. I couldn't have been more wrong.

Kobi had puppeteered us, domineered us, manipulated us, and everyone around him for his own devious plan of obtaining the Ultimate Weapon.

I hated him. And I hated the very powers inside me.

Electric sparks flew out against us, violent, manic, and uncontrolled. They zapped along the walls, electrified and faulty, but Red remained against me, unwilling to let go, unwilling to falter.

Breaths pounded unevenly from my overworked lungs as I shifted back, my head inches from hers. I glanced down at her full lips. I wanted to touch her, to taste her—*badly, deeply, sincerely.* I wanted to drown in my feelings of Red and never be resuscitated.

We were two lost souls trapped within the bodies of profound powers. Connected on a level unable to be understood by humankind.

The pull I felt towards her was unmistakable, undeniable, unable to be ignored. With our powers interlocked, we could rewrite history. We could create a new world, a better existence, a safer biosphere. She was the omnipotent power the world had spent an eternity trying to materialise. She held the ultimate power; she *was* the Ultimate Weapon.

And she was all I had ever wanted.

We could revolt against the system, we could overthrow the government, we could change the world.

No more meaningless deaths, no more needless suffering, no more senseless wars. We could create global equality—feed the poor, teach the uneducated, heal the sick.

We would be an unstoppable force, an unchallengeable opponent, an inalienable influence.

I lifted my gaze as Red hesitantly smiled, her hazel eyes uncertain. I reached for her hand and hurried into the open space. "Ace, I—" Stanley began. I shot him an unpleasant look and he fretfully stilled, darting his faded eyes away.

"*No!*" Red shouted, breaking away from my touch. I glared at her with a sudden confusion that burned hot within my energised mind.

"What?" I bellowed breathlessly. "What's wrong?" I heaved a breath from my overworked lungs as adrenaline pumped through my entire system at a record-breaking pace. My hands twitched, my body trembled, my thoughts twisted.

She held her palm, looking uncomfortable. "I feel your power, Ace. It isn't safe." Her eyes met mine, her words spoken so surely of themselves.

Felix hurried into the room, watching between us with deep unease. His dark hair was overly ruffled, his eyes bloodshot, his stance apprehensive.

"Ace, calm down," he instructed, stepping past Red.

My wild eyes pierced against his, the anger I felt sputtering and bubbling within me like that of an over-boiled pot as haywire sparks surged through my veins visibly. My knuckles opened, my power jolting violently around the room as my blue eyes faded to white.

As if on cue, the downlights exploded.

Felix gasped, racing to Stanley's side as he cowered away from the shattering fragments. Red refused to take her eyes off mine as broken glass fell around her, glistening like diamonds against her magnificent form. Her eyes remained with a comforting glimmer, her stance fearlessly unafraid, her presence calming my troubled soul.

I shut my eyes tight as agitated breaths tore from my lungs and bolts of electricity bounced around the room with a piercing squeal. I was coming undone. I couldn't control it, not anymore. I was more powerful than I ever could've imagined. The ability was within me; it had *always* been within me.

My colourless eyes sharply opened as Red wrapped her slim arms around me, her breath hot against my neck. "You're having a panic attack, Ace, you need to slow your breathing. Breathe with me, in, and out, in, and out," she uttered against me firmly.

I concentrated on her words, breathing as instructed. My heart rate slowed as the erratic volts within the room subsided. I stumbled against my weakened posture, falling atop her.

Felix grabbed my arm, heaving me up. I weakly stood, glancing defeatedly down at the broken glass as Red sat upright. She shook her body, removing the jagged fragments that snatched to her oversized jumper. I felt humiliated, selfish, pathetic.

I couldn't bring myself to glance over at Stanley, to witness his sorrowful expression before I ran away with my tail tucked between my legs.

"I have to go," I announced as I turned and activated the elevator key, awaiting the ding. I stepped inside and looked up, my regretful gaze meeting Red's.

Her cinnamon-hued eyes were filled with disbelief, her mouth fallen agape, her stance wary. I felt like a stranger to her, a mysterious being in the night, an unrecognisable version of myself.

The doors closed and I breathed out a pitiful sob.

I sat atop the concrete bench, ignoring the whistle of the wind, the chirp of the birds, the far away nicker of horses. My body restlessly squirmed as I fought back the urge to cry. I felt so stupid, so shameful.

I wanted to hide under a bridge and start my life anew as a troll or run away with the circus and become their most laughable act. I hated myself for what I had done, for what I had allowed Red to bear witness to.

"Hey, kiddo." I glanced at mum as she stood within the light of the lamppost. "Marty told me you were out here," she conveyed as she sat alongside me, two cups and saucers secured within her bony fingers. She passed me one and it rattled against my shaky palm. I stared down at the green tea, hoping to drown in it.

She lifted her hand and tucked a loose strand of blonde hair behind her ear. "Do you want to talk about it?" she asked as she neatly crossed her slender legs. I snorted, looking out at the darkened gardens. I felt numb, emotionless.

She sipped her tea, placing the cup down with a slight clink against the saucer. "Bad day?"

I laughed humorously. "The worst," I quipped as she doubtfully humphed. "I really fucked up." I looked down at the drink once more, taking a reluctant sip. I pulled a face. "Yep, still dislike tea." Mum smiled, looking across at the gardens adoringly. Immersed in shadows and illuminated by sparse lighting, these gardens were a spectacular sight to behold. She'd spent a lot of time and money to keep the estate looking its best throughout the many years of residency. Especially this section.

Gardening was her passion and this garden her paradise.

"We all make mistakes. I doubt you've ruined anything beyond repair," she reassured, watching me with a comforting look. Abruptly, it shifted. "Is this about Red?" I looked to her in haste.

She smiled against her porcelain cup, her green eyes knowing. "Kobi's mentioned her. I plan to meet her after the board meeting," she paused, breathing in the nippy air. "She definitely sounds incredible."

"She is."

I looked down, eyeing the ripples within the tea as a soothing silence overtook our conversation briefly.

"It wasn't always easy for your father and I," she quietly spoke. I glanced across at her eagerly, my wide eyes yearning for more as an ominous breeze blew against us.

"You never talk about him," I voiced, longing and slight irritation against my tone. Mum breathed a long breath, the faint wrinkles on her face shifting.

"It's difficult," she confessed as owls uttered hoots within the distance. "After the wedding, we decided to start a family. In the beginning, I struggled to fall pregnant. We saw an infertility specialist, tried IVF, but nothing worked. Then suddenly, there you were, two beautiful little bundles of joys developing within my stomach." She shivered, securing her hands firmly against the cup.

"When your father died, I wanted to go, too, but I knew that I couldn't. I knew I needed to live for you two boys, but it was hard, I struggled a lot," she hesitated. "The money from your grandparents greatly helped, but the life Stephen and I had dreamed of creating together—it was gone." She looked down at her tea sadly, reminiscing of times gone by.

"The powers certainly didn't help." She softly laughed. "I was so lost when Kobi came along. I know it's been... hard, for you and Felix, but I really do feel like he rescued us." She eyed me with a hopeful glance as I snorted curtly, looking away.

She knew how I felt about Kobi, by now I had hoped she would have accepted that fact. I wasn't sure how Felix truly felt, he was so secretive and defiant, and at times intolerable. He was exhausting, Kobi was exhausting.

I wasn't sure if Mum was aware of even half the tests and procedures our powers had undergone under the instruction of Kobi, and part of me hoped she never did.

Her mind was still active and alert, but some days it felt as if I was talking to an apparition. Like she was physically here, but mentally miles away. She loved her gardening, and her painting, both things gave her boundless joy and purpose.

I loved watching her paint. Her precision, her dedication, her talent. It was inspiring. Her flower arranging business was also no small feat. A colourful flower stand often stood at the front gate, filled with bouquets for every occasion.

Felix and I had had the privilege of helping her paint that very stand when we were five. Our sections were atrocious, and I'd always wondered why she never painted over them.

"Whatever you feel you did wrong, talk to her about it. Don't bundle it up, Ace, don't ignore it." She smiled alongside the darkened skies, breathing in the cold air that prickled against her throat.

"When you met my dad, how'd you know he was the one?" I asked nervously, afraid she would brush the question off like she always had.

She stilled, lost in thought. Suddenly, she glanced my way, her eyes glassy, her lip shaky. I wasn't sure if that was from the cold or from stifling her sobs.

"I can tell you all the usual things, like the way he loved me, the way he accepted me, the way he valued me, but honestly," she briefly paused. "It was the way he made me unafraid of death." I narrowed my eyes in confusion.

She smiled affectionately, continuing. "It might sound absurd, but loving your father gave me hope for what happens after we leave this world. Something I was truly terrified of for a very long time. It ignited this deep feeling within me that we would always find one another, no matter what universe, what time, what life." She placed her hand against her heart as teardrops slipped from her eye sockets. "Come, we should head inside."

I breathed in deep, valuing her rawness and honesty.

She had never spoken of my father like that, so lovingly or so openly. There was so much about him I longed to know, so many endless details. I wanted to know his favourite colour, his preferred footy team, his meal of choice. I wanted to know his fears, his loves, his motivations.

I longed to know everything there was about this man who was robbed of meeting his own two sons and stripped of growing old with the woman he loved.

The cup rattled within my hands as I stood to follow, but my mind hesitated. There were so many unknowns. My father, the power, this girl—*this girl?*

What the hell did Red really mean to me, and why couldn't I figure it out? Why had I gotten jealous of Felix for only looking into those gorgeous brown eyes of hers? And why did I constantly find myself thinking about her infrequent smile?

She was the Ultimate Weapon. She was the foretold, the legend in skin and bone. I was nothing compared to her. I was a meaningless imbalance that had unintentionally locked this girl into an eternity of despair. I was the one who caused this, I was the one who sentenced her to a forever-long purgatory. A punishment she did not deserve.

"Ace?" I glanced across at her suddenly.

"I want to go to her," I spoke the words urgently.

She nodded, a kind and understanding smile meeting her lips.

"Then, go to her."

CHAPTER 20

RED

I sat against Ace's bed, irregular breaths thumping from my chest. I was worried about him, worried about what had transpired between us. I needed to know if he was okay, but what could I do? He would return once he was ready, I just had to be patient.

An annoyed moan escaped my lips as I slammed back on the mattress. I hated being patient, I hated waiting around to learn of horrific happenings, I hated feeling so useless and being so ineffective.

I had refused his request to take me away, and all because I'd trusted my gut feeling over him. Was that so wrong of me to do so?

His power felt wrathful, erratic, unpredictable. I was scared, scared of the dangers it pulsated through my very core, scared of the ghostly white eyes that pierced against mine.

He had no idea how powerful he truly was. He could level continents, cause catastrophic quakes, cataclysmic events.

Together, Ace, Felix, and I, we could become unstoppable, ungovernable.

If only they could remove the restrictions against their powers, the limitations that had been so unfairly placed upon them.

There had to be a way to isolate the capabilities within them, a way for me to pinpoint where the powers resisted, a way to identify whether they're being triggered by a drug, a serum, an altered lapse within the brain.

I knew I was no doctor, but I also knew I had a power within me that rivalled all scientific research. I wondered then, of this other doctor Felix spoke of. Could they be the one responsible for creating this otherworldly substance?

I eyed the happy photo pinned against the back of the door as my mind quieted and my thoughts drifted within a calmed limpidity, allowing sleep to overtake my inhuman form.

My body shivered as I awoke to an uneasy chill.

I stood and left the room, embarking towards the cell. A gasp fled my lips as I eyed Ace fast asleep on the thin and unpleasant mattress.

I paused momentarily, watching the way his body relaxed, the way his mind stilled against his energised thoughts.

The door swung inward as I strode past and scooped my hoodie off the floor, flipping the soft and cosy cotton against myself. I tucked my hair neatly within the collar and pulled the hood over my forehead as the lights within the bunker clicked, turning on.

I winced at the harshness of them as Ace stirred, sitting up. He huffed out an irritated breath, stilling when his tired eyes met mine. "Red," he mumbled, surprise against his sleepy features.

"Hey," I muttered, leaning alongside the uncomfortable bars. "When did you get back?"

"Around three, I think." His eyebrows creased. "I visited the estate, and had a decent conversation with my mother, believe it or not." He exhaled hard and stretched. "Mum's looking forward to meeting you."

"You mentioned me?" I asked a little too hurriedly as hopefulness filled my troubled mind. I swayed, trying to act unfazed by whatever response he dignified that foolish question with.

Ace smiled playfully against my suddenly anxious mindset. "Mum did, actually. She already thinks you're incredible."

A doubtful snort escaped me as I stepped towards him, the cheap mattress squeaking with my added weight. "Stanley's really worried about you. Felix, he—" I hesitated, unsure how he was going to respond to my upsetting news. He eyed me restlessly, his grin slightly fading. "Felix had to take Stanley to the hospital." Ace gasped, shock and terror sprawled across his face.

"Hey, it's okay." I reached for his hand as he started to hyperventilate. "The shattered glass, it caused him to bleed, a lot, and we weren't entirely sure what to do... so, Felix took him to the hospital. I have no way of contacting him, so I don't know how it went exactly, but I'm sure everything's fine." I forced a smile as he whipped out his phone, dialling frantically.

Felix answered with an abrasive grunt.

"*Stanley*—is he okay?" Ace questioned, his breath jagged and harsh.

"Yeah, old mate's fine," Felix mumbled wearily. "He needed a few stitches." Ace exhaled slowly, relief coursing within him. "The nurses are a little concerned about some irregular heart palpitations, so they wanted him kept in overnight," he added. "I decided to stay, just in case. We'll be back later today, after the doctor's checked in on him."

"Okay, thanks. Bye." He lowered the phone, ending the call as Felix's reply echoed through the electrical device.

"You were by yourself almost half the night," Ace muttered suddenly. I nodded keenly. "That doesn't scare you?" My eyes narrowed unsurely as I shook my head.

"No, why would it? This is probably one of the safest places I've ever been." I glanced around the cell once more, observing the main room through the thick and heavy bars.

This bunker was safe, fortified, elusive. I may have feared man, but I didn't fear the structures they built. "I tried to wait up for Felix and Stanley to return, and of course, for you, too." I drifted my head back around slowly.

"You're like no one I've ever met before." He tilted his head, watching me with an expression I couldn't place, an expression I didn't recognise.

My eyes widened as he reached his arm forward and placed his hand gently against my face, rubbing his thumb clockwise upon the surface of my cheek. His fingers as smooth as butter along my heated skin, his pastel-blue eyes bright and adventurous.

My lips parted as I watched him closely, an overwrought feeling deluging my senses.

My mind raced and thrashed as if I was being held captive underwater. Unable to swim, unable to breathe, unable to ascend.

Ace moved his head towards mine, my heartbeat quickening at a supersonic pace as a million different emotions surged through my nervous system.

What do I do? What do I do?

His lips met mine, and I closed my eyes, melting like ice in the summer heat against him. His touch, his hands, his lips. They were all I could think about. This boy—*this generous, handsome, confident boy*—wanted me. *Me.*

It felt impossible, unbelievable, and insanely good. He felt insanely good, this felt insanely good.

Everything within my insignificant life had been leading me to this one crucial moment, to a connection I would no longer run from, to a love I would no longer fear, to a peacefulness I would no longer impede.

Ace was my safe space, my person, the prevailing strength to my devastating weakness. I wanted to safeguard him, to exist with him, to pour my bleeding, bruised, and broken heart out to him. I wanted to shout to him all the things I was scared to even whisper. I wanted to lay beside him, just to stay forever and watch the world go round.

He pulled back, watching me with rising trepidation. "Red?"

Tears built behind my brown eyes as my entire body fearfully trembled. I reached up slowly, placing my hand beside his cheek. My head bowed forward, my forehead resting on his.

"I needed you years ago," I muttered dryly.

"You have me now," he breathlessly reassured.

I paused midmotion, unwillingly remembering all those times I had inflicted my skin with bloody wounds and near-permanent scars. Those near-fatal times where I had watched the blood drip along my arms, and thighs, and pool in puddles I wrongly thought had the power to save me.

All along, I'd been killing myself, and I hadn't even realised it. I hadn't even stopped to comprehend the doings of my own blood-lusted actions. I was miserable, manic, monstrous. I'd made it out alive, but at what cost? I had lost everything—*my mind, my body, my faith.* I'd lost the ability to feel, the capability to trust, the propensity to love.

Ace shrieked as a pulsating force field entrapped us, capturing us within a ball of pure electricity and scintillated light. I placed my hand hesitantly on the unnatural surface, feeling its strength, feeling its power.

Orange tears slipped from my tattered being as the outside world faded into obscurity. Ace reached for my hand, entwining his fingers with mine as everything violently shone within our fearful eyes. An abrupt force snatched our physical forms, hauling us against an abandoned roadway as my body surged with abstracted radiance.

Rain ricocheted against the bitumen road as hail fragments fiercely dotted the ground around us. I deftly stood, pulling Ace to his feet as deafening thunderbolts boomed within the vast skies above. The trees aggressively shook, weaving almost inhumanly against the ferocious winds that tackled them.

I eyed Ace, who peeked around fearfully, terror embedded within his perfect features. "The fuck are we, Red?" He shuddered against the roaring chaos.

The thunderous noise faded as I scanned the broken fenceline, its discarded planks forming a lopsided cross. My eyes widened as I looked beside it, my vision colliding atop a rusted-out bucket that hung from the ageing post.

"*No—*" I sobbed as I stumbled back. Ace turned towards me as my alien glow intensified. We stood within the heart of the storm but somehow remained unaffected by its freezing touch.

A sudden motion startled me, and my body reacted instinctively.

I raced towards Ace and grabbed him harshly, forcing us away from the roadway as a car swerved and rolled, colliding violently against the chaotic night.

We tumbled against the embankment, tyres skidding and windows shattering as broken headlights weaved impaired patterns against the asphalt.

Ace's fearful expression flared as I kicked my feet, digging my shoes into the mud, and dirt, and pebbles. I propelled myself towards the vehicle and urgently screamed, falling to my knees as colourless tears flooded from my eyes. I sobbed and wept as the car sat idle, and broken, and mangled before me.

Ace ran up behind me, a hand placed against my shoulder. "I know where we are," I forced the words free. He peeked down at me, his blue eyes limitlessly concerned.

We both harshly gasped against the atmosphere as a young girl emerged from the wreckage. She weakly stood up, bloodstains against her clothes, glass within her hair, cuts along her perfect face. My breaths vanished from my lungs as my limbs hung motionlessly by my sides. I eyed the girl with shattered hope, with broken faith, and dared myself not to cry.

"Mum?" she squeaked as blood splattered from her mouth. "Mum, it hurts." She held her stomach in tightly, trying to lure the pain out from within her. "Dad?" she gabbled against painful tears as she lost her balance.

I sprinted forward and caught her slow motioned form, laying her gently within my arms. Her eyelids began to droop as her irregular breaths fumbled from her lips, the beat of her heart growing weaker by the second.

"She's me." I sobbed alongside my younger self, holding her

closely, safely. I didn't want to let her go; I didn't want to leave her to a world that would beat her down until suicide became her only option.

Ace knelt silently beside me. "You?" he meekly whispered. I curtly nodded. He exhaled a horrified breath, eyeing the girl, then eyeing me. "We're in the past," his voice broke as he collapsed beside me.

Abruptly, the orange glow blinked into the void, drenching our bodies within the storms raging quarrel. I glanced across at Ace as its roaring commotion assaulted my eardrums, my lashes heavy from the fierce raindrops that soaked my face.

He watched me unsteadily as his soaked hair stuck to his skin, his cheeks reddening. "We can't be here, Red, we need to go!" he bellowed over the mayhem that surrounded us.

I blew out a harsh huff and reluctantly placed my younger self against the ground, watching her face as she winced and moaned in pain. My fingers lightly brushed the damp hair away from her cheeks before I leaned in, kissing her wet and blood-covered forehead.

Headlights pierced through the darkness, and I screamed, on my feet in seconds as our bodies were heaved and thrown against a dark and dirty basement. Blood spluttered from my mouth as I sat against my knees, watching Ace, watching his fear fester into ugly distortions as the alien glow returned to me.

It illuminated the underground room with a faded glimmer of orange pulsations. It was just as I remembered, the cobwebs, mould, the rotten beams that somehow kept the house above from caving in.

My old pocketknife had remained within its hiding spot, concealed in a hollow pipe. I reached forward, instinctively wrapping my hand around its steel frame.

I glanced at the weapon atop my palm as my posture straightened. My mind abnormally still, my thoughts unusually quiet, my emotions strangely mute.

My mouth opened, my eyes flared, my hand shook. "First attempt," I uttered as I closed my trembling hand shut around the knife.

I remembered the light-headedness, the feeling of floating, becoming weightless. Blood had trailed along my wrist, vengeful and tragic. I was prepared to die, prepared to ascend into a peaceful oblivion. I was to rise above, to start anew.

The one moment I'd dared to be something more and something greater. If only my foolish mind had known.

Ace's terrified shriek pierced the exosphere as blood oozed and spat from my enclosed fist. I opened my hand timidly to an onslaught of blood that waterfalled down along the basement floor, spluttering against my arms and face.

Ace rammed back, stepping atop the broken staircase that had once led me to the devil himself. "*Red!*" he choked as his knuckles gripped white against the handrail. "What the hell is happening?" He darted his eyes around timorously as blood lapped along the skirting boards.

The timber railing broke under his forceful touch as I held my breath and dived beneath the growing pool of red beneath me.

I exhaled hard against the atmosphere, temporarily blinded as my younger self reared into view, shaking manically against the flimsy bed.

I stepped towards her, watching as she rocked forwards and

back in a rigorous pattern, unable to break away from the sudden shifts within her fearful and broken mind.

The room was all too familiar. The stained comforters, torn curtains, mice infested carpets. And the smell, the unmistakeable scent of faeces and roses. I dry-heaved.

My younger self placed her hands to her ears and whimpered as wails of complete terror escaped the lips of the girl outside the locked and bolted door. I could feel her excruciating pain, could sense her longing to leave this cruel and violent world.

I looked to the wooden door, remembering all those times I had before. All those times I'd been powerless to help, powerless to change the outcome for a girl I would've died for.

Ace mirrored my actions, trying desperately to understand this unravelling disaster before it fully disentangled. "Who's out there?" he begged as dried blood latched against his blood-soaked hair.

I turned back to myself, eyeing her fragile form, her dirty face, her messy hair, her bruised limbs. This was the night she made it out alive.

"Tiffany." *Tiffany did not.*

Pallid tears escaped my scarlet eyes as I swallowed hard, forcing the power within me to cease. I did not wish to see my past, I did not wish to see all the evils I had endured, I did not wish to relive a life I died to escape.

Grit overtook me as I twisted around and grabbed Ace's cold hand, kicking the door open with a powerful boot. The deadbolt easily faltered as I furiously charged into the abandoned room, colliding against an orange and inhuman mist.

As the eerie fog settled, I eyed myself at the end of the corridor, crouched low beside the front door. She slid a butter knife and ace of hearts card within the lock, frantically trying to open the latch and escape the torment, the pain, the abuse she faced every single day within this horrific household.

Her busted lip, her swollen eye, her putrid scent, a forgotten lapse within the system, or maybe just a neglected one… I cried and ran towards her, Ace in tow. I was desperate to free myself from their hateful and furious violence.

The door swung open, and we stumbled, falling flat on the bunker floor with a violent snap of bones.

I groaned and forced myself up, puking acid. I looked down as orange ooze escaped my bottom lip.

"*Ace!*" I clambered towards him, shoving his lifeless body atop its back. "Ace—" I cried, frantically checking him over for any fatal injuries. "*No, no, no!*" I screamed from the depths of my agonising core.

Ace coughed and sat up urgently, vomiting blood beside me. "I am *so* sorry," I whispered hopelessly as my fingertips hesitated against him, my mind uncertain if he wanted to be touched.

Touched by something as ugly and disgusting as me.

He eyed me directly, his expression chaotic, his hair messy. "We went into your past," he mumbled, wiping the blood from his lower lip. "How much pain did you feel?" He grunted, forcing himself near the wall for support.

"Physically? None."

"Do you know what that means?" I slowly shook my head. "You can go into the past. You can rewrite everything the world has ever known. You can go back and change your fate; change the way you died." He exhaled against the bunker air, frantic and hopeful.

"A power strong enough to send us back to the Stone Age or millenniums into the future." He eyed me buoyantly. "It's not fictional. It's possible."

Anger flashed within my brown eyes as I scrambled onto my sneakers. "Where are you going?" Ace hurried behind me like a lost puppy. I twisted around furiously, my knuckles tightening.

"I was abused every day!" I screamed hatefully against him, causing him to flinch. "It hurt, it hurt like fucking hell, and when I *finally* built up the courage, when I *finally* went to the shop, they told me to get in line and be grateful." I fretfully gasped.

"I remember hiding in that basement, unsure why I was so afraid to die when every day felt like death! I had bones that were never supposed to heal, cuts that were meant to scar me forever, burns that were meant to scorch my skin for the duration of my pathetic existence!" I quarrelled, fury engulfing me from within.

"*You* have no idea what I have gone through, no idea what I have done. If I went back, it would be for one thing and one thing only." I exhaled raggedly, my vision blurring with rage.

"For what?" Ace shook his head desperately.

"To kill every last one of them."

CHAPTER 21

RED

I breathed the warm outside air in deep, filling my lungs with a fresh, flowery, and familiar scent as I tuned into the bustling activity around me. I faded into the sounds, into the smells.

I floated above this clustered square and eyed my tomboyish self from above. I ran my eyes up my arm, focusing on the sporadic droplets that splashed upon the watery surface, flickering me with a cool sensation. I shifted my attention towards the fountain, observing the naked lady who stood within its centre point. Such a beautiful re-creation, this statue of a woman I would never come to personally know. It seemed sad, and I couldn't help but think I had much the same fate in store.

Would I also be displayed, be taken advantage of, be used for nothing more than my ability?

It felt like no one would stop to think who I was behind this title. No one but Ace, of course.

A cold wind blew as I promptly stood and fixed my trackies, pulling the drawstring taut. Right now, it didn't matter what the world wanted from me, not when I was screwing up everything with Ace.

He could barely look at me after what I'd said. After my accusation of my own action if I returned to a past that sealed my fate with blood and sacrifice.

I huffed, curiously watching a large dog that ran the length of the park, determination against his focused features to capture the Frisbee from the whipping air. I held my breath as he leapt, his jaw strong and fierce as he seized the toy in one swift motion.

A sudden movement caught my eye, and I looked sideways, my vision colliding against Felix as he urgently sprinted across the park, his boots thudding coarsely on the pavement below.

"*Felix!*" I yelled, my tone laced with confusion. He halted, skidding to an unsteady stop. He looked around frantically, his blazing eyes crashing upon mine. His face etched with worry, his eyes swollen, his hair ruffled.

He exhaled hard, like a knockout punch against the atmosphere seconds before he sprinted towards me. I stepped in his direction doubtfully as he slammed against me like an out-of-control plane along the tarmac.

We stumbled backwards as he held my waist and the back of my head desperately. His fraught puffs hot and uncontrolled beside my ear as sweat trickled against him.

My body froze, my mind hyperaware of his dire touch against my tiny and perplexed form. People from afar watched us curiously. Half with judgemental stares, others with sympathetic glances.

I squirmed as Felix's hand gripped the back of my head, grabbing a fistful of hair.

Suddenly, he took a step back, his hand against my waist retracting as he hastily checked me over. His cheeks flushed from overexertion as I eyed him sharply, awaiting an answer to his brazen act.

His breathing smoothed and evened against the crisp air. "I couldn't feel you. I couldn't feel Ace," he gabbled as tears filled his emotional eyes.

"Someone blocked the car in; Ace wouldn't answer his fucking phone. I thought, I thought—" Shaky breaths pounded from his lips once more as he reached up with his free hand, embracing my cheek.

I stiffened, remembering how Ace had caressed me like that only moments before his lips met mine. I swallowed hard, uncomfortably shifting my focus to anywhere else.

"Where did you go?" Felix blurted as the morning sun shone harshly against us. "I felt your power. It was strong, demanding, and then, it was gone." He shook his head, eager to find the truth. "I felt *nothing,* I felt empty," he cried as his hand tightened around my hair.

"Felix," I managed, trying to sound confident, but his touch was unnerving. I trusted Ace enough to touch me, within him, I felt a promise of safety, within Felix, I didn't know. "I went into the past," I muttered, my voice low to avoid the eavesdroppers that encircled us.

Felix's expression shifted. "The past?" he echoed, disbelieving. "You went into the past?" I nodded, feeling exposed. "What did you see?" he questioned as his worried eyes searched mine for explanation.

"I, *um,*" I forced a breath. There was no point in lying to him. "My power returned me to the most brutal and unkind moments of my life... to the night my parents died, to where I committed my first attempt, to the night my best friend was murdered, to the moment I escaped my abusive fosters."

I wasn't quite sure how the last one fit, how it entangled itself within those similar memories of love and of loss. That ace of hearts, that playing card I'd used to escape, had that been a sign of what was to come? Had my subconscious been trying to warn me of the powers within from the very beginning?

Felix's eyes narrowed. "Did you change anything?"

"No, I don't even think I could've. It was like watching a 3D movie, I could reach out and touch what was around me, but I couldn't interfere, couldn't change the outcomes. There was so much blood. And Ace... Ace was there, and he witnessed those things. Things I've spent years trying to suppress." I closed my eyes, feeling Felix's hands fall away from my tattered form.

I breathed in deep, continuing with a shaky tone. "Ace told me to go into the past, to change my death. I told him if I was forced to reexperience that same abuse, I would kill every last one of them."

My eyes met Felix's as his body involuntarily shivered. He took a step back, watching me with doubt. "You really were abused."

I shrugged contemptuously. "What does it matter now? I can't feel pain, I can't die, can't bleed. Can't do *anything*—" I snapped at myself with abrupt anger. "I can't even use this so-called incredible power." I snorted humorously, like it was all some big joke, and I was the star of the shitshow.

"Stanley might be able to help," Felix offered optimistically. "They're not sure if he'll be home today, but you can come with me back to the hospital and talk to him there. It's worth a try," he expressed, watching me with a steady and understanding expression.

Could it be that Felix wasn't as much of an arsehole as I'd first thought? Could it be that I had just misunderstood him?

I nodded after a heartbeat. I still wasn't entirely convinced, but Stanley seemed knowledgeable enough.

If anything, he could at least show me a different way to view my power, a simple way to understand it, maybe even a guide to being able to control it. He was a doctor, after all, and someone who had studied the powers of the Ultimate Weapon for decades. Surely, he would have some solid advice regarding it.

I had to at least try.

The board meeting was tomorrow, and Kobi expected compliance, expected perfection. He had no idea how fucked he really was.

We journeyed down a long, dull, and busy hallway within the hospital. Nurses with trays and clipboards, as well as the occasional patient, roamed the active passageways. I kept my head low, my eyes shielded.

"Want to know why I hate hospitals?" Felix looked my way unsurely, but still, he nodded. "They remind me of death, of how fragile and fleeting life is. They remind me that we are unimportant, that death is imminent and inescapable."

"I believe hospitals offer hope," Felix declared. I looked across at him, surprised by his optimism. "They heal the sick, bandage the sore, fix the broken. They help bring new life into the world and they assist when lives are fading away. Human beings are here for only moments, for mere blinks within the time continuum. They're not like you, or like me, they're not immune to ageing, or sickness, or injury."

I jammed my fallen lips together, staring into his pale eyes soundlessly. "I deal with darkness every day, I face a power inside me that echoes death," he paused, his tone uneasy. "What's more depressing than that?"

I fell silent, unable to form a reasonable response as he half-smiled indifferently and shrugged in my direction.

"Your words are mostly true, but what is humankind if they don't have hope?" he questioned, watching me with a steady expression.

I replayed the sentence within my mind, trying to understand the philosophy within those words.

"You and Ace aren't immortal, are you?"

Felix shook his head. "No, we age like normal, but we heal extraordinarily quickly. We can die, but who knows what will become of us when we do. You—" he hesitated.

"—You died. You changed the entire equation. It's hard to say what will become of you. If you'll age, if you'll die. But you're already dead, to die again would be an impossibility. You feel pain, yet it'll never be enough to kill you."

"I'm going to end up all alone like I've always been," I muttered gravely as Felix clicked his tongue, dismissive of my negativity.

"Hey, I wouldn't worry too much about it. For now, we're all here, we're all learning. And I'm sure you won't always be a fan of mine, but I'll always be here for you." I glanced up and met his kind expression. His pale eyes purposeful, hopeful. I smiled despite my growing fears.

If I lived for an eternity, I would have an eternity to figure it out. I could bring wars, could bring peace. I could bring about human extinction. I was powerful beyond measure, and I now had my entire lifetime to fathom what the Legend of Millennia truly meant. I had the means to solve the mystery.

We rounded a corner into a stuffy room, causing Stanley to look up from his tub of custard. "Felix, Red," he exclaimed. "And here I was thinking the idiot box was all the company I would have." He chuckled coarsely.

He looked so pale, his usual bright and cheery clothes replaced with a sad and flimsy hospital robe.

"How are you?" I asked as Felix ushered me into the bedside chair. I sat down cautiously against the leather material as the beeping monitor assaulted my eardrums.

"Only the usual aches and pains," Stanley proclaimed with a cheeky smirk as Felix placed another chair against the opposite side of the bed.

My tired eyes traced along Stanley's old, wrinkled, and sun-damaged arm, silently criticising the large white bandage that was tightly wrapped around the wound. My eyes lifted, trailing from the inserted needle to the strident machine.

"Nothing to worry about, my dear." I met Stanley's assuring smile, but something felt amiss. "I'm as fit as a fiddle. They're all just paranoid folk around here." He playfully winked.

I smiled at him warmly, but it didn't quite reach my eyes. This room didn't match him, didn't feel like him. It was cold, colourless, cramped.

"I read those magazines," I voiced, trying to bring some cheer within this lifeless space. His pale eyes lit up magically, like a child waking on Christmas morning to a tree huddled with gifts.

"All of them?" I nodded keenly.

He grinned as a warm cheeriness returned to his face and circled within the bleak room. "I've been trying to get Ace and Felix to read those for years!" He chuckled, side-eyeing Felix with a playful stare. Felix wrinkled his nose in response.

"I didn't understand a lot of it, but I tried. It was a good distraction," I admitted.

Stanley nodded, understanding my cryptic words. "Ace tells me you can utilise their powers," he mumbled, seemingly anxious. I nodded, and his warmness dulled. "Anything else you've noticed?" His tone now serious.

"I can't taste." I shrugged a shoulder like it was meaningless information. Felix and Stanley's eyes flashed with worry between them. I decided to move on quickly, reluctant to discuss it any further.

"I'm able to harness their abilities and feel them within myself. When I use my own power, it's usually because I'm angry, because the agonising pain doesn't distract me, it fuels me."

My hands fiddled within my lap as I exhaled a shaky breath. "My skin melts away, and I become pure energy. I feel invincible, I feel the pain of self-inflictions consume my body, and I let it. It feels intoxicating, agonising. It makes me feel powerful. My mind is struggling to comprehend that."

Stanley gracelessly coughed, avoiding eye contact. I glanced at Felix then, but he looked away as well, his expression conflicted, uneasy.

I swallowed the lump within my throat, analysing my perfect hands. They wouldn't have any idea of the hurt these knuckles had caused, any idea of the pain they had brought down upon me.

For the first time in my life, I was my ideal character. I was beautiful, healthy, unharmed. My complexion was radiant, my face void of imperfections, my naked skin flawless.

But it was all fake.

I may have escaped those abusive homes, but those abusive homes hadn't escaped me. They still caused me harm, still made me sick, still festered within my broken mind like a perpetual parasite.

"I can go into the past," I muttered anxiously, my eyes fixated down. "I can rewrite history. I can make humanity suffer, or I can set them free."

The monitor suddenly screamed, piercing the air with its worried wails as Stanley started to convulse. Vomit spluttered against him as he groaned, and grunted, and garbled.

I screamed and stood as Felix sprinted for the doorway, yelling for help. I glared at Stanley fearfully, for a passing millisecond frozen stiff.

"No, no," I cried, grasping his wrinkled hand, trying in vain to calm his erratic motions. His eyes were fearful and big as his limbs thrashed against the bed manically.

Nurses invaded the room instantaneously, ready for action. *"No!"* I blindingly screamed as a stranger's arm wrapped around me. I shoved them away, stumbling against the cords.

"Get her out of here!" a man roared as the room erupted into chaos, faces distorting before my anxious brown eyes.

Felix reached across and snatched me, shoving me from the room and into the passageway. I tripped on a shoelace, smashing my face against the far wall. "What the fuck is wrong with you?" he howled against me, his cheeks flushed, his eyes angry.

I meekly faced him, my broken nose readjusting. He glared at me like I was the enemy, like I was the forsaken one. And maybe I was—*what did it even fucking matter?*

"Why did you tell him all of that? His heart is weak!" Felix slammed his fist against the wall, breaking the flimsy signage that sat between his blow and its target as heightened voices echoed from Stanley's room.

"Because he asked!" I clenched my knuckles and screamed as nurses scurried around us. "You said he could help me. You didn't tell me to be dishonest!" I sobbed despairingly, unable to stop the onslaught of orange droplets.

Felix closed the space between us, his enraged face inches from mine. "If he dies, *you* will pay for it," he snarled.

He turned sharply and left, leaving me all alone in the blank and tormenting hallway.

I pushed my fingertip against the doorbell and waited. "Hello? *Oh,* hi, Red." The young man warmly smiled, his friendliness refreshing. "Come on in, I'll get Max ready."

My mind quieted as I stepped inside the two-storey villa, hovering within the cluttered entryway piled high with moving boxes. Blake hurried about, collecting Max's collar and leash.

I was two hours earlier than my normal pick-up time, but I could only sit against that bench for so long. Ace was mad at me, and Felix was downright furious.

I'd screwed up everything. I felt I had no right to return to that bunker, no right to resume the affection I felt towards Ace. Within that kiss, I had thought differently, but this was reality, and I'd be delusional if I thought it could be so easily so.

"Here you go." Blake passed me the leash.

"Thanks," I voiced as we trekked down the front porch and onto the newly laid concrete path.

Max was just a puppy, ten months old. He was a Golden Retriever and lived up to all their expected perks. He was gentle, affectionate, and intelligent.

Our first couple of walks had been a challenge, but he soon learnt the obedience training needed. Now, he was nothing but a joy. Nothing but a big, fluffy, playful pup.

Blake was in his thirties, worked in a stuffy insurance office, and spent most of his weekends away with Max. This dog had travelled further than I ever will. It was one of Blake's dreams to explore the Australian outback, and that was what he did, with Max in tow, of course.

He had recently moved to the newest estate within the city. The houses were all identical. With no driveways, hardly any front gardens, and rows of fake grass between them. I stood out like an eyesore every time I ventured there.

Max tumbled and played, socialising with the other canines in the dog park. I breathed the air in deep, listening to the echoes of a faraway city. I wanted to crawl under a rock, to drown in my own self-imposed pity.

Was Stanley going to die because of me, because of the truths I had so willingly told? Had I just ruined my only chance of figuring out what the Ultimate Weapon was truly created for?

This title, these abilities, my inability to bleed—*what* did it all mean? What was my endgame? What was the purpose of my rebirth? What was the *point* of my existence? Was it remission, absolution, exoneration? Was it learning to forgive, was it easing the anger inside me, was it solely just to exist as *this?*

I wasn't even an imbalance like Ace or Felix, I was the byproduct, the side effect, the useless afterthought. Why was it so imperative for me to even exist?

Had the other Ultimate Weapons felt this way, had they been as miserable as I was? As defective, as scared? Had they even been aware of the supreme abilities within them?

A hard exhale left my lips as I collapsed on the bench, laying back against the metal frame. I watched the clouds roll in, the birds zip past, the leaves tumble by.

This was existence. *Meaningless but purposeful.*

This unmatched power, I needed to understand it. Needed to know why it had brought me back from imminent death. My road was set, my route fixed, my path aligned. I had freed myself only to end up in another hell. One not as easily escapable.

I needed to start anew, to flourish within a life I irrefutably belonged. Was this my chance—my first *real* chance—at achieving all those things I'd been denied, refused, prevented from? Part of me couldn't help but think that it was, but as much closure as that should've brought me, it brought me nothing but dread.

CHAPTER 22

RED

I pounded my fist against the flimsy door, knocking loudly.

The door shuddered and shook, rattling against the tarnished doorsill. I exhaled a curt breath and stepped back, peering up at the decayed and damaged tunnel.

"*Lira!*" I bellowed, stomping my foot with frustration. It was a regular weekday, a basic noontime diurnal, there wasn't any reason for her absence.

She was always there, manning the front desk during the day to help with her parents' finances. Although, if they hadn't wasted so much on materialistic and unnecessary things for her, they would've been just fine hiring somebody to do it.

I picked up the 24-hour phone, huffing with aggravation at the inactive beep that typically assaulted my eardrum. An annoyed groan escaped my lips as I slammed the receiver down hard. The cord sprang and tangled, seemingly possessed.

Birds chirped overhead as I strode within the car park, confused by its ghostly abandonment. Sure, it was a cheap motel in a troublesome part of the city, but it was usually busier. Situated just outside the city limits, the price of accommodation almost halved.

There wasn't a single vehicle nearby, nor their family car. I narrowed my eyes in doubt, staring at the rooms distrustfully. Curtains all drawn, windows all cleaned, gardens all tidied.

Pebbles crushed beneath my worn sneakers as I marched across the parking lot. I stepped before room five, eyeballing the replaced door. My hand tried the handle fruitlessly. I squared my posture, then slacked. There wasn't any point breaking in, and I didn't need to inconvenience Lira's family with another meaningless cost.

Her parents had already been kind enough to let me stay, albeit within the worst room possible. But it was a roof over my head, a place to escape the dangers that lurked behind every street corner.

I sighed defeatedly and slipped against the side of the door. I didn't know where else to go, who else to ask for help. I was all alone, Lira my last resort.

I was still so angry at her, but maybe I needed to try seeing it from her perspective, see the way I had acted from her point of view. She couldn't have been all wrong, especially considering how I had once valued my scars.

My bare skin was now faultless, fictitious, and it felt wrong when it should've felt right. I lifted my sleeve to my elbow and traced along the freckles gently.

I was unable to be harmed, unable to be abused, unable to be mutilated. I was finally safe, finally free. So, why did I feel so unsettled? Why was there this displacement of loss within me? I had made it out alive. Something so many kids within the system had been robbed of, including Tiffany...

I had once prayed to be in this exact position, to be unable to feel pain. Maybe I had pleaded for it because I knew it was impossible, because I knew it was hopeless.

Death was the only thing that could save me, and look where I ended up, right back where I fucking started.

I woke up.

Woke up from my own successful suicide attempt. It was so messed up. I couldn't even pretend to be surprised that these powers of the Ultimate Weapon inside me were so unstable, so unpredictable, and so unhinged. This power had violated every private part of me. It had brought me back to life when living had been the hardest thing of all.

I slumped beside the weak frame and exhaled a mouthful of breath, hearing a vehicle turn against the harshness of the entryway. I ducked low as the black car slowed into the parking lot, crunching discarded pebbles below its wheels.

It idled there for a moment as I squinted my eyes, trying in vain to analyse the make and model. The car door opened, and stark white sneakers emerged.

"Ace." I stood and he twisted around, eyeing me with a saddened expression. I waited, unsure if he wanted me any closer.

"Felix blames you."

It was a fist full of sand inside my windpipe, a sharp pierce within my shattered heart, a bullet against my bleeding lungs... Stanley was gone.

A dry sob escaped Ace's mouth as orange teardrops dotted my pale cheeks. A cold wind suddenly blew, wrapping itself against our mournful figures.

I couldn't believe it. Taken all too soon.

There was so much I needed to learn from Stanley, so much I needed to know. He had so much wisdom, so much insight into my omnipotence. Now all that vital information was gone.

Did he leave behind a wife, a child, a grandkid? Did he own a house, did he have a dog, did he have anyone to pass on his research to?

Maybe Felix had the right to blame me. Maybe it really was my fault. Maybe I had shared too much, too soon.

Stanley had spent his entire life investigating the powers of the Ultimate Weapon, only to meet me for mere moments of his existence. I should've tried harder, should've done better. Now the opportunity was all but dead and gone.

"Felix can hate me for the rest of time." I looked up at Ace as my voice cracked, meeting his impassioned blue eyes. "But not you. Please, Ace, not you."

Ace wiped beneath his watery eyes, looking away. "Stanley was like a father to me," he voiced as the wind ruffled his hair. My chest tightened, and I promised myself that no matter what he said next, no matter how gut-wrenchingly painful, I would accept it. "But no, I don't blame you, I don't hate you. In all honesty, Red... I need you."

A held breath left my lips as I ran to him, my heart unafraid. I slammed within his open arms, my face buried into his chest. "I need you, too." I hugged him tight, breathing in his familiar scent against me. I felt relieved, reassured. I felt loved in a way I hadn't been for years.

Everything within my life had destroyed me, abused me, tormented me, but it had led me here. It had led me into Ace's life, into Ace's arms, into a love I didn't have to be so afraid of.

No matter what happened from here on out, I would keep Ace safe. He was the light within the dark, the calm within the storm, the quiet within my raging mind.

He hesitated, and I quickly pulled back. "There's something else." My expression shifted. "Kobi's moved the board meeting to today. Three o'clock. He has something planned, something big. When he found out about Stanley's passing, he wasn't even upset. Just demanded this stupid meeting be scheduled sooner." Ace exhaled harshly against the chilled air, kicking at the loose gravel underfoot.

"I don't know how to save you from this," his voice faltered.

"You can't save me from this, Ace. You can't save me from a power that brought me back to life." I eyed him straight on as the wind weaved through my red hair. "Kobi can't kill me, can't hurt me. He can't control me. He should fear me, not the other way around. This power can save me, but it can't save him," I stated.

"Felix once told me I'm just a player in a game," I continued as Ace's face shifted with confusion. "He told me I could choose to be good or choose to follow along. That sounds a lot like defiance or compliance to me." I glanced at him sharply as he ran a hand through his blond hair restlessly. "Let us defy them."

"Kobi will do whatever he can in this board meeting to destroy your mind, do you not understand that? In the Legend of Millennia, your power was never meant to materialise within the living world," Ace tried to reason. "Kobi wants you to be nothing more than his lethal weapon! He wants to *own* you. He wants to become the most powerful man in history."

"Let him challenge me, let the world see how powerful I really am!" Ace shook his head, dismissive of my resolve. "Let me *prove* myself," I fiercely begged.

"You know that's impossible; you know you can't use your power without your anger," he acutely snapped. "That's what controls you and you *know* that uncontrollable emotion's what will drive you to global eradication!" He fell quiet suddenly, watching me with a sad and apologetic expression.

I wanted to defend myself; I wanted to scream against the universe his misperceptions. Only, they weren't incorrect. He was right, and he knew he was right.

He may have regretted the tone, but his words were nothing but the truth. I couldn't control the anger, the hate, the fury within me. I was knocking down all the wrong doors, looking outward when I should've been looking inward.

A folklore, a prophecy, a legendary tale. I was no longer Red, no longer Johanna, no longer a mistreated little girl within the system. I was the Ultimate Weapon. And my mind wasn't going to let me make it out alive.

CHAPTER 23

RED

My breath ascended my windpipe at an increasingly unsteady pace as my feet fumbled beneath me. My eyes darted around the building, momentarily meeting those of others around me.

My knuckles clenched as I tried to prepare myself for the unknown. I shut my bloodshot eyes briefly, focusing my breath to slow as determination invaded my bones.

I lifted my chin, my eyes growing dark as Ace and I entered the elevator. The silver doors closed as I stared forward with a blank expression. Whatever happened, I'd be alright. I was the Ultimate Weapon after all. Maybe this was the moment I was going to prove it.

The elevator dinged on level 34 moments before we strode into the hallway with fastened footsteps and hyper heartbeats. Chatter billowed from the room next to us as we darted our eyes around anxiously.

"You need to do whatever he demands." Ace nodded across at me sternly as the thoughts within my head poked and pried into my subconscious.

I eyed him with a deep-rooted unease. I knew he wouldn't lead me astray, but just what in the hell was about to go down, and was I to submissively conform or unyieldingly flout?

I breathed in, hoping it would suffocate me as we rounded the doorway into the colossal room.

Men, and a few women, dressed in business suits examined us with hungry eyes like that of vultures circling their prey. Their sharpened gazes inspected every inch of me, from my frizzed hair to my worn and ratty sneakers.

I glanced across at Felix suddenly, his stare piercing, angry. I gulped, feeling vulnerable as I ran my eyes up and down the long, wooden table. I squirmed, the anxiety within my stomach twisting into a tight and rigid knot.

Kobi sat perched within a leather chair with one designer shoe rested atop his knee. His suit pristinely pressed, his face charmingly charismatic, his manner strikingly savage.

The crooked smile that grew along his thin lips was untrustful, deceitful. No one could take away the power he held, and he knew it. *No one except me.*

Ace walked in front of me, taking the vacant seat alongside Felix. He gave me a reassuring nod and a positive smile, but it did nothing to calm my jittering nerves.

"Ladies and gentlemen," Kobi began as he fixed his tie and swiftly stood. Everyone looked to him with eager attentiveness, their faux leather chairs softly squeaking.

"First and foremost, I sincerely wish to thank you for joining us today, and of course, for the patience you've displayed during this time. This, I assure you, is a day of great excitement. A day we have waited many, *many* years for," he proudly announced. "Today, I am honoured to finally introduce—" He motioned his outstretched arm to me. "The Ultimate Weapon."

The businesspeople gasped in a unified display of awe and disbelief as their mouths dropped, eyes widened, and thoughts spiralled. Avowedly stunned into amenability.

I anxiously stood; my mind disinclined to proceed. I felt like some pathetic little prize out on display. One handed out so those who won would feel accomplished. The type of prize that held no genuine importance, just the fake façade of one.

I took an unsteady breath, trying to read the room of their intensions. I had a bad feeling within my gut, one I didn't know how to decipher, one I didn't know how to decrypt. It felt like I was out of the loop, cast away from the elite, left to my own tarnished will.

Kobi smugly stood, watching on like a king would his kingdom.

It gave me an ick, an odious feeling of satire and disdain. He planned to parade me around like a newly acquired piece of property, just like how my foster families had treated me.

The feeling made me furious. It filled me with a hatred that flooded through my veins like a deadly toxin.

I wanted to riot; I wanted to rage. I refused to obey; I refused to oblige. This was not a situation I would adapt. I would stand against them, fight against them, I would wage the war I knew I was capable of bringing.

Kobi gestured to Felix, and he stood, his conceited smirk warping his attractive features. Ace and I eyed him with escalated breaths and tunnelled vision.

"As you are all aware," Kobi continued. "Ace and Felix were believed to be the only ones with superhuman abilities, the Ultimate Weapon nothing but mere speculation. However, I can now confirm the existence of this sovereign entity with one hundred percent certainty," he paused for effect. "Our soldier, our super, our saving grace—" He motioned to me once more. "Our Ultimate Weapon in flesh-and-blood."

I bit down on my lip, my heartbeat pounding as frightened tears built behind my brown and bloodshot eyes. I could feel my pupils dilate. I could feel the slow burn throughout my entire body as I started to furiously shake.

"A demonstration," Kobi proclaimed as the room broke into hushed whispers and excited murmurs. "Do it." He signalled to Felix. Ace glanced up between us, his eyes glassy and scarlet.

Felix stepped towards me as I rooted my shoes stubbornly into the carpet. Was he going to hurt me? Was I reading this right? He met my shaky eyes and stilled.

His expression pierced against mine. Dark, deadly, and disastrous. He wanted to hurt me; he wanted me to pay for what I had brought upon this doomed and dying world. He wanted revenge for what I had done to Stanley.

But he hesitated, his demeanour conflicted.

Kobi suddenly laughed, motioning to his intrigued and impatient audience. "Stage fright," he declared. They returned the laugh, forced but on cue.

Felix's eyes darkened exponentially as grotesque inky lines invaded his pale complexion like a hazardous poison. A few of the businesspeople gagged, unable to hide their repugnance.

I'd told myself to prepare for war, to prepared for violence. Within him, there was a dormant rage both deep and sentimental. Not only would he hurt me, but he would take pleasure in it. I forced myself to stand unafraid, to dilute my fears, to bolster my own hostility.

Ace stood, his heart beating in haste.

Felix shot him a sharp and threatening look. He swallowed anxiously, momentarily weighing up his options before he slunk back within the chair, defeated and meek.

I squared my posture, facing Felix straight on. I had dealt with worse, had danced with those more fearsome, had stood face-to-face with wickeder foe. I refused to cower; I refused to be made a fool out of.

Dark power expelled from his fingertips, encircling me in a black and lifeless fog. Only this time it didn't feel safe. The sensation prickled and pierced against my skin. Uncomfortable, unkind, unbalanced.

My eyes squinted through the unseeable mist moments before a whiplashing wind knocked me downward. I grunted and toppled towards the floor, my head smashing against the side of the table.

I winced, unable to sense the pain, but able to sense the orange droplets that stuck against my dishevelled hair.

The board members gasped but remained seated, unbothered by the brutality. They resumed their silent observation as I clambered to my shaky sneakers, meeting Ace's worried expression through the declining haze.

"Come on now, don't be shy! Show us what you're capable of," Felix snickered as his eyes grew dark. "For *Stanley*."

I snapped, the anxiety within my body fracturing as anger, and hate, and rage surged through my veins like fuel spilled within a calmed bonfire.

Fury blinded me as an electrified shriek escaped my lips. The sound ricocheted off every wall, bouncing across the room like a deafening echo.

I outstretched my shaky arm, Felix my only target, my one fixation. My power surged from against my palm, spewing out an alien glow like ripples upon the water. Entrancing, thrilling, terrifying.

Felix slammed into the far wall with my scintillated glow tightly wound around his neck. It pressed him into the structured frame with a hefty force as his legs kicked and dangled.

It was all I could think about. *The rage. The hate. The fury.* It burned hot within me like an everlasting flame.

I wanted Felix dead. I wanted them *all* to suffer for what they had done, for what the world had done! For the abusive foster home after abusive foster home, for the fake promises of safety, for the false façades of love. I wanted revenge. I wanted the world to burn, and flame, and sear for what it had done.

"Get off of him!" Kobi bellowed furiously as I swung my free arm against him. I slammed his entire frame into the far wall, hearing something snap.

The board members wildly shrieked, flinging themselves from the leather chairs. "*No!*" I roared, my face etched with unmistakeable fury as my hair whiplashed against my head, my arm sweeping across the room in a vehement manner.

My power scorched against the table, scattering documents and tossing files, as it simultaneously flung the businesspeople back into their seats. Their fearful cries falling upon deaf ears.

Ace urgently stood as a wave of electricity collided against the windows. The glass shattered in a synchronised display of chaos and oontrol, raining down upon the unsuspecting below like a crystallised waterfall.

Pain collided against my skeleton. It hurt, it burned, it tore my insides apart. Every bone split, protruding out my body as my remaining skin shattered and dissolved, revealing an entity of only pure untouched energy.

My face, my body, my hair, all pulsed with that same electric and petrifying glow that imploded almost gracefully from within my masked form.

Within that moment more than any, I felt like an alien. I felt like a supernatural being of immortality, of power and control. One unmatched by this world. One destined for more. One free of human impediments.

The room erupted into electric waves that rode against my inhuman form as pain drove me on. Further, and further, and further. It steered me towards total and utter destruction. It was intoxicating, hypnotising. I was ablaze with rage, with abstracted energy.

My power aligned and my body came undone alongside the erratic forces driving it to eradication.

"Red, stop! You're going to kill him!" Ace desperately cried. I ignored his plead, fury driving me forward.

The onlookers gripped their seats in fear, their fingernails tearing at the fine leather material as their once flawless faces became overtaken with panic. With any luck, this would teach them not to meddle with matters beyond them.

I wanted these people to fear me, to know exactly *who* they were trying to control. I wanted the world to know how powerful I truly was, to know exactly the weapon I was to become.

A weapon unable to be controlled, unable to be browbeaten, unable to be hurt by a corrupted system ever again.

They had the gun, but I had the ammunition.

"Red!" Ace pleaded once more.

I heard the worry, the unease within his shaky tone, but on I foolishly pressed. Felix mere moments from unconsciousness as the alien glow beamed out from within me, powering me on. I felt strong, capable, formidable.

A power strong enough to send us back to the Stone Age or millenniums into the future. It was within that precise moment that I found those words to be true.

I gritted my teeth, my fingers violently shaking as the Earth around us quaked and quavered. The businesspeople shrieked, thrashing themselves in vain against the glow that entrapped them.

The entire building shook, causing lights to sway, walls to creak, people to scream. I could feel it within my bones, I could feel the universe shifting, rotating, wobbling. I was linked to Mother Nature, it ran through my veins, it gifted me this power beyond means.

I needed to accept it, needed to choose to accommodate to these burning and breaking superhuman abilities within me, no matter how unstable or unbalanced they may be.

"*Stop!*" Ace bellowed as a wave of unfamiliar sparks flashed against me, bathing my overheated body in a curious sensation.

I gasped and stilled, my power blinking out of existence as flickering spangles collided against me with the most soothing and peculiar touch.

Felix dropped from the wall, coughing and splattering, as the board members dashed from the room desperately.

My inhuman form shuddered, my pale skin reappearing just as swiftly as it had vanished. I breathed out a long breath, the feeling of power rushing against me, hot and untamed.

Felix grasped Kobi deftly, helping him stand. He slung his arm around him for support, aiding him from the wrecked room with his newly acquired broken wrist. I scoffed angrily, watching them hobble away.

They did this to me. They forced me to use my power, to oppose them, to combat them. All my life I had trained for an unseen enemy, and there they were. As brutal as each other, as defiant, as obsessed. I refused to sink, *refused* to go down with this cracked, broken, and damaged ship. I would be the last one standing, even if I had to take them all down myself.

Ace grabbed my face abruptly, forcing my backbone to immediately straighten as he pushed me against the inner wall of the building. He was terrified, fearful. His hair ruffled, his blue eyes pale, his lips parted in angered confusion.

I leaned forward and kissed him.

My lips locked against his, kissing him deeper than any Seventh Sea could hope to reach. I needed him, needed to feel him, feel him with an intensity no one had ever before.

I wanted all his attention, all his affection. I wanted this boy with the safest and kindest blue eyes to *feel* how much I needed him.

He embraced me with the same fiery desire as his firm grip against my face loosened, his hands trailing down my body. I wanted to seep within his skin, to forever voyage within those charming blue eyes.

My hands tangled within his smooth and silky hair, pushing him further against me like he was the vital water to my devastating drought.

In the few days we had known one another, he'd made me feel more secure than any home, more understood than any therapist, more listened to than any hotline.

I longed to outright express how much time I had yearned for someone as tender, caring, and raw as him to come into my life. It gave me hope that my shattered, neglected, and closed off heart could once again hold the feeling of love.

Ace pulled back slightly, our lip lock unwillingly parting.

"Do you want me?" I muttered daringly.

He nodded breathlessly. "Yes."

CHAPTER 24

ACE

Police sirens echoed around us as we twisted and turned within the damaged room. Air whistled against the destroyed windows, squealing alongside the newly broken compounds.

A policeman escorted us to the ground floor by foot. Thirty-four dirty, smelly, seemingly endless stairs we descended.

I eyed my cell phone, tapping against the screen urgently. I needed Aunt Emma to swoop in and save us, to be our getaway driver within this moment of unrest.

All hell was about to break loose. I knew Kobi wouldn't let Red leave, knew Felix wouldn't let Red be. These were testing times and she no prisoner to the antics of humankind.

Her anger wouldn't allow it, wouldn't allow her power to be suppressed. She had the fury to destroy herself, to abolish this entire globe, to end civilisation with the snap of her petite fingers. I had to help her before it was too late. Not just for myself, but for the good of an entire nation.

After the twelfth storey, I was more than ready to haul myself out any given window without an ounce of hesitation. But I kept myself poised, vigilant, and my unmanaged breaths low.

Red shot me unsure gazes every few minutes, but I couldn't communicate my plan, not with this heavily wheezing man between us.

"Mr Holloway," the officer breathlessly averred as we wandered into the congested lobby. Kobi tore his gaze away from his fellow dishevelled businesspeople, glowering at us with a furious stare as he clutched his saggy wrist tightly.

I did not wish to wait around to witness his vengeful wrath.

A sudden breath escaped me as I grabbed Red's dry hand within my sweaty palm. I led us towards the outside world, not daring to glance back at the enraged echoes that boomed from both Kobi and Felix.

My cell phone rang, and I quickly answered. "We're coming out now. Don't turn the engine off," I instructed as Red side-eyed me quizzically.

Emma's bright car pulled alongside the kerb; her worn face etched with worry. "Over here, Ace!" she called over the lowered window as her brunette hair shifted across her shoulders.

We manoeuvred past the sporadically placed emergency vehicles, momentarily blinded by their pulsating lights of red and blue. We hurried over patches of shattered glass, hearing the satisfying crunch beneath the tread of our sneakers.

I slid my hand from Red's and ushered her into the backseat. She fell against the leather material with a thud as I reached over and opened the passenger side door, slamming into the seat with an abrasive huff.

"Go," I commanded, flinging my fringe away from my fearful blue eyes.

We pulled away from the kerb as Felix sprinted towards us,

stumbling as he eyed our getaway vehicle with contempt.

"Fuck," I exclaimed as I sank into the chair with a feeling of both relief and distress. "That went as bad as you could've expected." I exhaled gruffly as Emma weaved us through the busy streets and out of harm's way. "And thirty-four flights of damn stairs," I added angrily as I rested my head against the side of the window, and my feet against the dashboard.

Emma looked across at me worriedly, her tight grip on the steering wheel loosening. "Talk to me," she begged.

I sighed once more and eyed Red within the side mirror. She was fuelled with anxiety, her tiny mind overworked and overpowerful.

I had to figure out how to help her, how to guide her into calming and controlling the anger that triggered the untameable powers within her. I couldn't allow myself to be blindsided by that intoxicating kiss we had shared. Red needed my help, and God only knew how much I truly wanted to assist her.

"I wouldn't even know where to start." I glanced across at her timidly. "Except that Red is no doubt the Ultimate Weapon, and humanity may just be completely done for."

Emma eyed me anxiously. "What is that meant to mean?" I exhaled hard against the warm car air, then breathed in deep, the scent of her perfume subtle against my nostrils.

"She can't control it. And she can't be controlled." I placed my fingertips against my forehead.

"What about Stanley? He knows this power better than anyone," she fussed, her green eyes stubborn and wide.

I hesitated. "Stan's gone." Emma gasped, placing a hand to her mouth in disbelief.

"Oh, my gosh, *what*—what happened?" She shook her head, her chestnut locks shifting as tears built behind her emerald eyes. She turned into a parking lot, pulling into a vacant bay.

She faced me straight on, touching against my hand gently. "Ace, what happened?" I shifted towards her and peeked back at Red, observing her stone-cold stare as she fixated on the world outside, absentminded and numb.

"Heart attack." Red trembled.

"I'm so sorry, Ace. I know how close you two were," Emma paused, contemplating her words carefully. "How's Felix taken the news?" I swallowed hard, avoiding her piercing and unknowing gaze.

"He blames Red." The back door opened and slammed shut. "Shit," I muttered, exiting the vehicle as Emma glanced around questioningly. "Red, what are you doing?" I eyed her across the parking bay.

She stood with her hands in her pockets, staring out at the busy peak hour traffic. She felt far away, disengaged, alienated by her own brutal reality.

I placed my hand against her shoulder, but she was unresponsive to the gentle touch. My eyes narrowed in doubt as I moved in front of her, her impassive expression unchanged.

"Red?" I mumbled, moving my hand to her cheek.

"All I do is hurt people... I'm better off dead." I lowered my head, trying to meet her empty stare. She was worlds away, antipodes in distance. I ran my thumb along her thick, bottom lip. *Nothing,* not even a shiver.

I gasped worriedly, dropping my hand like it was infected. "What the hell is going on in there?" I snuffled as my blue eyes shook against her. It was like conversing with a mannequin, a dummy, a cardboard cutout. Not one single emotion behind those wide brown eyes of hers. "You mean a lot to me, Red. You mean a lot to the world." She snorted dully.

I swallowed hard, readjusting my encouragement. "I'm glad you woke up, I truly am. I'm glad I was given the opportunity to get to know you, the real you, the unfiltered you."

Her hair fell gently across her face, shifting ever so slightly alongside the zephyr that blew. "I don't want to do this anymore. I don't want this power, I don't want to be the Ultimate Weapon," her voice trembled.

"My anger is destroying me, and I'm letting it." An orange teardrop slipped against her unwillingly, and she shuddered, releasing a held breath. I wiped the droplet away, desperate for her to reconsider.

She was so hopeless, defeated, beaten down to her delicate heart. She was worth so much more than she thought, so much more than she knew.

"What do you need right now?" I uttered, touching along her soft and messy hair. She sighed gently and eyed me then, her expression disheartening. It was unemotional, empty. It struck pain into my very core at just the sight of it.

"I need to stop killing myself."

She was the Ultimate Weapon. A power unmatched, an omnipotence so rare. And yet, she hated herself. She drowned in those emotions that killed her; she gave in to those torments that caged her. She was at the end of her rope, admitting defeat to the noose that loomed above.

She had shared with me her distrust for superpowers, for fairy tales, for fabricated fables. And now, I could see and understand why. I admired her perseverance, her willpower, but I feared the emotions she held captive within herself, feared the moment she snapped under the weight of it all.

She was losing her mind like I knew she would.

"We're going to stay at my Aunt Emma's tonight," I stated, smiling her way before I glanced back around. Red followed the movement, eyeing my aunt who stood leaning against the car's shimmering roof. She nodded her agreement and waved to Red a silent introduction, to which Red nodded compliantly.

Emma was my only aunt and the older sister to my mother. They weren't close anymore, but they had been in their teenage years. The bulk of the stories I'd heard of my dad had come from her recollection, but regrettably, she couldn't remember much. My parents had run away together at age eighteen to start their lives anew.

After my dad's death, mum had financially struggled, so she returned to her hometown and made peace with her parents. Apparently, they'd been incredibly surprised to learn of mine and Felix's existence.

I reached over and wrapped my hand gently around Red's. Her fingers twitched, but she didn't enclose her hand against mine. I led her back to the car, and she reluctantly climbed into the backseat. The door shut as I smiled Emma's way unsurely.

"They will come for her," she warned. "Felix knows my car."

I sighed defeatedly. "I know, but if Red doesn't get the help she needs, she's going to eliminate the entire cosmos." I trembled, placing my forehead against the hot surface of the car. It was a frightening reality that awaited humankind.

Red, an abused teenage girl destined to fulfil a legend created millenniums ago...

It should not have been her responsibility, her fight, her problem. She had enough problems of her own, enough problems to sink a cargo ship.

She was pained by her past, by toxic emotions that pressed tight against her bleeding heart. She wasn't even an adult yet, two months shy, but still she was expected by the universe to wield such destructive powers.

Had Felix been right? Was the pain only because of her suicidal act or was there more? Was Red causing the unbearable agony when the power erupted from within her?

I sighed dismissively, lifting my face from the warm exterior. I highly doubted this was anything self-induced. She hated the anger, the pain, the alien glow.

She would persevere, I knew she would. Only, how far was she willing to go before breaking point beelined her straight towards a cataclysmic end?

CHAPTER 25

RED

"We're here," Ace announced as the car slowed to a gentle stop. I tiredly glanced across at the house. Two-storey, upper class, modern. It looked so bleak, blending in perfectly with its lifeless shades of grey.

Guess it was perfect for a suicide survivor.

I ran my shaky hands through my messy hair and huffed out an exhausted breath, readying myself for the inevitable.

Ace's door opened and then closed shut. I followed the motion, colliding against the cold air instantaneously. I breathed in deep, inhaling the scent of newly cut grass as Ace stepped up the kerb. He trailed my nervous glance to the front door.

My stomach twisted into a tight knot as anxiety pulsed beyond my empty stare. I had to stay calm; I had to be collected. I would walk into that house, I would nod, be respectable.

I could do this... *couldn't I?* If only it didn't feel like déjà vu. Like the walls inside my mind were closing in, like the air was suddenly unbreathable, toxic. Like every other home I'd been forced into before. I was unlovable. *They* told me so. They had me browbeaten down until I believed it myself.

I would ruin this boy, ruin this second chance at life, ruin everything this power tried so hard to gift me.

Stanley's life ended because of me. The feeling of guilt was overwhelming, the pain excruciating. He had been nothing but kind to my tarnished and troubled mind.

It was *me* who should've left this world, *me* who should've suffered. Now I had his blood against my hands and Felix's target against the back of my head.

The perfectly kept gardens caught my attention briefly. I'd survived when I should've been dead. I had stood, unaffected, unbruised, unbroken, whilst the world had fallen apart around me. I had glowed, and radiated, and shone. The power an intoxicating phenomenon within my broken mind.

The evening sky darkened as the world grew silent once more. I tightened my oversized jumper around myself, sinking into its protective layers as I forced my feet up the pathway.

We stepped into the warm interior, lingering within the entryway. Emma shut the door quickly as a Maremma Sheepdog bounded towards us.

"Tilly, no," she fussed, reaching for the overly excited dog's collar. Tilly resisted, rearing against the hold as her tail slapped noisily against the staircase, her hungry eyes yearning for my attention. "She's very friendly, but also very big." Emma laughed, struggling against the persistent yaps and whines of Tilly. "I'll put her outside. Ace, why don't you show Red the spare bedroom?"

"Sure," Ace agreed, eyeing the pooch with a playful smile. I turned to Ace and huffed out an exaggerated breath, trying to conceal my anxiety over this whole screwed up situation.

A new house had always meant new struggles, more abuse. I

knew this wouldn't be the same, I honestly did. But my mind couldn't comprehend it, couldn't block out the past, couldn't forget.

I'd lived my life of abuse and solitude for far too long. It wasn't something I could easily overcome, something I could effortlessly chase away. It was rooted within me; it obtruded from me. It *was* me.

I wanted to be cured, of course I did, I wanted to be healed. I wanted to do better, be better. I just wasn't sure if after all that had happened, I still could.

"The bedrooms are up there," Ace spoke gently, nodding his head towards the second storey. "I'll give you the official tour tomorrow, but for now, I'll just show you upstairs."

I soundlessly nodded, following him up the bleak-looking stairway, my eyes fastened to my feet. *One step, two steps, three steps, four.* I stilled abruptly and looked up, my hand holding tight to the wooden handrail. I watched Ace ascend, his motions fluent, relaxed.

He knew this home. It was familiar to him, it was safe. I was a stranger within these confined walls, a prisoner of whatever evils awaited me, of whatever malignant forces revealed themselves from shadowy corners.

I hesitated, doubt clinging to my bones, stuck like glue. "You good?" Ace murmured, giving me a puzzled look from the second storey. I nodded stiffly, tearing my mind from its current fixation.

I reached the top of the staircase and awkwardly stood, awaiting instruction. Ace gave a reassuring nod before turning to the hallway that loomed before us, dark and unnerving.

"That's Aunt Emma's room, bathroom," he began, casually

pointing at the doors. "That's me, and you're here." He stilled and faced me, a sure smile meeting his perfect lips.

I nodded curtly, my anxiety seizing up as fear entwined within me. It was just a door, a stupid room, in a dumb house. I shouldn't have felt this uneasy about it.

"It's okay," Ace uttered reassuringly. "I get it, it's scary, but you don't have anything to worry about. Emma's a saint, and I'm right here if you need anything."

He motioned to the door behind him once more. "I guess," I mumbled uneasily, adjusting my eyesight to peer down the darkened hallway. So many houses, so many rules, so many consequences.

I jumped, twisting around quickly as Ace placed his hand upon my shoulder. "Don't do that." I huffed, shifting back.

I didn't deserve his touch, his affection, his promise. I had been ready to annihilate this world, to kill Felix, to end all the pain of human existence. I'd kissed him so selfishly. The power a thrilling thing within my fractured mind, Ace's kiss the very same.

I yearned to drown in both of those intoxicating feelings, but I knew I couldn't. I'd screwed this one up good and proper.

Ace looked conflicted suddenly, but he didn't mention anything as he lowered his hand. "If you want to check out the room, that's fine, but come back downstairs once you're done. We need to organise something for tea; I'm hoping for pizza." He chuckled casually as I reached for the doorknob.

I twisted my wrist and opened the door, pushing it back gently. As soon as my feet stepped within the carpeted room, the entire ceiling fictitiously caved in from above. Surrounding me in dust, debris, and disappointment.

Nowhere was safe. Nowhere was home. Nowhere was everywhere. I didn't want to constantly feel like this. I didn't want to keep running to destinations I didn't even know of, to destinations I knew would do nothing but destroy me.

The door shut behind me as I sank into the carpet, crying against my jumper sleeves, begging for all this to be nothing but a nightmare I would soon awaken from.

I trekked down the staircase timidly, stilling near the last few steps. I could hear Ace and Emma bustling around in the kitchen, could hear the clinging of utensils and the steady flow of a relaxed conversation.

I slunk against the stairs, their wooden surface uncomfortable beneath my weight as I rested my head beside the railing, my mind tuning into the sounds around me and the warm air that cycled above.

A knock suddenly echoed from against the front door. Anxiety seized me as Ace entered the room and gladly answered.

"Delivery for Ace?" He keenly nodded.

The delivery boy passed over the pizza boxes. Abruptly, he stilled, his limbs frozen in place, his gaze fixated. "Talk Back?" I quickly stood, eyeing the boy with his thick afro hairstyle and skin tanned brown.

He glanced across at me curiously, his eyebrows creased in concentration. Ace stepped back, his pastel-blue eyes darting between us as he held the boxes unsurely and leant against the timber door.

"Thomas," I breathlessly mumbled, worry playing within my

mind as the sweet smell of hot food invaded my nostrils.

Thomas inched further into the artificial porch light. "You made it out," he mumbled as Ace's eyes met mine. His expression tense, unsure. I faked a smile as he glanced back.

"I'm Thomas, Talk Back's friend," he introduced nervously, fiddling with the zip against the pizza bag.

"Ace," he politely conveyed, but his voice remained hesitant.

Thomas nodded dismissively, his worn-out stare watching me steadily. "I always knew you'd make it out," he voiced with a hopeful expression against his tired face. "Flynn did, too. His new family is loaded." He wheezed, chuckling, the sound all too familiar. "He's enrolled in state university, studying criminology. He'll be able to put all the bad guys away," he said proudly.

Flynn had always talked about making a better life for himself. Even at the young ages we were, he knew he was destined to succeed. He wanted a wife, a few kids, an eminent career. He wanted to prove to the system that we could be neglected and still accomplish great things. I was glad he never gave up on that.

Emma strode into the entranceway, looking between the three of us unsurely as I stepped anxiously from foot to foot.

"Yeah," was all I was able to manage, the air between us filling with tightness as a rapid chill weaved in through the open doorway.

There had been a moment, back in the past, where I stupidly believed Thomas and I could run away together and escape all the cruelty of the world. We got caught, of course we did, and I lied until my tongue bled. I wouldn't let him take the fall for an idea that had been mine.

After that, I was involuntarily removed from the household.

I should've acted better; I should've begged them to let me stay. I had Thomas, and Flynn, and Lira, all within the confines of that rotting and deteriorating house. We'd made a pact to stay together; we set promises in stone with our blood to bind the contract. I was a foolish fourteen-year-old...

Thomas cleared his throat, causing me to crash back into reality head-on. "Anyway," Ace cut in. "We should start on the pizza," he ushered me to end the awkward conversation.

I stepped down from the remaining steps and stood before Thomas, the harsh manufactured light highlighting his imperfections. His cut lip, his tangled hair, his torn uniform.

"Can I see you?" he asked of me desperately.

"Thomas." I inhaled sharply. "We were fourteen, that life we dreamed of—*it's gone.*"

My feelings towards Thomas had all but faded when I was forced into my fourth foster home. It was the first one I'd witnessed sexual abuse, but it hadn't been towards me. Tiffany was the one who suffered, the one who bled for weeks...

That home changed me. It made me numb to the pain, to the abuse, to the neglect. It made me question God, and ultimately decide there wasn't one.

There was no greater power than man; there was nothing but natural disaster that could subjugate humankind. Humanity behaved as if they were untouchable. And for the most part, they were.

"We made a pact," Thomas declared, his voice trembling.

"It's over," I spoke obstinately, pulling the door closed.

Ace passed the pizza boxes to Emma before she hurried into the kitchen and away from earshot.

I stayed by the door for a moment longer, hanging my head low, ashamed of how I'd so easily disregarded everything we'd gone through. But it had been years ago... I was different now, I was changed.

The only reason I wasn't dead was because of this power, and the only reason I wasn't lost to insanity was because of Ace.

Short and panicked breaths rapidly pounded from my lips, and I winced, unable to control the unmanageable bursts of air from my tarnished lungs. I spluttered and shook, my mind distorting at a rapid pace.

"Red, Red, breathe," Ace instructed, his tone kind but firm. "In and out, in and out," he repeated, over and over, until my breathing slowed and my heartbeat soothed. I opened my eyes wide and met his worried look.

"Do you want to talk about it?" I rolled my head to the side, watching him through my drooping eyelashes and jaded expression. "Do you want to clarify what Talk Back is?" He was definitely curious about that one.

"It's me," I replied breathlessly. "It's not a hard one to figure out. I ran my mouth, I refused to obey, I talked back like I had the right to. After a while, the nickname Talk Back just stuck, I guess." I shrugged and sighed a heavy huff. "Haven't heard it in years, though," I murmured, my attention trailing back to that messy and malodorous house.

Our foster mum was known to us only as Ms Tay. She was a small and slender woman, her face bony and her eyes too big for her head. She was neglectful and rarely abusive.

The four of us had been forced to huddle within a group to stay warm, to scavenge for our own food, to comfort one another when the nightmares became all too real.

They were the family I never even knew I needed.

We had made a pact because we thought it logical. We had talked, expressed so much about our lives that we couldn't imagine a time we wouldn't all be together.

The police had pulled me punching, kicking, and screaming out of that house.

"It must be hard," Ace abruptly voiced, placing his hand upon my shoulder comfortingly. I swallowed the lump within my throat, feeling thwarted.

"It is," I confessed. "And every day, I don't know if it's going to be better, or if it's going to get worse," I regretfully admitted. "Sometimes, I feel like I'm never going to find my footing. Like I'm suspended in midair, unable to come down, unable to be in one place for too long." I snivelled, my eyes filling with tears. "Most of the time, I think I'm better off alone."

"I don't agree. I don't think anyone is better off alone."

Silence fell between us for a fleeting moment, and I briefly thought back to the simulation, to the feeling of waking up in a worn and decayed hospital room, with flowers that bloomed and died in seconds. Was that a reflection of human life, of how short and delicate it truly was?

"Come get some pizza," Ace offered hopefully.

I eyed him sadly, my body immobilised. "Do you think I'm a bad person?" His expression curiously shifted as I looked away sheepishly, afraid of the judgements I had just lined myself up for.

"I think your past forced you to survive, and with that came a lot of sacrifice," he paused. "But no, I don't think you're a bad person, Red. I think you're a girl within the system who's been treated unfairly her whole life, who's only now been given the chance to be anything more." He smiled my way so soothingly I wanted to cry.

I wrapped my shaky arms around him, pulling him in close. "Thank you," I breathed against him, burrowing within the crook of his neck.

CHAPTER 26

ACE

I stared at the ceiling, unsure of the thoughts that pounded within my troubled mind. I'd seen Red interact with Lira, and now Thomas. Two people from her past that brought out the worst in her. I had read about them, of course, Red had met them during her third foster home.

Flynn now attended university in another state, Lira was adopted out to the owners of Cassio Motel, and Thomas remained within the foster system. He had recently gotten a job as a delivery boy at a local pizzeria.

Tiffany was the only other child Red had lived with during her time in foster care. That little girl had suffered the worst, her gut-wrenchingly wicked tale one I did not wish to ever repeat. And Red had experienced that firsthand with nowhere safe to fall.

A deep breath escaped me as I tried to imagine all the horrors within her mind, of someone who had lived through those years of abuse and maltreatment.

She was an iron soldier, a tough recruit, a stone-built warrior. For too long she had borne bruises that didn't belong to her, contusions she foolishly believed would save her.

My hands rested against my forehead as I exhaled defeatedly. Why did the universe choose her? Why did it pick such an abused girl to handle such an omnipotent power?

She clearly didn't want it, clearly didn't want to be granted the indestructible powers of the Ultimate Weapon. She was on the verge of collapse, wielding a power her anger continuously faltered to. Did the universe want the world to end, for civilisation to be erased?

I sat up quickly, eyeing the door with a knowing look moments before a tiny knock whispered against the room.

"Yeah?" The door slowly opened.

Red stood meekly, peeking in curiously. "You free?"

"Sure, what's up?" I sat cross-legged upon the sinking mattress as she lowered her shaky form against the bed, her tired eyes filled with worry, her jumper wound tight against her.

"Is everything okay?" She shrugged, eyeing me worriedly.

"You know about them, don't you?" I smiled anxiously and nodded, feeling guilty of my excessive research into her life. "Are they doing okay? I know about Lira, but the others... is it true about Flynn?" she asked nervously as I noticed her bitten down nails and aglets chewed through.

I nodded, her tension easing. "It's true. He's studying interstate. Thomas is doing okay, too. He's still within the system, but he's been with the same couple for almost three years, and there haven't been any incidents or reports of mistreatment. He started working at the pizza place about six weeks ago."

"You knew?" she snapped.

Nervously, I squirmed. "I did, but Emma ordered the pizza, I didn't know he—" I fumbled over my own words. "I'm sorry about what happened tonight. I didn't mean for that."

Red exhaled, chewing once more on the frayed aglet. "Did you look into my parents?"

"I haven't yet, I'm sorry. Everything's been so crazy since you arrived," I confessed. She breathed out a long breath, looking against the room blankly. "I'll make it a priority. I'm just not sure when we'll be back at the bunker." She seemed different, felt different, like her mind was closing itself off, becoming numb, unresponsive.

"How are you handling things?" I asked, eyeing her expression uneasily.

She shrugged dismissively, unable to find the right words. I placed my hand against hers and felt the electric pulse of her power from within. She eyed me restlessly, her mind electrified. "I don't want to be alone tonight," she muttered timidly. "Would it be okay if I stayed with you?"

I nodded after a heartbeat, shuffling across the bed, reaching for the blanket to share. She flipped her jumper and tee shirt off, along with her pants, revealing a loose singlet and a pair of pyjama shorts before she slipped in next to me.

I held my breath, her tiny frame overtaken with so much agitation and anxiety. I wanted to ease her mind, wanted to mend her worries.

She sighed heavily and cuddled up beside my chest, resting her head on my heart. I stilled anxiously, eyeing the frizzy red hair that spilled from her scalp.

"I'm not handling any of this well," she mumbled against my torso. "I'm losing my mind." She stirred and eyed me straight on with a disheartened look. "I feel guilty for Stanley. I feel like Felix has the right to blame me, but I don't want him to. Back at the hospital, before we entered Stanley's room, he said he would always be there for me. After this, I doubt that's still true."

She looked so defeated, so deflated. I tilted my head to the side, watching her against the light of the moon that illuminated her pale face through the window.

Stanley's passing weighed heavy against my heart. He was an incredible old man with a heart of gold. A man who had unintentionally raised Felix and I for the latter part of our lives.

There was so much about Red he wanted to understand, so much he wanted to research and document for the future millenniums. But the way things were going, the universe may not even reach the next one.

I placed my hand beside Red's cheek, and she stilled. "I can't speak for Felix, but I'll always be here for you. And what happened to Stanley was nothing but a tragedy, you shouldn't feel guilty, or responsible, for that. We've all been on edge since you arrived, but that doesn't mean you caused his heart to worsen."

Her bottom lip trembled as orange tears cascaded from her eyes. "I didn't do it on purpose, but I caused it. And now, I've ruined my chance of learning all the things Stanley knew. Things that could've made this so much easier for me. Sure, I could demand this other doctor explain, but—" she broke off.

I sat up abruptly, eyeing her with confusion. "What are you talking about? Is there another doctor who knows about all this?" She stilled anxiously, her eyes wide and uncertain, her body tense. "Red?" I begged, placing my hand over hers. She trailed her gaze to meet mine, her irises the perfect blend of cinnamon and honey, and nodded gently.

"Kobi has another doctor. Felix told me the night of the accident, when I drove us into that building, but I wasn't meant to tell." She shook her head frantically, her fingers fidgeting. "Please don't tell him! He already hates me," she pleaded as she clambered onto her hands and knees before me.

Felix had been keeping secrets, I wasn't surprised really, but I was puzzled as to why he told Red. Maybe he had a soft spot for her. He was usually so private and guarded, but with her, he seemed unlike himself. Maybe he harboured resentment towards her for a completely different reason, maybe Stanley's death was just an easy and convenient cover.

"I won't tell, but I am curious who this doctor is," I admitted. Red relaxed, a relieved sigh escaping her now unpinched lips.

She slipped back down against the covers, throwing them over her tiny form like a wave about to submerge her. "I can no longer dream. Is that normal?" I hesitated, and she noticed, exhaling noisily. Like it was just another defective trait to add to her ever-increasing list. I laid back on the mattress with a nervous twitch, eyeing the way her cheek squished against the pillowcase.

No matter what I did, what I distracted myself with, I couldn't get this girl out of my head.

I reached over, almost instinctively, tucking a loose strand of hair behind her ear. Her eyes lifted sharply, watching me silently as my fingers hovered beside her face. "You really are beautiful," I whispered, daring myself to be dauntless as I caressed her cheek.

She pulled away sheepishly. "You know that isn't true."

"It isn't?" Our eyes met once more.

Red shifted restlessly, hiding her face beneath the feather duvet. "You saw me... before. There wasn't a single beautiful thing about me. This power has fixed all my imperfections, has healed all my wounds. I look in the mirror, and a stranger looks back." She stilled, breathing unevenly.

"Being the Ultimate Weapon, it's all that I have now, and I don't want it," she continued. "I don't want the ability to annihilate this world every time I feel wronged by it, every time my emotions become too much to handle." Tears filled her scarlet eyes. "I told myself I wouldn't trust anyone anymore, and then, you came around and messed that whole thing up. I'm in bed with you right now, and part of that fucking terrifies me."

"Why does it terrify you?" I asked gently, watching her face against the lamp's artificial brightness.

"Because I don't trust myself around you, and all I want is to be around you." She breathed in deep, sitting up. I mimicked the motion. "You make me feel human."

I held back tears as she pushed my fringe away from my glassy blue eyes. "You make me feel the same way, Red. You have ever since the day we met. And that feeling excites me, it makes me want to be around you, it makes me want to kiss you, to touch you. Don't you feel it?"

"I do. I feel it." She trailed her eyes along the wrinkles in the bed sheet. "But what if I'm not what you want?" She looked up shyly, her cheeks lightly blushed.

"How could you not be?" I hiccupped a happy laugh. "You're gorgeous, authentic, outspoken. I admire the way you rival the world, the way you challenge it. Most people dread that, but you run straight towards it," I expressed adoringly.

"You don't think I'm a fool?"

I smiled awkwardly. "You might be, but you're the bravest,

most beautiful fool I've ever met." I reached my hand forward and embraced her cheek, pulling her face towards mine.

A fierce electricity jolted through my system as my lips met hers. I felt love drunk, high on drugs I had never once tasted. I craved her, I needed her, needed her with a fearsome desire that sparked along my heated skin.

She was all I'd ever wanted. The girl of my dreams. My greatest weakness, my biggest strength. She was rare, and honest, and fearless. And within that moment, she was mine—*all mine.*

We dropped against the bed, her hair like a sail surrounding us as I buried her beneath my firm hold. She was like an addiction I couldn't get enough of, like a compelling punchline to my dull and meaningless life.

She had no idea of the secret I held, the secret I couldn't dare tell another, the secret I thought I would take to my grave. But within her arms, against her heartbeat, surrounded by her scent, there was an unspoken part of me that suddenly longed to tell her everything.

I awoke the next morning to an empty bed. I stirred and sat up against the warm covers, eyeing the room with a dreary haze. I quickly got dressed and headed downstairs.

"Aunt Ems?" I asked as I rounded the corner.

Emma glanced up, currently occupied with pouring herself a coffee. She twisted to face me and held up the kettle. "Do you want one?" I shook my head, and she turned back. "How did you sleep?" she asked, mixing the milk within her vibrant mug.

"Yeah, fine," I murmured, shielding my pink tinged cheeks. She strode over to the bench, wrapping her cold hands around the beverage as she blew against the billowing steam.

"So, what's up?" she queried as I slipped up onto a bar stool.

"Where's Red?" I tried to sound blasé. Emma sipped her coffee, her emerald eyes knowing.

"She said she had something important to take care of this morning," she voiced, casually shrugging. "She was acting weird, so I didn't push it." She flicked her wavy hair behind her shoulder. "What's the deal with you two, anyway?"

"There's no deal," I fibbed, trying to hide my reddening cheeks. She smacked her lips together, unconvinced by my vagueness.

"My dear Ace, it's going to take more than that to persuade me." She playfully chuckled, placing her hands upon the bench. "Although," her cheerful tone faded. "She does seem troubled." I huffed and slouched against the chair.

"She is," I admitted. "That delivery boy from yesterday, they grew up in the system together."

Emma's eyes widened in surprise. "Wow, that must've been tough for her." She plucked her mug from the bench, taking a mouthful of the caffeinated drink. "I'm guessing she isn't taking the whole 'Ultimate Weapon' thing very well?"

"That's an understatement." I snorted, regretting my pejorative tone instantly. "She's trying, at least, but it's challenging for her. The circumstances she died... it wasn't great." Emma eyed me sharply, unsurely.

"*Died?* She died?" I nodded meekly as her body trembled, her green eyes growing wide. "I think that would mess up even the sanest person, Ace. That goes against everything we know as human beings, no wonder she's struggling." She stilled and placed a hand to her lips worriedly. "Stanley's passing, Felix's accusation, Kobi's demands," she paused momentarily. "They're not making this easy for her, are they?" I shook my head defeatedly, but she already knew the answer to that.

When it came to Kobi, Emma understood. Unlike Mum, and her rose-tinted glasses, my aunt had seen and heard of the terrible things Kobi had done. And she judged him accordingly.

"I want to help her. I just don't know how," I fussed, running my hand through my dishevelled hair anxiously.

Emma glanced across at me despairingly, her pinched lips unsure. "I'm sure you'll figure it out. Maybe all she needs is time," she offered, trying to remain hopeful.

I appreciated her optimism, but she didn't know Red like I did. She didn't know that the last thing Red needed was time. In time, she would blow this entire planet to smithereens.

Unfortunately, I needed answers now, I needed to help her now. There wasn't time to plan, time to prepare, time to strategise. *The Ultimate Weapon was a failing mission, and I, its comical captain.*

"*Open up!*" Felix roared as the front door shook with an almighty wallop. "I know you're in there!"

I shot Emma an unpleasant frown before I ventured into the hallway, unlocking the bolted door. Felix barged in, armed and ready. "Where is she?" he demanded.

"Kobi's waiting in the car, we don't have all day." He peered around insolently, scanning the kitchen and lounge for any signs of movement.

"She's not here." I arrogantly shrugged.

His face twisted with rage as his knuckles clenched, and his eyes darkened. "Then where the hell is she?" he bellowed furiously. I shrugged once more. "How could you not *know?* You're meant to be watching her; you're her damn babysitter!"

I crossed my arms in front of my chest, leaning against the handrail. All this time, I'd hoped for my brother, for Felix. Now I only hoped for Red. "I don't know what you want me to say, she isn't here." Felix glowered at me.

"She is the most unstable *bitch* this world has ever seen, are you seriously telling me that you don't know where she is?" he spat through gritted teeth.

I sighed, shaking my head. "She's not a bitch."

Felix suddenly screamed, causing Emma to jump. "I will tear this fucking house apart if you don't bring her here right now!"

I leant off the banister, facing him dead on. "Red isn't here," I snarled as my eyes grew dark, contempt coursing through my veins. "Take your entitlement, take your anger, and get the fuck out of this house."

Felix twitched, his mind thrashing within his dense skull as he reached across and shoved me back. I slightly stumbled, regaining my footing quickly. "She needs to pay for what she did to Stanley," his furious voice trembled.

I watched him with an amusing expression. "You know that wasn't her fault; you need to *stop* blaming her for it! You have no idea how guilty she feels." Anger surged within me, my fists tightening as Felix scoffed dismissively.

"She *should* feel guilty! Stan had no idea what she was capable of. It overwhelmed him, sent his heart into overdrive," he snapped as the room shook around us.

"That isn't Red's fault!" I fired back.

"*No?* Then whose is it?"

I exhaled hard against the atmosphere as disbelief flooded through my system. "You want to blame someone, Felix—*blame* Kobi. Blame Mum. Blame the whole fucking world! I really don't care, but you leave her out of your tyranny. You leave her *out* of your cruel and conceited plans. Red is nothing but an innocent girl within all of this!" My tone wavered as my stomach heaved in and out with agitated breaths. "Keep pushing, Felix, and you won't only destroy her, you'll ruin any chance she has of gaining control over these powers."

Felix watched me unsteadily, fury pounding within him like a beating drum about to burst. He shrieked, throwing his fist in my direction.

I ducked low as his knuckle collided against the wall. Ripples broke out from against the deepened indentation, trailing along the exposed surface with a fierce impel.

Emma gasped, looking away gravely. "Red needs to be under constant control and strict supervision!" Felix turned on his heels and left the house like a steaming pot.

His enraged aroma lingered within the entranceway as I fell back upon the staircase, placing my head within my hands.

He had no idea how stupid he was being, no idea how Red's life had been undeniably flipped. His mind was set, his manner irrational, his emotions bottled-up.

How could I get him to understand? How could I show him there was so much more to this strong-minded girl than meets the eye? So much more than he could ever truly imagine.

CHAPTER 27

RED

I was an imposter within my own skin, unrecognisable no matter what direction I looked. I was weak, senseless, and living a lie.

Suicide should've taken me, should've wrapped me up in a graceful and safe embrace and delivered me to the end of time. But instead, I was tormented with these unmatched powers of the Ultimate Weapon, deadly abilities that drove me towards inescapable self-eradication.

I was getting too close to Ace, my emotions fuddling within my overloaded mind at a rate I couldn't comprehend them.

The way he made me feel was unlike any other, the way he undoubtedly believed in what I believed to be my biggest inabilities. These emotions were unstable, chaotic, irrational. And I hated myself for them, hated myself for falling in love with him when I *knew* I didn't deserve him.

There was too much at stake, too much to risk. I had no right to bet the survival of the entire universe against something as useless as love... *but I never asked for this. I never even wanted it.*

In my human life, I didn't even know Ace existed. I was content with leaving this world behind, with soaring above, but the universe wouldn't let me go. I was more valuable in death than I had ever been alive.

I just wanted to scream, to breakdown and collapse alongside my bare and naked body. I wasn't what the world needed, wasn't what it signed up for. I was a sin bigger than the Earth, shunned by God, punished by my own foolish act of rebellion.

I hated the words within my mouth, within my head, hated the way my mind was shutting down and closing off.

I was dissociating, disconnecting, unable to cope with the responsibility of a power not made for this world. A power not designed for me. I was meant to be dead... not falling in love with the one stranger who'd been nicer to me than anyone had in years.

Car horns blared, and I gasped, tearing my gaze from the reflection against the window. I looked up warily, watching the construction workers as they laboured above, fixing the windowpanes my power caused to shatter.

I knew I shouldn't have been this close to headquarters, this close to Kobi, but it was one of the only places that felt like a home. Within that bunker, I felt safe, my power concealed, my mind determined.

My palms flaked and peeled, and I picked at the dead skin rigorously, eager to tear every inch from my inhuman flesh.

My brown eyes looked up sharply as laughter filled my eardrums. A family of three strode down the sidewalk with a small and enthusiastic child. She was walking between them, holding tight to both their hands. They looked so cheerful, so content.

I couldn't even begin to express how much I missed my own parents; how guilty I felt over an accident I had been the only survivor. And now, I was struggling to hold onto my shattered mind, struggling to hold onto this second chance at life I didn't even want.

None of this would've happened if our car hadn't collided against the night. I wouldn't have been left orphaned, unloved, alone. I needed my mum's affection, my dad's protection. My heart filled with uncertainty; my mind lost within the haze of my own emotions.

I needed them now more than I ever ha*d*.

A sharp breath escaped my lungs as I felt Felix's cold power seep within my bones. I clenched my knuckles, feeling the uncontrolled darkness from within him. It zapped and flickered along my energy-filled veins.

He would come for me; I knew he would. He blamed me for Stanley's death, and I knew I deserved to be blamed. Deserved more than a fractured nose that realigned in seconds.

I shut the feelings out, desperate for the world to give me a much-needed break. I died. I ended my sad existence to ascend above, to escape the pain of being human. Only, I couldn't have been more wrong, I couldn't have screwed up any worse. I was moving through the fire, running barefoot along the brimstone. I hated myself for it, for the mistake I made the moment I collided against that train.

I had pushed myself too far, had clambered for the closest thing to redemption and scuffed the very fabric of time in doing so.

"Watch out!" a scream pierced the air with desperation.

I gasped, breaking away from my obsessive state as a panel of glass knocked me down forcibly, shattering against my form with a hefty and hell-bent punch.

"Call an ambulance!" someone cried as I shook the broken fragments off myself and timidly stood, my cheeks reddening with embarrassment.

The men in high-visibility uniforms shuddered to a sudden stop, glaring at me like I was a figure torn straight from their nightmares. "You're... okay?" I eyed them watchfully, their faces twisting with distress and disbelief.

"Unfortunately, yeah," I uttered as I slipped my hands into my front pockets, feeling shards of glass between my fingers.

A bald man with a neat appearance stepped forward, eyeing me worriedly as his steel caps crushed the debris beneath his tread. "How are you still alive? I saw it, that panel, it took you out. At the very least, you should be injured."

A dull laugh escaped my lips as I shrugged in response to their troubled expressions. If only something as simple as that could end the powers within me.

"I'm the Ultimate Weapon; I can't fucking die." I outstretched my arms, smiling despite myself, high on an inebriated feeling that tumbled against my better judgement.

I turned and started up the pathway, pulling my hood over my frizzy hair as my emotions jumbled within my head. I felt so lost, so unfulfilled and worthless.

Suddenly, I stilled, eyeing the building where the labourers remained, dumbfounded, relieved, confused. It was something they would never come to understand. It was something inhuman, demonic, possessive.

Well, at least they didn't have a lawsuit against them for my ill-timed demise. I scoffed, trailing my wide eyes up the building's shimmering frame.

The feeling of retribution knocked against my petite figure, and I gasped. I darted towards the building, dodging, weaving, manoeuvring past the bustling flow of commuters.

I raced for the emergency stairwell, swiping an unrestricted card from atop the housekeeping cart. I impelled the hefty door open and hurried up the foul-smelling stairs, desperation clawing from within as my mind silenced and my heartbeat leapt.

Marked floor numbers loomed above me as I bunched my jumper sleeves against my elbows and forced my feet faster beneath me.

The emergency lights flickered on with a static buzz as I ascended at a rapid pace. Abruptly, I stilled, puffing hard against the 35th floor landing as I placed the stolen card flat alongside the scanner. It beeped green, unlocking.

I stepped inside the apartment and screamed, clutching my overexerted heart as it pounded fiercely within my chest.

The room unfolded before me, manic and uncontrolled, as I zeroed in on the floor-to-ceiling windows nearest the far wall. I swallowed hard and jammed my dried lips together, grabbing a knife from the kitchen bench.

Chaotic warfare bombarded my brain as I ran full speed and leapt towards the windowpane. I collided against the ruptured compound as adrenaline engulfed my entire failing form.

My hair whipped backwards, weaving manically within the air that whistled against me. I glanced up, eyeing myself within the reflection of the windows. *I was unrecognisable.*

This wasn't me; this wasn't who I wanted to be. I thought I knew myself, thought I could find myself within the thickest of forestry, the deepest of caves, the darkest of nights. But unfortunately, I was wrong. I didn't know this girl, I didn't recognise this beast, I didn't consent to this weapon of war I was to become.

A teardrop slipped from my eye socket as the ground beneath grew closer, and closer, and closer.

People gasped, ramming backwards with fearful and stunned expressions as I plummeted towards the solid soil.

I slammed catlike against the pavement, my bones snapping like twigs as cracks rippled out from the indentation. I stood, un-bruised, unharmed, the knife securely within my grasp.

My devastated scream pierced the atmosphere as the glass waterfalled around me almost poetically. Police sirens echoed from far away, filling the air with desperate wails of salvation as onlookers stilled and eyed the knife within my firm grip.

My glassy eyes pierced against my open palm, daring it to glow as people grouped and bunched around me, watching on fearfully. Their curiosity too great for their common sense.

An agonising screech filled the atmosphere as power expelled from my nail-bitten fingertips. It wrapped itself against me with a cogent familiarity.

I felt engulfed within the fatal flames, felt electrified within the tormenting torture.

Suddenly, Felix's power knocked me off my feet. My body flew through the air, slamming forcefully against a concrete pillar. I hurriedly stood, eyeing him with an agitated snarl.

"What the fuck is wrong with you?" he furiously bellowed as Ace appeared alongside him, watching me with an alarmed ex-pression that overwhelmed his perfect blue eyes.

I shrieked and flung my arm forward, wrapping Felix within the electric and haywire buzz that surged through my veins intoxicatingly.

My eyes shone, my body torn apart by the alien glow inside as my skin seared away, revealing an entity of pure energy that radiated inhumanly against the pathway.

My breath shuddered as I tightened my hand around Felix. He kicked and spluttered against my forceful hold as I moved towards him. "You do not challenge me," I threatened, my tone dark and foreboding. "I am the Ultimate Weapon. You bow to me!"

My entire frame violently shook as a silence I had yearned for overtook my fractured form. I begged for nothing more than the numbness to permanently overtake my rage-fuelled mind, no matter the cost.

I could no longer control this power, these emotions, my will to live. I no longer cared to rewire my brain and start anew. *I was done.*

"Red!" Ace bellowed urgently, dodging the zaps and pulsations my power electrified against the biosphere.

"*No!*" I cried as I held the knife against my skin and sliced. I gasped fearfully as the wound instantaneously healed. "No—" I muttered, stumbling forward.

Fear welled within my stomach as orange teardrops cascaded from my shaky eyes. I cut the knife against my skin once more, desperate to sense the pain, frantic to feel human, dying to change my fate.

Nothing, absolutely nothing. *Again, again, again.* My dire mind shrieked within the void spaces of my consciousness as my hand instinctively carved. My naked skin laced with cuts for mere milliseconds before invisible fingers stitched the scars into oblivion.

Escalated breaths escaped my lips as tears collided against the knife's surface.

I stilled and angled the weapon towards me, the reflection revealing a disgusting and ugly girl ready to implode. Could this really be what I wanted? Was a war inside my mind really the solution? For the longest time, I had thought suicide was the answer. Turned out, it wasn't. It was a question, an idea, a deadly longing. But suicide hadn't saved me, hadn't eased the pain, hadn't healed the animosity. In fact, I'd foolishly trapped myself within circumstances far worse than humanity ever had, and I had no one else to blame but myself for this eternal suffering.

Maybe Ace was right.

Maybe I needed to go into the past to change the future. But no matter what I did, or what I changed, this power would be waiting for me. *Endlessly and always.*

I was the Ultimate Weapon, dead or alive. Only in death could I harness these abilities, and only whilst alive could my body ache, and age, and bleed.

"Red, stop!" Ace cried out desperately.

I looked up, fear colliding within as he slammed against me, holding my flushed cheeks as my arms dropped from exhaustion. Felix crashed against the ground, bones snapping, as the knife clattered upon the pavement.

"Please, Red, don't do this. Do not lose control of yourself." I hiccupped an electrified chuckle, my mind coming in and out of consciousness as I melted against his soothing touch.

"I give up."

Tears slid from Ace's pastel-blue eyes as he pinched his lips together and frantically shook his head. "No, Red, *please,* you don't want that—you can't. You are stronger than this, I know you are," he begged as the world unravelled before us.

I blinked a painful force field into existence as my scarlet eyes rolled into the back of my head, my knees weakening. I fell against his strengthened hold as my body violently trembled.

"Red, you can't give up," his voice hitched in uneven patterns. "*Please!*" Ace rested his forehead on mine. "Stop hurting yourself," he pleaded against my depressed and distorted soul.

"I'm falling in love with you," I muttered with an unwilling stutter as the powers surged within me.

Ace sniffled, a warm smile spreading along his perfect lips and against his tearful features. "Me, too," he confessed as I slunk against his entire body.

"Lock me up. Throw away the key. I am coming undone." I shook as the power blinked out like a broken bulb. "End me," I breathlessly begged as I fell against the ground next to him, my head hitting hard atop the concrete as the hazy blur within my eyes faded to black.

Within that misgiving moment, I had given up, had lost my mind, had endangered the untameable powers within me. I was exhausted, weak, and I was done with the perturbed whispers within my broken mind when all I wanted was to scream, and screech, and shriek.

I was done fooling myself, done believing I would improve. My heart was jaded, blackened, scarred. I was done masquerading as this all-powerful weapon. My body was untouchable, my skin impenetrable, but I couldn't survive without the pain, without the hurt, without the ache against my skin.

I had let Ace down, had let my parents down, but I knew, I had let myself down even more.

CHAPTER 28

ACE

"Get her on the table, now," Kobi commanded as I heaved Red onto the metal compound. Felix scurried behind us, watching on with an unsettled and uncertain expression.

Kobi reached across and grabbed Red's hand, analysing the flaked and dried skin along her palm.

"Fuck," he uttered, throwing her arm back against the table. "We need this under control. We need to limit her powers."

I scoffed, eyeing him unsurely, noting the cream-coloured cast against his wrist. "You're insane. You can't restrict the unmatched powers of the Ultimate Weapon," I curtly objected.

"Felix and I are an imbalance, our abilities susceptible to inter-ference, but Red's—" I broke off, shaking my head. "You can't limit her powers."

"You saw her. She is *unhinged.*" Kobi eyed me with daggers, his expression fearsome, his mind avid.

"Kobi's right," Felix casually interjected. I glanced back at him with angered irritation, but he just coolly shrugged. "It's only a matter of time before she turns her power against you," he stated, eyeing me arrogantly.

Doubt festered within my mind like a growing infestation as I peeked at Red's pretty and pale face.

It was evident she was unable to control her abilities, and it was ridiculous to think our small amount of guidance could ever measure up to the omnipotence she held. She was consumed by her emotions, by her inability to die and inability to hurt.

Maybe this method towards her madness was best suited. I just hoped she didn't fault me for complying. "How do you even plan to do this?" I asked of Kobi.

He ran his hand along his jaw restlessly. "It's a liquid injected into the bloodstream. I don't know how it works, just that it does," he quipped.

So, that's how our powers were being restricted. Honestly, I expected more, expected worse. But now that I'd had the time to process it, I knew Stanley wasn't at fault. Sure, he was compliant with the enemy, but he did it for the right reasons. He did it for us.

Kobi turned to Felix. "Get me Stanley's things." Felix rushed towards Stanley's chemical cupboard, reaching for the neat basket of syringes, test tubes, and liquid solutions.

I looked away as Kobi searched through the information on the bottles. "Got it," he said triumphantly as he slid a syringe within a colourless liquid, filling the barrel. He eyed the dosage before fiddling with Red's arm, pressing around her inner elbow to locate the vein.

"Here. Hold her," he instructed, eyeing Felix narrowly. Felix nodded, resting his hands gently against Red's shoulders.

A little *too* gently for someone who wanted her to pay for

Stanley's untimely death. It just didn't sit right with me, none of this did. I watched him so unsurely, at the way he observed Kobi, at the way he held Red.

He was meant to be so angry at her, so outraged, only times like now you wouldn't even think it. His grasp against her was near pointless, his fingertips barely brushing the thick material of her jumper. What kind of twisted game was he playing? What logical sense did this make inside his egocentric mind?

Red stirred and Felix jumped.

Kobi eyed her urgently, plunging the last of the liquid within her vein. "Get her to the underground cell. We can't risk anything." Felix nodded his agreement as he lifted Red into his arms.

He looked down at her and trembled. And if I didn't know better, I'd think he had feelings for her. But that couldn't be right, Felix only cared about Felix. There had to be something else at play here, but what? And why couldn't I figure it out?

I stepped before Felix, leading him to the fortified cell below. This was the serious one, the one constructed beneath the bunker, protected by a code, and built with the strongest elements against man and superhuman.

He rested Red's body gently upon the thin mattress, placing her limbs cautiously by her sides. "Why do you care so much about her?" I hissed, leaning against the bars. Felix exhaled an aggravated huff and turned to face me. His eyes dark, ominous, his stature boorish. I shrugged disdainfully, a bitter taste filling my mouth as I eyed him loftily. "What? You're meant to hate her, remember that?"

He scoffed and airily shook his head, his black hair shifting with the swift movement. "You sound jealous." I laughed dully, trying to act unfazed. "Whatever," he muttered gruffly.

"You blame her for what happened to Stanley, just admit it!" I fired at him, leaning off the bars. Felix rounded the cell wall, inches from my angered stance.

"Yeah, I do, I blame her, but—" he broke off abruptly, shaking his head in irritation. "It's none of your goddamn business, Ace, so stay the fuck out of it," he snapped before he turned and exited the room.

The monitor beeped, followed by an arrogant slam of a closing door. I exhaled hard and glanced across at Red, my anger subsiding as I watched her tiny form shiver.

In a way, I felt I'd failed her. I knew her mind would destroy itself, and it had.

I felt responsible. I should've protected her, should've tried harder to ease her tormented and destructive mind.

She was an abused girl who used self-harm to lessen her own pain, a foolish pastime for a girl with so much potential. She was wounded in a way I feared I would never be able to wholly understand.

She stirred, weakly pushing herself from the mattress. She clambered to her knees and tumbled across the floor, glancing up at me as her bottom lip slipped open, her eyes wide and unsure.

"Ace?" she questioned timidly. I crouched against the bars and levelled myself to her eyesight as she crawled closer.

"What happened?" she whispered as she placed her hand to her forehead and groaned, her tiny body suppressed with so much nervousness, pain, and despair. "I don't remember… I recall dog walking that morning, and then," her voice fell away like a wave lashing against the shore, her mind struggling to recount the brutal happenings of something so illogical.

"Wait." I heedlessly chuckled. "Did you say dog walking?"

She pulled a face. "Yeah, but I wasn't meant to," she muttered dryly as her cheeks blushed with embarrassment.

"So, that's how you survived at the motel," I thought aloud.

Red reluctantly nodded. "Cash in hand, no one's the wiser." She shrugged. "I wasn't paying much for the accommodation, but I needed food," she muttered, her defeated, drained, and worn-down tone filling the bunker. "What happened to me? I feel so weak."

She lifted her hands to her face, peering down at them with confusion. I eyed her unsurely, watching as her skin flaked and peeled. She picked against it hastily.

"I'm shedding," she hissed, then stilled, slapping her hands against the floor in defeat. The sound rang loudly around us as she glared at me with a hopeless look. "Ace, what the hell happened to me?" she begged as I observed her through the bars with an empathetic expression.

All I wanted was to wrap my arms around her fragile form and tell her everything was going to be okay, even though not an ounce of me believed it.

"Okay." I swallowed hard, preparing myself for the uncomfortable conversation. "You jumped from Kobi's penthouse," I delicately expressed. She gasped, covering her mouth. "You cut yourself with a knife. Multiple times…"

I looked down, unable to hold eye contact any longer. She stifled her tears, trying to remain strong. "Talk to me, Red, about the abuse, about the self-harm, make it make sense to me." I glanced up and met her bloodshot brown eyes, begging for her to let me in, pleading for her to bare her soul.

If she couldn't recall jumping, or the knife, she wouldn't have remembered those words spoken. Maybe that was a good thing, for now. I couldn't let our feelings interfere with this rescue mission. Red needed my help. And she needed it before the entire universe suffered her destructive and violent wrath.

"Make it make sense?" she echoed my words. I nodded, dying inside from the sorrowful look that flashed against her defeated features. "Ace, it doesn't even make sense to me." She lifted her glassy eyes and met mine. "But if it's an answer you need, then here goes..."

She breathed in deep, bracing herself. "My life was perfect, and then we crashed. In that moment, everything I knew, everything I loved, was gone. Taken by an unkind and unknown force. I experienced abuse for the first time in my second foster home, and it only got worse from there. I was just a kid, gullible and stupid. After a while, I placed normality within the abuse, and I started doing it to myself just to pass the time." She exhaled raggedly, looking away like she was ashamed.

"Even when I escaped, I didn't. I thought it would be easy to heal. I thought that once I took myself out of the foster system, I would be okay, but sadly I wasn't. I was already too far gone." Her voice shuddered and shook. "I thought suicide was the answer. I thought it was my only answer."

I wanted to be as vulnerable as she was. I wanted to express my mistreatments and connect with her on that same level, but my past was nowhere near as soul-crushing or gut-wrenching as hers.

She was forced to put her faith within the system, and the system did nothing but fail her. Sure, I missed my dad, but it was hard to mourn a life I never even knew.

I wasn't abused like Red, wasn't passed from home to home like a hot potato that nobody wanted.

The tests Kobi forced us through were strict, challenging, fatiguing, but scarcely violent. We didn't break bones, we didn't scar skin, we didn't worsen wounds.

When we got hurt, we shook it off, and our healing capabilities took care of the rest. Kobi rarely harmed us, but that didn't stop his hateful words, his short-tempered reactions, or his decisions over our lives that were indisputably final.

He had manipulated Felix and I into disliking one another, a ripple effect from the constant comparisons over our inhuman abilities. He planted the seeds long before we even knew what they were for.

To be taken away so brutally from this life, from Felix, from Stanley, would've condemned me to the far reaches of my own tarnished mind for eternity.

So, I couldn't blame Red for retreating within herself, for concealing her past within that fragile form of hers. She had so much potential, so much drive to reinforce change, to inspire revolution, but she was trapped. Trapped within the abuse she could never outrun, the abuse she could never undo.

She cupped her hands and pressed her lips tight against her thumbs, restraining her tears. Hastily, she dropped her arms, eyeing me straight on. "And it didn't work," she voiced tonelessly, her eyes unreadable.

"What didn't work?" I eyed her unsurely.

She chuckled dryly. "You cannot limit my power, Ace. You cannot suppress it; you cannot restrict it." She weakly stood. "I felt the pull, the burn. I am the Ultimate Weapon, and I am one hundred percent of this entity. Impediments will only falter." I shifted uneasily from foot to foot.

She knew, but of course, she knew.

Her bloodstream wasn't filled with blood, wasn't filled with plasma. Nothing but haywire electricity zapped and pulsed within her veins. There was no way the solution could've gone unnoticed within her. It was a foolish thing to think.

She sighed suddenly as conflicted thoughts flashed within her honey-brown eyes. "I grew up thinking there were only ever heroes and villains. That the line between was so obvious and distinguishable, but it was never that simple. It's hard to be a hero, it's vain to be a villain. I don't know what I am, but I know I have the capability to be either. And that scares me." She smiled awkwardly and shrugged empathetically.

"I have the potential to be exceedingly good for this world or exceptionally bad. And someone like me, someone who has seen the worst of humankind, I don't believe I should have the option to choose. Because either way, I end up losing." Her dismal tone filled the air around us.

I eyed her with a steady expression, watching as her hair tumbled by the sides of her face, perfectly framing it. "What do you lose?" I asked curiously. She lifted her chin to meet my jaded blue eyes, her smile unsure, her expression conflicted.

"Myself."

CHAPTER 29

RED

I tossed and turned against the uneven mattress, missing the safe feeling of Ace's arms around me. I sat upright and scoffed, anger momentarily flooding my weak system as I swiftly stood.

I paced the cell uneasily as overwhelmed agitation overtook my listless thoughts. "What are you doing?" I gasped and froze, looking into the darkened passageway.

"Felix?" I asked with a curious tone as he turned the flashlight on and skimmed it against my tense form.

"Yeah," Felix responded as my eyes flinched from the unexpected intensity. "I needed to talk to you." He placed the torch beside him, its artificial glow lighting up the room at a strange angle, its tunnelled brightness an abstracted display.

I straightened, watching him with confusion. "If you want to fight me, you should come this side of the cell." He laughed, the sound odd within my eardrums. "This about a truce?"

He shook his head. "It's about Ace, sort of," he voiced, clicking his tongue nervously as I lessened the space between us and silently slipped against the floor.

"He likes you, obviously." He hiccupped a sudden chuckle as I smiled and rested my chin upon a horizontal bar. "Problem is, now he thinks I like you, too."

My doubtful eyes narrowed. "Do you?" I criticised; my tone laced with unhidden judgement. Felix laughed once more.

"Not like that." His cheeks blushed. "Look, I blamed you for Stanley's death, and that was wrong of me to do so, but the only other person to blame was myself." He stilled thoughtfully, running his thumb along his pierced lip. "I don't want a rift between us, you're the Ultimate Weapon, you're linked to my powers no matter what I think, no matter what I do. And I…" his voice trailed off. "I feel your power within me, and it gives me hope."

I chuckled despite myself. *He wasn't serious, was he?*

"I know it sounds dumb," he continued. "My power is dark, defiant, disruptive, Ace's is just intrusive, but yours—" He eyed me through his darkened fringe, leaning in closer. "Your power feels strong, capable, rebellious. It feels hopeful." I lowered my uneven breaths, watching him steadily within the strewn light. "Ace is going to think whatever the hell Ace wants to think, but I wanted you to know the truth."

I adjusted my posture and tilted my head, smiling across at him. "I appreciate that," I uttered. He chuckled softly and sat back, stretching his legs.

"Kobi's *real* pissed about the broken wrist." He smiled teasingly as he placed his hands by the back of his head and glanced up at the ceiling, the manufactured light illuminating it poorly. I exhaled a repressed laugh and lifted my chin, copying Felix's motion.

"I'm sorry about Stanley," I whispered as I ran my chipped nails through my hair, catching on the tangles.

Felix lowered his head, our gazes colliding. His pale eyes were vulnerable. A way I'd never seen them before.

He wiped at his face as a stray tear escaped. "I should go." He stood hurriedly, coughing awkwardly. "Here." He passed me the torch, causing our fingertips to graze.

He glanced up, his breath hitching in an awkward pattern as I eyed him warily, watching the wheels in his mind smoke like rubber against asphalt. "Red?"

"Yeah?" I held my breath, unsure of the words that awaited.

"I'm sorry I hurt you." I tilted my head in wonder, analysing his sympathetic features.

"Yeah, Felix. I am, too." His eyebrows creased in confusion. "I shouldn't have—" Suddenly, the scanner clicked green, the door opening.

"Felix?" Kobi queried as the fluorescent lights switched on. I winced at their sudden harshness as Felix slid his hand from the torch and brushed by Kobi, not another word or second glance escaping him.

Kobi spun to face me, striding towards the chair that rested before the cell. He sat down, eyeing me quizzically. "Ace tells me it didn't work." He slid a hand along his gelled hair, then sat them neatly in his lap, as neatly as he could with the inconvenient cast.

"It didn't," I confirmed. "And now, I know how you're limiting their abilities."

He eyed me with an angered and apprehensive expression. "You best not threaten me, Red," he cautioned, his demeanour unsettled.

I sat upon the uncomfortable mattress and leant against the wall, bringing my knees to my chest. "I'm not trying to." I calmly shrugged. "I wanted to know how you were restricting their powers, and now, I do," I muttered, placing my head by the wall. "It doesn't do me any good, though, not when I can't control my own abilities."

"Speaking of, I have another doctor who will be examining you," he instructed. My eyes widened as I looked to him in surprise. Felix *was* right.

He stood, patting the unwanted creases from atop his trousers. "Her name's Dr Cleo Jenson. Keep the information to yourself for now. I don't need—*or want*—any unnecessary input from either Ace or Felix." He rolled his eyes, his expression soured.

"Now, if you'll excuse me, I'm off to clean up that unfortunate mess you caused our neighbouring building. Quite the expensive bill you've cost me." My mind fell quiet as I watched him steadily, ignoring his comment about my careless and costly crusade. "This doctor, can she help me?" A sliver of hope laced my dull tone.

Kobi stilled and glanced across at me, his face unreadable. "I'm counting on it," he confidently stated before he swiped his card and flipped the switch, leaving me alone once more within the dark and silent cell.

I snuggled into my jumper, reaching for the flashlight. I activated the power button, observing the manufactured light as it danced along the lifeless and cream-coloured walls.

Since my conversation with Ace, I had remembered every penitent detail of yesterday's happenings. The way the glass panel had shattered around me, the way I'd irrepressibly leapt from the highest storey, the way I'd slashed the knife against my exposed skin…

I was ashamed of my behaviour, regretful of Ace's presence when it was done. I had never intended for him to see that, to see me cutting, carving, slicing my own flesh.

There were execrable capabilities within me that I had never wished for Ace, or anyone else, to bear witness to. And sadly, that was one of them. I needed to apologise to him... but I knew that meant having a conversation about it. I didn't even want to think about it, let alone discuss it. I wanted to forget.

Forget like I had tried to do so many times before.

It was wrong the way they treated me, it was wrong the way I treated myself. Those beatings were never mine to take, those crooked views were never mine to express, those hateful words were never mine to hold. And yet, I had, and to this day, I continued to let them overwhelm and overtake me.

I was free of the past, free of the torments and pains I had so unfairly suffered. This power had the potential to save me, but it also had the potential to ruin me.

My eyes examined the faint lines and wrinkles buried beneath my flaked skin. I had once believed that those lines could tell my future, believed that they could guide me to the great beyond. I had no idea of the powers I would one day come to possess.

I *was* the Ultimate Weapon, a legendary tale. My birth alone marked an epoch within time and history. I was unlike anything the world had ever seen, had ever known. I was special, vital for the survival of the universe. So then, why did I continue to view myself as insignificant, irrelevant, worthless?

No self-respected deity would ever act like this. They knew their worth, they inspired change, they led revolutions. I had to have a meaningful purpose within this world, a reason to be, a place where I belonged.

I needed to stop hurting myself; to stop the hateful speech I spoke within my tarnished mind. I needed to learn my worth, to stop pretending I didn't have any.

I curled my fingers, eyeing my jagged nails bitten down to their nubs. It was hard to know when to stop chewing when I couldn't feel the pain.

My hand dropped as a frustrated exhale escaped my lips. I stared at the tunnelled light as it propelled from the torch, re-membering the way the sunlight had reflected against the surface of this building.

Why did I do it? Why did I jump? Why did I grab that knife? I was so angry at myself for the pathetic answers I devised.

And then there was Ace...

To him, I had naïvely voiced that I was falling in love, and in return, he revealed his true feelings towards me.

I didn't quite know what to do with that information, didn't quite know how to handle it. It was clear we felt the same way, but could it even work out right between us? Ace was so kind and gentle, I was so loud and arrogant.

I sighed and rested against the mattress, flipping the woollen blanket over my trembling silhouette.

From here on out, no more self-harm, no more degrading talk, no more anger-induced breakdowns. I had to improve my mind, strengthen my power, enhance my knowledge.

I was reborn for a reason, I was awakened for a cause, I was saved for a purpose.

An orange glow abruptly shone from my naked skin. I sat up urgently, throwing the blanket down on the floor. I watched my palm, studying the pulsating flickers upon my peeling skin. My shaky breaths lowered as I concentrated on my hand.

A haywire buzz jolted from within and against the room, filling the space with a bright, electric, and awe-filled radiance. I laughed gleefully and stood as illuminated spangles twinkled within the concealed room.

I pushed my palm outward, propelling the orange waves to encircle the space as my scarlet eyes watched in amazement, a joyful smile spreading along my lips.

I transformed the powers within the room, creating multiple sized force fields that ballooned out around me. It ignited a safe and secure feeling inside my heart, the alien glow soothing upon my heated skin. I wanted to hold onto this moment, wanted to lock it up safely within my misused heart and throw away the key.

Inside myself, I felt divine, ethereal. Was it truly possible for me to wield these powers without pain, to dabble within these superhuman abilities without excruciating consequence?

All I had to do was believe in myself, believe in this power, believe that I could speak to myself with the very same positive assurance as my parents did.

I inhaled a large lungful as a force field grew exponentially around me, sucking me in like a deadly vortex. I gasped for breath, spinning, spiralling within the agitated glow before I was hauled against the floor like a lifeless rag doll.

An annoyed huff escaped my lips as I stood, inspecting my shadowy and ghostlike skin. I felt weightless, floaty, like I was wide awake in a lucid dream.

"I feel her, but it doesn't *feel* like her," Felix loudly voiced.

I glanced up, eyeing around the bunker with sudden scepticism. "I don't understand it, either. We need to go to her," Ace declared.

"No, she needs time by herself in a secure location," Kobi instructed as I rounded the corridor, watching them through the faint orange glow of my cornea.

"Why are you huddled in the hallway?" I judged mockingly, my voice angelic and airy. They gasped, slamming their shocked gazes against me as I squirmed uncomfortably, glancing between their doubtful and dumbfounded expressions.

"*What*—what the fuck?" Felix shuddered frightfully as he stumbled back. I watched them steadily, unsure of their sudden terror-stricken looks and tentative reactions.

"Red," Ace whispered worriedly, stepping between them.

"Why are you so afraid of me?" I watched Ace's throat shift as he swallowed hard, a trickle of sweat forming against his brow. "Ace..." I muttered anxiously, trying desperately to understand their peculiar body language.

"You're translucent."

I paused midstep, stifling an uncomfortable laugh as an insecure and exposed feeling grasped hold of me. I peered down at my skin, observing sallowed flesh before I aimed a fingertip against my arm and pressed. It dived right through the bone. A terrified gasp filled the air as I stared in disbelief. I turned and ran for the below cell, unsure how I even knew what direction to take.

They followed behind as I sprinted down the staircase and slammed against the hefty door.

The scanner rapidly blinked against my faded eyeballs as I impelled the door open, stepping into a room thick with electric pulsations.

I moved towards the cell with a hesitant wobble as they entered, watching me unsurely. I met Ace's expression, his wide eyes intense and terrified. I swallowed hard and forced myself to peek beyond the bars.

My eyes fearfully widened as I watched my other self within the cell. She was afloat, suspended midair on her back like she was fast asleep. Her limbs hung motionless as a piercing glow protruded from her chest and waves levitated across her.

She was so peaceful, so safe. Surrounded by the one thing that was strong enough to protect her from anything.

I placed my hand over my heart, feeling the heat, the pulse, the power. "Are you in pain right now?" Ace asked hesitantly. I looked back to him, eyeing the three of them clustered within the corner of the room, and shook my head.

"The power feels stable, freeing," I breathlessly voiced, my heartbeat pulsing at a steady rhythm. "Come look." I held out my hand to Ace, but he hesitated, an encouraging smile meeting my lips.

He stepped towards me with a doubtful stagger, fear breaking through his tattered being as he glimpsed my other self within the cell. He rammed back with eyes wide and unaware as panicked breaths ascended his windpipe.

My hand dropped as I exhaled a breath, realigning my centre with the powerful abilities that surged within and around me. I shut my eyes tight and gasped as I morphed against my other self, falling from the air manically.

I whimpered and sat upright, the orange light blinking out of existence as my translucent skin changed back to its original opaque.

Ace tiptoed towards the cell, watching me through the bars with a nervous glance. I looked across at him and smiled shyly.

"What—*in the actual fuck*—was that?" Felix unexpectedly bellowed, and I couldn't help but laugh.

CHAPTER 30

ACE

I tapped the pen against the desk absentmindedly, listening to the rhythmic clank against the metal surface as my mind repeated the uncanny events of yesterday's happenings. I couldn't help but think of the way Red had appeared so supernaturally and ghost-like.

It wasn't possible to appear in two places at once, wasn't possible to detach from your own self and exist within both entities concurrently. It reminded me of when we'd gone back in time to the places that had most affected her life. That definitely shouldn't have been possible, either.

The powers of the Ultimate Weapon were never predicted to be this powerful, this reality bending and bizarre. She could challenge the very meaning of time itself. She could rival anything the world has ever known. She was an inhuman force not to be reckoned with.

"What are you doing?" I fearfully jumped as Felix drummed against the surface of the desk mischievously. He slipped into a leather chair and scooched behind me, reading the computer screen over my shoulder. "This about Red?"

I exhaled sharply. "It's none of your business," I snapped, angling the monitor away from his pressing stare. He huffed and relaxed, spinning in the chair playfully. I rolled my eyes and refocused myself, scanning the various documents.

Red seemed to be doing better, her mind improving, her self-esteem increasing. It was good to finally see her adjusting to the profound powers within. She had been practising her abilities, learning to control them without pain or disfigurement. I was proud of her for that.

"Have you spoken to Lottie, or Marshall?" Felix asked suddenly. I stilled and glanced across at him with a worried look.

Stanley's wife and grandchild... it was surreal to think of them within this world without him.

Lottie was a darling old lady, and Marshall a downhearted and unhappy soul. But he wasn't always like that. Seven years ago, Marshall had lost his father in a tragic accident. To Stanley and Lottie, they had lost their only child. No one saw it coming.

He was there one day, gone the next.

In all the years I had known Stanley, I had never seen him that closed off or depressed. And for the painful months that followed, I worried I would never see his smiling face or hear his cheerful laughter ever again.

Lottie had very much done the same. She had retreated within herself, leaving the house only to visit the local church and cemetery.

It was a horrific time in their lives, and a few people speculated their marriage would end because of it. They took some time apart to grieve in their own ways, unable to unitedly cope with the weight of their son's loss.

They reconciled after a belated time, finding comfort within the arms of one another. Stanley adored his wife, and she adored him just the same. They refused to allow their grief to break the foundation of their marriage.

Marshall was fourteen when it happened, now twenty-one. I tried to reach out a few times, but he found solace in drugs and alcohol. After a year had passed, Stanley forced him into a drug rehabilitation program.

The whole thing had gone south quick, and for a few years after, Marshall had resented him for it. But thankfully, the treatment worked. He was clean now and had even thanked Stanley for the push towards sobriety.

"I haven't." I shook my head regretfully. "I called Marshall, but it went straight to voicemail," I muttered truthfully. "Have you?"

Felix tapped his fingers gently against the arm of the chair, then nodded. "I talked to Marshall. He relapsed." I eyed him sharply as my mind shook. *That couldn't be right.*

Felix clicked his tongue nervously. "He doesn't even want to think about it. Lottie's putting on a brave face, but I doubt that holds behind closed doors. They've already started preparing for his wake."

I sighed and buried my head into my hands. I didn't even want to think about the funeral, about laying Stanley to his final resting place.

I hated the way the depressed and debilitated thought entwined within me, tightening around my bones. I wanted to ignore it, disregard it, to stay concealed within my misconception.

"We should go visit Marshall," Felix suggested as he leant against the chair and crossed his arms in front of his chest.

I stilled my restless motions and raised an eyebrow in surprise. "What?" I snapped as curiosity piqued my interest.

He heedlessly shrugged. "We should take Red to meet him," he concluded. I stood, watching him like a hawk. "I *might* have mentioned something about blaming her." He looked away as I exhaled hard, anger flashing against my features.

"You told him it was Red's fault?" I zeroed in on him, eyeing him down like a bull did its red flagged target.

Felix scoffed dismissively and stood to stand equal against me. "I was angry," he barked.

"That's a pathetic excuse," I snarled, crossing my arms.

"It wasn't my finest moment, I'll give you that." He huffed, shaking his head. "Look, I'm sorry. I didn't mean to throw her under the bus, I just started venting, and then—" he broke off abruptly. "I got caught up," he admitted, his pale eyes expressive and regretful. I calmed my attitude, relaxing my wound-up mind that was ready to strike.

"You really think introducing them is a good idea?" I analysed his conflicted motions.

He shrugged obliquely. "Yeah, I think so. We don't want to risk a scene at Stanley's memorial service."

I hesitated. "I thought it would be best if she didn't attend." Felix stilled, watching me with a bitter expression as tension sliced between us, thick and unmoving.

"And why the hell is that?" he snapped.

I was worried about Red, about her mind deteriorating. She was finally improving, finally becoming an Ultimate Weapon to be adored across the globe. I couldn't risk anything derailing that, anything snatching her from that path of self-resistance she now trekked.

She was finally stabilising her powers, finally learning control over the formidable abilities she unwillingly kept. There was finally hope, finally acceptance within Red's tainted and turbulent mind.

I feared Stanley's wake would unravel all that progress, but I wasn't the one to make that decision, and I knew it.

"I'm just worried about her," I said vaguely, eyeing Felix.

"So am I," he spoke with aggravation lacing his tone. "Stanley spent his entire life dedicated to researching the Legend of Millennia. He would want her to be there. I mean, what the hell makes you think you're the one that gets to make that decision?" His tone shook irately.

"You hated her, you *blamed* her, and then just like the flick of a switch, you decided differently. Who are you trying to fool? What even changed your mind? He died two days ago, so make up your fucking mind what you think, because right now, you're looking like nothing but a deluded follower," I snapped, shaking my head mordantly as anger surged through my veins. "You're a loose cannon, and I refuse to clean up your mess."

Felix glowered at me, his knuckles clenching hard, his nostrils flaring. "You think you're so fucking perfect! I've seen the way you look at her, Ace, the way you drool. How can you even think you stand a chance with her, with the almighty Ultimate Weapon? You're a fool, and you know you're a fucking fool!" He twisted against the desk and stomped down the hallway.

"Fuck." I collapsed into the chair, my hand to my forehead. I was ruining everything... and I didn't know how to stop.

I felt so lost without Stanley, without the old man's persevering optimism through all my tragedies and doubts.

He was always there for me with a shoulder to lean on and an ear to listen. He had helped me through so much, as I did when he lost his son. Well, best I could at age ten.

Those were the dark times; the times I met a whole new Stanley. One that I didn't recognise, one that I didn't know. But he had pulled through, and so would I.

Only now he was gone, a large part of my heart was missing. A large part now filled with nothing but regret for the last conversation we'd shared. It never should've ended like that; I should've barged into that hospital room and apologised profusely for my actions.

I felt so unlike myself, so plagiarised and faux. I knew I had to remain strong. These were still testing times for the powers of the Ultimate Weapon, and I knew Red would need me now more than ever. The least I could do was find her mum and dad's final resting place.

I turned back to my research, clicking a few times against the mouse. I analysed the files that flashed across the brightly lit screen, examining the findings.

It was unusual, to say the least. There was no record of her parents' burial site, and the more I studied her mother's death certificate, the more I wondered about its authenticity. If it was a fake, it was exceptionally well done.

There were little things about it, like numbers that didn't quite align under magnified inspection, and fonts that seemed the slightest bit off. I had to be imagining it, right? What possible reason would there be for a false certificate?

My mouth dropped as tears built behind my wide blue eyes. I

tore the printed page from against the printer, peering down at one Lucinda Zimm. I steadied my uneven breaths, analysing her information.

She was the one I had to find.

"Where are we going?" I glanced up as Red's uneasy voice filled the vast space. Felix led her into the room, his strides long and determined.

"You need to meet someone."

I swiftly stood, stuffing the sheet of paper into my pocket as Red's uncertain eyes met mine.

I couldn't help but immediately notice the way she firmly held her jumper against herself, the way her untidy hair cascaded across her shoulders. She seemed unusually anxious.

"We're going out." Felix eyed me with daggers, his tone arrogant and snappy.

"I'm coming with," I uttered, my tone almost inaudible. He angrily huffed, shaking his head, but he didn't argue.

"Hi," Red mumbled timidly as I stepped beside her.

"You alright?" I asked, feeling apprehensive about her meek behaviour.

She soullessly shrugged and looked away. "It's hard staying positive. My power feels stronger, more stable, and I can sense that, but..." her voice trailed away as I reached for her delicate hand and squeezed, feeling an electric spark between our skin.

I smiled her way reassuringly. "I'm worried about my anger." She lifted her chin, her eyes raw and bloodshot. "About something setting it off, and all this being for nothing."

I could sense her concern, sense the conflict within her tiny and overworked mind.

"I get it, Red, I understand how you're feeling, but I don't think you should worry so much about it," I offered, watching her with a steady gaze. "Your training is important, and if you try your best to stick with that, you'll be just fine." She forced a smile, her lips thin and unsure as we entered the elevator.

I watched Red with an unsettled feeling as Felix pulled against the kerb. I breathed in deep, reaching for the handle hesitantly. I collided against the morning sun, feeling its persistence stab on the back of my neck.

Marshall had relapsed; I couldn't believe it. He had worked so hard to combat the deadly and addictive habit, and now, he was right back where he started.

Only this time, without Stanley's much needed assistance.

Marshall trudged down the front wooden steps, watching us with a blank expression.

His face was swollen and puffy, his brown hair tousled and messy, his clothes old and worn through.

I smiled and waved, but he didn't return the favour. I swallowed hard, feeling even more apprehensive of an oncoming battle between him and Red.

"Who's that?" He nodded towards Red sharply, flicking his cigarette towards the ground.

Felix hesitated, clicking his tongue anxiously. He wasn't too sure about this plan now, not with the way Marshall sized him down like weakened prey.

"Red," he squeaked timidly.

Marshall's face flared with anger as Red's eyes flashed with worry. "You killed my grandpa!" he screeched, stomping towards her with fury etched across his fatigued features.

I stepped in front of her, Felix mirroring the motion as Red gasped anxiously, the sound breaking against the atmosphere with a harsh shrill. I held my tongue as my wide eyes flickered between them.

"Marshall, I was wrong," Felix confessed daringly. Marshall ignored his words, his enraged temper zeroing in on Red with a blinding fearsomeness. "Marshall," he snapped and grabbed his shoulders, forcing him to a standstill. "It was *not* her fault!" Their eyes locked, the space between them intensifying.

Marshall snarled, watching him with a spiteful and furious look. "Then why the hell did you tell me it was?" he shouted, his tone sharp and fierce.

Felix kept his posture firm, his face as hard as stone as his voice trembled. "Because I was angry, and it was easy to blame her for it. Easy until I realised, she's just a victim in all of this."

I looked back to Red, observing the way she glanced across at Felix abruptly. "I'm not innocent," she breathlessly snapped. Felix and Marshall turned towards her with perplexed expressions, their anger momentarily quelled.

She unclasped her knuckles restlessly. "I'm trying to be better; I'm trying to understand my mind," her tone shuddered. "I didn't want Stanley to die; I didn't want to be all alone with this ability that I don't even understand."

She twisted her palm upward, intensely eyeing against it. "I hate myself for having this, because I know I don't deserve it." She swiped her hand down quickly, her wide brown eyes meeting Marshall's. He swayed unsurely, his mind wasted and wrecked.

"I know Stanley didn't deserve it. So, if you want to be mad at me, then be mad at me. If you want to direct all your hate towards me, I'll take it. Because when Felix blamed me, I was angry, I was hurt and bitter, but I soon realised, he was right." Her glassy eyes flashed against Felix's as he stifled a sob and shook his head.

"Red, don't you dare!" he roared with a breaking voice box as I anxiously glanced between them. "Don't you dare tell me I was right! I was wrong, and I know I was wrong. People die every day—we all know that. If it wasn't for this imbalance, you'd be six feet under as well." He stilled, watching against her longingly.

"Maybe that's where I deserve to be," she murmured as the hope faded from Felix's pallid eyes.

"Red, what are you talking about?" I interjected worriedly as she lifted her shaky eyes to meet mine. "Positive thoughts, remember? You're healing, helping your abilities. Why are you talking like this?" I shook my head sharply.

She watched me for a moment longer. "If I give into my anger, I won't be the only one punished for it. If I give up, if I let my misery overthrow me, I'll be the only one who suffers. You tell me which ones best for humankind," she remarked bitterly, straightening her backbone to meet my unsure expression.

Suddenly, Marshall gasped. "You're the Ultimate Weapon," he uttered, startling realisation against his unsteady tone. He chuckled manically, his facial features twisting with rage. "I might be high, but I'm not that fucking high!" he shrieked. Red recoiled, guilt-stricken and mournful.

"My grandpa spent his entire life trying to find you, and you killed him the moment he did!" Marshall howled, his bloodshot eyes piercing against hers as she violently shuddered.

"I didn't mean to!" Red breathlessly gasped, fighting back the orange teardrops that invaded her remorseful expression.

"*Save it,* we are done here." Marshall shook his head irately. "You are not welcome at his wake, you are not welcome at his grave, you are not welcome at this home!" he callously roared.

Red's tearful eyes widened as she bit against her bottom lip, stifling the incoming sobs. She darted her eyes downward before she turned and ran, sprinting up the cracked and uneven pathway with the echoed thuds of her sneakers sounding loud.

CHAPTER 31

RED

My breath hitched in an uneven pattern as I flipped myself up and over the barrier rail, sitting cross-legged upon the concrete slab, dauntlessly close to the edge.

The water below lapped and splashed upon the solid pillars, vehicles zipped and chugged along the roadway, as birds flew whilst overhead with extraordinary speed and precision.

So much had happened since I threw myself off this ledge. So many bizarre, beautiful, and baffling things I never could've imagined coming to pass.

I'd died, been gifted an indestructible power, fallen in love, dared myself to change for the better. It was a crazy ride, and I still doubted it was true.

It was hard to remain positive, to speak within myself with kindness and truthfulness. It made it easier to wield the powers inside me, easier to stabilise and control my own fearsome abilities.

If only I wasn't left feeling so lifeless, like a hollow shell, a void vessel, an empty carapace. I felt meaningless without the anger inside me, urging me on, driving forward my determination and recklessness.

I stood and turned my back towards the river, outstretching my arms horizontally as my battered lungs breathed the warm air in deep. I opened my eyes and fell back, feeling the harsh rush of the haphazard winds frantic against me.

My hair tangled across my face, whipping like an untamed sail out at sea. I squinted, the sunlight burning my brown eyes as I hit the surface with a sizeable splash.

It sucked me in like a vortex, the liquid compound suffocating my fragile form. I breathed out a stream of bubbles, distraught by the startling realisation that I could breathe.

My legs kicked urgently beneath me, my body rising to the top. I emerged from the surface with a conflicted quarrel as my mind struggled to understand it.

My arms treaded against the glistening water as I looked up at the bridge that loomed above, intimidatingly immense. My soaked hair stuck against my flushed cheeks as I wrestled over how to feel about this new and defective trait.

I could no longer taste, no longer dream, no longer drown.

I couldn't tell whether my body was protecting or attacking me. I was the furthest thing from a human being. I was flawed, perfect, useful, useless, whole, and broken. I was everything and nothing, all at once.

The sunlight shimmered along the surface of the river as I swam across to the solid ground. I shook myself dry, clambering once more up the steep and muddy hillside.

Once I reached the top, I stilled, looking out at the bustling world around me. Everyone with their own purpose, their own mission in life. I was a castaway, shipwrecked and marooned.

Without the anger inside me, I felt pathetic, insecure. Like a ball of thread just waiting to be unwillingly unravelled. It was inevitable, unavoidable. I was not made for this world, yet I was forbidden to abandon it.

I was immortal, eternal, endless. Only, what the hell was I supposed to do with so much useless time? And what if I didn't die when time ticked by its thousand-year cycle? What if the Ultimate Weapon was plunged into an everlasting purgatory?

If I lived forever, the universe would have its balance, its weapon, its almighty power. It would win, but I would lose. I would lose everything I ever knew, everyone I ever loved, every part of myself I ever recognised.

Forever seventeen—forever looped within an infinite cycle. I was never going to age, to grow old, to die. Would never be laid to rest in a cemetery, never be buried alongside my parents, never retain a tombstone above my grave.

I had once read stories of vampires, of fairies, of mermaids, of mythical creatures that outlived time. In my wildest dreams, I never imagined I'd become one. In a way, I was like a phoenix that arose from the ashes, reborn anew from its own fatal destruction. There was something strangely poetic about that.

And what of heroes and villains?

I had always known of a villain dormant inside me. I'd spent most of my life trying to will myself a hero to battle that force. It was tiring, exhausting, wearing thin.

What would become of me if I just gave in, if I just gave up? If I outright accepted those villainous urges that infiltrated my daily thoughts? Who would be able to break me, to defeat me? What atrocities would I commit? Would I kill, would I murder, would I seek revenge?

But then again, it didn't matter what shoddy scenarios my tarnished mind created, I would never allow myself to give into such a corrupted state of mind, to become such evil.

I wouldn't allow myself to manipulate Ace in that way, someone who believed in me, who trusted me, who valued me. It wasn't an option, wasn't a possibility. I had promised Ace I would try.

So, I was.

"Red?" a confused voice filled the air, and I hesitated, looking across at the café.

Lira stood, holding a takeaway cup within her petite hands. Her blonde hair was tightly pinned back, her face blushed from the heat of the beverage, her eyes wide with worry. "Why are you wet?" I huffed, turning away. "*Wait, Red*—how are you?"

She stepped beside me, watching me steadily as the walkway around us filled with impatient people insistent on their caffeinated fixes.

"Fine," I muttered, darting my glassy eyes away. She sighed, stepping closer.

"I ran into Thomas. He said he saw you." I exhaled sharply and turned away, heading for the parklands. "Hold up!" She jogged alongside me, holding her cup cautiously. "Red, *please,* talk to me, how are you going?" Her gentle voice sounded loud as I stilled and exhaled hard against the atmosphere.

"I told you, I'm fine," I snapped, annoyed at myself for this pointless conversation.

I didn't care about her. I didn't care about Thomas. My life had been completely changed, completely flipped. I no longer needed them; I no longer had any oath to that empty promise we sealed in blood a lifetime ago.

"Ace tried to explain it," she began warily.

I halted, turning back. I hated the way his name sounded on her tongue, the way it floated up her windpipe with such effortless ease and flowed into the compacted space around us.

My eye twitched as frustration seeped within my bones like an oil spill within the ocean. She had no right to speak Ace's name, no right to speak of him at all. My eyes darkened, watching her with a bitter and brooding expression.

She squirmed uncomfortably, biting against her bottom lip. "He tried to explain the power," she spoke of him once more.

"Don't talk about him!" I yelled irately, my face enraged, my stature standoffish.

Lira hiccupped a surprised squeak, her eyes flashing with irritation and disbelief. "You don't *own* him, Red." She huffed. "But I should've known, you've always been possessive," she hissed, her pretty features twisting with frustration. I breathed in deep, trying to control the fury that banged within my mind like a piñata about to burst. She hovered against me, her eyes wide and provoked.

"Leave me the fuck alone," I sneered, stepping past her as I dug my hands into my jumper pockets. Lira laughed hysterically.

"Running away, like always," she jeered, her ladylike voice toxic and warped against the air as strangers turned their heads in our direction.

I lowered my chin, feeling exposed as I fruitlessly shielded myself from the intrusive stares that lingered for far too long. I yearned to fade away, to disappear, to wrap invisibility against my failing figure and then blink out of existence like a bubble.

Lira's hateful words ricocheted against me as I peered at my flaking palm, focusing my mind to still and my anger to calm. I exhaled a slow breath and shut my eyes, removing myself from my physical form. I drifted through my empty mind like it was an ethereal voyage above the stars.

Orange clouds draped soothingly around me as I breathed the serene sensation in deep, feeling the phantom prickle upon my bare skin.

People screamed and fled as my eyes shot open in haste. I examined my skin urgently, eyeing the translucent flesh.

I spun around as Lira stumbled against the cracked and muraled wall. Her eyes wide and fearful, her coffee a mess against the ground.

A sly chuckle escaped my lips as a wide smile beamed from ear to ear. I could feel the power encapsulate against my bones and flood my system. I felt ultimate, untouchable.

Adrenaline pumped through my veins as I pushed my invisible form forward, breaking out into a hurried run. I could do anything I wanted, go anywhere I deemed to go, be anyone I thought to be. *My options were limitless.*

Where had I always wished to go? What location had always been unobtainable? It needed to be somewhere grand, somewhere fun and thrilling. A place I had longed to venture but was never able to visit. I gasped, happiness bursting through me as I bee-lined for the amusement park.

My oversized jumper thudded against me as my shoes slapped stridently upon the pavement, excitement bounding from within.

The sunshine loomed above the entryway as I stilled within the shadows of the renovated car park, the towering structure soaring above.

I had forever stood this side of the fence, looking in with a disappointed hopefulness, but today would be different.

Today I would finally enter.

I slipped in line, bypassing the pay stations and staff members that fumbled about with transactions. Families bustled around me, chatting and laughing amongst themselves as the line inched forward. I could hear their cheerful babbles echo within my eardrums as I stepped past the iron gate and into the tunnelled entryway.

Themed mascots in loveable costumes paraded the streets as children and adults alike roamed the walkways with enthusiastic grins and eager-filled eyes.

Acrobats entertained and performers danced. Adults laughed and children played. Cameras flashed and smiles brimmed.

I could smell the warm aroma of freshly cooked foods, could feel the slight tickle of bubbles as they popped against my skin, could hear the far away music of rides as people bellowed their excited and nervous cries into the crowds below.

The day was hot, the sun glistening within the clear blue skies with a rich and beautiful scent. I breathed the refreshing odour in deep, grateful to have finally made it past the strong barrier between. My younger self would've thanked me for it.

A young couple laughed with one another, catching my attention off guard. Their hands intertwined as the girl directed their journey with an amusement park map.

She had bright pink hair and a frilled dress; he had blue hair and studded clothing. They looked so happy, so in love, and care-free.

A twinge of jealousy surged within me, the feeling strange and unkind. I placed my hand against my beating heart, feeling the electrified pulse that quickened against my touch.

I would live forever. Ace wouldn't.

He would grow old and withered, whilst I would never age beyond my seventeen years. It was a doomed love. Hopeless, cruel. But I knew Ace, and I knew his love would be worth the inevitable heartbreak that awaited.

For him, I would suffer that fated torture a thousand times over, because within his arms, I felt a love and happiness that had forever eluded me. Was it selfish to think that way? Was it heartless to corner him into a futile relationship that wouldn't last his lifetime or produce any offsprings?

It was impossible to bear children without a menstrual cycle, and I no longer bled. So, it made sense that I would never be able to conceive. I wasn't sure how I felt about that; I was still just a kid myself. It wasn't something I had thought about, or something I had cared about.

Maybe one day my opinion would change, but so what if it did? I no longer bled, I no longer reproduced, and there was no point in adopting when I would only outlive them.

My body would never age, but my mind would. From the outside, Ace and I would be judged, ridiculed. I was seventeen years old, not even an adult. How long could I be with him before the cracks started to show?

And if I couldn't age, where would I go once people started to notice? It seemed foolish to think I could live forever within that underground bunker, but what other choice would I have?

What would become of me, of an entity so powerful, and capable, and formidable?

I would never cease being the Ultimate Weapon, I would never die, would never succumb to the limitations of humankind.

But that didn't mean I couldn't love or be loved. And I loved Ace. I was sure of it. I knew I was mad, unhinged, inhuman, yet at the end of the day, I was still just a traumatised and lonely teenage girl.

There was so much good and so much evil I had yet to face, and I knew I wouldn't be able to manage those treacherous and terrible feats without Ace by my side.

He accepted me for all I was. He didn't judge me for the past I ran from. He offered me his help, his time, his effort. He brought forth the good within me, a good I thought I'd banished years ago.

I glanced down at my slender arms, their translucent surface unharmed. This body still didn't feel like mine, didn't look like mine, didn't bear the collection of scars like mine. I realised then that I had to see this naked body anew. I had to learn to accept it, to stop being so afraid of this irreversible change. And I knew Ace was the one to help me do it.

My thoughts unwillingly drifted to the previous night, to the heart-stopping moment Ace had laid me down beneath his embrace. A euphoric and thrilling moment seconds before my anxiety attack had ruined the whole rendezvous.

My cheeks blushed with embarrassment as my hands fidgeted with irritation.

No matter my attempts, my mind was constantly under attack, like a broken record stuck on repeat, like a merry-go-round on a malfunctioning streak, like a teetotum on a nonstop rotation.

But I never wanted it to be like that, I wanted to heal myself, to trust my heart. I wanted to stand before Ace with my body as naked as my mind.

A burning sensation suddenly erupted from within me as a fearsome heat made me dizzy and a forbidden desire scorched along my fingertips.

I trusted this boy.

Trusted him with everything I was and everything I wasn't. I trusted him with every damned detail of my abused, neglected, and fucked up past. If I was ever going to allow someone into the deepest and darkest parts of myself, it was going to be Ace.

I wanted *him.* I *needed* him. Needed him with an intense desire that insisted, begged, demanded to be obeyed. And I knew, I had to listen.

CHAPTER 32

ACE

"Who's next?" the receptionist called.

"Hi, I'm hoping to speak to Lucinda Zimm, I believe she works at this facility." I forced a smile as my fingers drummed nervously against the front desk.

"Sure, let me check." The lady returned the smile, hers undeniably pleasant, as she swiftly tapped upon the keyboard.

The hospital was currently an active jumble, everyone with something urgent to do and somewhere important to be. Shoes clicked hurriedly across the tiles, the wide-open space echoing against the crisp noise as people openly conversed.

Doctors, nurses, patients, and visitors, all occupied the vast first storey with their fastened paces, rapid babble, and voluble jargon as various aromas intruded my nostrils. Perfumes, colognes, chemicals, freshly brewed coffees, just to name a few.

"She works in ICU." The receptionist pulled me back in with her verifying words. "I can give her a buzz if you'd like?" I nodded across at her eagerly.

The young lady was attentive and vibrant. Her dark-brown hair a curled bob, her eyeglasses circular and thin, her makeup strikingly executed. Dark eyelids and bright lips.

"Who shall I say is waiting?" She removed the phone from her ear and placed her hand against the receiver.

I squirmed restlessly. "Ace Hart," I replied, trying to fake my own confidence. The lady pinched her lips and smiled thinly. It was a common reaction; many thought I was pulling their leg.

"Yes, hello, it's Alex from reception, is Lucinda available?" There was a brief pause. "Yes, I see. I have an Ace Hart wishing to speak with her," she communicated, the sentence followed by yet another pause. "Yes, will do. Thanks, bye." She hung up the phone, the cord recoiling.

"She's currently on her lunch break, but you can find her in the food court. If you follow that hallway down to your left—" She pointed instructively. "You'll see the elevators; food court is level 3." I smiled and nodded keenly.

"Appreciate it," I expressed before I turned and started up the hallway.

A long and nervous sigh escaped my lips as the blank and lifeless corridors extended out before me almost menacingly.

I stepped into a vacant elevator, awaiting my destination with a deep-rooted restlessness.

The doors dinged open, but I just stood, frozen in place as a surge of anxiety invaded my core. I breathed in deep, forcing my feet to move beneath me as a group of people began filing into the congested space.

It felt wrong, being here, doing this, investigating a person who I believed to be—a razor-sharp intensity swiftly brought me to my knees as I clutched atop my heart urgently, inwardly sensing a spiral of Red's untameable power from within. It was fierce and formidable, electric and erratic, powerful and perturbing.

"Let me help," a kind voice rang loud as a gentle, yet firm hand wrapped around my forearm, guiding me up.

I tidied my clothing and fixed my wonky sweater, trying to brush off the embarrassment. "Thank you." I glanced upward, meeting the wide brown eyes of an older woman.

Her features were soft, her presence warm, her demeanour welcoming. Freckles laced her nose as strands of brunette hair cascaded down her cheeks. She looked to be in her mid-forties.

She smiled my way with a toothy grin, her blue scrubs glistening against the dull and colourless walls. She had a lanyard and stethoscope perched around her slender neck.

I absentmindedly tilted my head, my focused eyes reading the name on her ID. "Lucinda?" I queried, uncertainty lacing my tone.

She eagerly nodded, her glossy fringe shifting. "Yes, that's me," she declared. "You don't happen to be Ace Hart, do you?" She eyed me closely.

A nervous chuckle left my lips as I ran my hand through my loose and tumbled hair. "Yeah," I muttered.

She smiled once more, her hazel eyes widening with gladness. "One of my co-workers told me you were looking for me. Although, I can't say I recall an Ace Hart from anywhere, and you don't seem familiar." She slanted her head, her lips pursed in thought. "Nevertheless, let's go find a quiet place to chat."

It was evident she knew her way around the vast structure as she navigated the long and lifeless corridors with nothing but her memory. Occasionally, fellow nurses would nod and smile in her direction, along with a few visitors that motioned quick waves and uttered greetings.

She led me from the building and into a warm and tidy garden area situated within the centre of the bustling hospital. It was a large and peaceful area, with a wooden pathway, alfresco seating, and an outdoor café that was currently closed.

I glanced skyward, eyeing the large and panelled windows that ran the length of the entire building against all four sides. It was crazy to think how enormous this place truly was.

Hallways that seemed to never end, car parks that stretched on for miles, enough staff to ward off a zombie attack.

Lucinda sat by a shaded concrete bench. "So, how can I help you today?" She placed her hands within her lap and crossed her ankles, curiously awaiting my response.

I swallowed hard and took a seat beside her, the concrete cold against my sweaty palms.

"You have a daughter." I spoke the words in haste; uncertain they would leave my lips otherwise. She briefly froze, her eyes wide and mouth agape.

She exhaled a hard chuckle, her motions stiff and forced. "I don't, no," she insisted as she darted her eyes away from my lingering stare.

"Not biologically, but you adopted her." I watched her with an unpleasant expression, zeroing in on her fluctuating mood. "Why did you allow Johanna to believe you were dead this entire time?"

She quickly stood, her movements frantic, her mind shaken. "This conversation is over," she stated, sweat against her brow as her hands nervously trembled. "You need to leave. If you refuse, security will be called, and they don't take kindly to those who harass the staff," she threatened with a shuddering tone about to shatter.

It was crystal clear to me now; she was truly Red's mother. It was a heartbreaking discovery, a gut-wrenching find. This selfish woman had faked her own death and started anew. She had deserted Red, leaving her to fend for herself in one of the cruellest ways possible.

Her whole life could've been different; it should've been. It should've been happier, safer, filled with an abundance of love that I knew she undoubtedly deserved.

Red adored her parents. She idolised them; she *mourned* for them. All she'd ever wanted was closure. All she'd ever wanted was to visit their graves and grieve their losses. To sit by their decayed tombstones and reminisce of better days, days when they were together as a loving and united family.

And now, now I knew the devastating truth.

A truth I didn't know if I could ever speak of. A truth that I knew Red would go berserk and go ballistic over. There was no doubt, she would fly off the handles, blow a gasket, hit the roof. And she would bring the whole damned universe down with her.

Her mother was alive, living in the same city she killed herself in. The same city she awakened in as the Ultimate Weapon. The same city she obtained the omnipotent power within.

I leant back against the concrete surface, frustration fuelling my veins. "You were admitted into a psychiatric hospital after the accident," I boldly spoke, eyeing her with an intense demeanour. "You blamed yourself for killing your husband, and you abandoned your daughter because you couldn't deal with the responsibility of caring for another human being."

She fiercely shook, her once sophisticated and joyful manner completely shifted. "Please, no," she uttered despairingly.

I continued despite her request. "I know your daughter, and she's a beautiful but troubled soul. She tried to kill herself just to be reunited with you. It's been almost eight years, and she doesn't even *know* you're alive."

"It's better this way," she murmured weakly.

"You shouldn't get to decide that!" I spat, the sentence spilling from my mouth like word vomit. "How could you even do that to her? How could you abandon her so easily? How could you so unremorsefully renounce her to a life filled with uncertainty and danger?" I bellowed, the unpleasant words piercing my throat as teardrops stung behind my eyes.

Lucinda collapsed soundlessly upon the bench. Her body immobilised and brittle, her face sickened and pale. "She wasn't my daughter," she whispered harshly. "She *wasn't* my responsibility."

She referred to Red so emotionlessly, like she had been long gone for eons. Nothing more than a throwaway object intended to be ridiculed and ignored. It made me sick; it made me angry. Red deserved so much better, she deserved a mother who loved her, who adored her, who fought for her.

I sat forward suddenly, watching Lucinda with a distrustful and repulsed expression. "I hope Red never meets this version of you," I carelessly expressed as she curiously lifted her chin. "You are a horrible person for the deplorable thing you did to her." I stood, heading for the exit with an untamed fury that burned hot within my breaking heart.

"Did you say Red?"

I stilled momentarily, my hand hovering atop the doorknob. "Yes." I opened and then slammed the glass door shut, proceeding to the underground car park.

This place was toxic, suffocating, poisonous. The people the very same. I couldn't believe the words Lucinda—no, *Luciana*, had spoken of her own daughter. They were vile, selfish, and I vowed Red would never hear of them. If I could help it, and I intended to, she would never discover the deceitful and dreadful actions of her own mother.

After the accident, within the confines of that psychiatric hospital, Luciana had rebuilt her life and discarded Red. She obtained a new name, a new identity, a new life for herself. All whilst her naïve daughter had rotted away in abusive, neglectful, and hateful foster homes, never knowing the truth of what had happened after that fateful night.

Red was a gorgeous girl, filled with potential and promise. She was a determined force, an outspoken personality, a headstrong character. She was never built to be caged, or confined, or constricted. She was formed to be omnipotent, outrageous, obtrusive. To stand out and stand against. Daring to the point of utter recklessness, brave to the point of plain foolishness, but she was indisputably herself. She disregarded norms, ignored rules, snubbed laws.

"*Ace!*" Luciana desperately called, clutching her lanyard.

I turned around sharply, my stature unapproachable and unkind. She recoiled before me, her cheeks brightly flushed as she exhaled a long and ragged breath.

"I did, what I did, for a *reason*—" her voice choked against the unpleasant word. "I don't hate her, but I don't love her. Not anymore." She shook her head as crocodile tears slipped from her brown eyes.

Fury overtook me, ravenous and resolute, as I propelled my

hand forward, my fingers outstretched. My power jolted from my trembling palm and forcefully slammed against her, knocking her to the ground with a vicious thud. She screamed out a terror-stricken echo, alerting others.

My irises turned a ghostly white, my skin zapping with inhuman wrinkles of electricity as I lowered my arm in haste, her wide and terrified eyes piercing against mine.

I turned and hurried down the hallway, letting Luciana's far away cries become nothing more than meaningless white noise.

CHAPTER 33

RED

I glanced once more at my translucent flesh, noticing the faded freckles and tiny hairs that remained visible to no one except me.

I couldn't wait to show Ace this new ability, couldn't wait to see his shocked expression when I unexpectedly blinked into view and flashed my daring smile.

Of all the powers I had created, this was undoubtedly my favourite. To exist without existing, to be without being, to appear without appearing.

This was one of the supernatural abilities I longed for, one I knew would help my conflicted mindset in accepting these unnatural powers within. It was still insane to think about, still crazy to envision my life before.

I'd never really thought that much about death, about what happened in the moments after the Grim Reaper gained ownership over your soul.

Was it a peaceful feeling or a malignant one? What had my parents experienced? Were they welcomed into heaven with open and loving arms, or were they denied? Would I have been blessed with the same outcome?

An irrational thought, I grumbled. I was never going to see them again, was never going to be accepted into the heavens above, and I knew I had to accept that unfortunate fact pronto.

The reflection within the window was unable to locate me, unable to perceive my ghostlike figure against the landslide of pedestrians around me. I shook my head and smiled.

I was truly invisible to the outside world.

"Hey!" I shouted, wondering if I could be heard in my hidden form. Not a single person stirred. I triumphantly chuckled as my spectre self slipped into the rhythm of passer-by's footsteps, just an added nobody within a faceless stream of city dwellers.

I darted sideways and into the street, twisting and turning. I stilled, my red hair jutting out as I eyed Ace. He trekked along the busy pathway, for the first time, unrecognisable.

My face fell as I observed the anxious way his eyes blazed. He looked agitated, upset, angry. His body tense and stiff, his usual smiley self reduced to a thin and unpleasant frown.

I held my breath as he stepped past me, his mind focused. He didn't even notice me... I turned my head, watching as his sweater shifted against his slender figure.

My eyes narrowed in confusion. What had caused him to be so unapproachable?

I stepped in line with the men and women against the walkway, eyeing Ace's blond hair from afar. He departed the crowded footpath and made his way towards the high-rise building. I followed suit like an undetected snooper.

I hurried behind him, slipping into the elevator unnoticed as the doors clunkily closed.

Suddenly, Ace screamed, his controlled composure breaking

apart at the seams as he furiously threw his fist towards the side of the mirrored glass. It instantly shattered, raining down on the metal floor below.

I pressed my body tight alongside the metallic surface, the congested air growing thick as he slumped against the side of the lift. He looked defeated, done. He squeaked out a cry, placing his hands flat against his forehead.

The doors reopened as I reached across to console him. He stepped out urgently, crunching the glass beneath his speckless shoes. "*Felix!*" he boomed as the sliding doors opened.

Fearfulness and confusion overwhelmed my brittle core as I inched further into the bunker, watching as Felix flipped himself up and over the old, worn couch.

"What's up?" he asked, eyeing Ace with an uncertain look.

Ace slammed his fist against the metal desk, his knucklebones breaking. I gasped, my eyes wide and fearful. "What the hell happened to you?" Felix proceeded closer as Ace collapsed against the floor, his blond hair tumbling in front of his tearful blue eyes. "*Whoa,* hey." Felix crouched beside him, placing his hand upon Ace's shoulder.

"I messed up," Ace shuddered, placing his forehead against the desk's hairpin leg.

I slipped down to my knees, observing him with deep apprehension. I wanted to soothe his worries; I wanted to wrap him up within a blanket of safety and protect him forevermore. I crept closer, my palms hesitant against the cold flooring as I watched Felix comfort him like never before.

"Ace, what's going on?" Felix spoke gently, his features kind and soft. "Talk to me," he begged.

Ace glanced across at his brother timorously, his eyes wide and bloodshot, glassy and raw. He looked troubled, upset, betrayed. Just what the hell had happened to him?

"I met Red's mum. I met Luciana."

Anger exploded from within me as my eyes widened and an enraged shriek left my lips. I stood as the powers within me buckled, and seared, and burned against my tattered being. I glanced down at my body, watching as my translucent flesh pierced and electrified with untamed flickers of my erratic ability.

Ace and Felix gasped fearfully, glancing around as I flashed in and out of view. "Red?" Ace stood and desperately yelled, eyeing my angered and mortified expression.

I screamed once more, the power morphing, and warping, and contorting within me. It seared hot, burning against my flesh like molten lava. I cried out in agony, the feeling engulfing my entire fragile form as the orange glow protruded from my naked skin, my flesh cracking and liquefying.

"No, Red!" Ace shrieked, running towards me.

"*No!*" I roared, outstretching my arm.

Ace flew through the air, slamming against the far wall. He tumbled towards the ground below, a painful moan escaping his lips as he felt impact.

My entire frame vigorously shook, my translucent flesh returning to opaque as orange teardrops slipped uncontrollably from my bloodshot eyes.

Ace forced himself up and winced, holding his side sorely. Felix stood like a deer stuck in headlights, his frightened stare darting from mine to his brother's. "Please, Red, don't do this," Ace pleaded, forcing himself to stand unaided.

He stood haphazardly hunched as the bones within his body started to heal. "Yes, Red, your mum is alive. She didn't die in that car accident."

"You lie!" I foolishly shrieked, refusing to hear Ace's words, refusing to believe my mother was alive and had been alive this entire time.

Ace shook his head urgently. "No, Red, I don't!" Tears built behind his pastel-blue eyes as haywire sparks shot out from against me, darting within the room at a supersonic pace.

Agony spiralled from within me, encapsulating my broken and brutalised mind. "Why would she *leave* me?" I sobbed as I looked directly at Ace, begging for the answer.

Ace's eyes were wide with understanding, filled with nothing but concern. I wept, wiping wrathfully at the alien droplets that splashed against my reddening cheeks. "Where is she?" I cried as my larynx burned at a brutal temperature. "*Tell me!*" I glared at Ace and outstretched my arm once more, pinning him to the nearby wall.

My eyes narrowed with determination, filled with a mix of fury, and fear, and frustration. Ace kicked against my powerful hold, struggling, wrestling against my control.

"The Royal Hospital," he shouted hesitantly. "She works in ICU," he weakly added, his troubled expression meeting mine.

I gasped, my arm dropping. All this time she had remained in the very place she found me. She had returned to her normal life and forgotten all about my existence.

Now I was positively fuming, the anger the only emotion surging within my damaged mind.

Ace fell harshly upon the ground, his body limp as Felix ran to his side, aiding him to a sitting position against the wall.

He looked across at me, his dull eyes wide, his black hair tousled. "You will *kill* everyone," he fired a warning shot against me.

"They all deserve to die!" I furiously roared as every light bulb fractured and every electrical device exploded, bathing us in nothing but my unstable glow that wildly weaved within the enclosed room.

The lift malfunctioned, opening and closing in a rhythmic pattern as the sliding doors shattered. My body darted sideways, my feet stepping loudly against the fractured glass as I clambered into the elevator. I slammed my palm in vain upon the ground floor key, my power forced to lift the broken box.

I screamed and grasped at my stomach, feeling a harsh rush of agony as I ascended to the ground floor. I leapt from the congested space as the elevator plummeted behind me, smashing fiercely against the ground below.

Onlookers screamed out manically, darting in all directions as I picked myself up and ran for the hospital. I observed myself against the large mirrors, the alien glow shining alongside my baggy clothing.

People sprinted out the way as I shook my head furiously, pumping my elbows harder and my feet quicker. I stumbled into the roadway, urgently racing up the asphalt as my skin radiated, and glowed, and pulsed with erratic flickers. All whilst my mind remained permanently numb.

I couldn't think, couldn't stop, couldn't control the intense power that tore against my broken heart. All this time she had been alive. Alive in the very city I lived. The very city I was passed from foster home to foster home.

Why had she never rescued me, *why* had she never protected me, *why* had she never bundled me up and taken me away? Was I that much of an inconvenience to her, that stupid and dumb, that meaningless and useless?

I had spent most of my life begging for my mother's tender touch, for her loving words and encouraging smile to get me through the brutality of living within those toxic homes.

Alongside that, the strength and resilience I'd summoned from my father, daring myself to be as courageous as he. *To speak my mind, to stand unafraid, to question everything.*

That Christmas I spent in the care of that awful case worker, that had been the most brutal night of all... I had blamed myself for the accident, blamed myself for killing my parents and ending our perfect existence.

I was young, weak, naïve, delusional. I had fought my way to heaven to be reunited with them, but she had been right here this entire time. I had never hated anyone more.

All I had wanted was for Ace to find their burial, their final resting place. Instead, he found *her.* I had wanted closure, but instead, I received an invitation to war.

Car horns blared as my body shuddered, but I forced myself on, ignoring the blurred reflections of my inhuman form that glistened against every reflective surface.

CHAPTER 34

ACE

Felix forced me up the emergency stairwell, holding tight to my prickly sweater. We impelled the hefty door open, hurrying across the crowded footpath as my bones fused and strengthened. We neared Kobi's car that shimmered under the warm sunshine.

Felix shoved me into the passenger seat, then climbed into the driver's side. He revved the engine as people screamed and ran. I looked up, eyeing Red, watching as her glowing form ascended the roadway ahead.

Sparks jolted from against her as haywire bolts of electricity flickered upon her. If I wasn't so terrified, I'd be awe-struck. If I wasn't completely responsible, I'd be proud.

I grabbed my mobile, twisting it around the right way. I dialled Kobi's number, slamming the device against my ear as an anxious breath escaped my lips. "What?" he cruelly snapped.

"We have a problem, a big fucking problem!" I struggled for breath as I adjusted my sinking posture. "Red found out her mum is alive. She's beyond furious, and *glowing,* and headed for the Royal Hospital!" I howled as Felix raced up the road, changing gears in rhythm with the building speed.

A moment passed, the phone rustling. "Shit," Kobi's voice shook. "It's on TV." I leant forward and looked up, eyeing the news helicopter that circled the towering buildings above.

I slammed back into the leather chair, breathing haphazardly as uncertainty crept within my bones. "We need the Army, or the SWAT team, *something*," I snivelled. "She's going to end the entire fucking world!"

Kobi hung up quickly as I dropped the phone against the floor, screaming at myself for being so fucking stupid and careless.

I *never* should've researched that woman... I should've stayed far away from that open and painful wound. I had put Red in danger, had sentenced the entire world to a cruel and debilitating fate, had signed the death certificates of so many innocents.

"Ace, relax, we'll help her!" Felix shouted as we neared Red.

She glanced back at us, her eyes wide, and enraged, and radiant. She forced her legs harder, her glowing form fastening its inhuman pace as a train horn bellowed before us.

A panicked breath escaped me as I looked up, watching the boom gates lower and the red lights flash with danger. I held my shaky breath, looking to Red as she pushed her body harder with a determined sprint unwilling to falter.

"*Felix!*" I cried as I grabbed the seatbelt and clicked myself securely in place. My knuckle paling as I grasped the dashboard for support, my eyes darting between Red's tiny figure and the oncoming train. "We won't make it!" I forewarned with a high-pitched shudder.

"Yes, we will," Felix firmly stated, shoving the car into sixth gear. I held my breath and eyed Red as she leapt in front of the train, missing it by mere centimetres.

Her bravery was godlike. I couldn't help but be enthralled by her power, her presence, her perseverance.

Abruptly, the car piercingly spluttered, rapidly skidded, and violently lurched. Felix gasped, reaching his arm against my chest protectively as he lost control.

The vehicle slammed against the railway sign with a deafening crunch. We jolted forward as the airbags imploded, filling the car with a dusty mist and ear-piercing blast.

The flashing lights against the railway sign blinked out, the pole crashing atop the car with a thunderous crack. Felix and I gasped, ducking low.

We had lost; we had doomed the entire universe.

Red would destroy herself, and she would take the whole world with her. Whether she meant to or not, she would annihilate humankind. She would end the possibility of the next generation. She would force time itself to an indefinite standstill. She was a powerful antihero with an unwanted role within this world, and I was sure the girl beneath, the girl I'd come to personally know, was gone. Her mind broken beyond repair.

The Ultimate Weapon was a captivating omnipotence, one unable to be commanded or controlled. She existed outside the laws of nature. She created her own destiny and designed her own limitations. *Of which, she had none.* She was a force bigger than Kobi, greater than the Armed Forces, superior to the entire universe.

Her powers needed to be mastered, needed to be managed in a way that caused her no harm, and assisted her in understanding just what she had been gifted.

I glanced up weakly as the mist within the car settled and the train passed. I heard sirens and saw flashing lights of red and blue pulsate with urgency around us.

"Felix?" I winced, moving against the crumpled mess.

"Yeah?" he weakly muttered, coughing coarsely.

"I'm sorry, for everything," I forced the words free.

If this was truly the end of time, the end of life as we knew it, then this was the moment I had to say I was sorry. To apologise for all those times I'd disregarded him, all those times I'd valued the Ultimate Weapon above him, and all those times I'd foolishly thought someone else would swoop in and save us.

A heartbeat passed before he responded. "Same here, bro." I smiled to myself, feeling an ounce of relief.

"Are you okay in there?" a paramedic bellowed.

"Yes!" I shouted as I shifted against the door, wrestling my way through the smashed window and away from the broken pole. I crawled into the open space covered in scuff marks and debris as a firm hand reached down and offered its assistance.

I weakly stood, my lungs filled with dust, my clothes coated in glass. I coughed a few times, squinting against the severity of the sun that blazed against the globe.

"Ace Hart?" an officer asked as I twisted around to face him, looking away from the mangled carnage. I feebly nodded. "You have any idea what this so-called 'Radioactive Menace' is?" he sternly spoke, his tongue catching on the foolish title.

Ah. So, that's what the news crew was calling her.

"Felix." The officer addressed my brother, looking across at him directly. Felix nodded mutely, his expression strained, his eyes unreadable.

"She's one of us," I admitted with a twinge of guilt.

The officers humphed and nodded as the leading paramedic

checked us over. "I need that car," I swiftly ordered, angling my head towards their work vehicle.

The officer laughed, loud and rumbly. "I don't think so, kid. That's a police vehicle." Felix side-eyed me disbelievingly.

"I'm not asking," I reiterated. "That 'Radioactive Menace' is headed for the hospital and if we don't stop her, all hell is going to break loose, and this very world may become obsolete."

The male officer shifted uncomfortably, eyeing his partner for back-up. His partner shrugged unsurely, her eyes aglow with confusion. The officer sighed. "Bring it back in one piece," he uttered with a pleading hopefulness.

I gasped inwardly as excitement mixed with panic fuelled my failing system. "Felix, in the car, *now*," I instructed as I leapt into the front seat and anxiously stilled, observing the control board, radar, and radio that buzzed with a static noise.

Felix slipped in beside me, his demeanour skittish and unsure. I released the handbrake with a slight shake, pulling onto the roadway as the officers watched on with inner turmoil.

A booming laughter suddenly rolled off Felix's tongue. "How the fuck is it possible that *you* scored a cop car? This is seriously insane," his loud voice rumbled playfully within the vehicle.

A wide smile beamed across my face as I shrugged impishly, my mind running at a million miles per hour, and for the briefest moment, forgetting the danger that loomed before us.

"Do you have a plan?" Felix's tone dramatically shifted.

"Unfortunately, I don't," I confessed. "There's no how-to for something as fucked up as this. Red can't be killed, so we don't have to worry about that, but I don't know how to stop her."

I breathed in deep, trying to remember Stanley's teachings.

"We don't know of any weaknesses, nothing that could benefit us in any way." I exhaled an annoyed breath, frustrated at myself for being so unprepared in the face of true danger. "We need to work together, that's all we can do. We'll figure it out. We have to."

Felix nodded solemnly. "Whatever you need, Ace, consider it done."

I breathed in deep, begging myself for the strength to take her down, to stand against her if the situation became dire enough.

Within my heart, I felt a way towards Red that couldn't be denied, couldn't be ignored. I adored her, admired her… I loved her. And I promised myself I would one day give her that happily ever after she'd forever been kept from.

I refused to lose her, not today, not tomorrow, not ever. I refused to even consider it. I would protect her, I would bring her back from the brink, I would gamble with the devil to save her. She deserved to be loved, to be protected, to be defended.

My heavy heart pressed tight against my chest as I blinked away the tears. I needed her to hang in there, I needed her to fight, I needed her to try.

I needed her to survive.

EPILOGUE

RED

I darted inside the hospital, the lifeless walls closing and caving in around me. I gasped frightfully, my legs skidding and stumbling beneath me.

I slammed my weakened palm upon the blank wall, bouncing myself off hurriedly as invacuation alarms pierced through my ringing eardrums.

Anger spiralled from within me, burning, and bellowing, and blatant. I *refused* to let her win, I refused to let my mother have her perfect little world, whilst I had rotted and decayed in filthy, traumatic, and abusive foster homes.

The endless corridors extended out before me as I sprinted irately towards my destination. Doctors and nurses shrieked, shielding themselves from my glowing alien form.

I hurried around the corner, hell-bent on finding my mother as I slammed against the front desk. The receptionist screamed and backed away, her gaze darting against me fearfully as escalated breaths tore from her windpipe.

"Where is Luciana Tolmer?" I roared, throwing my fist against the desk. My knucklebone split, the wound stitched and healed in a matter of seconds.

The lady's fearful eyes grew wider, her lips pinched harder. "Tell me where she is or I will bring this whole goddamn hospital down right now!" I threatened as my scintillated glow encircled the vast and colossal room, weaving like spilled water within the modern structure.

"You can't!" someone shouted from behind me.

I spun around sharply, eyeing the doctor with a malicious and insistent snarl. He shifted uncomfortably, his arm frozen in its outstretched manner.

He swallowed hard, composing himself. "Who do you wish to see?" he asked sternly as the faintest drop of sweat rolled against his brow. He was tall and foolish, with short black hair, hazelnut eyes, and large glasses. He was no match for the powers that jutted out from against me and threatened this entire medical institution.

"Luciana Tolmer," I repeated myself, his silence infuriating my tarnished mind. "Where is ICU!" I screamed. He jumped, breaking away from his overloaded thoughts.

"Level 3. Take that hallway, right at the elevator. Once at level 3, turn to your left." He breathed harshly, his body trembling.

I sprinted for the elevator, my heart beating at an abnormal rate as my power followed frantically against my erratic form. Tears stung behind my shaky and bloodshot eyes, but I refused to let them fall as I rode the elevator up, bursting into the third storey unsteadily.

I eyed the intensive care unit with determination, my heart fracturing and failing, but on I pushed. I forced my feet forward and ran into the hallway, my unstable ability surging, and flickering, and pulsating with electric waves.

I froze and urgently exhaled, eyeing my mother through the spotless windows. She stood with a nervous, grim, and fearful expression. She'd barely aged. Her features similar to the way they were before, her scrubs highlighting her slim and healthy figure.

Orange teardrops spilled upon the ground as I sobbed and wept. I held my stomach in tightly, releasing an ear-piercing roar. Hundreds of windows shuddered and shattered, plummeting within the building's centre point.

The waves of fractured glass roared to the ground below as I met my mother's wide eyes through the chaos. She stepped back and placed a wrinkled hand to her mouth.

My legs gave way beneath me as I clung against the wall for support, my power grasping at my heart with a desperate and strong-handed fist.

It was true. It was all true...

She moved on, she started a whole new life without me. She discarded me, deserted me, dejected me. She forced me into those homes and forgot about me.

Was I truly that repulsive? My expression flared with fury, my fists clenching hard. *"How?"* I screamed, zeroing in on her meek and anxious form. She flinched, her brunette hair shifting. "How could you abandon me like that? How could you leave me to fend for myself? To grow up within a world I believed my parents to be *dead* and *gone!"* I bellowed, my shaky voice echoing throughout the broken corridors.

I exhaled hard against the atmosphere, watching her notice something within the adjacent room. She hurried away quickly, unhesitantly.

"No!" I screamed forcefully and ran forward, determined to keep her here. Determined to get answers. Determined to find out why she decided she didn't want me anymore.

Officers in SWAT uniforms invaded the floor with a quick and swift motion. They wore full protective gear, their darkened suits thick and heavy, their guns drawn and aimed.

I lowered my chin angrily and screamed, flipping my hand skyward as a powerful force field darted outward manically. The burn seared against my fragile form, breaking, tearing against my inhuman flesh as rage blinded me.

Bullets ricocheted against my power, the gunfire thunderous within my ringing eardrums as empty shells darted in all directions, clanging across the ground.

"I want Luciana!" I yelled and stepped forward firmly, my ability unwavering against their strong weaponry and fortified shields. Even combined, they were no match for the powers of the Ultimate Weapon. I was unaffected by their useless ordnance.

They surrounded me then, guns firing off in all directions as my power encapsulated me, protecting me within an electrified bubble that pulsed grotesquely along my blazing skin. I ducked low and dashed forward, jumping from the structured frame as the SWAT members frantically roared.

I dropped through the air, my power encircling me as I was gently guided to the floorboards below. My torn sneakers trod atop the broken glass as I hurried from the open space and into the deserted passageways that stretched out like unfulfilled dreams.

I was so enraged, so furious, so angry. I wanted the world to pay for what it had forced me through, for the endless pain, the ongoing abuse, the vile mistreatment.

It was all a *mistake*—I never should've woken up! I never should've been reborn into a world that had cast me out, denied me everything, and turned its back on my neglected and abused mind when I had needed it most. Where was the justice, where was the fair fucking treatment? I was only a child!

I ran into the abandoned city roadway, one that was usually packed with cars, and buses, and impatient pedestrians. It was now filled with only the ghostly remembrances of one.

Distant alarms echoed against the atmosphere, growing louder, and louder, and louder. I shuddered, observing the SWAT vehicles near the hospital's entryway before I turned on my heels and ran like hell. I sprinted halfway across the city, desperate to reach Coombe Park.

It was the one place I felt welcomed, the only place that felt like mine. For days on end I had rested against that neglected park bench, eager to forget my past, eager to rewrite my future.

Now all I needed was a safe place to fall. A secure location to collapse against and blink out the brutality that fatigued my body and mind.

I had thought suicide would save me, that my death was the answer to all. It was comical how wrong I had been, how foolishly I had thought, how recklessly I had doomed myself.

There was no saving me now.

Helicopters circled above with piercing spotlights as I ran the empty and deserted roads. The usual overbearing sounds of a faraway city were for once completely silenced, my own constant puffs and frantic splutters the only noise that invaded my eardrums.

A large exhale left my lips as I collapsed against the bench, my body alight with radiance, with electrified flickers, with the relentless agony of a death that even hell didn't want. I gripped my knuckles hard, bellowing my desperate echoes against the empty world.

I was inhuman. I was pathetic, useless, tragic... my own two mothers had abandoned me. How the hell was I supposed to feel? *Thankful, grateful? No.* My mind was beyond anger, far past fury. The emotions I felt inside, the untameable and unstable feelings within my heart that demanded to be avenged, were fearsome, and deadly, and powerful.

I felt psychotic, detached, impulsive. I felt the world weaken at its knees, bowing only to me. To the great powers of the indestructible Ultimate Weapon. A power I held within myself. A power that would never break, never fail, never weaken.

My rage imploded as I vowed to destroy this world, to terminate its futile existence, to drive my power so far into its core it shattered against the unrestrained momentum. I would never again cower away in fear, never again wince from their brutal blows, never again beg and bargain.

I was the villain of this story.

The monster under the bed, the unknown behemoth that spied from shadows, the evil apparition that longed for nothing but sweet revenge.

My mind was resolute, my heart failing to palpitate. I was never the hero, never the idol. I was a loser, a failure, a mistake. Why did I deny everything they told me, everything they swore to be the truth?

I was an error, a 404, a fault within the system, a weakened link within the chain, a broken cord that sparked a house fire. I was the common denominator that ruined everything.

The sun shone upon me, blazing its hopeful glow against me. I hated this world, I hated myself, I hated the people who forced me into this cruel and compacted life without a single consequence of their own.

I was a victim—but I didn't have to be. *Not anymore.* I was a villain, a criminal, a sociopath. I would rise above all those that hurt me, all those that stood aside as I was dragged through hell, all those that denied me my salvation, my retribution.

This was my war zone, and this my undisputed battle royale.

"*Red!*" Ace yelled desperately, leaping across the pathway. I eyed him sharply and stood my ground. "What's going on inside your head?" he bellowed, his voice trembling. Felix halted beside him, just as unsure and unaware.

"They will never take me!" I furiously shrieked. "I am the Ultimate Weapon; I will never be controlled!" The alien glow seared within me as I lifted my arm upward, power expelling from my tarnished fingernails and into the exosphere.

A great force field boomed against my hand, entrapping the entire globe.

Orange waves pounded, protruded, projected against the universe, eclipsing the world within a deadly and shadow-like force. It blocked out the clouds, the sky, the sun. It beckoned to be seen, demanded to be believed.

Thousands of birds took to the skies, squawking, screeching, carrying on as their peaceful world was consumed with an abstract matter. They twitched and flapped, their noisy nature ruining my perfect moment.

"*Holy fuck,* Red, no!" Felix's defiant power dived towards me as his eyes blackened and his skin pulsed with an inky texture. I threw my hand sideways, shoving the futile clouds away in one fell swoop. His power huffed and spluttered, zeroing in for another almighty blow.

I clenched my teeth and aimed, anger and fury hot within my damaged mind. My power wrapped against him, throwing him harshly through the air with a forceful impact awaiting.

Felix slammed against a brick wall and shattered it, bones snapping like twigs as his limp body dropped motionlessly.

"*No!*" Ace cried, his body staggering. "Red, what the fuck are you doing?" He eyed me straight on, his expression fearful and desperate. He held back an onslaught of tears as his body violently trembled. "Don't lose your mind, hold onto yourself," he begged as his dishevelled hair tumbled in front of his eyes.

"I am nobody!" I cried. "I was nobody then, and I am nobody now. I *told you* I had the potential to be exceedingly good for this world or exceptionally bad. And I choose bad. I choose to be a villain; I choose destruction, and carnage, and power!" I bellowed against the universe as a supernatural force snatched me into the air divinely, my inhuman form defying gravity.

My entire body glowed; it radiated with power and energy. It refused to be condemned, to be defined, to be controlled.

I glanced upward, the atmosphere pulsing with my incredible and supernatural power. Every single human being would witness my ability, would experience this significant moment before I wiped out their pathetic existence completely.

A hysterical chuckle left my lips as Ace's weakened power collided against my protective force field. "What the hell is wrong with you?" he cried manically. I smiled at him, a foolishly toothy grin against my disfigured features.

"Everything," I uttered, allowing the power to entrance me.

It was a thrilling feeling, intoxicating and inebriating. I refused to let it go. I was an all-powerful entity. Nothing and no one would ever harm me again. I was putting a stop to the vicious cycle. I was protecting myself from others and forcing my decision to be the only one that mattered.

Bullets blasted against me, useless and intrusive.

I screeched against the sky like a devil hell-bent on annihilation, like a demon filled with bloodlusted vengeance.

My baggy clothing seared away, leaving nothing but orange energy encapsulating my mutilated form. It pulsated through my frizzy hair, it seared against my eyeballs, it blazed out at my fingertips. I was truly invincible, insurmountable.

The world was done for. The universe at its end. The planet forced to a standstill. I would never again be challenged, never again be abused, never again be a victim. I was finally free. I'd finally discovered my purpose, had irrevocably uncovered the Ultimate Weapon's role within this doomed and dying world.

It wasn't love that had set me free. It was power.

All I had to do was close my fist and Earth would undeniably blink out of existence. And just like that, humanity would be finished. Their cruel, selfish, and greedy ways finally punished by the only one powerful enough to do it: *the Ultimate Weapon.*

My fingers curled closed around my hand, the feeling triumphant. What would become of me? I didn't know and didn't care. I was done pretending, done caring for the world as it had never cared for me. I was allowing my anger to finally be free, to finally have its outshining and victorious moment.

Yes, Ace and Felix would hate me for the rest of time. But I was a villain, villains did not care for heroes. I would continue to walk this lifeless and empty globe for the next one thousand years, most likely more. And that was fine by me. It was my own utopian world. I would never die, never age, never falter.

Ace's power knocked against me, and I shuddered, losing my balance momentarily. I threw my arm towards him, bringing him before my godlike figure suspended within midair. His darling blue eyes were deliciously frightened as I lowered my head and smiled deceitfully.

"Yes?" I asked of him.

He swallowed the lump within his throat, fear tight against his bones. "Red, please," he pleaded helplessly.

I huffed, blowing a stray hair from beside my cheek as my power enveloped around his firm body. He kicked restlessly, arms swatting the power away like it was nothing more than an irritating fly. I scoffed angrily, darkening my piercing eyes.

Unexpectedly, he stilled, eyeing me straight on, his expression raw, his emotions laid bare. "Red, I love you."

My eyes flashed with emotional turmoil, my power shorting out like a broken fuse as I gasped and eyed my surroundings.

Was this the way my story ended? Was this how I wanted to be remembered? Was this even what I *wanted?*

I panicked, conflicted and confused thoughts pounding inside my dense skull like a vigorous migraine. If anyone could save me, it was him, it was Ace. But this power wouldn't allow me to falter, wouldn't allow me to give into something so fleetingly unpredictable and purposeless.

My power was magnificent, unmatched. It fuelled my body and mind with control, and strength, and power. It threatened the world, it barred their relentless attacks, it suffered at no one's mercy.

My head slowly shook, orange teardrops slipping along my cheeks as I drifted Ace back down to the solid ground below. His eyes yearned to say more, his mind desperate to connect with mine and set me unknowingly free.

I loved him, I undoubtedly did, and I would until the end of eternity... but I knew what I had to do. I knew what the energy within me craved, what it desired, what it needed. It urged me on, it forced my hand, it bowed down to no one.

I breathed in deep and closed my fist, awaiting the end of time.

ACKNOWLEDGEMENTS

Thank you for reading this novel of mine. I began writing Force when I was fourteen years old, a story that has remained with me throughout my entire life, a story I have decided to finally share.

Last year, I set the goal for myself to make that happen. It was about time I finally finished this novel and allowed the world into the most personal parts of my mind.

I can now proudly say, at age twenty-seven—*I did it!*

Back when I first created Force, it was more of a diary. A way to express myself within the eyes and mindset of a character I built to be strong, fearless, and outspoken. Someone who wasn't so afraid and alone like I was. *Enter:* Red. A girl who I have come to love, admire, and cherish. A girl who made it possible for me to love myself again.

The two main characters, *Red and Ace,* have never changed from their humble beginnings. The main idea and powers of the Ultimate Weapon have also remained the same, minus the lore. Everything else has changed quite a bit, and I have the awful first drafts to prove it!

Anyway, there's a lot of people within my life, those living and those who have sadly passed, that I owe thanks to for helping me in one way or another in writing (and finally finishing!) this book. So, from the bottom of my heart—*thank you!*

A massive thank you in particular to my incredible husband, Hayden, for the continuous support you have given me and the positive encouragements to continue my writing. This wouldn't have been possible without you!

Also, a massive thank you to my best friend, Brooke, for forever listening to my rambles of made-up stories and worlds. You have no idea how much this helps.

To my darling Nan, Pauline, who passed away in 2020, your kindness, strength, and positivity continue to endlessly inspire me. I just wish you were here to see my accomplishments.

And of course, a huge thank you to my remarkable Mum and Dad, for all the support and wisdom over the years. I always knew I would become an author.

I also want to thank everyone in my brilliant writers' group. (*You superstars know who you are!*) Your feedback, advice, and suggestions have truly assisted me in diving back in and perfecting this novel. I can't wait to witness the undertakings of your own creative journeys!

Last, but certainly not least, a massive show of appreciation to the lovely and talented artist, Coffee Rain! For the gorgeous and eye-catching cover art. A wonderful soul, who I had the privilege of working alongside to bring Red and Ace to life in the Second Edition of this novel!

To all my readers, to those who have struggled with similar themes within this book, and to those that thankfully haven't, allow Red's story to hold nothing but inspiration within your own, valuable lives.

Let it encourage you, guide you, inspire you, to create and nourish a beautiful life, a happy world, an inspiring story. I, for one, know it's entirely possible.

Life is full of ups and downs, of wins and losses, of highs and lows. Always have faith in yourself. Learn to ride the moments as they come your way. We're all human beings; we all go through the same emotions, but in different ways.

Love the world, love your creativity, love yourself.

The Ultimate Weapon Book Two—*coming soon.* As well as many more! Keep an eye on my Instagram for updates.

All my love,
Candice Joargenson ♥